LUDMILA

Titles available in this series

Yannis
Anna
Giovanni
Joseph
Christabelle
Saffron
Manolis
Cathy
Nicola
Vasi
Alecos
John
Tassos
Ronnie
Maria
Sofia
Babbis
Stelios
Kyriakos
Monika
Emmanuel
Theo
Phaedra
Evgeniy
Ludmila

Greek Translations

Anna
published by Livanis 2011

LUDMILA

Beryl Darby

ISBN 978-1-9997176-50

Printed and bound in the UK by
Print2Demand Ltd
1 Newlands Road, Westoning,
Bedfordshire, MK45 5LD

First published in the UK in 2019 by

JACH Publishing
92 Upper North Street, Brighton, East Sussex, England BN1 3FJ

website: www.beryldarbybooks.com

Author's Note

There have not been any graves discovered in this particular area of Elounda.

The war time atrocities and events attributed to the villagers during the years of occupation are true.

For the purpose of this book I have made the legal processes that take place happen very speedily. I am sure in reality it would take many months, possibly years, for the legalities to be completed.

.

August 2015
Week Two – Tuesday

'I have nothing to do with "The Central" any longer, Dimitra. I cannot just walk in as if I still owned it. I'm sure Mr Kuzmichov would be most offended and annoyed.'

'Mr Kuzmichov was taken away in handcuffs. The staff know and trust you and someone is needed here that they can turn to for advice.'

Vasilis sighed. 'When do you have to make a statement, Dimitra?'

'The police told me it was necessary to report to the police station later today and if I did not go they would come and arrest me.'

'I'm sure you would not be arrested. They would simply ask you to accompany them and provided you did so they could not arrest you.'

'Please, Mr Iliopolakis,' Dimitra sounded close to tears. 'Please come up and help me.'

'I'll need to speak to my wife and make some arrangements down here. I cannot just leave her alone. I'll call you back. Just do whatever the police say and you'll not be in any trouble.'

Vasilis turned to Cathy. 'That was Dimitra.'

'I gathered that. What was her problem?'

'Kuzmichov has been arrested and there's chaos at the hotel. She has been told she needs to make a statement and has asked

me to go up and be with her and also see if I can be of any help
in the hotel.'

'So are you going?'

'I want to have a word with Panayiotis before I make a
decision. The hotel is really none of my business. If I have to
make a statement about the information that Dimitra gave me
originally and seeing Ludmila collect some men from the beach
I may have to go up to Heraklion anyway.'

'Couldn't you do that here?' asked Cathy.

'That's why I need to speak to Panayiotis. I certainly won't
consider leaving you here alone if I have to stay over night.'

'I could go and stay with Saffron and Vasi.'

'They're both out most of the time.'

'Marianne, then.'

'She has her mother staying so she hasn't a spare room at the
moment. If I do have to go to Heraklion the most practical solution
is for you to come with me. I'll see if Panayiotis is home yet. He
told me he was on duty down at the building site, guarding the
bones. As if anyone would want to walk off with them!'

Panayiotis was in his dressing gown when he answered the
door to Vasilis. 'I was just about to go to bed,' he remarked.

'I'm glad I caught you before you had gone to sleep. Can I
come in for a minute?'

Panayiotis opened the door wider. 'I was going to call on you
later. Some more men landed in the early hours and I understand
Chief Inspector Solomakis arranged to visit the hotel.'

Vasilis nodded. 'That was one reason I have come to see you.
I've had a call from Dimitra, the woman who mentioned the men
to me in the first place, and she said they have arrested Kuzmichov.
She has been questioned and asked to go to the station to make
a statement. She's in a bit of a panic and has asked me to go up
to Heraklion, not only to support her but also to see if I can be of
any help at the hotel. Is that permissible?'

'Go up and support the lady if you wish, but bear in mind that you will also have to make a statement. I'm afraid I have had to name you as being the previous owner of the hotel and being out in the boat with me when we first saw the car and men arriving at the beach.'

'Why can't I make a statement here?'

'You can, but it would be sent up to Chief Inspector Solomakis along with our surveillance reports. If your ex-employee has said that she spoke to you regarding her concerns he may well ask you to confirm that. He has the authority to insist that you go up to the station in Heraklion. Could save you a visit at a later date when it's inconvenient.'

'Have you any idea when the forensic pathologists are going to start excavating and how long they will take?'

'No idea. No one had arrived when I handed over to Achilles this morning.'

'So if I did stay up in Heraklion for a few days I wouldn't be able to get on with building?'

'No way. You can be prosecuted if you even set foot on the land, despite the fact that you own it.'

Vasilis sighed. 'I thought all my problems were going to be over when I retired. They seem to be multiplying. There's no way Cathy can stay down here on her own and it isn't convenient at the moment for her to go and stay with either family or friends. She'll have to come with me. A shame Kuzmichov also bought our apartment; she'll have to sit in a hotel most of the time and be bored to tears.'

The knocking on the front door woke Ludmila. Evgeniy must have forgotten his key. She crawled out of bed and stumbled through the hallway. She unlocked the door and turned to go back to her bedroom.

'Excuse me, Madam. We are the police and we need to speak to you.'

Ludmila stopped. 'Has something happened to Evgeniy?'

'Mr Evgeniy Kuzmichov is your husband?'

Ludmila nodded.

'He is helping us with our enquiries and we would like you to get dressed and come to the police station.'

'Are you arresting me?'

'Why should we arrest you, Madam? At the moment we would just like your assistance.'

Ludmila shook her head. 'It is not convenient for me to accompany you. I wish to go back to bed. You woke me up.'

'If you refuse to accompany us voluntarily I will have to arrest you. Please go and get dressed or you will have to leave here in your nightclothes.'

Ludmila gave the officer a venomous look and returned to her bedroom. Had one of the refugees demanded his money back and assaulted Evgeniy? Even if such an event had occurred it was unlikely that Evgeniy would have reported the matter to the police, but he had not returned from the hotel after settling the men into their temporary accommodation. Hastily she donned a pair of jeans and a T-shirt after washing her face and brushing her hair. She certainly did not want to be seen leaving the apartment in handcuffs and wearing only her nightdress. Picking up her handbag and ensuring that she had her mobile 'phone, the keys to the apartment and the safe she returned to where the officer was waiting just inside the doorway.

Vasilis returned to his apartment. 'It appears that I may be asked to corroborate whatever statement Dimitra has made and also give my version of the events that I witnessed when I was out fishing with Panayiotis. Chief Inspector Solomakis is in charge of the enquiry and I know how difficult he can be to deal with. It's better that I approach him before he sends someone to arrest me.'

'Why on earth would he want to arrest you? You have not done anything wrong.'

'I know. I have nothing to worry about. I am only concerned

about you. Can you get a case packed? You'll have to come with me and I'll find a hotel where we can stay for a few days.'

'So you are going to offer help at "The Central"?'

'I expect I'll have to ask Solomakis's permission to go there and see what the situation is and if I can help. If he refuses we can come straight back down here, but it's best to be prepared to stay.'

'Couldn't we stay at "The Central"?'

Vasilis shrugged. 'I don't know, but I'd rather know you were safely settled somewhere as I have no idea how long I will be at the police station. I'll call Vasi and tell him we're going up to Heraklion.'

'What's wrong, Pappa?'

'A number of things. Far too complicated for me to go into over the 'phone at the moment. Cathy and I have to go to Heraklion and I'm not sure how long we will be staying. There are problems at "The Central". Nothing really to do with me, but Dimitra has asked me to go up and I need to make a statement to the police. I'm not in any trouble.'

'Well that's a relief. When you mentioned the police I thought you might have gone down to your land last night and dug up all the bones you could find.'

Vasilis sighed. 'I'm not allowed to set foot on the land. There's a police guard down there. All I can do is wait and see what transpires. I'll call you this evening and tell you exactly what the problems at "The Central" are.'

Evgeniy was escorted to a holding cell and to his disgust made to empty his pockets and relinquish his mobile 'phone before being locked in. 'I am not a common criminal,' he protested. 'I wish to consult my lawyer.'

'All in good time, sir. Once we have finished our enquiries you could well be released and then you will have no need of a lawyer.'

Evgeniy glared at him. 'I will still need to consult my lawyer and ask him to start proceedings against you for unlawful arrest.

You have caused distress to my employees at the hotel and also to my guests. What will they have thought seeing me led away in handcuffs? I insist that you remove them immediately.'

'You will have to bear with me, sir. When I have finished itemising your possessions and you have signed to say the list is correct I will be able to go and obtain the key.' The officer waited until Evgeniy had read down the list and signed before he swept all Evgeniy's possessions into an evidence bag. 'These will be returned to you in due course.'

Ludmila was escorted to an interview room and her handbag was taken from her. The contents were spread out on the table before her. She wished she knew exactly what was happening so she could have her own version of events ready.

The officer emptied the contents of her purse, finding that it contained only a reasonable quantity of Euros and a credit card. The numbers stored on her mobile 'phone were scrolled through and the 'phone placed inside an evidence bag. The miscellaneous collection of tissues, nail file, lip salve, hand mirror, breath fresheners, mosquito repellent, headache tablets, elastoplast and two pens were replaced in the bag and handed to her. Finally the officer picked up her bunch of keys.

'These are the keys to your apartment?'

Ludmila nodded.

'And this key?'

'It opens the safe.'

'Thank you. That could save us a good deal of trouble. Mrs Kuzmichov, we have a warrant that enables us to search your apartment and that includes opening the safe and examining the contents. What are we likely to find in there?'

'I have no idea. My husband is the only one who has access.'

'Yet you have a key?'

'That is only for me to use in an emergency. I am not allowed to open the safe.'

'What kind of emergency would that be, Madam?'

Ludmila shrugged. 'The unfortunate demise of my husband. He keeps his business accounts in there and I would need access to those if such an awful event happened.'

'Quite. What business would these papers relate to?'

'I imagine they contain information about the purchase of his hotel.'

The officer smiled thinly. 'Very likely. We will be taking your key to open the safe and ascertain the contents for ourselves.'

Ludmila swallowed nervously. She had placed the envelopes and mobile 'phones from the refugees in the safe before going to bed. 'Can I speak to my husband?'

'Not at the moment, Madam. The Chief Inspector is with him.'

Chief Inspector Solomakis studied the man sitting across the table from him, whilst an officer stood just inside the door.

'I will be recording this interview. Please confirm that your full name is Evgeniy Kuzmichov.'

'It is.'

'And you are the owner of "The Central" hotel?'

'I am and I demand that I am allowed to contact my lawyer immediately.'

'Of course, but before you make your 'phone call I would like to ask you a few questions. To clarify the information you gave me earlier.'

'I am not answering anything that could incriminate me without my lawyer being present.' Evgeniy folded his arms and glared at the Chief Inspector. 'What exactly are you charging me with?'

'At present there is no charge against you. We have simply asked you to come in to help us with our enquiries.'

'So why was I brought here handcuffed and locked in a cell?'

'When asked to accompany us you refused so my men had no option. You told my officer that you went to the airport this morning and collected some men, but you were unable to tell him the number of their flight or from which country they had arrived. Is that correct?'

Evgeniy scowled. 'I am not interested in where my guests have come from. It is not my business.'

'Did you speak to any of the taxi drivers whilst you were at the airport?'

'No. I don't usually fraternise with them.'

'But they would be able to confirm seeing you there at that time? Your car is quite distinguishable.'

'They may have seen me. I doubt if they took much notice.'

'Quite. You also said that your wife has access to your car and she often went out during the night if she was unable to sleep. How frequently does she do this?'

'I wouldn't know. Fortunately I sleep well.'

'So where exactly would your wife go?'

'I've no idea. I don't ask her.'

'You and your wife are on amicable terms?'

'Of course. Sometimes she receives a call from a hotel where the taxi has not arrived and she is asked to collect the guests.'

'So if that was the case last night she would be able to give us the address of the hotel and they could confirm they had called her?'

'You would have to ask her. I demand to have my possessions returned to me. I want to contact my lawyer. I'm allowed a 'phone call and his number is on my mobile.' He would have to call Ludmila and tell her to leave the house and take the contents of the safe with her.

Chief Inspector Solomakis continued as if Evgeniy had not spoken. 'One of my officers has talked to your employee in the car park at the hotel. He says the car is often returned in a dirty condition when you have collected men from the airport and you insist it is cleaned immediately. If your wife went out for a drive last night why did you use it to go to the airport before it had been cleaned?'

'It was early in the morning. I didn't notice the condition of it. Had I done so I would have ordered a taxi.'

'Mr Kuzmichov, on a number of occasions your car has been seen in the Elounda area, driving across the Causeway and parking behind a windmill.'

'Then that is probably where my wife has driven some nights.'

'I am sure she will be able to corroborate that.'

'I object to my wife being disturbed.'

'It is just a matter of procedure, Mr Kuzmichov. Your wife has already been disturbed and is here to help with our investigation.'

Evgeniy's face purpled. 'She is to say nothing without my lawyer being present.'

'That will be at the lady's request, not yours. I'm afraid I am not completely convinced by your answers. We have warrants that allow us to search your hotel and also your apartment. I will return to you when the searches of both properties have been completed. I may well have some more questions for you then.'

Evgeniy shook his head. 'I am not answering any more of your questions without my lawyer being present.'

Chief Superintendent Solomakis ended the recording and requested that Evgeniy Kuzmichov be escorted back to his cell.

He returned to the reception area and spoke to the officer on desk duty. 'Provide the foreign gentlemen we brought from the hotel with some coffee and water. Take some money from the petty cash and buy three packs of biscuits. We do not want to be accused of mistreating them. Whilst you're about it find out if they speak Greek.'

'What about the hotel owner? Should I get some coffee and biscuits for him?'

'Certainly not. A bottle of water is sufficient. Give his wife a bottle also.'

Vasilis 'phoned Dimitra. 'I'm on my way. Are you still at the hotel?'

'Yes, sir. There's an officer on this floor and I'm not allowed to leave until I am ready to go to the police station. He will then escort me there.'

'Cathy is with me and I have to find a hotel where we can stay tonight. When I have done that I will 'phone you. Once I have spoken to you give me about an hour and then tell the officer who is with you that you are ready to go to the station and make your statement. I'll wait there until you are told you may return to the hotel.'

'You can't be with me when I make my statement?'

'That is not a good idea, Dimitra. The police may think we have colluded. You only have to tell them the same as you told me originally about the men staying at the hotel. You have done nothing wrong so there is nothing for you to sorry about.'

'If you say so, Mr Iliopolakis.' Dimitra sniffed dolefully.

Vasilis stopped at the "Excelsior" hotel and booked a room for himself and Cathy. 'I'm sorry, it's on the second floor and the outlook is the back of the houses behind. If we have to stay any longer than tonight I'll try to find somewhere more attractive for you to stay.'

'I have plenty of books with me and I assume there is a television in the room? I admit I'd rather be at "The Central". I know some of the staff there and feel at home.'

'I'll try not to be out for too long. By the time I have given my statement and then waited whilst Dimitra gives hers I'll probably be a couple of hours at least.'

'What about you going to "The Central" to help with the problems?'

'I'll have to ask the Chief Inspector if that is permissible. If he says that is out of order we can go home tomorrow.'

Cathy smiled. 'That's a nice thought. I hope he says you are not to set foot inside under any circumstances.'

'I'm a bit concerned about the staff,' frowned Vasilis. 'If Kuzmichov is detained for any length of time how are their wages going to be paid or the outstanding bills to the suppliers?'

'Vasilis, that is not your problem. I'm sure some arrangement can be made through Kuzmichov's lawyer and the bank. Promise me you will not guarantee any payments to anyone.'

Vasilis shook his head. 'I certainly won't do that. I'm sure Kuzmichov would never pay me back. Do you want me to order some food to be brought up to our room? I don't want you waiting around until I return and ending up starving.'

'That's a good idea. You ought to eat as well. There's no urgency for you to go to the station.'

The police officers arrived at Kuzmichov's apartment and opened the door with Ludmila's keys. Word soon spread amongst the neighbours and they began to appear in the street and cluster together speculating on the police presence.

Everywhere was clean and tidy and the police were unable to find any incriminating evidence of any kind, despite searching assiduously in the most unlikely places. Evangelos pulled his mobile from his pocket and called Chief Inspector Solomakis.

'We've searched all the rooms thoroughly. No sign of drugs or weapons. There are three new suitcases in one of the bedrooms, suitable size for taking on board a flight as hand luggage. We're just about to open the safe. Do you want me to stay on the line and tell you if we find anything in there?'

'It would save me from being interrupted again. I'm just about to take a statement from the previous owner of the hotel. I'll keep him waiting until I've spoken to you again.'

Evangelos nodded to his companion and handed him the key to the safe. 'Open it up, but don't touch anything until I've spoken to the Chief again.'

The door swung open and the officer gasped. 'There's hundreds of dollars in here along with some Euros and sterling. There are also some named packets.'

Evangelos relayed the information to Chief Inspector Solomakis. 'Do you want us to put it all in a bag and bring it in or should we count it here?'

19

'Take a photo of the safe and the contents before you empty it and make sure you are wearing gloves. Place everything on the table and photograph it again. We don't want Kuzmichov accusing any of us of helping ourselves.'

The coffee, biscuits and water had been received gratefully by the Syrians and Dawoud thanked the officer in Arabic and also asked if they could have their luggage to enable them to change from their wet trousers, socks and shoes.

The officer looked puzzled. 'Greek,' he said. 'Speak Greek.'

Dawoud shook his head. 'No Griq. Arabic. English.'

Nodding his comprehension the officer returned to the reception area and waited until the Chief Inspector was free.

'I gave the men the refreshments as you asked. From what I could gather they do not speak Greek, only Arabic or English.'

Chief Inspector Solomakis sighed. 'I only have two officers who are capable of interviewing them in English and one of those is out searching the Russian's apartment.'

'Could they not be questioned all together in the first instance? It will take all day if they have to be spoken to individually. They've all been in the same holding cell so they're bound to have talked amongst themselves and will all tell the same story.'

'We don't have enough cells to hold them separately and I don't want to put Kuzmichov and his wife together. I'll see if Orestes is willing to conduct an interview with me present.'

Dawoud and his companions sat in the interview room. Extra chairs had been brought in to accommodate them and the ceiling fan was working hard to move the hot air as much as possible.

'Explain to the men that we want to know exactly how they arrived on Crete.'

Orestes nodded and proceeded to speak slowly in English. Dawoud interrupted him.

'I have been elected as spokesman for us. We are quite willing to talk to you but would it be possible for us to have our cases brought here from the hotel? Our trousers are wet, along with our socks and shoes. It is most uncomfortable. Thank you for the biscuits, but we are still hungry. That is all we have eaten since yesterday evening.'

Orestes relayed the man's requests to Solomakis.

'I'm afraid they will have to suffer their wet clothes for a little longer. Once the interview is finished we can send out for a pizza or chicken kebabs and chips if they are happy to eat either.'

Orestes smiled at them. 'You will have some food when this interview is over and we will see about your clothes later. First I need to see your passports and I would like each of you to tell me your name and exactly how I should spell it.'

Each man took his passport from a pocket in his jacket and handed it to the Chief Inspector. They certainly looked genuine with the Embassy stamp embossed on each page.

Dawoud held out his hand. 'Please may we have our passports back?'

Orestes looked at Solomakis for confirmation. 'I think we should return them, sir. We need to keep them friendly so they will give us as much information as possible. We can always ask for them to be produced later if we need verification that they entered the country legally.'

The Chief Inspector shook his head. 'I want them all photocopied now. They could alter them and we would never know due to them being written in Arabic. I'll see who's free.' Solomakis rose and opened the door. 'An available officer here please.'

Two men arrived expecting to be confronted with a problem. 'Take these and make two photocopies of each one. When you have done so bring them all back here to me.'

He turned back to the men. 'We are going to record this interview with you. Please do not all talk at once and if I ask you a question you need to reply verbally. The tape does not record a nod or shake of the head. Do you understand?'

21

A chorus of "yes" answered him. Orestes switched on the tape recorder, gave the date and time of the interview along with each man's name and that Chief Inspector Solomakis was also present.

'We are taking photocopies of your passports and then they will be returned to you. Did you show your passports when you left Syria or when you arrived on Crete?' asked Orestes.

'We were not asked for them. We were told that we would be given new British passports so we could travel to England.'

Orestes spoke to Solomakis who made a note regarding passports on his note pad.

'Now tell me exactly how you left Syria, arrived on Crete and taken to the hotel where we arrested you.'

Dawoud sighed and proceeded to explain how they had paid to be brought across the sea, were subsequently rowed through a canal and met by a woman with a large car.

Orestes interrupted him. 'Do you know what kind of car it was?'

'It was dark, but I think it was a Mercedes.'

'You are certain it was a woman who met you?'

Dawoud nodded. 'She gave us suitcases that she had in the car and we had to put our belongings inside. She then placed them in the boot of the car and drove us away from the area. We stopped briefly when we reached a town. The woman got out and a man then drove us to the hotel. He gave us our cases and then took us up to some rooms. That was when you arrived and arrested us.'

Orestes conversed quickly with Solomakis who made some more notes.

'Let us return to when you left Syria. If you did not have to show your passport we can only assume that you were leaving illegally.'

'We would not have been given permission to leave the country. Some of our compatriots have tried and ended up in prison. We were told that we could have a safe exit if we had sufficient money to pay the boat man and our ongoing expenses.'

'So how much did each of you pay him?' Orestes looked from one man to the other.

'We all paid the same amount, twenty thousand American dollars. It was explained to us how much the journey was going to cost and we were told we would be given five hundred Euros to pay for our air fare to England and five hundred pounds in sterling to pay for us to have accommodation until we had found work.'

Orestes frowned. 'That was rather a lot of money. Having paid how did you know that the boat man would keep his side of the bargain?'

'We had to trust him. He put our money in separate envelopes with our names and mobile phones and placed them in his safe.'

'Was this money returned to you when you left the boat?'

Dawoud shook his head. 'We were told the money would be taken to the hotel where we would be staying to pay for our expenses there. A bag was thrown ashore to the woman who was waiting for us and we were told that contained our money and mobile phones.'

'Do you know the name of the man who owned the boat?'

'I believe it was Ivan. There was another man with him. He was the one who rowed us through the canal in a dinghy and I think his name was Panos. They spoke in Greek amongst themselves and the man called Ivan spoke to us in Arabic.'

'And the name of the boat?'

'I don't know.' Dawoud looked at his companions. 'There was a fishing net hung over the side when I went on board that obscured the name.'

'How many times did you go on board before you sailed?'

'Only once. Do you want me to ask my companions about the name and how often they went on board?'

Orestes nodded. If one of the men had spotted the name it could be useful. Dawoud spoke to them rapidly and each man shook his head and confirmed that he had only visited on one occasion before setting sail.

'Can you describe this boat for us? It was obviously not a rowing boat.'

Dawoud shrugged. 'It was a small sailing vessel with a motor. If you give Hazim a piece of paper he could probably draw it for you. He's a draughtsman.'

Orestes consulted with Solomakis who nodded and passed a sheet of paper across the table. Hazim drew swiftly and passed the paper back.

'I have no knowledge of boats but I am sure someone would be able to tell us exactly what kind of sailing vessel this is. Now let us return to your arrival. Were you told you were coming to Crete?'

'Yes; we were shown a map and Ivan traced our route for us.'

Orestes frowned. 'So if we had not arrived at the hotel this morning what would your programme have been?'

'I don't know. We were told that further instructions would be given to us when we arrived.'

'You say you were planning to go to England and find work. What made you think that was possible?'

'We had been led to understand that England needed professional men. We have our qualifications with us, showing where we studied and graduated and a record of our employment in Syria.'

'But you would be arriving as refugees. Why would you expect to be given work?'

'We were told we would have British passports. We would not have claimed refugee status.'

Orestes ran a hand across his head and spoke to Solomakis. 'I think we should terminate this interview until we have obtained more information from the other people we have brought in for questioning. Our enquiries are going to be more complicated and time consuming than we realised. Would it be possible for these men to be transferred to a hostel where they could be placed under guard before we return them to Syria?'

Chief Inspector Solomakis nodded. 'We can hardly keep them

all in a holding cell for any length of time. Arrange for some food to be brought in for them and I'll ask for their cases to be searched by one of our officers at "The Central". Provided they hold nothing more than their clothes they can be returned to them.'

'Thank you, sir. I'll explain to them.'

Vasilis arrived at the police station and was shown into Chief Inspector Solomakis's office. 'I understand that I need to make a statement regarding some events that I witnessed in Elounda.'

'I have had the initial reports from Inspector Antonakis's officers. Have you any objection to your statement being recorded?'

'None at all. I would also like to add some information that was given to me by a member of the staff at "The Central". I understand she has been asked to give you a statement regarding the events she witnessed over the previous few months.'

Chief Inspector Solomakis looked at Vasilis suspiciously. 'Is this something you have thought up between you?'

'Not at all. When she first spoke to me I took little notice. The hotel was no longer my affair. It is only now that I feel her observations could be relevant to your enquiries.'

'Follow me to an interview room.'

Vasilis waited until the recording had been started and then relayed to Solomakis the original conversation he had had with Dimitra.

'She was concerned that the guests who arrived and stayed in the rooms on the top floor and used the Conference room were not recorded in the accounts that she is responsible for checking. I assured her that it was not her business how Mr Kuzmichov arranged payment for his personal guests. I met with her once again after that and she was still unhappy with the situation.'

'Why did you instigate these meetings?'

'I happened to be in Heraklion meeting my architect. We completed our business earlier than I had expected and asked Miss Artimatakis if she would care to meet me for lunch; a courtesy gesture really. When I was out fishing with Panayiotis I observed men being rowed through the canal and met by a woman whom I believe to be Mrs Kuzmichov. I then asked Miss Artimatakis to meet me again. She confirmed that some men had arrived that morning and I passed this information on to Panayiotis who then spoke to Inspector Antonakis as he believed something illegal was taking place.'

Chief Inspector Solomakis continued questioning Vasilis until he felt he had elicited every scrap of information the man had and finally terminated the interview.

'You have been very helpful, Mr Iliopolakis. If you would leave me your address and 'phone number I will contact you if I have any further questions.'

'I am not sure when I will be returning to Elounda, but I can give you my mobile number. Miss Artimatakis asked if I could go to "The Central" and speak to the staff there. She said they were upset and worried.'

'What made her think your presence would aid the situation?'

'They trust me and would abide by my judgement. I am concerned about the welfare of the staff. She has asked me to wait and see her after she has made her statement. Please treat her gently; she is somewhat fragile mentally.'

'Assuming the lady has done nothing wrong she has no need to be concerned. You may wait for her if you wish and I will let you know if it is permissible for you to visit the hotel.'

Vasilis saw Dimitra arrive with the police officer and smiled at her encouragingly. She stopped as if to speak to him, but the officer took her elbow.

'Please go straight through. The Chief Inspector is waiting for you.'

Vasilis went outside and switched on his mobile 'phone. 'I'm still at the police station, Cathy. I've given my statement and been told I can leave but Dimitra has just arrived and I said I would wait for her. I also need to know if I can visit "The Central." It might be possible for us to go and stay there if I have to be in Heraklion for any length of time. I'll call Vasi whilst I'm waiting and explain to him why we are here.'

'I hope we can go home tomorrow.'

'So do I. Had I not gone out fishing with Panayiotis I would not be involved. How are you amusing yourself?'

'I'm sitting on the bed reading. I'm about half way through my book, so provided you are back here before I finish it there is no problem.'

'I hope it's a thick book,' smiled Vasilis. 'The Chief Inspector interviewed me for almost an hour and I really had little to tell him. Goodness knows how long he'll keep Dimitra.'

'Let me know if you are going to be really late. We can always have a take away if the dining room is closed when you arrive.'

Dimitra finally emerged from Chief Inspector Solomakis's office and looked close to tears.

'You may take the lady home, Mr Iliopolakis. She has been very helpful.'

'Am I able to visit the hotel?' asked Vasilis.

The Chief Inspector shrugged. 'I see no reason why not. Obviously you must not discuss the case with the staff.'

'Is "The Central" able to stay open and operate as normal?'

'The manager has been told that he cannot accommodate any new arrivals. He will have to arrange for them to stay elsewhere. The guests who are currently in residence may stay for the duration of their holiday.'

Vasilis nodded. 'Thank you.' No wonder Dimitra had said there was chaos at the hotel and she thought it was going to be closed down. 'I'll see if I can be of any assistance to them. Will you be requiring my presence again or can I return to Elounda?'

'Unless you become pertinent to our enquiries you may go wherever you wish provided you do not leave Crete without notifying us.'

'I understand. Come, Dimitra, I'll take you back to "The Central" and have a quick word with the manager. Then I will have to return to the hotel where I left Cathy. She has probably finished her book by now.'

Chief Inspector Solomakis looked at his watch. He had been due to go off duty twenty five minutes earlier. He would tell his officers to lock the money and 'phones they had found in Kuzmichov's apartment into the safe and examine the items the following day. He would have to ask Evgeniy Kuzmichov for details of the ownership and that could take him the remainder of the evening. Depending upon the information the man gave him he would then have to interrogate Ludmila Kuzmichov. He shook his head. He was not prepared to tackle those interviews tonight.

Vasilis gave Cathy a resume of his interview with the Chief Inspector whilst they ate a meal in the hotel dining room.

'I called in briefly when I took Dimitra back and spoke to Giorgos. The poor man is so harassed. The travel companies are complaining that it is short notice and it is not their problem to find alternative accommodation. They are muttering about compensation. His assistants had been working all day to book the guests who wished to leave into suitable hotels locally and they all looked exhausted. I've said I will go in tomorrow and see if there is any way I can help. I could at least make some telephone calls on their behalf.'

'Don't get too involved, Vasilis. You don't want the managers relying on you to sort out the problems.'

August 2015
Week Two – Wednesday

Chief Inspector Solomakis read through the notes that had been left for him by his officers who had been on duty overnight. Both Mr and Mrs Kuzmichov had complained about being detained and also about the quality of the meal they had been given and the facilities of the holding cell.

'They should think themselves lucky that they were given a meal and a bed to sleep on. We could have left them locked in an interview room with just a bottle of water until the morning. No doubt they would have claimed that was torture and against their human rights. Have they been given breakfast?'

'Yes, sir.'

'The other men were safely transferred to a hostel?'

'They were no trouble at all and they understand they are under guard and must not leave the premises.'

Solomakis nodded. 'Then we'll examine the contents of the safe and ask Mr Kuzmichov for his explanation of the items.'

The Chief Inspector watched as his officers laid the bundles of notes out on the table before him. Six named envelopes contained mobile 'phones and American dollars and he pushed them to one side. 'They can be examined later. I want the money counted and double checked. Kuzmichov may know how much the value is to the last dollar.'

'I think he may have the amount recorded in this cash book.'

Solomakis took the book and opened it. There was a date followed by some cryptic entries and a final number being recorded before a line was drawn beneath it and the entries were repeated. Each few lines appeared to be a copy of the ones above with the only difference being the date of the entry.

$$6 \times 10 \ 60,000$$
$$R - P.Port \ 2,000$$
$$6 \times 2 \ 12,000$$
$$Eu \ 6 \times 500 \ 3,000$$
$$GB \ 6 \times 500 \ 3,000$$
$$52,000 \ exp \ 1 \ max$$

He frowned and placed the book to one side. 'We'll examine that later. Once we have counted the money I'll confront Kuzmichov with the total and the book and ask for an explanation.'

Vasilis rose early and drove into the car park behind "The Central". Lanassakis came hurrying towards him.

'You cannot park – oh – Mr Iliopolakis. I didn't realise it was you.'

'Is it alright if I stay here, Lanassakis? I don't want to have taken a reserved space and upset Mr Kuzmichov.'

Lanassakis shook his head. 'Mr Kuzmichov is not here. The police came yesterday morning just as he arrived back from the airport. They would not let me clean the car and then they took it away to be examined. A policeman stayed and talked to me after they took the car away. He said that Mr Kuzmichov had been taken to the police station along with his visitors. I expect he will arrive back soon and then I will be in trouble for allowing the car to be taken away and not cleaning it for him,' he finished morosely.

'I don't think you have anything to worry about, Lanassakis. I will try to find out what is happening with the car later today and let you know. You just carry on with your usual jobs and you'll not be in any trouble with anybody.'

'If you say so, Mr Iliopolakis. I was never in any trouble with you.'

Vasilis walked into the hotel foyer from the rear entrance. He took in at a glance the piles of luggage that were placed around and the disconsolate looking guests who were beside it. The reception desk was surrounded by people and the harassed employees were on the telephone or trying to placate an irate customer. Vasilis strode over and pushed his way to the desk, ignoring the complaints of those around him.

Giorgos looked up and a relieved smile crossed his face. 'Are you able to help, Mr Iliopolakis?'

'I'll try. Help me up.' With Giorgos's assistance Vasilis climbed onto the reception desk and stamped his foot up and down until he had attracted the attention of all those milling around. He held up his hands and raised his voice.

'Please listen to me. Up until a few months ago I was the owner of this hotel. There was never any problem at that time. I am not allowed to discuss the present situation with you but I do have the assurance from the police that no guest is involved in any way nor are you in any danger. The enquiries that are taking place relate to a personal problem with the new owner.'

'Why were the men taken away in handcuffs then? Were they planning a terrorist attack?' A man interrupted Vasilis.

Vasilis shook his head. 'There is no suspicion of terrorism. Our police often take innocent people to the police station in handcuffs. They seem to think this will make them look more efficient to any onlookers. You are all welcome to stay for the duration of your holiday. Those of you who wish to move elsewhere please be patient. The staff are working as swiftly as possible to satisfy everyone. I will be here to answer any further queries that you have. I trust you have all had breakfast. If not, please go to the restaurant. They will be serving breakfast until the usual time and after that soft drinks will be available until the bar opens.' Vasilis repeated his message in Greek and then looked at Giorgos. 'Who are your most proficient linguists for French, German and Italian?'

'Andros speaks French and German.'

'Then ask him to repeat my message in the languages. What about Italian?'

'Ariadne.'

'So ask her to speak when Andros has finished. Now, help me down and let me know exactly what the situation is.'

Vasilis watched as the customers conferred together, some drifting off to the restaurant and others listening intently as his message was repeated in their own language and they were able to fully comprehend.

Giorgos sank gratefully into a chair. 'This has been going on all night. Some of the guests saw Mr Kuzmichov being led away in handcuffs along with some other men. The police refused to allow anyone to leave yesterday until they had examined their passports. It unsettled everyone and some travellers probably missed their flights. Then we were told that no new visitors could be accommodated until the police had completed their investigations. We've had to 'phone the travel companies and they're not happy. They say it is up to us to arrange somewhere for the guests to stay and if it is not up to the standard expected not only the customers but the companies will be claiming compensation.' Giorgos ran his hand across his thinning hair. 'Then there are the customers whom we cannot contact. They have made their arrangements themselves.'

Vasilis frowned. 'Don't you have a contact number for those who have booked independently?'

'For some, but not all. Those who were travelling yesterday could not be contacted until they actually arrived here. I was tempted to accept them.'

'That would have been a sensible solution.'

'Until the police found out,' replied Giorgos miserably. 'They have a record of all the guests who were staying here yesterday and those who were due to leave. If they then saw any names added they would know I had disobeyed their instructions.'

'So is there any way I can help?'

'If you could man one of the phones and contact some of the hotels they would probably be more accommodating for you. It would also enable one member of staff to have a break for twenty minutes. When they return another could have some free time.'

'I think you need a break more than anyone else, Giorgos. I'll go down to the kitchen and ask for coffee and soft drinks to be brought up for the staff. You cannot be expected to work for hours without anyone relieving you so you must have the first break.'

'I'd be grateful, but I'll not take longer than twenty minutes.'

'Just before you go, ask Andros to ask the French and German speakers to go to one side of the lounge where he will be able to converse with them and then ask Ariadne to say the same for the Italian speakers and go to opposite side of the lounge. That should take some of the pressure off the reception desk. I'll help deal with the English and Greek speakers and also be able to phone the tour operators once it is a little more peaceful here.'

Chief Inspector Solomakis watched his officers count the money, placing every thousand dollars in a paper band with their initial. They would then pass it to their neighbour who would check that the amount was correct and add their initials to the band before placing them in a plastic box at the side of the desk.

'This is going to take all day,' grumbled Solomakis. 'I'll make a start on counting the Euros.'

'We should have asked a bank cashier to come and help us. They would have been quicker.'

Solomakis looked at him sourly. 'We can't use outsiders to deal with evidence.'

The officer bent his head back down over the dollars and continued to count assiduously. On two occasions his colleague had returned a bundle and asked him to recheck the amount.

It was mid day by the time all the notes had been counted and the total calculated. Along with the dollars that amounted to five hundred and thirty six thousand there was also one thousand two hundred and seven Euros and three thousand two hundred in sterling.

'Now for the envelopes.' Solomakis laid them out in front of him. Each one bore a man's name and when he opened it there was a mobile 'phone inside along with ten thousand American dollars. 'I want to place these items in new envelopes and seal them with sticky tape and sign over it. They can then be placed back in our safe until we have interviewed the men. In all likelihood this money belongs to them.'

'What about the other money?'

'I am going to contact the bank and ask if they will place it in their strong room. Our facilities are not sufficiently secure to have this amount on the premises.'

'Will that mean we have to count it again in front of them?'

'I hope not. Provided they are willing to accept it as a sealed parcel there should be no problem.'

'I've never seen so much money in all my life,' remarked Manos. 'Do you think it's real or counterfeit?'

'I am assuming it is real, but I am sure its authenticity will be checked at a later date. Now envelopes and tape, please. I want to ask Mr Kuzmichov for an explanation.'

Whilst the envelopes and box were sealed the Chief Inspector opened the small cash book. Although the entries were cryptic he was sure now that they related to the amount of money that each man had paid to Kuzmichov and the remaining amount was the profit on the transaction. He shook his head. He was not at all sure that his police were capable of dealing with the situation; it could be sensible to call on Athens and ask for their assistance.

Evgeniy Kuzmichov glared at Chief Inspector Solomakis as he entered the interview room wearing handcuffs.

'What is the meaning of this? Why am I cuffed like a common criminal?'

'It is customary when moving a person from a cell into an interview room. Please sit down and be aware that we are planning to record the interview.'

'I still want to call my lawyer. I have been held here against my will for over twenty four hours. I know my rights.'

'Quite, Mr Kuzmichov. I am now commencing the recording.'

Kuzmichov glowered at Solomakis as he entered the details of the date and time into the machine. He held up his hand as Kuzmichov was about to interrupt.

'Mr Evgeniy Kuzmichov is assisting us with our enquiries regarding the discovery of illegal immigrants at his hotel. The men were witnessed arriving and taken to the top floor of the hotel where they were subsequently apprehended. Where did these men come from, Mr Kuzmichov?'

'It is not my business where visitors to the hotel come from.'

'You do not check their passports when they arrive?'

'I leave that to my staff when they check the visitors in.'

'That is quite customary, I believe. There is just one problem here, these visitors did not check in with reception when they arrived.'

'They were not given the opportunity,' replied Kuzmichov with alacrity.

Solomakis nodded. 'I appreciate that was the case yesterday morning, but I also understand that since you became the owner of "The Central" hotel at the beginning of March there have been a number of visitors whose details have not been recorded at reception.'

'They were my private guests.'

'And where did these guests come from?'

'Various countries. I have been an international business man for many years.'

'And you provided these guests with free accommodation and meals for the duration of their visit?'

'Of course.'

'So that would be why they are omitted from accounts?'

'Evidently.'

'How can you explain the large quantity of American dollars that were in the safe at your apartment?'

Kuzmichov's face purpled with rage. 'You had no right to go to my apartment and break into my safe. That is a violation of my privacy and is also criminal damage.'

'Your safe has not been damaged in any way. We used a key to open it.'

Kuzmichov clenched his fists. Ludmila must have provided the key for them.

'There was a very large sum of money in there. Please explain where it has come from.'

'As I have told you I am an international business man. Many of my clients stem from Russia. The international currency for trade is the dollar.'

'I understand that,' replied Solomakis, 'but why should you have such a vast sum in your private safe?'

'I had not had the opportunity to go to the bank.'

'So where did all this money come from?'

'Various places and transactions.'

'And you have the supporting paperwork, invoices and orders to confirm this?'

'Probably.'

'Probably is not good enough. If you are in business it is customary to keep copies of your invoices and mark them appropriately when the bill is paid.'

'My colleagues and I trust each other. Our word is our bond.'

'Then maybe you would be good enough to give us the names of these associates. They would then be able to confirm any payments they have made to you.'

'I would need to return to my apartment and consult my records. You cannot expect me to remember information like that off the top of my head.'

'And the notebook with amounts recorded? What exactly did those amounts refer to?'

'Probably transactions I had made or repayments that I was expecting.'

Chief Inspector Solomakis nodded. 'Interesting that the amounts were all exactly the same. In my experience it is rare to have two bills for identical amounts, but we can return to that problem later. How do you account for the named envelopes that were in your safe, each one containing a mobile 'phone and ten thousand dollars?'

'They were in there for security.'

'So who placed them in there? You say you met the men at the airport and drove straight back to the hotel. You did not stop off at your apartment.'

Kuzmichov shrugged. 'I expect my wife placed them there. She deals with a good deal of my financial affairs.'

'I am sure she will be able to corroborate this, but I still have a problem. Your car, with your wife driving it, has been under surveillance. In the early hours of the morning she has been seen driving to Elounda, across the Causeway and parking behind the windmills. She has then been observed walking a short distance up the road to a small deserted beach where she has waited until a dinghy appeared carrying some men. The men were escorted to the car and subsequently driven to Heraklion. If your wife met them and drove them up to Heraklion you cannot have met them at the airport.'

'Those men must have arrived earlier in the morning.' Kuzmichov rubbed his thumb and forefinger together, leaned forward and spoke quietly. 'I am an innocent business man, and I would like to return to my apartment. How much do you want to release me now? A year's salary? Two?'

The Chief Inspector shook his head. 'I am not open to bribery, Mr Kuzmichov. You may have been able to buy your way out of any previous problems that you encountered, but the immigration authorities in Britain are also involved. They are holding a number of men who have applied for refugee status and asylum. All these men say they entered Britain after travelling to Crete and staying at your hotel whilst arrangements were made for them to continue their journey.'

Kuzmichov glared at the Superintendent. He had expected to be able to talk his way out of the problem or offer a bribe sufficiently large to have the matter ignored as he had in the past when his business activities had been investigated.

Kuzmichov folded his arms. 'I am not answering any more questions without my lawyer being present.'

'Very well. I will telephone the Russian Consulate in Heraklion and ask them to provide you with a lawyer. You will be detained until further notice on suspicion of bringing illegal immigrants into Crete and attempting to bribe a police officer. I am terminating this interview with Mr Kuzmichov and he is being returned to a holding cell.'

Chief Inspector Solomakis waited until Kuzmichov had been taken from the interview room. 'Before I make that telephone call I think we'll have a few words with the wife and see what she has to say.'

Ludmila sat in the interview room picking at her fingers nervously whilst Chief Inspector Solomakis started the recording and entered the usual formalities.

'You are Mrs Ludmila Kuzmichov?'

Ludmila nodded.

'Please make a verbal answer.'

'Yes, I am,' replied Ludmila.

'Can you tell me exactly what you were doing in the early hours of the day when our officers visited your apartment and asked you to come to the police station.'

'I was asleep.'

'I am referring specifically to the hours between midnight and six in the morning.'

'I'm in bed during that time.'

'Do you sleep well?'

'Usually.'

'According to your husband you do not sleep well. You often go out during the night. If that is so what do you do when you are out?'

Ludmila shrugged. 'Walk around, sit somewhere, then return and go back to bed.'

'Your husband says you often take the car and go for a drive.'

'Sometimes.'

'How often would you say you did that? Once a month, once a week, every other night?'

'I don't keep a record.'

'So if you have taken the car where do you drive?'

'Just around.'

'Would that include a journey down to Elounda?'

'Maybe. I don't take a lot of notice where I am going.'

'We know that you have driven to Elounda on a number of occasions during the early hours of the morning. Once there you have driven across the Causeway and parked behind the windmills. Why would you do that?'

'I expect I needed to stretch my legs or a bathroom.'

'There would be no bathroom available over there at that time of the morning.'

'Then I would have to use the area behind the windmill.'

Chief Inspector Solomakis nodded. 'Having relieved yourself why did you not return to the car and commence driving back to Heraklion?'

'I probably wanted to walk around for a while.'

'And whereabouts did you walk?'

'Just up and down.'

'Up the road as far as the beach?'

'Maybe.'

'There is no "maybe". You were watched on a number of occasions walking up as far as the beach where you waited until a dinghy arrived carrying three men. The men waited there with you until a further three arrived. You then led the men to the car and subsequently drove them up to Heraklion. Who were these men?'

'I have no idea.'

'So why were you meeting them?'

'I wasn't told the reason.'

'Who told you to meet them?'

'My husband.'

'And do you always do as your husband tells you without question?'

Ludmila leaned forward. She knew Evgeniy would implicate her in an attempt to extricate himself. She had no hesitation in blaming the whole venture on him and claiming ignorance.

'You have to understand, my father was Russian and my mother Syrian. I am married to a Russian. In both cultures the woman has to do as she is told whether she wants to or not. If I disobeyed my husband or refused to comply with whatever he asked of me I would suffer.'

'Are you telling me that he would be violent towards you?'

Ludmila nodded vigorously. 'I disobeyed him on one occasion and I would not want to risk incurring his displeasure again.'

'I believe you have been married to Mr Kuzmichov for quite a long time. Why have you stayed with him if he mistreats you?'

'Where would I go? I have very little money of my own. Evgeniy always paid for everything and gave me an allowance. Provided I did as he requested I could certainly not complain about his behaviour.'

The Chief Inspector sighed. 'So you were told to drive to Elounda and collect these men. Who brought them through the canal to the beach?'

'I don't know. I never saw his face and he didn't speak.'

Ludmila was not prepared to implicate Panos. She could well need his help once she was able to leave Crete.

'What was in the bag that he threw across to you?'

'The mobile 'phones that belonged to the men.'

'And what did you do with these?'

'Took them back to the apartment and placed them in the safe.'

'You declared earlier that you were not allowed to go to the safe despite having a key, but your husband says that you often deal with his financial affairs.'

'That is quite true. I assist him in agreeing his business accounts but I am only allowed to open the safe to place the mobile 'phones inside. Once Evgeniy returns home I have to give the key back to him.'

'So what else is there inside the safe?'

'Some money. It is probably from the hotel.'

'Have you ever taken any of this money?'

Ludmila looked at the Inspector scathingly. 'I would not dream of taking money that did not belong to me. I would ask my husband if I needed money.'

'He would give you whatever you asked for?'

'Within reason. He is a generous man.'

'I see. I think that is all for the time being, Mrs Kuzmichov. We will terminate this interview now.'

'Are you releasing me?'

Solomakis shook his head. 'Not yet, Mrs Kuzmichov. We have further enquiries to make.'

'I need to go back to my apartment and collect some clothes and my toiletries. You cannot expect me to remain in the same clothes indefinitely.'

'I will arrange for the police to go to your apartment and collect basic necessities for you and your husband.'

Ludmila glared at the Chief Inspector. She was obviously not going to be released for some time.

Thranassis Solomakis waited until Ludmila had been escorted

back to the holding cell then he turned to the officer who had attended the interview.

'Having listened to the interviews given by each suspect what is your opinion?'

'I think they are both trying to claim innocence and both are equally guilty.'

Chief Inspector Solomakis nodded. 'My conclusions also. I will contact the Russian Consulate and ask them to provide Mr Kuzmichov with a lawyer as he has requested. We are obviously not going to get any more information out of him until they have conferred together.'

'And Mrs Kuzmichov?'

'She has not requested a lawyer so we will interview her again tomorrow. Another night in detention might make her decide to give us some more information in the hope of being released. Then I suppose I ought to go and interview the men who are in detention again. They may be able to furnish us with some more details about their trip over and we ought to tell them that we have their mobile 'phones and their money here.'

'Won't they expect to have their phones returned to them?'

'I'll explain that at present they are being held as evidence and they will certainly be returned to them when our enquiries have been completed.'

'They'll probably ask for their money also.'

'That is also being held as evidence and will not be returned to them until we have decided how to proceed. They are crucial witnesses once we have sufficient evidence to charge Kuzmichov. We cannot release them or they will probably disappear and our case against Kuzmichov will collapse. I'll send a message telling them to expect a visit from me tomorrow morning.'

Vasilis telephoned Cathy. 'I'm planning to leave "The Central" in about an hour. Start thinking where you would like to go this evening for a superb meal. You deserve it having been left alone again all day.'

'Is everything settled at the hotel?'

'Not really, but it has quietened down. The guests who are already here are now happy to stay on. It is only the ones who are due to arrive within the next few days that are the problem.'

'It is not *your* problem, Vasilis. You are not to agree to stay up in Heraklion and run the hotel for an indeterminate amount of time. It belongs to Kuzmichov, not you.'

Vasilis sighed. 'I know, but I feel a degree of responsibility towards the staff. I'm going to talk to Giorgos for a while and then I'll be only too pleased to return to our hotel and have a shower before we go out. Tomorrow we can go back down to Elounda.'

'Do you mean that, Vasilis?'

'Yes, I don't see that there is anything else constructive I can do here.'

Cathy smiled with relief. She had been terribly bored all day and had dreaded that Vasilis would decide to stay in the city longer.

'I'll call Panayiotis later and ask if there is any news from my building site. Provided they haven't found any more bones they could well be finished there.'

'He may be at work,' Cathy reminded her husband.

'In that case I'll call again tomorrow.'

'Why don't you call Vasi? Surely he would know if excavation is continuing.'

'That's a good idea. If he says the site is deserted I'll call Panayiotis then and ask if I am able to proceed with the work.'

Before leaving "The Central" Vasilis sat in the office with Giorgos. 'I'm planning to return to Elounda tomorrow. I don't think there is anything more I can do here to be helpful.'

'I have appreciated having you here, Mr Iliopolakis. You took some of the pressure away from the reception staff and calmed the visitors who were staying here. I will have to contact the police to see if we are able to accept the new guests. If we are refused then the hotel will have to close.'

Vasilis nodded understandingly. He would go and speak with

Chief Inspector Solomakis and see if he could persuade the man to allow the hotel to continue to function. He felt sad. He had loved his hotel and the thought of it closing down due to him selling it to a Russian was a bitter blow.

He drove to the police station and requested an interview with Thranassis Solomakis. The Chief Inspector frowned at him.

'I am a busy man. Have you any relevant information to give me?'

Vasilis shook his head. 'No, and I am not trying to ask for information to which I am not entitled. I understand from the manager of "The Central" that he has to cancel the bookings for the visitors who were planning to visit in the future. Is that strictly necessary?'

The Chief Inspector shrugged. 'Why would this concern you?'

'The travel companies are asking for compensation for the cancellations and if there are no customers where will the money come from? I do not have any knowledge of Mr Kuzmichov's financial position but I was assured when I sold him the hotel that he was a man of considerable wealth. If he is detained for any length of time would it be possible for his lawyer to make an arrangement with the bank so the money can be released? Also the staff salaries need to be paid and the suppliers who are owed money at the moment. If the hotel can remain open there should be sufficient money coming in to pay the current expenses and the travel companies will have to be asked to be patient. It may take a while for them to trust the hotel again, but provided the bookings they have in place for the future are honoured this event could be explained away as an unfortunate misunderstanding.'

'I am not sure if this proposal is as simple as you seem to believe. There are a number of other factors that have to be taken into account.'

'Would you consider it? I would be willing to speak with Mr Kuzmichov's lawyer and explain the accounting system that I used.'

The Chief Inspector hesitated. If the lawyer from the Russian Consulate was able to negotiate the immediate release of Kuzmichov or even manage to have the charges against him dropped there would be repercussions and he could well find he was accused of mismanagement and dismissed or forced to resign. He had only three more years before he could retire and did not wish to lose his pension.

'I suppose it might be possible. I will have to speak to the legal department at the Embassy in Athens. It could not be my decision.'

'I'm happy to wait whilst you do that.'

Solomakis looked at his watch. 'The legal department may well be closed by now. I will contact them tomorrow.'

'Then I will return tomorrow morning. Time is of the essence for a decision to be made regarding the continuing function of "The Central".'

Chief Inspector Solomakis sighed. He was expecting a lawyer from the Russian Consulate during the following morning and he would have to spend time apprising him of the charge against Kuzmichov; he also wanted to interview further the men who were staying in the hostel and try to elicit more information from them.

Cathy was not happy when Vasilis told her that he had to return to the police station the following day and depending upon the outcome of his visit he would then have to visit the hotel.

'You said we were going back to Elounda tomorrow.'

'We will. It just means that we are unable to leave as early as I had planned. I'm going to 'phone Panayiotis and see if he has any information for me. If he isn't available I'll call Vasi.'

He was unable to contact Panayiotis that evening and Vasi had not been very helpful. He declared that the land was still cordoned off, but he had no idea how quickly the work was progressing.

'I'll go down tomorrow and see what I can find out for you. It's possible they may have finished but not yet removed the police tape. It has caused a good deal of local interest. People have been coming down from the village to have a look at the proceedings and the tourists are fascinated by being so close to an archaeological site that is being excavated.'

'They might be, but I'm not,' answered Vasilis crossly. 'I just want to be able to progress with the building. I'll see if I can talk to Panayiotis tomorrow morning. He may have some up to date news and we should be leaving Heraklion in the afternoon.'

'What's the situation with the hotel?'

'Complicated. I'll be able to tell you more when we get home.'

August 2015
Week Two – Thursday

Vasilis had slept badly, turning the problem of the hotel over and over in his mind. If the legal department in Athens rejected Solomakis's request there was nothing he could do. It was with trepidation that he entered the station, prepared to wait until the Chief Inspector was available.

Having told Cathy that they would return to Elounda that day he hoped he would not be kept waiting for hours and that there had been a positive outcome so he would be able to call in at "The Central" and give Giorgos some good news.

He waited for over two hours before Solomakis appeared accompanied by a smartly dressed man carrying a briefcase. They carried on a quiet conversation for a few minutes before the Chief Inspector turned to Vasilis.

'This is Mr Propenkov from the Russian Consulate. He has agreed to represent Mr Kuzmichov. I have spoken with our legal department in Athens and provided Mr Kuzmichov and his lawyer are in agreement we have come up with a solution. I apprised Mr Propenkov with your proposal and I understand that Mr Kuzmichov is in agreement, although somewhat reluctantly. It is fortunate that you are here so he can speak with you about the arrangements for the hotel.'

Vasilis looked at Mr Propenkov hopefully. 'Is the hotel able to remain open?'

'There are various conditions that have to be complied with. If we could go into a private room I can explain the situation to you.'

Solomakis led them both to an interview room. 'This is the best I can do, but we will have some privacy.'

'You understand that I can discuss nothing to do with any charges that may be brought against Mr Kuzmichov,' stated the lawyer.

Vasilis nodded. 'I am only interested in the hotel.'

The Chief Inspector indicated that they should each take one of the uncomfortable chairs that were in front of the table and also sat down.

Mr Propenkov took a seat and placed his briefcase on the floor. 'Without going into any legal or confidential details regarding the charges that the police are thinking of making against Mr Kuzmichov the full enquiry is likely to take a number of weeks. The Chief Inspector has refused to allow Mr Kuzmichov to be released on bail during that time, although, of course, we will be challenging that decision. As I understand it the legal department in Athens has agreed that the hotel may remain open and trade as usual. This brings us to the financial arrangement. Mr Kuzmichov will be unable to deal directly with the finance, but he is willing for an administrator to be responsible for the payment of expenses provided proof of all income and outgoings are given to the bank and the information regarding the transactions passed on to him on a regular basis.'

Vasilis nodded. He would have some good news to take to Giorgos.

Mr Propenkov continued. 'Mr Kuzmichov has suggested that you should be the administrator, Mr Iliopolakis, as you are obviously conversant with the running of the hotel and the financial arrangements you instigated are still in place. He would be reluctant to make the agreement otherwise.'

'Me! I have retired. I do not want to return to Heraklion.'

'There should be no need for that. I gather that you had a system in place whereby the accounts were dealt with by staff at the hotel and only scrutinized for accuracy by you. Once you ascertained that the accounts were correct you would authorise the payment of bills, arrange transfers to the appropriate staff for their wages and withdraw cash for those who were paid weekly. Mr Kuzmichov has continued to use this system. You would be able to complete the financial transactions as you had in the past without having to be in Heraklion.'

Vasilis ran his hand across his head. If he refused the hotel would close down, the staff would be unemployed and suppliers who had bills outstanding would not be paid. This would cause considerable hardship to a number of people and they should not have to suffer due to the actions of Kuzmichov.

'Kuzmichov's bank would honour the arrangement? I am not prepared to use my money with no realistic expectation of being reimbursed.'

Mr Propenkov nodded. 'Provided you are agreeable to act as the administrator I will draw up a legal document with Mr Kuzmichov and this will be presented to the bank.'

'I am not prepared to commit myself to the arrangement until it has been agreed by the bank. How long is this procedure going to take? I have promised my wife that we will return to Elounda this afternoon.'

Mr Propenkov looked at his watch. 'I can return to my office now and have two agreements drawn up. I will then need to return to obtain Mr Kuzmichov's signature on both documents; one for the bank and one naming you as the official administrator. It will be necessary for you to sign both of them. If I leave now I should be back here by five at the latest. Once the signing has been completed you can return to Elounda. I will then visit the bank tomorrow and officially register the agreements.'

Inwardly Vasilis groaned. He had hoped to leave Heraklion as soon as he and Cathy had lunched. 'I would like a copy of both the agreements and how will I know if the bank has found the arrangement acceptable?'

'If you would give me your mobile 'phone number I can call you and I can ask the bank to do the same.'

Vasilis shook his head. 'I would prefer that you and the bank e-mailed me so I have an accurate record. Telephone messages can be misconstrued.' Vasilis gave Mr Propenkov his business card. 'My details are on there.'

'I will telephone and e-mail you, Mr Iliopolakis. That way you will receive the information immediately even if you do not have access to a computer at the time.' Mr Propenkov rose. 'If there is any delay in completing the agreements or should they be ready earlier than anticipated I will call you. Provided all goes smoothly I will see you again at five. I will now speak briefly with Mr Kuzmichov and advise him that you have agreed to the proposal.'

Vasilis let out a breath and looked at Solomakis. 'I wish I had never become involved. May I go to the hotel and tell the manager that he may accept the visitors that are planned to arrive in the near future?'

The Chief Inspector shrugged. 'I see no reason why not.'

Vasilis hurried to "The Central" pleased to find that the reception area was much quieter and calmer than on his previous visit.

'I have good news, Giorgos. The hotel is staying open and you may accept new guests.'

'Really? How did you manage that, Mr Iliopolakis?'

'I have come to an arrangement whereby I will act as administrator for the hotel whilst Mr Kuzmichov is otherwise engaged. All the accounts should be completed as usual and sent through to Dimitra and on to me for authorisation. Mr Kuzmichov and I will have signed an agreement later today and provided the bank finds that acceptable the arrangement will commence tomorrow.'

'Will the staff be paid as usual?'

'Priority will be given to the payment of the staff wages and the suppliers whose bills are outstanding. If you have some money in the safe you can start to make up the wage packets for those who are paid weekly. I will return tomorrow with a substantial sum so you can finish the wages and have a reserve in the safe. Once outstanding bills have been paid I will have to negotiate refunds and compensation for those visitors who were sent to other hotels. The travel companies affected will be advised that the situation arose due to a misunderstanding which has now been sorted out and the hotel is trading as before. I hope they will not press for large sums in compensation as it will only have affected them for three days. I do not want to become involved in extensive correspondence with them. You have a list of the companies involved and I will draft a letter that you can send out to them. I will also need a list of the hotels where the customers were transferred for the duration of their holiday along with the names of the guests.'

'Thank you, Mr Iliopolakis. I do wish you were still the owner here. I have to admit that I do not like Mr Kuzmichov.'

Vasilis shrugged. 'You have not known him for very long. You may well revise your opinion in time.'

Giorgos shook his head. 'Somehow I do not think that will happen. He does not appear interested in the hotel.'

Vasilis gave a small smile. He knew exactly how the manager felt. 'Mr Kuzmichov has never been responsible for a hotel before. He was a business man. I'm sure he will realise that the personal touch when dealing with employees and guests is essential.'

'The only time he came here was when he had men staying on the third floor and he said they were his private guests,' grumbled Giorgos.

Vasilis was not prepared to become involved in a discussion regarding the short comings of Mr Kuzmichov. 'I am going up to tell Dimitra that she has to send the accounts through to me again whilst Mr Kuzmichov is indisposed, then I must go and face my wife. She was expecting us to be able to return to Elounda this afternoon and I will have to explain that I am going to be delayed. I do not think she will be very happy.'

Chief Inspector Solomakis sipped his coffee slowly. There was no point in trying to elicit more information from Evgeniy Kuzmichov until his lawyer from the Russian Consulate was present during his questioning. His visit that morning had been spent agreeing the financial arrangements that were to be put in place and Kuzmichov complaining about the charges that he was facing. Mr Propenkov had requested bail for his client but the Chief Inspector had refused to contemplate the idea at present.

'When you have had the opportunity to discuss matters more fully with Mr Kuzmichov I think you will understand that we need to make further enquiries into the situation with both the Embassy in Athens and also the Immigration Authorities in Britain. We are holding some men who have entered the country illegally, apparently with the help of Mr Kuzmichov. If this is so, he cannot have been working alone and we do not want him contacting his associates so that they disappear. If you are able to complete the arrangements for Mr Iliopolakis to be the administrator for the hotel in the interim that will be something that Mr Kuzmichov does not have to worry about. You are welcome to return tomorrow and spend time with Mr Kuzmichov and I hope he will then agree to being interviewed and supplying us with more information.'

Mr Propenkov had protested, but conceded that until he was more conversant with the facts he could not insist that bail was granted.

Vasilis returned to the hotel where Cathy was waiting eagerly for him. 'I've packed everything except your washing kit and a clean shirt. I thought you might like a shower before we leave'

Vasilis shook his head. 'A shower will be welcome, but I have to return to the police station later this afternoon.'

'Why? You said we would go back to Elounda as early as possible today.'

'I know, but I have to return to the police station at five and meet the lawyer from the Russian Consulate again. To enable "The Central" to remain open Kuzmichov had to agree that it was put into administration otherwise it would have had to go into liquidation.'

'Is his wife going to take over?'

'No, he stipulated that he would only agree to this on condition that I was the administrator. He doesn't want his wife involved in any way.'

'Oh, no. Does that mean we have to stay in Heraklion?'

'No, the accounts can be dealt with by me as they have been in the past. Once Dimitra has checked them she will e-mail a copy to me each week and once I have agreed them I will authorise Kuzmichov's bank to pay the outstanding bills along with the staff wages. Mr Propenkov has returned to the Consulate and is having the papers drawn up. They should be ready for signatures by five this afternoon. If we return to Elounda now I will only have to come back up to Heraklion tomorrow to collect them and go to the bank to complete the papers. This way I can collect some money so Giorgos can finish making up the wages for the staff who are paid weekly.'

'You should never have agreed to become involved, Vasilis.'

'I really felt that I had no choice. If I had refused the hotel would have been closed down and money owing to the staff and suppliers would not have been paid. I know I could say it was no longer my concern, but it isn't fair to put loyal, hard working people into that situation.'

Cathy shook her head. 'There are times when I wish you were not such a nice character and did not have a conscience.'

'I shouldn't be very long at the station. It will only take a few minutes to read the documents and sign my name. I can then go on to the bank tomorrow morning and make a quick visit to "The Central". We can then drive down to Elounda. We can stay another night at the hotel.'

Cathy wrinkled her nose. 'I don't like this hotel. I don't feel that it is very friendly.'

'Then we'll check out now and go and stay at "The Central" tonight.'

'Could we?'

'I see no reason why not.' Vasilis smiled at her. 'After all, I am the administrator, so it could be logical that I stay there and speak to relevant staff about the arrangement, put their minds at rest. I'll also be able to collect the relevant list of travel companies and the hotels where the guests transferred. I have told Giorgos that I will draft a letter to them that can be sent in my name. He should have time to compile that during the morning and then I can work on it when we are home in Elounda.'

'In that case I won't make a fuss about staying an extra night. But no more than that, Vasilis. If we are not driving back to Elounda by two tomorrow afternoon I am going to hire a taxi and return alone.'

Vasilis took Cathy in his arms. 'I promise we will go home tomorrow.'

Andreas collated the information he had received from the men of Kato and Pano Elounda. Even allowing for exaggeration on their part he certainly had sufficient information to write a play about their war time activities. According to them they had used every opportunity that arose to inconvenience and hinder the German and Italian soldiers.

Achilles had smiled, showing his toothless gums as he recounted how the boys had caught snakes out in the fields and then placed them beneath the seats of the jeeps. 'Sometimes they had wriggled away before the soldier returned, but if they were still there they caused a tremendous panic. They were mostly harmless grass snakes, but they did not know that.'

'What else did you do?' asked Andreas..

'We pretended to be playing tag and used their vehicles to dodge around. It was an ideal opportunity to push a stone into the exhaust pipe.'

'Didn't they chase you away?'

'Frequently and we would go away without arguing with them. Every day we would place boulders on the paths and tracks leading up to the villages so they were impassable. We used to watch the soldiers having to leave their vehicle and walk. Once they were out of sight we would put earth or small stones in the petrol tank or break the wing mirrors. We used to throw a stone at the windscreen. Even if it did not break completely it would crack and the driver would have difficulty in seeing where he was going. We damaged anything we could.'

'Weren't you caught?'

'We were well away by the time they returned. Sometimes we even risked stealing the spare can of petrol that they carried.'

'What did you do with that?'

'We used to hide it well away from the village and creep down at night to where they had their vehicles parked. Provided there was no patrol we would pour the petrol over the jeeps, lorries or motor cycles and set fire to them.'

'Weren't you punished by them?'

'They did not expect young boys to commit such acts and were sure there were andartes in the area. They spent a considerable amount of time searching for men that did not exist.'

'What about the women and girls? Did they also help you?'

Achilles nodded. 'They helped.'

'What did they do?'

A crafty look came over Achilles's face. 'You'd have to ask them.'

Chief Inspector Solomakis sighed; the morning had been virtually wasted due to having to be a witness to the agreement being drawn up for the administration of the hotel and now he had to be there until the Russian lawyer returned and Mr Iliopolakis was also there to check and sign the relevant paper work.

He had intended to visit, accompanied by Orestes, the men

who were being detained in the hostel. If more information could be gleaned from the men it could be helpful. They may have decided to be more forthcoming now they were no longer in a prison cell and being decently treated. He had tried in vain to contact the Embassy in Athens to ask if the British Embassy had any further news or information, but each time he had phoned he was told there was no one available and although he had sent an e-mail he had not received a reply as yet. They were quick enough to contact him when they wanted something but it was certainly not reciprocated.

The only interesting information he had received was from the passport office. It appeared that Ludmila Kuzmichov had made a number of visits to Syria, driving over land from Russia and through Turkey to reach the border. She would hardly be making the risky journey so frequently just to check on the well being of her brother when a phone call on a mobile would suffice. He was waiting for the results of the scrutiny of both her and her husband's mobile 'phones to see if there was evidence of any contact with the country.

Syria was in such turmoil that he felt it would be useless to try to make any enquiries and expect a sensible answer from the authorities there, even if he was able to contact them. Solomakis continued to make copious notes of questions whilst he waited for the two men to return.

Vasilis called in at "The Central" and booked a room for himself and Cathy for the night.

Giorgos looked at him in surprise. 'You are only staying for one night?'

'I have promised my wife that we will return to Elounda tomorrow. Provided I am able to sign the documents that have been prepared tonight I can then visit the bank tomorrow with the Russian from the Consulate and check everything is in order for me to arrange weekly withdrawals to cover the wages that are paid in cash and the tradesmen's bills. At the end of each month I will transfer money to cover the wages of the more senior staff. I will obviously advise you of the amounts once the accounts have been agreed by Dimitra. I will use Dimitra's weekly reports as I did in the past when I was the owner. Now I have to go to the police station and meet the Russian lawyer who has worked on this agreement again. He said he would return at five and I do not want to keep him waiting.'

Mr Propenkov, having gained the relevant signatures from Vasilis and Evgeniy Kuzmichov immediately left the police station; he was not prepared to stay and interview Evgeniy Kuzmichov further that evening. So much time had been spent agreeing the arrangements for the hotel to remain open that he had been unable to ascertain the full details regarding Kuzmichov's detention. As bail had been refused by the Chief Inspector he could only assume that there were more serious issues involved rather than a misunderstanding as Kuzmichov had claimed. He would visit the bank the following day in the company of Vasilis Iliopolakis to ensure the arrangement for the previous owner to act as administrator had been accepted and then return to question the Russian further.

'Hi, Marianne, it's Elizabeth.'

'Is anything wrong? You don't usually call me until the weekend.'

'Nothing wrong at all. In fact I have good news. Nicolas has been told by the heart specialist that now he has had a pace maker fitted he is fit to fly again. I haven't told Nicola that yet. I want it to be a surprise for her. We are planning to visit his sister in Athens and then come over to Crete.'

'That's wonderful. I'm sure she'll be delighted.'

'You won't tell her, will you?' asked Elizabeth anxiously.

'Of course not. We'll have to sort out a room for you as my

mother is still with us. I'm sure Yiannis can go back in with Nicola and John.'

'No, if you do that Nicola will realise there is something afoot. We'll stay in the self catering apartments if you have a room free or we could go and stay in Vasi's hotel. We're happy to pay our way; we don't expect any favours.'

'Of course we'll make certain you can have a room and there will certainly be no charge. You're family. Do you have a definite date?'

'Would a week on Monday be convenient? We leave for Athens on Tuesday. We'll spend the night in Washington and travel to Heathrow the following day. I've insisted that we stay the night in London as I don't want Nicolas overtaxing himself. All being well we should be in Athens on the Thursday. Four days there will be more than enough for me. I doubt we will go out anywhere much, just spend the time sitting around talking to Elena and she probably won't want to entertain us for any longer.'

'What about Eleanor? Is she coming with you?'

'No, she wanted to come, of course, but Nicolas refused. Her last semester's grades were appalling. She just does not have any inclination to work. We paid for her to have extra tuition during the summer break and Nicolas has said she has to improve her grades before he is willing to allow her to have time away from her studies. She's going to stay with our neighbours and they have assured us that they will see she attends college every day. They can't make her do the work, of course, but neither can we.'

'I'm sorry to hear that you are still having a problem with her.'

Marianne was not sorry that Eleanor would not be coming with her parents. The girl seemed content to sit around all day doing nothing but reading trashy magazines. If asked to help in any way she always had an excuse or complied with a bad grace and sulky expression on her face.

Elizabeth sighed. 'I really cannot see her ever having a career. We just hope that she might meet a nice young man and get married.'

'Do you think that is the answer?'

'No, but the thought of her living at home with me waiting on her for ever more is not an enjoyable prospect.'

Marianne smiled. Eleanor had been a lazy, difficult teenager and had obviously not changed as she became older, despite managing to go to college.

'I hope that she will mature over the next couple of years and cease to be a worry to you. I can't wait for you to arrive. If you have to change your dates at all to give Nicolas more time to rest that will be no problem. I can look at our bookings and easily juggle rooms around so that you have a ground floor.'

Marianne went to find her husband with a delighted smile on her face.

John opened his computer and was delighted to find that there was an order for ten of Uncle Yannis's pots from a shop in Heraklion. He printed off the details and went in search of his uncle.

'Ten more orders,' he announced triumphantly.

'For the pithoi?' asked Yannis immediately.

'No, smaller replicas, but that's better than nothing. You'll have to show me which ones they are and then I'll get them packed.'

'When will you be able to deliver them?' asked Yannis as he rose stiffly from his chair.

'We'll check that the money is in your account. Provided it is safely there I could take them tomorrow. I'll have to ask Dad. If necessary I could do an airport run at the same time. If he needs me here they'll have to wait until Monday or later in the week.'

'I don't want to lose the sale.'

'I'm sure you won't and we don't need to seem too keen. If they had to go by courier it would probably take a week so anything under that time is a bonus for them. You'll only have to pay Dad for the petrol.'

'That will eat into my profit.'

'You will already have been paid the cost of the carriage by the shop. The price of the petrol will cost less than postage or a courier so you'll actually make more profit.'

'If you have to make an airport run I shouldn't have to pay anything,' argued Yannis. 'You'll be driving up to the town anyway.'

'You'll have to sort that out with Dad. I'm just the errand boy and I don't know yet if there is an airport run due. Stop being so belligerent and help me find the pots. If I don't need to go to the airport to collect visitors I could take some other small pots up with me and go around to the shops that sell ceramics. I might be able to talk them into giving me an order.'

August 2015
Week Two – Friday and Saturday

Vasilis and Cathy had a leisurely breakfast at "The Central" and Vasilis fended off enquiries by the staff regarding the fate of the hotel.

'There is no need for any of you to be concerned. The hotel will be operating as usual and when Mr Kuzmichov has sorted out any problems that he has I am sure he will return to take over again.'

Although the news regarding the hotel was greeted with smiles, no one looked particularly pleased when Vasilis said Kuzmichov would be returning.

'Not the most popular of men,' murmured Cathy.

Vasilis frowned. 'So I have gathered. I begin to regret selling to him.'

Cathy looked at her husband in horror. 'You won't try to take it back, will you? I don't want to have to return to Heraklion to live and I certainly do not want you having to drive up each day.'

'No, I don't think I could afford it now I have invested so much money in Elounda. I just wish I had sold to someone who was more likeable and not involved with something rather dubious. I'll not try to purchase it back from him. If he decides to sell up it will have to go back on the open market.'

'You really mean that?'

Vasilis nodded. 'Now I've lived down in Elounda I realise just how much I dislike large towns. I'll be waiting on the doorstep for the bank to open and as soon as all the formalities there have been completed we'll go home.'

Cathy smiled in relief. 'Our cases will be packed and I'll be waiting on the doorstep here.'

'There is one person I want to see before we leave.'

Cathy's face fell. 'If you start to see people you'll become involved with something else.'

Vasilis shook his head. 'I just want to speak to Eirene. I don't know if word will have filtered through as far as the chambermaids and cleaners yet and I wouldn't want her worrying about being paid.'

'If I see her whilst you're out shall I tell her?'

'Certainly, although I doubt very much that many of the staff care who is in charge provided their wages are paid.'

Mr Propenkov arrived at the police station and asked to speak to Mr Kuzmichov. 'It will need to be a private discussion. I need to hear from him exactly why you are holding him. I know it is not necessary for me to add that if your suspicions and accusations are groundless he will be suing you for a very substantial sum.'

'That is a chance I have to take as a police officer,' answered Chief Inspector Solomakis. 'You may spend as long as you like with Mr Kuzmichov. We have visited the apartment and both Mr and Mrs Kuzmichov have been provided with clean clothes and some toiletries. They were both able to shower this morning and have been given a breakfast. I need to go out this morning and I will ask my staff to provide you with anything you may want in the way of refreshment.'

Orestes drove his superior officer to the hostel where the men from Syria were being detained. They looked clean and well fed, although each was evidently anxious when he entered the room.

'Are we under arrest?' asked Dawoud suspiciously.

'You are being detained as illegal immigrants,' explained Orestes.

'Please do not send us back to Syria. We would be arrested as defectors and placed before a firing squad.'

'If you co-operate with us we will deal with you as leniently as possible. The Chief Inspector has a number of questions he would like to ask you. First we would like you to tell us who approached you and offered you passage to Crete.'

'We've talked together and we were all approached by the same man at different times. He said his name was Ivan and made arrangements for us to visit him on his boat to discuss the conditions of travelling with him.'

'Did you all go aboard at the same time?'

Dawoud shook his head. 'Individually until the evening when we sailed. We were up on deck at first, then when it became dark we were sent below whilst we left the harbour. We had to stay down there until Ivan said we could go up on deck again for some fresh air.'

'How long were you kept below?'

Dawoud wrinkled his brow and looked at his companions. 'Three nights, I think.'

'Where were you when you were allowed on deck again?'

'In the middle of the sea. We were allowed to stay up there until land was sighted, then we were told to return below. Ivan came down and told us that we would be going ashore in the early hours of the morning and we would be met by a woman with a car. She would take us to a hotel and we would be able to stay there until we had new passports and could book a flight to England.'

'How were you going to pay for your stay at the hotel and a flight?'

'We had trusted Ivan with our money and he said that after he had taken the money for the boat trip the remainder would go to the man at the hotel. He would take his expenses and we would have the rest of our money changed into Euros and sterling.'

'How long were you going to stay at the hotel?'

'I don't know. You came and arrested us before we had received any more information.'

Chief Inspector Solomakis and Orestes conferred together quickly.

'They were very trusting,' remarked Orestes to Solomakis. 'This man Ivan could have taken their money and once out in the open sea murdered them and disposed of their bodies. No one would have been any the wiser.'

Solomakis grunted. 'Why didn't they ask for asylum here once they arrived?'

Orestes repeated the question to Dawoud.

'We did not want to stay in Greece. We do not speak the language and even if we had decided to stay here we had no opportunity to speak to anyone in authority.'

Orestes sighed. 'If you are granted asylum you will have to stay here or return to Syria. You will not be sent on to England.'

'How long will it take before we know?' asked Dawoud anxiously.

'I don't know the answer to that. In the meantime you are to stay here under house arrest. If you decide to leave and attempt to go elsewhere you will be found and then you will end up in a prison cell. The conditions there are not pleasant.'

Dawoud shrugged. The conditions in a Greek prison could not be worse than they were in Syria. 'Where would we go? We know no one here who would help us.'

'Then I suggest you just spend your time here quietly. It could be to your advantage to learn some of the Greek language. I can arrange to have some books sent in to you.'

Dawoud smiled. 'At least that would help us to pass the time. Knowledge of any sort is always useful.'

Mr Propenkov sat with Evgeniy Kuzmichov in an interview room. 'Now, Mr Kuzmichov, if I am to represent you I need you to be entirely honest with me regarding the immigrants who arrived at your hotel. This interview is not being recorded so you can speak freely.'

Kuzmichov shrugged. 'It is quite a long and involved story.'

'Then start at the beginning and I will only interrupt you if I need clarification.'

'Well, as you probably know, I was an international import and export merchant. I am not getting any younger and a few years ago I decided that I would like a change of occupation where I was not so pressurized and would be able to spend more time with my wife. I began to sell my contracts and fleet of container lorries on to other importers and exporters. I then found I was somewhat bored; too much free time on my hands.

'I looked around and investigated various possible business opportunities. I happened to stay at "The Central" and I was impressed at the way the hotel functioned so smoothly. I thought little more about the hotel until I saw the owner was offering it for sale. I contacted Mr Iliopolakis and we agreed on the figure over the 'phone, subject to all the legal formalities being satisfactorily completed. I then needed somewhere to live in the town and I was delighted when Mr Iliopolakis said he wanted to sell his apartment also as he would no longer need to live in Heraklion. Again the purchase was agreed over the 'phone and when I finally visited I was more than happy with my purchase.'

Kuzmichov smiled and sat back. He was warming to his story now, having spent most of the night considering how best to shift blame from himself and appear innocent.

'I could not believe my good fortune. It was not until after the transaction had been completed that I made the mistake of 'phoning my brother in law and told him of my change of occupation. We rarely meet and are not close. He immediately asked me to help him and if I refused he threatened to contact the authorities about an unfortunate incident that happened about a year ago.'

'What incident was that, Mr Kuzmichov?'

'I had agreed to arrange the transport for a consignment of car engines from Russia to Iran. At the last minute the driver was ill and my wife agreed to drive the consignment as far as Turkey. She was not prepared to enter Iran. She was met at the border of Turkey by a new driver, all the papers were in order and there was no problem. My wife then flew back to Moscow. As the lorry was stopped and checked upon exit from Turkey and before entering Iran sniffer dogs found a quantity of drugs hidden in the spare wheels. It was obviously nothing to do with my wife. The driver of the lorry was arrested, despite declaring that he was innocent, and is now spending time in jail.'

'So what was your brother in law planning to do?'

'He said he would tell them that I had arranged for the drugs to be planted in the lorry once it had passed over the Turkish border. He has influential friends and such an accusation would no doubt lead to a further investigation of the case. It would be all lies, of course, but I could spend some time in jail before I managed to clear my name and my reputation would be in shreds. I felt I had no option but to agree to his plan.

'He has taken it upon himself, in the name of humanity, to help Syrian refugees to leave the country. It is most commendable of him and obviously places him in danger. He sails across from Syria to Crete with a few men who have occupations that would be welcomed in England.'

'So why did you not issue a counter threat to expose his activities?'

'I could not do that. It would have meant his imminent arrest and he would probably have been beheaded. How would my wife have felt? She would never have forgiven me. She and her brother have a close relationship.'

Mr Propenkov nodded understandingly.

'I felt I had no choice. I agreed that each group could stay at the hotel for a few days before travelling on to England.'

'How was that going to be accomplished?'

'Once they had arrived I was to contact a man in Heraklion and he would come and provide false passports for them. My wife, who, although devoted to her brother, is completely subservient to him, would then take them to a travel agent to book their flights. I would finally take them to the airport and that would be the end of my involvement.'

'I see. A number of questions spring to mind. Firstly the name of your brother in law and also the name of his boat and where it is registered.'

'His name is Ivan Kolmogorov, but I have no idea of the name of his boat or where it is registered.'

'Do you have an address for him?'

Evgeniy shook his head. 'To the best of my knowledge he lives on his boat.'

Propenkov looked at Evgeniy sceptically. He thought it most unlikely that he would not know the name of the man's boat. 'So how do you contact your brother in law?'

'I cannot. After I had finally agreed to his proposal I had second thoughts and tried to telephone him back to say I had changed my mind and wanted no part of the arrangement. He had changed his 'phone number.'

'How do you know when these men will be arriving?'

'I receive a very quick call to say the time they will be put ashore.'

Mr Propenkov tapped his fingers together. 'So on the first occasion when you received this call why did you not refuse to be involved.'

'I was given no opportunity. I tried to call him back and the number was not available. I did not feel I could leave these poor men stranded.'

'Obviously these men were not landed at any of the ports or harbours along the coast or they would have had to show a passport or visa that allowed them to visit the country. Where did they land?'

'Ivan has a friend who is knowledgeable about the area and it was decided to land them in a secluded area down by the village of Elounda in Lassithi.'

'So how did they get from this secluded area up to Heraklion? I have a rudimentary knowledge of the geography of the island and Elounda is quite a long distance from Heraklion. I am assuming that they did not walk.'

'Having been advised that they were on their way I had to instruct my wife to collect them in the car when they arrived. I would then meet her and drive the final distance to the hotel.'

'Why didn't your wife take them straight to the hotel?'

'I needed to escort them in so that the formalities of registering could be avoided.'

'You have a rather expensive car, I believe.'

'I bought it to transfer guests to and from the airport.'

'I have been told that the police examined it and nothing incriminating was found. Why was the front seat manufactured in such a way that it could be lifted? What did you plan to use the cavity to transport?'

'I thought to use it as safety precaution when I needed to take sums of money to the bank.'

'Really.' Mr Propenkov raised his eyebrows and made a further note on his pad. 'And how did these men propose to pay for their boat trip and subsequent stay at the hotel and then their flight?'

'That was all arranged by Ivan. He deducted his expenses from the money they paid him and sent some on to me to cover their costs.'

'How much did you receive?'

'Approximately four thousand dollars for each man. Two thousand was the cost of supplying them with a false passport, one thousand was to cover their flight and ongoing expenses and the remainder covered their stay at the hotel with a small amount of profit for myself.'

'What exactly were the expenses that you incurred at the hotel?'

'I had to buy each man a suitcase, cover the cost of the petrol for the drive to Elounda and back, their food, of course, and then to have the rooms cleaned after they had left.'

Mr Propenkov sat back. 'So you are telling me that you are actually an innocent victim of the scheme and had no choice but to participate with no financial gain to yourself?'

Kuzmichov nodded eagerly. 'Exactly.'

'I see. I'll explain this to the Chief Inspector and ask him to reconsider your application for bail. It is unlikely that anything can be set in motion before Monday so I will visit you again then and advise you of the outcome.'

Vasilis returned to the hotel to find Cathy sitting in the lounge waiting for him.

'Have you been thrown out of our room? It isn't mid-day yet.'

'I thought I should leave the maids to get on. I could sit down here just as happily as up there. I saw Eirene and told her that she would receive her wages as usual each week. She was so relieved. She said she had heard rumours, but wasn't sure if they were true. A number of the chambermaids and cleaners are making enquiries at other hotels to see if there is any work available.'

'I hope you assured her that was not necessary. I don't want to find that we suddenly have no staff. I need to see Giorgos and hand him over some money. Once that has been done I can pay our bill, then I'm ready to leave unless you want to stay and have lunch here?'

Cathy shook her head. 'I don't want to stay any longer than necessary. If you are seen here there's bound to be someone who wants to speak to you. We can easily find somewhere to have something to eat in Malia or Hersonissos.'

Mr Propenkov left Evgeniy Kuzmichov with mixed feelings. He was not at all sure that he believed the man's story. He would ask if he could interview Ludmila Kuzmichov and also make some enquiries of his own about the incident in Turkey with the drugs.

Chief Inspector Solomakis agreed that he could speak to Mrs Kuzmichov provided she had no objection to speaking to the lawyer.

'First of all she denied all involvement with transporting the men. When I told her that we actually had proof she admitted that she was doing as her husband told her. She accused him of being rather rough with her if she disobeyed.'

Mr Propenkov raised his eyebrows. 'The impression I had from her husband was that she was dominated by her brother and was just doing as she was told. Kuzmichov also had no option but to participate in the scheme. I think I am justified in asking for bail to be granted for both of them.'

'I'm waiting for information from the British Embassy in Athens and until I hear from them I am not prepared to grant bail for either of the Kuzmichovs. I'll arrange for Mrs Kuzmichov to be brought to the interview room.'

Mr Propenkov looked at the woman as she entered, accompanied by two police officers, but not handcuffed. She looked composed and confident as she smiled at him and took a seat.

'I understand you are a lawyer from the Russian Consulate. Have you come to tell me I am about to be released?'

'I am afraid not, Mrs Kuzmichov. I am representing your husband. He has made a statement to me regarding his involvement in the arrival of Syrian men at his hotel. I would like to know how you became involved. This interview is not being recorded so you can speak freely and honestly to me.'

Ludmila began to pick at her fingers. She wished she could remember exactly what she had told the police inspector.

'I understand that you drove the car from the hotel down to an area on the coast and waited whilst the men were brought ashore,' prompted Mr Propenkov.

'I was told that was what I had to do.'

'Who told you that?'

'My husband. I had to drive the men up to Heraklion and then he would take them into the hotel whilst I went home to sleep.'

'How often did you make this journey in the course of a month?'

'I don't know, two, sometimes three times.'

'And how many men did you meet each time?'

'Six.'

'How many journeys did you make in all?'

'Ten, possibly twelve. I didn't keep count.'

'Whose idea was it to bring refugees from Syria over to Crete in this way?'

'My husband's. That was why he bought the hotel.'

'What about your brother? Was he involved?'

'Evgeniy, my husband, spoke to him about the idea but my brother refused to have anything to do with it at first.'

'What made him change his mind?

'Evgeniy said that if Ivan refused he would inform the authorities that he had used his boat to transport drugs to various locations.'

'And had he?'

'Of course not, but my brother knew that even if the accusation was mentioned to the authorities he would probably be placed in jail in Syria and even if enquiries were made it could take years to prove his innocence.'

'So, your brother was forced into agreeing to the scheme and then asked you to participate?'

'No, my brother did not want me involved in any way. It was my husband who insisted that I should meet the men initially and later take them to book their flights to England.'

'And you always do as your husband says?'

'I explained to the police that if I disobeyed my husband I would suffer the consequences.'

'How much were these men paying your husband for his hospitality?'

Ludmila shrugged. 'I have no idea. I was not told.'

Mr Propenkov looked down at his notepad. So far he had received conflicting stories from both Evgeniy and Ludmila Kuzmichov. He had an idea that if he was able to interview the man with the boat he would be told a different version again.

'Can we back track a number of years, Mrs Kuzmichov. I believe you drove a lorry with a consignment of goods from Moscow to Turkey. They were bound for Iran, but it was arranged for a driver to meet you and take over to drive from Turkey to Iran.'

'That was a long time ago.'

'Did you often drive lorries on behalf of your husband's business?'

'Occasionally, if there was no one else available to do so at that time.'

'On that particular occasion the lorry was stopped at the Turkish Iranian border and drugs were found concealed on board. Did you know you were carrying drugs?'

'Of course not. They must have been placed there when I stopped for the night in Turkey and handed the lorry over to the driver who relieved me.'

'No one approached you in Turkey and suggested that you hid them in the lorry?'

Ludmila shook her head. 'I am completely innocent. I had passed through the Turkish customs without any problems so any drugs that were on the lorry must have been placed on board after I handed over the consignment and it was signed for.'

Mr Propenkov believed that Ludmila Kuzmichov was telling him the truth; she would have been unlikely to have been cleared by the Turkish authorities if drugs were already on board the lorry.

'Were you ever stopped by the border controls on other occasions and found to be carrying something illegal?'

Ludmila shook her head. She had been fortunate each time she had delivered a shipment of arms carefully concealed amongst machinery and spare parts. After a cursory inspection by the border police she had been waved through.

'But you are not innocent of illegal acts at the moment. You drove down to a remote spot on the coast and collected immigrants when they landed and then took them up to Heraklion. I would like to contact your brother and ask him to help with our enquiries. Can you give me his address?'

Ludmila shook her head. 'He doesn't actually have an address. He lives on his boat.'

'So what is the name of his boat?'

Ludmila frowned. 'He must have told me at some time, but I've never really taken much notice. "Sprite", "Spirit", "Spectre", something like that.'

'Where is it moored?'

'I have no idea. He makes a living by taking people on fishing trips or journeys down the coast. He could be anywhere.'

'So how do you contact him?'

'I don't. He telephones my husband occasionally and I speak to him then.'

'Your husband gave me to understand that you have a close relationship with your brother.'

'I have,' Ludmila smiled. 'But that does not mean that we are continually telephoning each other. He would be distressed and horrified if he knew I was being held in prison. I knew what I was doing was wrong, but I had to obey my husband. Please believe me and allow me to be released on bail.'

'I am unable to do that at present, Mrs Kuzmichov, but I will have a word with the Chief Inspector on your behalf.'

'I would be very grateful.'

Mr Propenkov terminated the interview and went in search of Chief Inspector Solomakis.

'I have spoken with Mrs Kuzmichov and she insists that she had no choice but to obey her husband.'

Solomakis sighed. 'She told me that also.'

'So there should be no reason why she is refused bail,' smiled Mr Propenkov.

The Inspector shook his head. 'I'm not prepared to allow her to leave yet. When we first asked her to come with us to the station we also had a warrant to search the apartment. She had the key to the safe in her possession, although she claimed it was for emergency use only if anything untoward should happen to her husband. When we opened the safe a very large sum of money was found inside, along with envelopes bearing the names of the men who had recently arrived at the hotel. The only person who could have placed those inside was Mrs Kuzmichov. I believe that she is far more involved than she admits. I am waiting for the British Embassy to contact me. We were asked to be particularly vigilant at the airport as a number of men had arrived at Gatwick airport bearing false passports. Until I have heard from them I propose to keep both Mr and Mrs Kuzmichov here assisting us in our enquiries.'

Mr Propenkov considered the information. He would need to contact the authorities in Moscow and ask them to demand access to the Kuzmichov accounts. The procedure could be lengthy.

'Surely there is a limit to the amount of time you are able to hold them?'

'In Greece you can be held for an indeterminate amount of time whilst enquiries are being conducted.' Solomakis smiled complacently. 'I believe the same applies in your country.'

'It's good to be home.' Cathy looked around at their apartment and smiled happily.

'We were only away two days.'

'It seemed much longer; probably because I was bored sitting in the hotel. It was different when we lived there. You were usually around for at least part of the day and I had shopping, cooking and cleaning to occupy me.'

'What would you like to do this evening?'

'I don't feel like cooking as that would mean going to the supermarket and until I've checked the fridge I won't know what I want. Why don't we go for a meal locally? You can 'phone Vasi and I'll make out a shopping list ready for tomorrow. Then we can get back to normal.'

'I'll go and see if Panayiotis is around and if he has any information for me about the bones. If work is able to progress

I'll need to let Mr Vroukinas know. I don't want him to charge me for sitting there doing nothing and nor do I want him accepting another big job so that I am at the end of the queue.'

'Whilst you go and see him I'll unpack and put the washing into the machine; then I'll have a shower so it will be free when you return. Don't be too long. I'm hungry. The pizza we had in Malia seems like a lifetime ago. You could ask Panayiotis to join us.'

Panayiotis was at home, and accepted Vasilis's invitation to join them for a meal.

'I have to be on duty tonight so I will have to leave you by half nine to come home and get changed. I'm on bone watch.'

Vasilis groaned. 'I was hoping you would be able to tell me that the site had been cleared and I could continue building.'

Panayiotis shook his head. 'I'm afraid not. So far they have found ten graves and think there might be more. The excavation work could take a number of weeks as it has to be done slowly and carefully; everything photographed and recorded before it is moved.'

'Is Mr Vroukinas down there each day?'

'No, he was told he had to move his digger. I spend the night sitting close by in my car. There is a small tent that the archaeologists use to store some of their equipment over night. I wish they'd take it all away with them when they leave. I've had to confront prowlers on two occasions. I'm sure they were just after the tools although they tried to tell me they were just curious.'

'They'll be finished before the winter rains arrive, won't they?'

'I've no idea. You'd have to talk to the man who appears to be in charge and ask his opinion. He said they would be working over the weekend. I think they will be as relieved as you once they have finished. How did you get on up in Heraklion?'

'A satisfactory outcome, but not one I'm terribly happy with. The hotel is able to stay open, but I have to be responsible for the accounts. I'll tell you more over our meal. Cathy asked me not to be too long as she is hungry and I think she will appreciate an early night in her own bed. I also want to have a shower and 'phone my son and let him know we are home. Come round in about three quarters of an hour. We should be ready by then.'

Vasilis drove down to his plot of land on the coast road. He was pleased to see that there were men already at work and lifted the tape so he could gain access. He looked at the series of shallow oblong pits that were spread across the site where men were on their knees or lying down to gain access to the holes.

'You're not allowed in,' called a man who was sitting with a clipboard resting on his knees.

'I need to speak to whoever is in charge.'

'He's busy.'

'I am the owner of this land and if I am not allowed to have a conversation with the archaeologist in charge I will refuse all of you access.'

The man placed his clip board on the ground and rose to his feet. 'You might be the land owner, but this is an archaeological site and you cannot refuse to let us excavate.'

'So you are in charge?'

The man nodded. 'What do you want?'

'Firstly I would like to know if you have any idea how much longer you are going to be working here.'

The man shrugged. 'Impossible to say. Once we have cleared these graves we will investigate further back using GPR.'

'What is GPR?' asked Vasilis.

'Ground Penetrating Radar. It gives us readings of the area below ground. Saves us having to dig up the whole site. If we don't find anything then we're finished and our work will be in the lab, cleaning, cataloguing and writing up our notes.'

Vasilis sighed. 'Is there any way the process can be speeded up?'

'Not really. We have three volunteers working with us who remove the top soil from an area where the GPR alerts us to a possible grave. If they find any evidence of bones they tell us and as soon as an archaeologist is free he will commence the retrieval. It has to be left to a specialist. We don't want them to suffer any unnecessary damage through ignorance or clumsiness. Then there is the sieving that needs to be done.'

'Sieving?'

'All the soil that has been removed has to be sieved and examined for small pieces of bone, teeth, seeds and anything else that might be relevant. We then use that soil to fill in the excavated areas. The volunteers do the original sieving and then one of us examines whatever remains.'

'Couldn't one of your volunteers do that job?'

'We can't expect them to be responsible for the examination. They might not know what a tooth or piece of bone looks like. They remove the waste spoil and refill the empty graves.' The man waved his hand to four areas that showed where new soil had been placed.

'If you have dug holes in the ground and then filled them in will it be safe for me to build my house here? I don't want to find it subsides.'

'There should be no problem. The ground will be more stable when we have finished than it was before.'

Vasilis's shoulder slumped. 'If I give you my card would you be able to contact me and let me know how you are progressing? I can come down every day to have a look but I don't want to continually interrupt you if you have nothing to report.'

The man placed the card in the pocket of his jeans. 'Is that all you wanted to know? If so I'll get back to work.'

Vasilis nodded. It was obviously impossible for him to speed the excavation up.

Dispirited, Vasilis returned to his car and drove further along the coast road until he reached a convenient turning place. He wished he had bought the adjoining plot of land and then the problem might not have arisen.

Cathy took one look at his face when he entered the apartment and knew that he was not happy with his visit to the land.

'They don't know how long it is going to take them,' he complained. 'There's nothing I can do.'

'Now you're home will you come shopping with me? You can decide what you would like for a meal this evening and I can buy some fresh bread to go with our lunch today. I thought I'd 'phone Marianne and see if we could invite ourselves over there tomorrow afternoon. I'm sure Giovanni would be interested to hear about the hotel.'

'If you want,' replied Vasilis and then felt contrite when he saw Cathy's face. 'I'm sorry. None of this is your fault. I just feel so helpless and depressed and this afternoon I must work on the accounts that Dimitra has sent through to me.'

'Then it would be a good idea to forget about the bones and visit the Pirenzi's tomorrow,' said Cathy firmly.

August 2015
Week Three – Monday

Chief Inspector Solomakis examined the reports he had received after the mobile 'phones of both Evgeniy and Ludmila Kuzmichov had been examined. Ludmila's 'phone showed she had only made a phone call to her husband about every ten days in the early hours, and not communicated with anyone else.

Evgeniy Kuzmichov's 'phone showed calls both received from and placed to different mobile numbers, along with those received from his wife. As Solomakis looked at the details he saw a pattern beginning to emerge. The mobile numbers that were listed were different after they had been used three times. Two calls were received by Kuzmichov and some hours after the second call he would make one back. The call Kuzmichov had made to the mobile number coincided with the days his wife had called him in the early hours. All the calls were brief, none of them lasting for more than a minute.

Later, on the same day Kuzmichov would a call a land line number in Heraklion. The number in Heraklion was always the same and it would be able to be traced. The different mobile numbers that were listed would be impossible to trace back to their source. It was likely that the caller was using a cheap 'pay as you go' mobile that was being thrown away.

The Inspector was just about to give instructions to an officer to trace the call made to someone in Heraklion when a knock on his door interrupted him.

'There's someone here from the British Embassy in Athens who says he needs to speak with you.'

Solomakis gave a pleased smile. 'Please show him in.' He straightened his uniform as he stood up to welcome his visitor.

'How can I help you?' asked Chief Inspector Solomakis as he shook the man's hand.

'It's probably more how I can help you,' replied Mr Cavanagh as he took a seat and placed his briefcase beside him. 'I have been instructed to visit you by the Immigration Authorities in England. I believe they asked you to be particularly vigilant in checking passports for foreigners who were travelling to England.'

Solomakis nodded. It was a relief to know that the man spoke fluent Greek and he would not need to ask Orestes to come and act as interpreter for him. 'I placed extra men at the airport but they have not been alerted to any irregularities.'

'I think it was a little late by then for the Immigration Authorities to make the request.'

'So I can withdraw my men?'

Mr Cavanagh nodded and continued. 'As I understand it a number of men are being detained as illegal immigrants in England. They entered the country from Syria on false passports expecting to make a new life for themselves. When they were unsuccessful they finally confessed to the authorities and asked for asylum status. They have given statements, all of which are virtually the same regarding the circumstances in which they left Syria and their subsequent arrival on Crete and departure to England. You then contacted the Embassy in Athens saying you had illegal immigrants detained here who were expecting to travel on to England. I have been asked to co-operate with you in the enquiry. It appears that we have human traffickers at work, probably making excessive amounts of money at the expense of these unfortunate and desperate people.'

'I have made some progress in the investigation and we have two people in custody at present helping with our enquiries,' announced Solomakis. 'Unfortunately they are both Russian so their Consulate is also involved.'

'Really?' Mr Cavanagh raised his eyebrows in surprise. 'We did not receive that information from the men who are detained in England.'

Chief Inspector Solomakis sat back and began to make Mr Cavanagh conversant with the details of the arrest of the Kuzmichovs. 'I interviewed both of them separately and their stories are inconsistent. The wife insists that she knew nothing and was forced into driving the men to Heraklion due to her husband's threats of violence if she disobeyed. The husband insists they were his private guests and he met them from the airport at the instigation of his brother in law. A representative from the Russian Consulate has interviewed both parties but I do not know what they told him. He asked for both of the Kuzmichovs to be released on bail, but I refused.'

'Have you also interviewed the Syrian men?'

'Yes, but that was more difficult. They do not speak Greek and I had to rely on one of my officers to act as an interpreter.'

'Would you give me permission to speak with them?'

'Certainly. I can arrange that for this afternoon if that is convenient with you. You will be able to check their statements with those already in your possession from England. One of them is acting as spokesman for all of them. His name is Dawoud.'

'Do you have photographs of the couple you have in custody at the moment?'

'No. Photographs would only be taken once they had been convicted of an offence. Why?'

'It could be useful to send them to England to see if the men who are detained there recognise them as the woman who booked their flights and the man who owns the hotel.'

'We're holding their passports. Would those photographs be any use?'

'Better than nothing. Are you following up any other lines of enquiry?'

'I received their telephone records this morning. They make interesting reading. I was just about to ask an officer to trace a 'phone number when you arrived.'

'May I see them?'

'Certainly. I believe a 'pay as you go' mobile was used and subsequently disposed of. There is a definite pattern to the 'phone calls and a number in Heraklion seems to have been used on a regular basis. That is the one I am going to ask an officer to trace.'

'Do you have any information about the boat the men travelled in?'

Solomakis shook his head. 'They are unable to tell me the name of the vessel, only that the man who sailed them across was called Ivan.'

'Have they said how much they paid him?'

'Twenty thousand dollars each. Half was for the cost of the boat trip and the remainder was to cover the cost of their passports, flight and hotel expenses. We found an enormous amount of money in the safe at the Kuzmichov's apartment and that has been sent to the bank for safe keeping. There were also envelopes, each named and holding a mobile 'phone and ten thousand dollars.'

'Has that money also been sent to the bank?'

'I did not want the responsibility of holding such large sums of money at the station. The money from the envelopes was sent as a separate consignment to the bank.' Chief Inspector Solomakis smiled smugly. There could be no suspicion that any money had disappeared whilst at the police station.

'Did you keep the mobile 'phones?'

'They are here in the original envelopes. Now we have a record of the calls made on the mobiles used by the Kuzmichovs I can ask for the Syrian ones to be examined.'

'I think you are unlikely to find out anything useful from them. According to the men in England all the arrangements were made in person and their mobiles only returned to them just before they boarded their flights. The call that was made regularly to the same number in Heraklion could be informative. Whilst you deal with that and arrange for me to visit the men this afternoon I'd like to hear the interviews you recorded with the Russians and also have a look at those telephone records for myself.'

Dawoud and his companions looked at the photographs of Ludmila and Evgeniy that Brian Cavanagh showed them.

'The man, yes,' said Dawoud. 'We all recognise him. He was the man who took us into the hotel and you arrested. The woman, we can't be sure about. It was definitely a woman who met us, but she was dressed all in black and only spoke a few words to us. We sat in the back of the car so didn't really see her face at all.'

Brian replaced the photographs in the folder. 'I have read the interviews you gave to the Chief Inspector. I am going to ask you the same questions again as he had to work through an interpreter. I want to ensure that there are no contradictions due to translation difficulties.'

Dawoud nodded. 'We understand.'

Patiently Brian went through all the questions again about how the men had been contacted and were invited aboard the boat. They all confirmed that they had paid twenty thousand dollars to be taken to Crete and then travel on to England.

'Do you happen to know of anyone else who has made the journey?'

'Not for certain,' replied Chadhi. 'One of my colleagues disappeared. No one seemed to know what had happened to him and it isn't wise to make too many enquiries. He could have been arrested for some reason and if you ask for information you could be arrested as well.'

'Can you give me his name?' asked Brian. 'There are a number of men being held in England who claim to have arrived via Crete. I could check if he is one of them.'

'Jamal, he was a doctor.'

'What will happen to them?' asked Dawoud anxiously.

'They have asked for asylum and their cases are being investigated. At present they are living in a hostel similar to this one. I am sending the photographs that I showed to you over to England and the men will be asked if they recognise the couple. We are coming to the conclusion that this is a well planned operation and it needs to be stopped. Not only is it illegal to bring visitors into Crete without going through the official channels at airports and docks there is the additional concern about travelling across the sea in a small boat. So far the weather has been good for the crossings, but if a gale blew up a small boat would be extremely vulnerable. The safety of the passengers could not be guaranteed.'

The officer who had been asked to track down the 'phone number that appeared regularly on Evgeniy Kuzmichov's mobile placed a paper on Chief Solomakis's desk.

'According to the telephone company the number is of an artist who has premises on the outskirts of Heraklion and registered in the name of Rashid Maziar.'

'Any calls from him to Kuzmichov?'

'None that we can see. He calls a number in Iran almost every day, but his other calls are all incoming.'

'Find out his opening hours and then we'll pay him a visit.'

Brian Cavanagh returned from his visit to the hostel and sat before Solomakis. 'Has there been any reply from Immigration in England about the photos that I sent to them?'

'Not yet. What did the men here have to say?'

'They recognised Evgeniy Kuzmichov, but were unable to confirm that the woman was Ludmila. They said she was dressed all in black and hardly spoke. I'm hoping we'll be able to receive a definite identification of her from the men in England.'

'That would be helpful,' agreed Solomakis. 'The 'phone number that Kuzmichov called regularly belongs to an artist. We're going to pay the owner a visit. It's possible Kuzmichov was planning to have his portrait painted, but somehow I do not think he had that in mind. There must have been another reason for his calls.'

Brian Cavanagh raised his eyebrows. 'Interesting. Once I've heard from Immigration about the photos I'll put a call through to them and ask for details. Depending upon their information I'll then arrange to meet with Mr Propenkov. If he is confronted with irrefutable facts he may be more co-operative.'

John returned from Heraklion late in the afternoon feeling pleased with himself. Having delivered the collection of pots to the shop he had walked along the road looking for similar establishments. He had persuaded Uncle Yannis to allow him to take three other samples of the goods he had for sale, along with a folder of photographs. It was time consuming talking to the shop owner, showing the samples and the photographs and explaining that he was not the owner of the items, but working on behalf of his uncle who was now too old to continue with his business and needed to dispose of his stock.

The shop owners showed interest, two placing orders for some of the miniatures and another actually purchasing one of the pots that John had with him. Having left all of them with details of the web site and obtaining their e-mail addresses John felt that his efforts had been rewarded and planned to suggest that he should repeat the procedure in Aghios Nikolaos.

Uncle Yannis was elated when John placed the cash in his hand and pushed it into his pocket.

'You'll have to pay it into the bank,' John advised him.

'Rubbish. I am the only one who knows how many pots I have for sale. If they are not purchased through a transfer to the bank the money is mine. Don't forget to adjust the stock accordingly.'

'I thought I might try visiting the gift shops in Aghios and see if I could persuade them to buy some.'

Uncle Yannis nodded. 'I was well known in the town when I

had a shop there. They would know if they purchased anything from me it would of exceptional quality. They all have the seal attached to say they are museum replicas so they are better than the mass produced items they usually try to sell to the tourists. If you make a sale see if you can get them to pay you in cash.'

John smiled. His Uncle might be getting on in years but he was still an astute businessman. He would load up the car with examples and try his luck.

'Hi, Marianne. How is mother? You must be exhausted having had to look after her all this time.'

'She's fine; no trouble at all. Most days she goes down for a swim and she enjoys entertaining the girls and playing with little Yiannis.'

'Hmm.' Helena did not sound convinced. 'Greg has arranged some extra time off and we are going to travel to Washington and spend a few days there, then to London, Paris and Athens. We plan to arrive on Crete in about three weeks. We'll take mother home with us from there when we return. I'm sure you've put up with her for quite long enough and will be pleased to see her go.'

'I think you should ask her before you presume.'

'She needs to return and see that everything is in order in her house. It's been shut up for months.'

'I thought you were keeping an eye on it for her. I understood that you had keys.'

'That's true, but it's not convenient for me to keep having to go over. If Greg and I moved in it would be so much simpler.'

'That is something you would have to discuss with our mother when you are here. I think she appreciates having her own house where she can go to live if she decides to return home at any minute.'

'She would have a home with us,' answered Helena petulantly.

'That is not quite the same as living independently on your own. She doesn't need to be looked after as yet.'

'You are as impossible as she is,' snapped back Helena. 'It's ridiculous that she should expect to live alone without help at her age.'

'She is only seventy eight, healthy and sensible. In ten years time she might well appreciate your offer.'

'I might not give her the opportunity a second time. We'll see you in about three weeks and stay in the hotel down by the waterfront.'

'I'll do my best, but I do need definite dates from you. Vasi's hotel is very popular and is usually fully booked.'

'They are friends of yours so I'm sure you can arrange something with them. I'll e-mail you the dates as soon as we have decided how long we will spend in each city. Tell mother we will arrange for her to return with us.'

Marianne sighed. No guest who had already booked should be made to move elsewhere to accommodate her sister. 'You need to speak to mother before you start booking a return journey for her. She's welcome to stay here for as long as she wants.' She closed her mobile 'phone and went in search of Giovanni. 'Do you want to know who has just called me?'

'Just tell me.'

'Helena and Greg are coming over in about three weeks time. They want to stay at Vasi's hotel and Helena wants to take mother home with them.'

Giovanni raised his eyebrows. 'I thought she was busy helping Uncle Andreas.'

'I told Helena that, but she is proposing to book for Mamma to return to the States with them.'

'Is that what your mother wants?'

'She hasn't been consulted. I told Helena she should speak to Mamma before she made any arrangements and that Mamma was welcome to stay here as long as she wanted.'

'Are you going to tell your mother?'

Marianne nodded. 'It's only fair that she should know Helena's plans in advance and not have them sprung on her.'

Andreas read through the reply he received from his publisher in New York. They had read the draft of his play and considered that it had great potential, but it needed to be longer. After sitting at his computer and adding dialogue he was still not pleased with the result. He needed to be able to incorporate the reminiscences of the women and they still refused to talk to him.

Elena listened to the proposal that he made to her over the 'phone. 'I'm not sure if I could persuade the women to talk to me.'

'Would you at least come and try? I won't blame you if you have no success.'

'Can I come and discuss it with you? I may have a problem and helping you could be just the excuse I need.'

'Has Marianne said you have outstayed your welcome?'

Elena smiled to herself. 'She certainly hasn't said that to me and I hope I haven't been a nuisance to her. She told me a short while ago that Helena has called. She and Greg are planning a visit and want to take me back home with them.'

'So when will you leave?'

'I don't want to leave. If I can tell Helena that I am working with you it will be a good excuse to stay on until I feel ready to return home.'

'Come and visit me tomorrow and we'll make some plans.'

Vasilis drove down to his plot of land. It was still cordoned off and he could see the men were working there. He ducked beneath the tape and walked a short distance towards the man he had spoken with before.

'Have you made much progress?' Vasilis asked anxiously.

'Difficult to progress when we get continual interruptions.'

'I'm sure it is, but I need to know when I can get my workmen back on site. I don't want to find that you have been finished for over a week and no one has told me.' Vasilis knew this would not happen as Vasi passed the site each day on his way to his hotel and Panayiotis was on duty at night.

'Look, I can't tell you how much longer we are going to be here. I have your card and I agreed to 'phone you when we were finishing up.'

'I'd like to watch your procedure. I won't interfere with your work.'

'We don't want anyone tramping across the land just as they please. They could damage something beneath the soil. We make sure we walk around the perimeter and then go to the area where we are currently excavating.'

'I won't walk around. I'll just stand where you say and watch.'

'I doubt you'll find it very interesting.'

'In that case I'll leave.'

With a sigh Lambros led the way to where he was using a trowel to carefully dig the soil away from the bones until they were exposed. He then placed a measuring rod and number at the side and took a series of photographs. Satisfied that he had an accurate record he proceeded to brush away the earth and lift the bone carefully from the ground and placed it in a tray. He then added the grave number and a short description of the bone on a piece of paper from his notebook and added it to the tray where he anchored it with a stone.

Vasilis watched the procedure and he had to admit that seeing the same process repeated time after time it became boring.

'Thank you,' he said as Lambros rose and moved further up the edge of the grave. 'I think I have seen sufficient.'

'I'm just about to lift the skull. Don't you want to watch that?'

'Is it any different from the work I've seen you do?'

'I have to insert a bandage around all of it to ensure that it is removed as complete as possible. Stavros will help me. It needs two hands.'

'I'll wait until you have done that.'

Stavros walked over with a roll of bandage and tape. Lambros would lift the skull a few inches from the ground and Stavros would insert the bandage beneath it and across the front. The procedure was repeated until the whole of the skull was wrapped in bandages. Lambros then lifted the skull in both hands so it was clear of the earth and Stavros applied the bandages from the top of the skull to beneath the chin and up the back, finally securing them with tape and both men lifted it gently into a waiting tray.

Vasilis found he had been almost holding his breath until the skull, completely wrapped, was placed safely in the tray.

'Do you have to do that with all of them?' he asked.

'If they're broken into pieces we just bag the fragments and try to reassemble it later. When we find one that is virtually complete we don't want it to break up as we remove it. Once it reaches the lab they'll unwrap it and clean it up properly. It looks like a man.'

'What makes you think that?'

'Heavy jaw and brow ridges. Confirms the information from the pelvic bones.'

Vasilis ran his hand round his chin. Was that how he would look when he became a skeleton?

'Thank you. I understand now why it is taking you so long. I have work of my own that I should be doing so I'll leave you now.'

'Follow Stavros back to the tape. That way you won't cause any damage.'

Vasilis returned to his apartment and Cathy looked at him in surprise.

'You were gone far longer than I expected. Does that mean the archaeologists have finished?'

Vasilis shook his head. 'It will take them quite a long time. I stood and watched as they excavated a grave. It had to be done so carefully, everything photographed before they moved it. Then I waited whilst they removed a skull. It takes two of them and they have to cover it in bandages so it doesn't fall to pieces.'

'Didn't they mind you standing here watching them work?'

'Provided I stood where I was told they didn't seem to worry. They wouldn't want me to go down there and walk around on my own. I was a bit foolish to stay down there so long. I have more than enough work to get on with here. I'm beginning to get e-mails from Giorgos with replies to the letters I sent out to the hotels and guests. I'll need to contact all of them for details and work out compensation money for those who were inconvenienced.'

'Surely if they paid their bill before they left "The Central" it is only the cost of a taxi fare for the guests.'

Vasilis nodded. 'True, but I want to work out just how many people that involved. I'm not prepared to pay them an extortionate amount for a taxi that only took them around the corner. I think that ten Euros for the taxi and fifty Euros for the inconvenience is more than sufficient. If it involves two hundred people I may have to reduce the compensation. Some of them may try to claim more, of course. The complications arise for those people who had paid for their hotel stay in advance. They can't be expected to pay a second time and I will have to ask them for proof and also how much their new hotel charged them. I can double check their figures, of course, but it will be time consuming.'

'Couldn't Vasi help you?'

'I can ask him, but I feel it is my problem and not his. I need someone who has a good computer brain and a knowledge of the law.'

'So why don't you ask Marianne? She trained in International Law and she's proficient on a computer.'

Vasilis looked at Cathy. 'Why didn't I think of that? Do you think she would be willing to help? I just want advice regarding the compensation. I wouldn't want to be accused later of spending Kuzmichov's money indiscriminately.'

'You can only ask her. Why don't you call her and see if she has the time available.'

August 2015
Week Three – Tuesday

Chief Inspector Solomakis sent two officers to the artist's premises with instructions to bring Rashid Maziar back to the station to help with their enquiries.

As the officers walked in Rashid gave them a frightened glance. 'What can I do for you?' he asked, hoping it was just a general check on his legitimacy to occupy the shop.

'We would like you to accompany us back to the station. We are conducting some enquiries and believe you may be able to help us.'

'I'm in the middle of finishing some painting. The client is waiting. Can't it wait until later or tomorrow?'

'I'm afraid not. I suggest we give you a few minutes to finish up your immediate work; then we will have to insist that you close your premises.'

Rashid shrugged. Whilst pretending to finish some painting he would remove incriminating evidence and make a swift exit through the back door and disappear for the remainder of the day.

Manos followed him through to the empty room behind the shop. 'I thought you had a client?'

'I did not say they were here. They are expecting me to complete their commission this morning and be able to collect it later today.'

Manos looked at the icon that Rashid was obviously touching

up where the original paint had cracked and flaked off. 'Very delicate work,' he observed. 'It would be wrong to rush it and spoil such a beautiful item. I am sure that it will not come to any harm if it is left for a while. Please come along with us now, sir. If you resist we will have to arrest you.'

Sulkily Rashid allowed himself to be escorted to their car and climbed onto the back seat. This was obviously more important than a client complaining that he had not completed some art work to their satisfaction. He never kept more than six passports at the shop at any one time, but if the police had a search warrant they would be enough to convict him.

Chief Inspector Solomakis greeted him genially and asked him to take a seat in the interview room. 'I believe you speak Greek; is that so?'

Rashid nodded.

'Good, then we will not have to delay matters whilst I send out a request for an interpreter. I am going to record this interview as it could save a considerable amount of time at a later date. You understand?'

Rashid nodded again.

'I am now commencing recording.' Solomakis added the date, time and the name of the suspect he was interviewing. 'Please answer any questions verbally, a head movement is not recorded by the machine. Please state your full name and current address.'

Rashid complied and waited for the next question.

'Do you have a valid passport or identification papers that allow you to reside in Crete?'

'Yes, sir.'

'How long have you been in possession of those?'

Rashid shrugged. 'Almost a year now.'

'Do you have them on your person today?'

'Yes, sir.'

'Then please produce them.'

Rashid handed over a passport and Solomakis studied it. He

could not see anything obviously amiss. 'This will be photocopied before it is returned to you.' He handed the passport to the officer who was standing by the door.

'Are you familiar with Mr Evgeniy Kuzmichov, the owner of "The Central" hotel?'

Rashid looked down at his hands. 'No.'

'Would you like to reconsider that answer? We understand from Mr Kuzmichov's telephone records that he contacted you on a regular basis.'

Rashid gave a deep sigh. He had no choice but to co-operate. 'I do know him.'

'Can you tell us why he should be contacting you?'

'He said he might have some work for me.'

'Really?' Solomakis raised his eyebrows. 'I think you need to do better than that. We know that over the previous four months Mr Kuzmichov has contacted you no less than a dozen times. Rather a long time to consider whether to ask you to undertake some work. Why did he contact you?'

'He had some design work for me.'

'We happen to know that Mr Kuzmichov had gentlemen of a foreign nationality staying with him at the hotel during the times he contacted you. What exactly was the design work he was requesting?'

'Passports.' The answer was a whisper from Rashid.

'Please speak up and repeat your answer.'

'Passports.'

Chief Inspector Solomakis smiled. 'Now you have admitted that you were working on passports for Mr Kuzmichov we can progress with our other questions. Obviously you knew you were breaking the law so why did you agree to do this work? Monetary gain?'

'Not entirely.'

'Then please explain.'

'I was able to leave Iran legally and go to Turkey. I was unable to obtain valid passports or travel papers for my wife and son and naturally I want them to be able to join me. I was told by a woman that if I contacted Kuzmichov he would be able to help me.'

'Who was this woman?'

Rashid shook his head. 'I have no idea. I stopped in Turkey by the Iranian border in the hope that I would be able to find a way to bring my family across into Turkey and we could travel on together to a country in Europe. I watched the lorries as they went through the check point and they seemed to pass through unhindered. One evening a woman arrived having driven a container lorry into Turkey and was taking a break. I approached her and engaged her in conversation finally asking if she would be willing to bring my family out on her return journey. She said it was not possible as she was signing the consignment over to someone else for the remainder of the journey into Iran. We continued to talk and she asked my occupation. When I said I was an artist she seemed more interested and offered to contact someone she knew and ask if they could help me.'

'So who was this person she contacted?'

'I don't know. She spoke for some considerable time and I didn't understand the language. She finally told me that he was willing to help, but there were conditions attached. I had to travel across Turkey until I reached the coast. Once there I had to 'phone him on the number she would give me and he would arrange for someone to collect me by boat and take me to Crete.'

'What was the name of this man?'

'He never disclosed his name.'

Chief Inspector Solomakis frowned. 'So on the word of this unknown man you obeyed his instructions and subsequently travelled to Crete?'

'He told me to go to a small coastal village on the border between Turkey and Syria and contact him again when I arrived to arrange my collection. I did this and within a few hours a small sailing boat arrived and I went aboard. We sailed back down the coast and then out into the open sea and finally arrived at Crete.'

'So you spent some time in the company of this man. What was his name?'

'He said it was Ivan. He may have been the man I had telephoned but I'm not sure.'

'And whilst you were making this journey did he disclose the plans he had for you?'

Rashid nodded. 'We sailed into the harbour at Heraklion and went ashore quite openly. He took me to a cheap hotel that was used by the lorry drivers. The following day he took me to the bank where he arranged for me to open an account and he placed a large sum of money in it. He told the manager that I was looking for a property to rent to set up my art restoration business and he was subsidising the venture. He made it clear to me that the money was a loan, but he would accept repayments in instalments. Once I had established the business I should contact him again and arrangements would be made for my family to leave Iran.'

'So are they now here with you?'

Rashid shook his head. 'I was foolish. I should have realised that the offer was too good to be true, but all I could think of was that my family would soon be joining me. I found some small but suitable premises that were cheap to rent and bought the equipment that I needed. I had flyers printed advertising my work and I visited the shops that sell icons and religious paintings to tourists and asked if they might have any work for me. One gave me a photograph of an icon and asked me to paint a copy. They were impressed by my work and asked me to paint some others for them. I began to have a regular clientele. Once again I phoned the number I had been given and gave him the address of the premises. He asked for my 'phone number and I had no hesitation in giving it to him. I also offered to start paying back a small amount of the loan each month if he would give me his bank details. He said it was not necessary at this time and I should wait until I had more money coming in. I asked when my family would be joining me and he said arrangements were being made. I still call my wife regularly to ask if she has any news of her departure.'

Tears came into Rashid's eyes as he continued. 'I was contacted about a month later and told to meet a man who had profitable work for me. It was Mr Kuzmichov, but I did not know that at the time. He explained that he wanted me to take photographs of men who would be staying for a short while at his hotel. I was then to insert them into British passports, doctoring them in any way that was necessary but so that the authorities would not notice. A condition was that the work had to be completed within twenty four hours. I told him I had no British passports and he said he would arrange for them to be sent to me in small batches. He said if I wanted my wife and my son to join me I should do as he said. He explained that it would cost a great deal of money to bring them safely over here and I already owed money to the man who had paid for me to open my workshop.'

'So you agreed to work for him?'

'I had no choice. He showed me the amount that had been deposited in my account and the interest that had accrued. There was no way I could make that amount of money from my painting. However hard I worked I would not be able to pay the sum back in my life time.'

'So how much money were you paid to make these false passports?'

'Two thousand Euros.'

'For each one?'

'No, I had to make six at a time and my debt was reduced by two thousand Euros when I delivered them.'

'How many passports have you dealt with?'

Rashid calculated and tapped his fingers. 'Seventy eight,' he said finally.

'So you have been able to pay off your debt?'

'Some of it, but there is still the interest accumulating and I

97

was told I needed to clear all the money I owed before my wife and son could be brought over here.'

Solomakis had a certain amount of sympathy for the man. He had obviously been desperate to bring his family to Crete and as such had been taken in by the offer made to him. He had a suspicion that the unknown man was the elusive Ivan and no doubt the woman he had approached in Turkey was Ludmila. He wondered how many others had been duped in the same way.

'You obviously knew that the work you were carrying out was illegal.'

'Will I be sent to prison?'

'That depends upon your further co-operation with us. Do you still have the 'phone number of the man who brought you to Crete and funded you?'

Rashid nodded. 'When I reached Crete he insisted that I had a new mobile 'phone and he took my old one The only number I was allowed to put into it was the one belonging to my wife. When I called him I had to buy a cheap mobile and destroy it after the call had been made. I have the number written down.'

'Then for a start I would like you to give us this number and if you wish to avoid a lengthy prison sentence you never try to call it again.'

'I don't have it with me. It is back at the shop.'

'Do you have any passports there waiting for your attention?'

'Yes.'

'Then one of my men will accompany you back to the premises and collect the passports at the same time as you provide him with the number. I am terminating this interview with Mr Rashid Maziar.'

Elena sat with her brother and read through the manuscript that he placed before her. 'Those boys certainly got up to some dangerous tricks. Their mothers must have been worried to death that they would be caught.'

'Achilles may have exaggerated, of course. They may have put a snake into a cab on one occasion and he has told me they did it many times. The same with stealing the cans of petrol and damaging the vehicles. I cannot believe that the soldiers were so stupid that they didn't realise some off the incidents were due to the local boys and not the andartes.'

'Maybe they preferred to think it was andartes rather than little boys. To have to tell their commanding officer that their jeep had been put out of action by a child would have been rather embarrassing.'

'If you can get the women to confide in you they would probably know how truthful the stories were.'

'I'll do my best, Andreas.'

Andreas smiled. 'I knew I could rely on you. We'll walk up to Pano tomorrow and whilst I sit with the men you see if you can talk to any of the women.'

'Come along this afternoon, Vasilis, and I'll do my best to help you. I'll look up a few things on the internet before you arrive and that could clarify some of your queries.'

'Do you want to come with me?' asked Vasilis of his wife and Cathy shook her head.

'You and Marianne are going to be working. She can't sit and chat to me and work at the same time. I'll be happy to stay here and prepare our evening meal.'

Vasilis was relieved that Cathy was prepared to stay at the apartment so he and Marianne could be uninterrupted. He parked outside their house and with his lap top under his arm he made his way around to the patio.

'I'm pleased you're early.' smiled Marianne. 'Everyone has been fed and the oldies are resting. You can include Giovanni in that, he likes to have a nap after lunch now. Marcus is up at the taverna and Bryony has gone out with Nicola and the children. John is around somewhere. Have a seat and tell me your problem.'

Vasilis opened up his lap top. 'If the police had not made their presence so obvious the situation probably would not have arisen. The guests saw him and some other men led away in handcuffs. It panicked them. Some of the guests decided they wanted to leave and go elsewhere. The reception staff did a magnificent job 'phoning around to the other local hotels and arranging accommodation and taxis. The worst problem arose when new guests arrived and they were told they were unable to stay at "The Central"; some of them had paid their hotel bill in advance and then had to pay a second time to stay elsewhere. Then there is the question of compensation, how much should I give each person or should I limit it to whoever made the original booking?'

Marianne held up her hand. 'Now stop, Vasilis. Let's approach this systematically. Do you have a list of all the guests who were refused accommodation at "The Central"?'

'Giorgos has sent me through the names of everyone.'

'Firstly we'll make a list of those people who booked through a travel agent and paid up front. The hotel would have received that money so it should be sitting in the bank and quite easy to return to the travel company and they can then return it to their customers. For those who had paid and subsequently moved we need a separate list detailing how long they stayed at "The Central". We then need to find out if their new hotel charged them again for staying there. If that is the case the people will need a refund, and again, it should be able to come from the hotel accounts. In the unlikely event that the new hotel said they would bill "The Central" you ask them to produce receipts and pay them accordingly.'

Vasilis nodded. He had not made any lists, but these were the arrangements he had in mind.

'I really need to know how much compensation I should pay the guests who were staying there at the time and had the inconvenience of having to change hotels.'

'Strictly speaking, and under the law as it stands, you are under no obligation to pay them anything at all. They chose to leave; there was no reason why they should not stay until the end of their original booking. We'll make a separate list of those and deal with it in more detail later. Now, those who arrived and were subsequently sent elsewhere do deserve compensation. Obviously you will pay their taxi bill, which should be minimal but a compensation figure is more complicated to work out.'

'That's where I need your help.'

'I've looked up the guidelines for delayed flights but that doesn't really fit your case. Once the guests arrived they were only delayed a very short time before being accommodated and it would be more of a good will gesture on your part. I suggest you offer ten Euros per person. I would expect most people to accept that as it is virtually money for nothing. If you begin to get letters asking for more I'll help you compose a letter telling them they have no hope of anything extra and take it or leave it – you are not open to negotiation and you are definitely not admitting any form of liability.'

Marianne smiled at the look of relief on Vasilis's face. 'How much were you thinking you would have to offer?'

'I was expecting you to say fifty Euros.'

Marianne smiled. 'If you were taken to court the figure might be increased but I think that is very unlikely. There was no emergency whereby they suffered trauma of any sort. Now, the people who did leave of their own volition deserve nothing more than their taxi fare, but their plans for the day were probably disrupted and again I would suggest that you offer ten Euros per person as a gesture of good will; again take it or leave it. Make sure that you enclose a form that they have to sign to say they have accepted the payment. Does that make sense to you?'

Vasilis nodded. 'It seems fair. I've been given a position of trust and I don't want to be accused at a later date of abusing it.'

'I hope you are being reimbursed.'

Vasilis looked at Marianne in surprise. 'I've never considered that and no one has mentioned it.'

'You are virtually in charge of running the hotel. It might be for a week, a month or a year. How long will it take you to check the accounts each week? How long will you spend composing letters to the companies and guests and dealing with any other problems that might arise? You should be recompensed for your time. Speak to the bank and tell them how much you will be claiming for personal expenses each month, and don't stint yourself.'

'How much do I owe you for your professional advice?'

Marianne smiled. 'Nothing. I am doing this as a friend. If it occurs frequently then I might think about putting in a bill. Now, let's make those lists and you should have a clearer idea how to progress. Once you have composed the e-mails send them over to me and I will check that you have not said anything that could be challenged if the recipient did decide to ask for more compensation.'

'I suppose I can't ask for compensation from the travel companies who refused to take bookings as they were under the impression that the hotel was closed down?'

'I don't think you would get very far with that. You advised them as soon as possible that there had been a misunderstanding and you can ask Giorgos to check his advance bookings. They should only be low for no more than a week or two at most. It could be worth your while to contact them again and reiterate that everything is back to normal at "The Central".'

'Should I tell them that it is in administration?'

'You could say that the owner was temporarily indisposed and you have authority to act on his behalf until he is able to return. You don't have to go into detail. They'll probably assume that he is ill. The fact that they will know that you were the previous owner and they never had a problem when dealing with you should allay their concerns.'

John appeared on the patio with Skele at his heels. 'Hi, Vasilis. What brings you up here?'

'Your mother is helping me with a legal problem.'

John raised his eyebrows. 'Are you charging rent to those bodies found on your land?'

Vasilis smiled. 'Only you would think of something like that. I went down there this morning and watched them excavating. It was very interesting.'

John swung a chair out from the table and sat down. 'Tell me.'

Vasilis described the procedure he had witnessed and John listened avidly.

'Would they allow me to go down and watch? I've only been able to look from the road.'

'I don't see that they could refuse if you were with me.'

'When you've built your house down there do you think you'll have a ghost or two?' John was remembering the experience Ronnie claimed to have had on Spinalonga with her long dead great grandmother.

'I'm sure other people have their houses built over old graves and have no problem with ghosts. I'll ask the priest to bless the land before the building proper starts. That should get rid of any spirits that might be hanging around. Come down tomorrow and I'll take you down to meet the archaeologist in charge. Don't bring Skele. He might decide to make off with a bone.'

'As if he would,' said John, scratching gently behind the dog's ears. 'What's going to happen to them eventually?'

Vasilis shook his head. 'I don't know. The museum may put them on display or just keep them in their store room.'

'You could ask to have them back.'

'Why would I want to do that?'

'They were found on your land; you must have some claim to ownership.'

'What would I do with them?'

'I think it would show far more respect for them if you had them reburied in the area you plan to have as a garden.'

Vasilis gasped. 'I can't have a cemetery in my back garden.'

'I'm not suggesting that. There are probably some bones that are too badly fragmented to be of any use to the archaeologists. What would they do with them? Put them in a box and forget them. You would only need a small area where they could be buried all together.'

'The ground would not be consecrated. The priest would never allow it.'

'I doubt that the land was consecrated when they were buried originally. I just think it would be rather a nice way of keeping the useless pieces of bone all together close to their final resting place. Much better than a cardboard box in a museum.'

Vasilis left Marianne feeling much happier. He would e-mail Giorgos and tell him that he had taken professional advice regarding refunds and compensation and within the next few days he would have the appropriate letters composed to send out. He then e-mailed Dimitra and asked her for a list of pre-paid bookings that had been made for the hotel during August. Once he had that he could write to the bank and explain the amount of money he would be withdrawing along with a list of the recipients.

He decided it would be quicker to telephone the various hotels where visitors had been accommodated and ask them to send him the details by e-mail so he could make the appropriate reimbursements either to the hotel or the customer.

Once he was satisfied with the letter he had drafted to the list of visitors with details of the compensation he was prepared to pay to them he would forward it to Marianne for her approval.

'Don't do any more today,' said Cathy, after he had told her of the advice he had received.

'I'll just draft out the letter and send it on to Marianne. If she is able to check it later today or tomorrow I can then send a copy to Giorgos. Some of the customers who are still in Heraklion may visit the hotel and ask him about compensation. He can show it to any of them that turn up there. It's only fair that he should know exactly what is happening and be able to tell them that it is being dealt with. I can authorise Giorgos to pay them cash and also send him a form that they will have to sign acknowledging acceptance of the money. It would be quicker and easier to pay them immediately rather than have to ask for bank details from them and send it later. I'll then e-mail Dimitra and ask her for a list of customers who pre-paid for a stay during August.'

Cathy shook her head in despair. Vasilis was obviously going to work throughout the evening.

August 2015
Week Three – Wednesday

Vasilis worked far later than he had originally intended and even when he finally went to bed he was unable to sleep. He kept thinking of the letters he had written and wondering if the wording was correct, the amount of compensation he was offering was adequate and if he had acted swiftly enough to save the reputation of the hotel. He rose early and Cathy shook her head when she saw him sitting at his lap top, a cold cup of coffee at his elbow.

'What time did you get up?' she asked.

Vasilis shrugged. 'I don't know, but I was wide awake and I didn't want to disturb you so I crept out.'

Cathy sat down at the table opposite him. 'Vasilis, this has got to stop. You are going to wear yourself out trying to sort out problems that are not of your making. Close the lap top down and go and shower. I'll have some fresh coffee and a croissant ready for you when you're dressed.'

'I want to get all the problems sorted out as quickly as possible.'

'I appreciate that, but working yourself into the ground is not going to help anyone. You sold the hotel and retired, remember, so that you could have plenty of time to do as you pleased. Suppose Kuzmichov is sent to prison? What happens then? You cannot be expected to be responsible for the hotel indefinitely.'

'I know, and I don't want to be involved for any longer than necessary, but until I'm able to get on with building the house I may as well occupy my time.'

'I thought you wanted to sit on a jetty and fish,' remarked Cathy.

'Since going fishing with Panayiotis I have definitely gone off the idea. I'm going down to the land when John arrives. He's interested in seeing the excavations.'

'Surely he's been down by now to see what is going on?'

'Yes, but only from the road. He wants to watch a skeleton being removed from the ground. Do you want to come?'

Cathy shook her head. 'I'm not really interested. I could go to the museum in Aghios and look at skeletons.'

Vasilis smiled. 'These are ours.'

'Ours? What do you mean? How can they be?'

'I think they are rather special as they have been found on our land.'

'But we have no idea who they were. They're not like the bones that were removed from the charnel house on Spinalonga. John knew exactly which ones belonged to old Uncle Yannis and if he'd been given the opportunity to examine some of the others he may have been able to put names to them.'

'John suggested yesterday that we reclaimed any damaged bones that the archaeologists had no use for and reburied them in the garden I plan to have at the rear of our new apartment when I am finally able to build it. He felt it would be more respectful to have their remains together close to their original internment area rather than sitting in a box at the museum.'

Cathy looked at Vasilis in amazement. 'Are you serious?'

'I haven't really thought about it, but John was certainly serious when he suggested it to me.'

'Would you be allowed to do that?'

'I don't know, but it wouldn't be like having a proper burial ground. Just a small area where a casket was buried and with

107

some sort of commemorative stone saying that a certain number of skeletons were found on the land.'

Cathy sighed. 'I wouldn't want visitors tramping through to our back area.'

'They wouldn't. It would be entirely private and no one apart from the family would know anything about it.'

'If the skeletons are on display in the museum they will have the location of their burial ground.'

'They would only put the general location, not our address. I'll ask the priest on Sunday and see how he feels about it. If he disapproves or says it would be illegal I'll forget the idea.'

Chief Inspector Solomakis had allowed Rashid Maziar to return to his shop and continue with his work once he had produced the 'phone number that probably belonged to Ivan and handed over the passports that were in his possession.

'Your activities will be monitored. One of my men could arrive at any time and search your premises. If they find any indication that you are doctoring passports you will be arrested and will certainly not avoid a gaol sentence. If you are contacted for any reason by this man Ivan you are to inform me immediately.'

'How am I going to repay my debt?'

Solomakis shrugged. 'I can only suggest that you try to save some money from your legitimate work. You say you do not have any details of the man or his bank so it is impossible for you to make any repayments at present.'

Rashid had been profoundly relieved and grateful, but worried. 'Suppose this man 'phones and says that arrangements have been made for my family to travel?'

'I think it most unlikely and I would advise you not to believe him. To try to smuggle them across the border could place them in grave danger. They would probably disappear without trace.' The immigration of Maziar's wife and child was not his concern.

Once Rashid Maziar was back at his shop he used the 'phone number he had written down to contact Ivan immediately. It was unlikely that the police would be able to trace the call if he acted swiftly. His call was answered on the second ring.

'Yes?'

'It is Rashid here. I have been picked up by the police and questioned regarding the passports. I believe Mr Kuzmichov is being held by them. I had to disclose this 'phone number but I did not give them any other information.'

'Good. Keep it that way and do not try to contact me again as I will not be using this number.'

'What about my family?' Rashid began to ask as the 'phone line went dead.

Ivan smashed the mobile phone into pieces and dropped them into the sea. If the police tried to trace him by using that number they would find it was no longer in use. Now he knew why he had been unable to contact Evgeniy Kuzmichov to say he was leaving Syria with the latest group of immigrants. He was pleased he had had the foresight to withhold his number whenever he had called. It was annoying that the lucrative business he had set up was no longer viable and he would have to leave his current port and sail further up or down the coast. He had assured the immigrants that the delay would be no more than a day or two and he did not want them coming aboard to demand their money back.

Having sent Maziar away the Chief Inspector decided he would call Brian Cavanagh and ask if the men in England had recognised the photograph of Ludmila Kuzmichov as being the woman who took them to book their flights and check how much each man had paid for his new passport. If they confirmed that it was Ludmila Kuzmichov he would call Mr Propenkov and say he wished to interview the woman again.

Brian Cavanagh spoke cautiously. 'Apparently the men have been shown the photographs and are fairly certain that the woman was the one who took them to book their flights and buy some shoes.'

'Why aren't they certain?'

'They say her hair is different.'

'And the photograph of her husband?'

'Definitely the man who spent time with them at the hotel.'

'How much did each of them pay for their new passports?'

'Two thousand American dollars each.'

Solomakis whistled through his teeth. 'According to Maziar he was paid two thousand each time he delivered six passports. I have a suspicion that Kuzmichov held on to the extra money. I'll 'phone Mr Propenkov and ask him to come to the station. I'd like you to be here to tell him that Kuzmichov has definitely been identified. He can then speak with the man and see what excuses he manages to come up with.'

'Does Mr Propenkov speak Greek or English?'

'He speaks Greek. I don't know about English.'

'I'd like to talk to both the Kuzmichovs,' said Brian. 'As a courtesy I will tell Mr Propenkov that he can sit in whilst I conduct the interviews. It's unlikely that either of them will talk to me without him being present. I just hope he won't continually interrupt in Russian and tell them what to say.'

'The interviews can be recorded. I have no one on my staff who speaks Russian but there is sure to be someone at the British Embassy in Athens who could translate. Don't make Mr Propenkov aware of that. He may give up some useful information if he thinks his words will not be understood.'

'See if you can arrange something for this afternoon. I'll have cleared my desk by then.'

John drew up outside Vasilis and Cathy's apartment. 'I have my bike with me so we can ride down and I'll bring you back before I go to collect Skele.'

Vasilis shook his head. 'We'll take my car,' he said firmly. 'I'm too old to ride pillion nowadays.'

'I offered Grandma Elena a lift one day and she was about to accept when Mum stopped her. She's much older than you and willing to take the chance.'

'Hmm; obviously older and more foolish. My car is just along the road. You can leave your bike in the space whilst we're gone.'

John grinned. He had known it was extremely unlikely that Vasilis would accept his offer. 'I'll just get my camera.' He removed his camera from the pannier on the back and placed his helmet inside before locking it securely. With his camera hung around his neck he wheeled his bike along the road to where Vasilis's car was parked.

'Will my bike be safe here? I don't want to come back and find it has been removed.'

'There should be no problem. Anyone can park along here, although it is mostly the residents who do so.'

'Useful to know when I have to come into town. Save having to pay in the car park.'

'Do you pay?' asked Vasilis.

'It just depends,' replied John cheerfully. 'If I know I am only going to the chemist or baker I usually take a chance or double park. If I'm blocking someone who needs to get out the keys will be in the car and they can move it a short way.'

'Suppose they damaged it?'

'They're not likely to do that moving it forwards or backwards a few yards; besides I use Dad's old work car, not the decent one he uses on an airport run.'

John looked at the site as they drew up. 'It doesn't look any different from when I came down to have a look last week. Leave me to do the talking.'

Lambros looked up and scowled when he saw Vasilis and John approaching. 'We've not finished if that's what you've come to ask,' he announced.

'I'm so pleased you haven't,' said John with a smile. 'Mr Iliopolakis told me how he'd watched you remove a skeleton and how fascinating he had found the procedure. I hoped I might be here at the right time to see you lift another.'

'Won't be for at least another half an hour. Lefteris is just finishing cleaning it.'

'Really? May I take a photograph of the skeleton before you move it?'

'Why would you want to do that?'

'As you know, Mr Iliopolakis owns the land and is planning to build a house here. He would like a photograph of one of the skeletons that I can enlarge and he can have hanging on his wall as a memento.'

Vasilis looked at John in amazement. He had never mentioned having such a photograph. He was about to protest when John bumped his arm and winked.

'I suppose so, although I don't really understand why anyone would want that kind of photograph on their wall.'

'Mr Iliopolakis is something of an eccentric.'

Lambros looked at Vasilis and shrugged.

'He also had another idea,' continued John. 'What happens to all the little bits of bone that have broken off over the years and you don't know exactly where they come from?'

'Our forensic archaeologists can usually tell which bone has been damaged.'

'I'm sure they can, but what do you do with those bits and pieces? Do you glue them back in the appropriate place?'

'That depends upon the state of the skeleton. If it is going to be placed on display it will be made to look as complete as possible. If it is just going to be stored for future reference they usually go into the box along with the rest of the skeleton.'

'Does anyone ever look at them again?'

'I've no idea. Why?'

'Mr Iliopolakis had the idea that if you have little useless pieces of bone he would like to have them. He would provide a casket and bury them in his garden with a small memorial plaque to say they had come from this site with details of their approximate age.'

Lambros looked at Vasilis warily; the man was more than an eccentric. 'I don't know if that would be allowed.'

'Oh, well, it was worth asking you. Maybe you could find out at a later date.' John smiled and appeared to dismiss the idea. 'Please can you lead us to where your colleague is cleaning the skeleton.'

Lambros led the way to an oval hole in the ground where Lefteris was lying down and carefully brushing away the soil from the bones. John took his camera from the case and adjusted the view finder.

'Looks like a man,' he observed.

'How would you know?' asked Lambros.

'I helped remove some of the bones from the charnel house on Spinalonga. I was shown how to differentiate between a man and a woman by a friend of mine who used to be an orthopaedic surgeon.'

Lambros regarded John with slightly more respect. 'So what makes you think this is a man?'

'The sciatic notch, the brow ridges and the fact that the bones look generally sturdier than those of a female. Have you any idea how he died?'

'Nothing obvious at the moment,' added Lefteris. 'Most likely old age or illness. There doesn't appear to be any damage on the bones to suggest he was in a battle.'

John knelt down and began to take a series of photographs and then rose and took a shot of the extended body. 'The light is not perfect but I hope these will come out decently.' He rose and stood beside Vasilis. 'You don't mind me watching the procedure you use to remove the bones? At the charnel house it was very difficult to say which bones belonged to which skull. They were so jumbled up. At least the skulls and the leg and arm bones were able to be preserved and the other remains were given a decent burial, not just left in a box.'

Lambros glared at him. 'You can watch the removal and then I'll ask you to leave and allow us to continue with our work.'

'Of course. I appreciate the time you have given to me. I certainly do not want to be a nuisance.'

John stood quietly beside Vasilis as Lefteris removed each bone, marked which side of the skeleton it had come from and placed it inside a bag. John looked at the leg and arm bones, hoping he might see some of the tell tale signs of leprosy, but they all looked healthy. Finally the skull was bandaged and lifted and Lambros turned to the two men.

'That's it. I don't want you down here every day expecting to take photographs whilst I work.'

Once back in the car Vasilis turned to John. 'Why did you tell them I wanted a photo of a skeleton on my wall? I wouldn't dream of having it hung up anywhere.'

John grinned. 'I doubt if he would have allowed me to take photographs. I had to make him think that you were the one who wanted them.'

'You made me sound like a senile old man. Suppose he ever came to my house? He'd see that I didn't have a photo on the wall.'

John sighed. 'You'd have to explain that I'm not a very good photographer and they were so out of focus they were useless.'

'Why do you want all those photos?'

'I want to show them to Saff. She might be able to tell if the person who has just been removed from the grave was suffering from leprosy. If he was, the chances are that all the others were also.'

'You really are the most devious young man I have ever met.'

Mr Propenkov and Brian Cavanagh met at the police station and Chief Inspector Solomakis arranged for Ludmila Kuzmichov to be brought to an interview room.

'I would appreciate the whole interview being conducted in Greek as I am not conversant with the Russian language,' said Brian, 'and I would also like to record it. Do you have any objection?'

Mr Propenkov shook his head. 'If I feel you are asking the lady leading or irrelevant questions I will advise her not to answer them. If you wish to ask her to elaborate on any information I will not interfere.'

Ludmila sat before the men and looked at them warily. She must remember the answers she had given in her previous interviews and not contradict herself.

Brian Cavanagh smiled at her, trying to put her at her ease. 'The interview will be recorded; you know the procedure. Mr Propenkov is here with me and if he considers that I have asked you something inappropriate he will advise you not to reply. This can sometimes be construed as admitting guilt, so please be as co-operative as possible.'

Chief Inspector Solomakis switched on the recorder and after the usual formalities Brian Cavanagh began.

'A copy of your passport photograph was sent to England where there are a number of men being held in secure accommodation having applied for asylum. They all claim to have travelled from Syria by boat to Crete and we know that you collected them and took them to your husband's hotel. They were able to identify you as the lady who took them to book their flights to England and also to buy some shoes. Out of curiosity I am asking why they needed shoes. Surely they did not arrive bare foot?'

'They only had canvas deck shoes and they were wet from where they had come ashore.'

Brian nodded. 'Thank you. As I said, that was just curiosity on my part. Now you took them to a travel agent and they booked their flights. Who paid for the flights?'

'They paid.'

'And where did they get the money from?'

'My husband had changed some of their dollars into Euros for them.'

'Did he do the same for the purchase of the shoes?'

'He gave them an amount each to cover the cost of the flights and their shoes.'

'Was there any money remaining?'

'Some.'

'Was that returned to your husband?'

'No, the men were able to keep it to buy refreshments at the airport or on the 'plane. It was their money.'

'Did you buy anything else for them?'

'No.'

'What about the suitcases? They said you took them from the boot of the car and gave them one each.'

'My husband told me to buy the suitcases.'

'Where did the money for those come from?'

'He gave it to me.'

'Before you took these men to make their travel arrangements it was necessary for them to have new passports. Who supplied those?'

'I have no idea.'

'No problem, I expect your husband will be able to help us there. Now, if we can return to their journey across the sea. I understand that the boat they travelled in belongs to your brother, but you do not know the name of the craft.'

'I've told you that.'

'You have also told us that you are unable to contact him.'

'That's correct.' Ludmila hoped the police had not found the private number she had for Ivan.

'I have looked in my previous notes and I do not appear to have a record of his full name. Please tell us.'

'Ivan Kolmogorov.'

'I would like you to spell that out, please.'

Ludmila complied and Brian Cavanagh made a note of the name.

'Do you know the name of his sailing companion?'

Ludmila shook her head. 'I have no idea,' she lied.

'What about the man who rowed them through the canal? He threw a package across to you. Surely you must have seen his face when he did that?'

'It was dark. I did not see his face clearly and if I had it is unlikely I would have known him.'

'Did you know what the package contained?'

'My husband said it would be their mobile 'phones.'

'And what were you to do with these packages?'

'Use the key to the safe and placed them inside.'

'Was this the usual procedure?'

'Yes.'

'You then gave the key back to your husband when he returned to the apartment?'

'Yes.'

'Did you ever see your husband open the safe and examine the packages?'

'No, but he may have done that when I was out. I don't understand why you are asking me all these questions a second time.'

'It is just a formality in the hope that you may have remembered something that could help us.'

Ludmila glared at them. They were trying to trap her into contradicting herself or extract information that she was not prepared to give.

'I'm not answering any more questions. I have a question of my own; when am I going to be released and allowed to go home? You should be talking to Evgeniy. He arranged everything. I just did as he told me.'

'We will be interviewing him later. He claims that it was your brother who made the arrangements.'

Ludmila shook her head. 'I've told you, I had nothing to do with any of the arrangements. As far as I am aware it was Evgeniy who arranged everything. There's no point in you asking me any more questions.'

'Very well. We will terminate the interview, but I have to advise you that we will be unable to release you until we have concluded our enquiries.'

Mr Propenkov turned to Solomakis once Ludmila had been led away. 'You really have no grounds for keeping her locked up. The poor woman obviously had to do exactly as she was told by her husband.'

Chief Inspector Solomakis shook his head. 'She is guilty of bringing illegal immigrants ashore. That is a crime.'

'You could release her on bail and allow her to return to the apartment. Provided you continue to hold her passport she would be unable to leave Crete.'

'Not at the moment. She claims she has to do exactly as her husband tells her, her husband says she does whatever her brother says. I don't believe either of them. Until we can get to the truth of the matter I would prefer her to stay in a holding cell. I'm sure she is not enjoying the experience and it might persuade her to finally tell us the truth regarding her involvement.'

Mr Propenkov shook his head. 'I will be asking the Russian Embassy to contact you. She is entitled to their protection and under the circumstances I think they would press for her release.'

Chief Inspector Solomakis looked at Mr Propenkov sourly. 'She cannot complain about her treatment. She has had her own clothes and toiletries brought in for her, fed adequate meals each day and given an extra blanket when she complained she felt cold at night. We'll take a break and let Kuzmichov eat his lunch then see what he has to say about the passports.' The Chief Inspector knew that if the Russian Embassy became involved the Greek Embassy would not want to cause an unpleasant incident by refusing the release of Ludmila from custody.

Evgeniy Kuzmichov tried not to show his annoyance when he was told that Rashid Maziar had confessed to taking the photographs of the men and providing false passports.

'I was acting on the instructions of my brother in law.'

Brian Cavanagh nodded. 'How did you receive these instructions?'

'He would call me and say when he was leaving Syria with his passengers. He would then call again when he was off the shore of Crete and then Ludmila would drive down to collect them. Once they had arrived I would call Rashid and ask him to come the following day.'

'All these 'phone calls,' remarked Brian. 'Can you please give us the number that was used so frequently?'

Evgeniy shook his head. 'Whenever Ivan called he either withheld his number or used a throw away 'phone. I was only able to receive incoming calls from him.'

'How much did the men pay Maziar for their new passports?'

'Two thousand dollars.'

'Was that the cost to each man or the total cost?'

Evgeniy hesitated. 'The men paid two thousand dollars each.'

'Really?' Brian raised his eyebrows. 'Maziar says he was only paid two thousand in total. He claims to have supplied seventy eight passports over the past three months. Now mathematics are not my forte but if each man paid two thousand that would make a total of one hundred and fifty six thousand dollars. If Rashid says he only received twenty six thousand what happened to the other one hundred and thirty thousand?'

'The man is lying.'

Brian sat back with a sigh. 'I think a lot of people are lying. I believe that everything you have told me so far is a pack of lies to try to cover the illegal activities of you and your wife. You have been participating in human trafficking for monetary gain, obviously with the assistance of your brother in law.'

Evgeniy's face purpled. 'Human trafficking? That is ridiculous.'

'You met illegal immigrants and gave them sanctuary at your hotel. You then arranged for them to have false passports enabling them to book flights to England. You were well aware they would be unable to find work that suited their qualifications and abilities so they would be forced to take menial jobs giving them only a subsistence wage.'

'I did not traffic these men. I treated them as guests at my hotel. They had bedrooms with all amenities. They ate good food, often down in the dining room amongst the other hotel guests. That is not trafficking. I did not force these men to work for me.'

'How much did you charge these men to stay in your hotel?'

Evgeniy shrugged. 'The going rate.'

'Really? According to our information no payment for these men was ever shown in the hotel accounts.'

'I kept it separately.'

'Would that be because the amount they paid was so exorbitant that both your accountant and the tax man would want to have details of the transactions? A very large sum of American dollars was found in the safe at your apartment, along with the mobile 'phones that belonged to your most recent guests. Twelve thousand would be the amount the men had to pay for their passports but how do you explain the remainder, Mr Kuzmichov?'

Evgeniy looked at Mr Propenkov who shook his head. 'Mr Kuzmichov is under no obligation to answer these questions regarding his financial affairs.'

'If Mr Kuzmichov was an English man I would be requesting that his financial dealings were scrutinized closely. He could be involved in any number of transactions that fall outside the law.'

Mr Propenkov shrugged. 'I have already passed that request on to Moscow and I am awaiting a response.'

Evgeniy banged his manacled fists on the table. 'My previous business accounts have nothing to do with either of you.'

'In that case, Mr Kuzmichov, you have nothing to worry about on that score,' replied Brian Cavanagh smugly.

Once Kuzmichov had been escorted back to his cell Brian Cavanagh looked at Solomakis. 'Have you tried calling the number that Maziar gave you?'

Chief Inspector Solomakis nodded. 'I did so as soon as I had a line free at the station. It was not recognised.'

'So either Maziar gave you a false number or he managed to warn Ivan Kolmogorov.'

'I think it most likely that Maziar had been given an incorrect number.' Solomakis was not prepared to admit that he had eaten his lunch before attempting to make the 'phone call.

August 2015
Week Three – Thursday

Elena walked up to Pano Elounda with Andreas. He greeted the men they encountered by name and nodded to the women who appeared in their doorways. At the kafenion Andreas announced his intention of stopping there to spend time with the men whilst Elena walked further into the village to see if she could find any women who were willing to talk to her.

'The men will say nothing in front of you and likewise the women won't speak to me about their experiences. It's better that you go on alone and see if you can find out anything.'

'What kind of questions should I ask them?' asked Elena.

'Just get them talking. The questions will follow naturally.'

As she wandered through the narrow streets she bade the women good morning in Greek and tried to engage them in conversation. Finally their curiosity got the better of them and one asked where she came from.

Elena smiled, fanned herself and asked if she could sit with the woman on the step of her house. Immediately she was offered a chair and a drink of water. Elena accepted the water, but declined the chair.

'I know my mother always sat on the doorstep when she lived in Aghios Nikolaos. She was a fisherman's daughter.'

'You live in Aghios now?'

'No, I live in New Orleans in America.'

'So you are on holiday here?'

'I am staying with my daughter and her family. You may know them, the Pirenzi's?'

The woman shook her head. 'I don't go outside the village these days. My son does my shopping and takes me up to church on a Sunday.' She gave a gap toothed smile. 'I'm too old for travelling now.'

'I expect your son knows them. They have self catering apartments and a snack bar and small shop that caters for the tourists. I am sure you would be made very welcome if your son was willing to take you down there.'

'Maybe. Why don't you take me now? You must have a car.'

Elena shook her head. 'I have a car in America, but I don't drive over here. My grandson drove me to Kato Elounda to meet my brother and then he and I walked up here.'

'Your brother does not live in America with you?'

'Not at the moment. He has a small house in Kato and is talking to the men in the villages about their war time memories.'

'What for?'

'He is a writer. There is a tremendous amount written about Crete and the suffering of the people during the war, but he wants some personal stories from the boys and girls who were growing up here at that time.'

The woman sighed. 'They were not good times.'

'I'd be interested to hear how they affected you.'

'So you can tell your brother?'

Elena shrugged. 'Maybe, if they are interesting.'

The woman gave her a scathing look. 'If your grandfather was a fisherman in Aghios why are you living in America?'

'It is an interesting story. Would you like to hear it?' Elena hoped that if she told the woman about herself she would be more forthcoming with her own life story.

The woman shrugged. 'If you like.'

'My mother was betrothed to a local man who became ill and

was sent to the island.' Elena hesitated and waited for the woman to realise the implication of her words.

'You mean Spinalonga? He was leprous?'

Elena nodded. 'My mother was training to be a nurse and she went over to Athens believing him to be in the hospital there and expecting to nurse him.'

'You don't nurse lepers,' replied the woman scornfully.

'She found that out, but continued to work in the general hospital in Athens. She happened to meet a young man who was involved in microbiological research and she suggested that he tried to find a cure for leprosy. She left the hospital and became his assistant. He was offered a scholarship to America to continue his research and asked her to marry him and go with him.'

'He didn't find a cure,' remarked the woman triumphantly.

'No,' admitted Elena, 'But much more was found out about the disease and now there is treatment available to halt the spread of it throughout the body. After the war my father released all his research papers to the man on Spinalonga and it was due to him that the government agreed to test everyone. Many were found to no longer have active leprosy cells in their body and all of them were moved away from the island.'

'Where did they go?'

'Some lived at the hospital in Athens and others returned to live with their relatives.'

'What about the man your mother knew?'

'He went to live in the hospital, then he received some money owing to him from during the war and bought a small apartment.'

'Did you visit him?'

Elena shook he head. 'Unfortunately I never had the opportunity. My father met him once when he visited Athens.'

'And your mother? Did she visit?'

'No, she asked her father to take her over to Spinalonga before she agreed to marry my father and spoke to Yannis from the boat.

He said he released her from their betrothal agreement and wished her every happiness.'

'Yannis? You mean the Yannis who came from Plaka?'

'That's right.'

'I've heard about him.'

'Really? Who told you?'

The woman shrugged. 'Someone I knew.'

'From Spinalonga?'

'Maybe.'

'I would be interested to know. My grandson has done a considerable amount of research about the people who lived over there.'

'So tell me more about your family. I know you have a brother; do you have sisters?'

'I had two sisters; one became an assistant to a missionary and the younger one died.'

'I had three sisters and four brothers. Why didn't your mother have more children?'

'She hated having children.'

'The pain?'

'No, looking after them. She loved us all dearly, but she did not want to be at home with us every day. She wanted to be in the laboratory with my father.'

'A mother's place is at home,' the woman said smugly.

'We were not neglected. The problem was solved when my grandparents came to America. My grandmother looked after us and our mother was happy spending most of her day helping my father.'

'How many children did you have?'

'Three; twin girls and a boy. They are all married with children, and John, my grandson who lives over here, has twin girls and a little boy. Now, I have told you my life history, please tell me yours, particularly what it was like to be a child growing up during the war when you were occupied.'

The woman shook her head. 'Not today. I'm tired and it's hot sitting here. Next time you come, maybe.'

'Who shall I ask for if you are not sitting here?'

'My name is Evangelica. I'm called Evi.'

'I am Elena. I look forward to talking with you again.'

Mr Propenkov had no intention of contacting the Russian Embassy but he knew his threat would make Chief Inspector Solomakis think twice about refusing bail for Ludmila Kuzmichov. Having received an initial report into Kuzmichov's previous business transactions there was nothing to implicate her except occasionally driving a truck to a destination and handing over the cargo it contained. It would take a considerable amount of time before all Evgeniy Kuzmichov's accounts had been fully examined and investigated. If illegal dealing and bribes paid to customs officers was confirmed he would be charged and sentenced in Russia and nothing to do with the Greek authorities.

In his opinion there was no reason why Ludmila Kuzmichov should continue to be held in custody. He was sure the woman had been forced into complying with the arrangements for the arrival of the illegal immigrants and had no more useful information to give them. When the case against Evgeniy Kuzmichov was finally taken to court that would be the time to contact the Embassy and attempt to negotiate a lenient sentence for him and a complete exoneration for Ludmila.

He made his way to the police station shortly before mid-day and was annoyed to find that Solomakis would not be available until the afternoon. The young policeman he spoke with shook his head sadly.

'The Chief Inspector is a very busy man. Before he left yesterday Mr Cavanagh made an appointment with him for this afternoon. I understand that you are involved with the case they are dealing with so I suggest you return about three when both gentlemen will be here.'

Vasilis spent the morning examining the accounts that Dimitra had sent through to him. Once again everything appeared perfectly in order. He telephoned Giorgos and asked how much he needed from the bank to make up the wages for the staff who were paid in cash each week and promised to have the money available to him within the hour.

'I'll also arrange for the tradesmen's bills to be honoured. At the moment the hotel is still making a profit and there is no cause for concern. When the visitor numbers dwindle the travel companies will pay for the summer bookings and I'm sure you will soon be asked to book some conferences.'

'Are we allowed to use those rooms?' asked Giorgos. 'I've not heard anything back from the police.'

'I'll check it out with them. They should not need access any more so there is no reason why they should not be cleaned and prepared.' Vasilis ran a hand over his head. If he had not sold the hotel this situation would not have arisen and he hoped that he would soon be able to discharge his duties back to Evgeniy Kuzmichov.

Ludmila was delighted when Chief Inspector Solomakis declared that she was to be released and allowed to return to her apartment, although her passport would be held and she would be unable to leave Crete.

'I will arrange for a taxi to take you home as soon as you have packed your belongings.'

'Who is going to pay for that?' asked Ludmila. 'The only money I have is in my purse. How am I going to pay for my food once that has gone?'

'Do you not have a bank account?'

Ludmila shook her head. 'My husband gave me an allowance each week to cover our living expenses with a little over that I could spend as I wished.' She was not prepared to admit that she had a bank account in Russia with a very healthy balance that she could have made arrangements for Mr Propenkov to withdraw money from.

Mr Propenkov looked at Solomakis. 'I can only suggest that Mr Iliopolakis arranges for her to have a monthly income from the hotel. Her husband is the owner of the property so that should not present a difficulty.'

Chief Inspector Solomakis sighed. The woman would need some money to enable her to live, but this was yet another job that he really should not have to deal with. He was a policeman, not a social worker.

'I'm sure Mr Propenkov can speak to Mr Iliopolakis. Four hundred Euros should be more than sufficient for your expenses each month. You do not have any rent to pay.'

'How will I be able to receive that as I haven't a bank account?'

'It would be most practical if Mr Iliopolakis arranged for you to collect it from the hotel. Opening a bank account under the current circumstances would be time consuming and not necessarily granted.'

Ludmila nodded. She had hoped that she would be able to receive the money in cash as she certainly did not want to become involved with a bank. They would be forced to make enquiries in Russia and very likely discover the account she held in her maiden name. Four hundred Euros a month was not a vast sum, but she knew she would be able to manage until she had contacted Ivan and he arranged for her to leave Crete.

'Am I able to leave my apartment as I wish? I do not want to be confined there all day every day.'

Chief Inspector Solomakis nodded. 'You are not under house arrest and may go wherever you please in the town. Remember that you do not have a passport so you cannot leave Crete.'

'May I have my mobile 'phone back?'

'Of course it will be returned to you. Would you like to visit your husband before you leave? I would have to be in attendance, of course.'

Ludmila shook her head. Unless she was able to have a private conversation with Evgeniy there was no point in her visiting him.

'Not today. Maybe a meeting could be arranged in a few day's time when I have recovered from this ordeal. I would like you to tell him that I have been released and am able to return to the apartment. I am sure it would put his mind at rest to know that I am safe.'

Mr Propenkov raised his eyebrows. From all Evgeniy and Ludmila Kuzmichov had said about each other it was most unlikely that either was concerned about the welfare of the other. 'I am sure that can be arranged. Telephone me when you feel ready and I will contact Chief Inspector Solomakis.'

Ludmila smiled sweetly, disguising her annoyance. She had hoped that by arranging to see Evgeniy later in the week she would be able to discuss the events that had overtaken both of them and he would be able to tell her how she could help him to ensure the charges against him were dropped. If the man from the Russian Consulate was going to be in attendance and understanding the language a private conversation would be impossible.

Ludmila was escorted back to the holding cell but the door was not locked behind her on this occasion. She packed her clothes and toiletries quickly; she did not want the decision to release her to be reversed. Carrying the case she made her way back down the corridor to where a guard sat on duty at the desk.

'I understand that a taxi will be arranged to take me home. I would obviously like to leave here as soon as possible.'

'Of course, madam. I will have to ask you to sign to say all your belongings have been returned to you.'

He produced the keys to her apartment, her purse and mobile 'phone from beneath the desk. Ludmila examined her purse and as far as she could ascertain the amount of money inside was correct. She checked the numbers on the mobile 'phone and was satisfied that it belonged to her. She was certain the police would have examined it and recorded the numbers that were stored, but she had no intention of using any of them.

Ludmila perched uneasily on the hard seat and tried to curb her impatience. Half an hour later a taxi arrived and a surly driver placed her case in the boot and she was ordered to sit in the back. He ensured the glass panel between the driver and rear passengers' seats was closed and locked all the doors. She had a moment of panic. How did he know where to take her? She rapped on the glass division, but he ignored her. Trying to compose herself she watched as they entered the suburbs of Heraklion, finally taking a deep breath of relief when he drew up outside her apartment.

Without switching off the engine he removed her case from the boot and placed it on the pavement before unlocking the car doors and waiting for her to alight. He slammed the door behind her and climbed back behind the wheel, immediately putting the car into gear and driving away.

Ludmila opened the door to the apartment and carried her case inside. She slumped down in an easy chair and placed her head in her hands. She needed to think and plan her actions carefully.

Chief Inspector Solomakis, Brian Cavanagh and Mr Propenkov sat in the Inspector's office.

'What is going to happen to the Syrian men you have detained?' asked Brian.

Solomakis shrugged. 'They are not my problem. They have been told they can request asylum and it will be up to the authorities to decide whether this can be granted or if they should be sent back to Syria. It is not a police matter.'

'Will their money and 'phones be returned to them?'

'In due course.'

Brian Cavanagh looked thoughtful. 'I will contact the authorities in England. If they are willing to grant the men who are detained over there asylum would that influence the decision of the Greek authorities?'

'Who knows? Our laws differ from yours in some respects. I am now more concerned about bringing Evgeniy Kuzmichov to trial and ensuring he receives a prison sentence. It may be necessary to produce the information given by the men in England as further evidence against him.'

Mr Propenkov cleared his throat. 'Having released Mrs Kuzmichov I think the same leniency should be applied to her husband. It is the man called Ivan Kolmogorov who needs to be found and interrogated. I understand that you have inserted a device in Mrs Kuzmichov's mobile that will enable you to trace any calls that she makes. If the same is done with her husband's 'phone and he is also released it is more than likely that one or the other would try to contact Kolmogorov.'

Chief Inspector Solomakis shook his head. 'I think it could be most unwise to release Kuzmichov at this stage and I am not prepared to authorise the action. Once he and his wife were together they could well disappear.'

'You will be holding their passports,' Mr Propenkov reminded him.

'They could well have other contacts who would be willing to help them. No, Evgeniy Kuzmichov will remain in custody until I am certain there is sufficient evidence against him to ensure a conviction. Should you find out that he has committed any illegal activities in Russia before he comes to trial here you are at liberty to contact the Russian Embassy and make a request for his extradition. I will have no objection.'

Ludmila finally roused herself. She checked the fridge and removed the milk that had soured into a solid mass, the mouldy cheese and hard bread along with the fruit and vegetables that had turned to a disgusting mass of pulp. She threw all of it into a carrier bag and wiped the fridge clean. She needed to go to the supermarket and get some basic food items or she would have nothing to eat.

She took her clothes from the case and placed them into the washing machine before stripping off those she was wearing and adding them to the load. Checking that the water was hot she entered the shower, washed her hair thoroughly and scrubbed her body until the skin felt sore. Although she had been able to have a quick shower each morning whilst staying in the holding cell she had never felt clean.

Once dressed in clean underwear, trousers and a T-shirt she switched on the washing machine, picked up the bag of mouldy food that was already beginning to smell and opened the door to the apartment. She looked up and down the road, but there seemed to be no one loitering who might be watching her movements. Ensuring that she had her keys and purse with her before she closed the door she walked down the road and threw the carrier bag into the first rubbish bin she saw before rounding the corner to the row of shops.

Inside the supermarket she hesitated. What did she need? Having turned out the fridge she had not thought to check her cupboards. There was probably cake, bread and biscuits that were quite uneatable. She walked around slowly, placing items in her basket and then replacing them on the shelf. She would only buy milk, cheese, cold meat and tomatoes and some fresh bread from the baker. That would be sufficient to make a meal for herself that evening and she could make a comprehensive shopping list the following day.

She would have to be careful with the money she had in her purse. For years she had not needed to think twice before she spent whatever she wished. Once she had spent her current funds she would have to go to the hotel and ask if arrangements had been made to provide her with some money. How degrading to have to go and beg for what was rightfully hers.

Returning home Ludmila made a sandwich and ate it slowly. She needed to think carefully. Although she had seen no sign of anyone watching her whilst she went shopping she must act with caution and give Solomakis and Propenkov no cause for suspicion.

Vasilis was not amused when he had a telephone call from Mr Propenkov requesting that he made arrangements for Ludmila to have four hundred Euros each month from the hotel income.

'Having spoken to the hotel manager I have finalised the amount of cash that needs to be withdrawn from the bank this week,' remonstrated Vasilis.

'I'm sorry, but I will have to ask you to make a separate arrangement for Mrs Kuzmichov. She has been released and allowed to return to her apartment. Her husband is still in custody and she has no access to any money. It is not a vast amount, but it will enable her to purchase her food until such a time as the case against her husband is resolved.'

'How will this money be paid to her. Is she opening a bank account in her own name?'

'That would not be easy under the circumstances. I have told her she can visit the hotel and the money will be passed over to her there.'

Vasilis looked at his watch. 'It is too late for me to make the arrangement today. It will have to wait until tomorrow. Does she have sufficient money until then?'

'The lady does have some cash on her person which will be sufficient temporarily. If you can make the arrangement for Monday that should not cause a problem and I can advise her that the money will be available as from Tuesday. Thank you for your help, Mr Iliopolakis.'

When Ludmila's mobile 'phone rang she looked at the unknown number suspiciously. Much as she wanted to speak to Ivan she did not want Chief Inspector Solomakis to be able to trace where he was calling from.

'Hello?'

'Mrs Kuzmichov, it is Mr Propenkov here. I wanted to tell you that I have spoken to Mr Iliopolakis and arranged for him to make a monthly withdrawal for you from the hotel funds. The money will be available for you to collect on Tuesday. Go to the hotel and speak to the manager. You will obviously have to sign for the transaction.'

'Yes, thank you, Mr Propenkov.'

'Is there anything else I can help you with?'

Ludmila hesitated. 'I do have one question. I was told I could move around freely in Heraklion. Am I able to visit the other towns in the area?'

'Where are you proposing to go?'

'I have not decided, but I cannot spend all my time sitting in the apartment waiting for my husband to come home. I thought if I could go out for part of the day to somewhere I was unfamiliar with it would help me to pass my time.'

'You realise that without your passport you cannot hire a car.'

'On the allowance I have been given I certainly could not afford to do that. I would travel by bus.'

Mr Propenkov considered; the woman was not under house arrest and there was no reason why she should not go wherever she pleased.

'I think that would be quite acceptable.'

'Do I need to tell you or Chief Inspector Solomakis where I intend to visit?'

'I see no necessity for that.'

'Thank you Mr Propenkov.' Ludmila ended the call and sat back with a pleased smile on her face. She was beginning to formulate a plan, but it could take a few weeks before she could finally bring it to fruition and she would have to ensure that she was not being watched or followed whenever she went out.

She would check her cupboards before visiting the supermarket the following day and replenishing items as necessary. If she considered she still had sufficient money for food until Tuesday she would call in at a newsagent or bookshop and purchase a map of the area. She had plenty to keep her occupied over the next few days; she needed to iron her newly washed clothes and also clean the apartment. She would then check the map and decide on her next movements. A visit to the bus station would then be essential to pick up a bus timetable and ascertain the cost of the bus fare to the various towns.

August 2015
Week Three – Friday

Elena picked up her stick from behind Andreas's door and then replaced it. She had not admitted to Marianne that she had succumbed to using one at Andreas's suggestion and she certainly found it easier when walking up the steep hills, although she still needed to stop frequently to regain her breath. If Marianne was taking them up to Pano Elounda she would not need it today.

'We're ready,' she announced and settled herself in the back of the car, leaving the front seat for Andreas.

'Where would you like me to drop you off?' asked Marianne.

'The kafenion would be ideal,' answered Andreas. 'It's only a little further up the hill for Elena to walk.'

'Are you sure, Grandma?'

'There's no need for you to take me any nearer to Evi's house. You know how narrow the streets become. You'd have to reverse back down as there's nowhere up there to turn.' Now she regretted her decision to leave her stick behind.

Elena waited until Marianne had reversed a short distance to where she could turn and drive back down to the main road to Elounda and then turned back to Andreas.

'Vasilis and Cathy visited us yesterday,' she said. 'They had to go up to Heraklion last week. There's been some trouble up at Vasilis's old hotel. He said he couldn't go into details about it, but apparently the hotel was going to be closed down. He has agreed to act as the administrator until the new owner returns.'

'Rather irresponsible of the owner to go away without making adequate arrangements for the running of the establishment. Where's he gone?'

'From the little that Vasilis told us I think he may be in prison, or at least detained to help the police with their enquiries.'

'Sounds serious.'

Elena nodded. 'I believe that Vasilis is involved in some way. Nothing criminal, of course, but he had to go to the police station to make a statement. We were all curious, but Vasilis wouldn't say any more than that. I think he's more concerned about the bones that have been found on his building site. He just wants them removed so he can continue with the construction of his house.'

'Don't know why he's bothering. The apartment he and Cathy have in Elounda is perfect just for the two of them.'

'You know Vasilis; he has big ideas.'

'So why didn't he move back into his house up on the hill? That's plenty big enough for Vasi and Saffron to live there as well.'

'Cathy wouldn't be able to manage the hill even with an electric wheelchair.'

'Has she become that incapacitated?'

'No, but Vasilis is thinking of the future. Cathy uses her three wheeler to go out on flat ground in the village, but crossing the road to get to the waterfront would be difficult for her because of the traffic and she doesn't want to be dependent upon Vasilis all the time. If they were living further along she would be able to cross the road easily and sit beside the sea.'

'How would she get into the village?'

'She has a light wheelchair that she can propel by hand on flat ground. She'd be able to go along the seafront road using that.'

'She'd still have to cross the road to get to the shops.'

'She could use the crossing and the traffic would give way to her wheelchair.'

'I wish they would give way to me when I wave my stick.'

'I expect they think you are waving hello to them. I'll walk back down to the kafenion to meet you when I've finished talking to Evi.'

Elena continued up the hill and rounded the bend in the road. It was steeper here and she leaned against a wall frequently to regain her breath. She could see Evi sitting outside her house and waved to her.

'I expected you to be back before now,' remarked Evi as Elena stood before her. 'Do you want a chair?'

Elena nodded. It would be easier to talk if they were on the same level rather than her sitting down on the doorstep.

'Bring one out,' commanded Evi and Elena entered the small room that was crammed with furniture and picked up a folding chair. She placed it on the uneven ground outside and hoped she would not over balance.

'Thank you. That will be more comfortable. I didn't want you to think I was pressurizing you into talking to me by coming back too soon.'

'It's up to me what I say to you. You can't make me tell you anything.'

'Would you prefer that I go away and come back another day?'

'Now you're here you might as well stay,' said Evi grudgingly.

'And you'll talk to me?'

'Maybe.'

'I'm sure some of your memories are quite personal. I just hoped you would tell me about your childhood when Crete was occupied and how it affected you and your family, but it sounds as though I'm wasting my time.' Elena rose. 'I'll go and find someone else to talk to.'

'You'll not find anyone else who knows as much as I do.'

'I don't think you know anything of interest or you'd be willing to tell me.'

'You don't know that until I've told you anything. Sit down and listen.'

Evi broke into a rhyming song, her voice cracked with age.

'He's a fat faced fool, smells like a mule;
Cut out his liver and drown him in the river.'

'Goodness, Evi, I'd almost forgotten that silly song.' A woman had rounded the corner.

Evi scowled. She wanted to be the centre of Elena's attention. 'Good morning, Maria. What brings you up here?'

'I heard there was a lady asking for information about our lives over here during the Occupation. I thought she might like to talk to me.'

'I'm sure you don't remember as much about those days as I do.'

Maria shrugged. 'I probably remember different things.'

'Come and join us,' said Elena. 'I'm sure Evi won't mind if I get another chair. Then I want to write down the words to that rhyme Evi was singing.'

Maria waited until she was seated in a chair on the other side of Elena and ended the rhyme, smiling triumphantly at Evi.

'His feet smell of meat, left out to rot;
Rancid and sweet, he ought to be shot.'

'Did you really sing that at the soldiers?' asked Elena. 'Weren't you frightened?'

'We were at first. Every time we saw them approaching the village we would run and hide in the house. They didn't seem interested in us children, all they wanted were our animals and any food we had stored. Gradually we became braver and began to ignore them, then we tried to be a nuisance to them'

Maria nodded. 'We used to join hands, four or five of us girls, and dance around in a circle. One would sing the first line and as soon as she started the second another girl would sing the first line and so on.'

139

'Like a round,' remarked Elena.

'It seems rather childish and silly now, but we thought we were being clever and the soldiers used to smile thinking we were innocently playing a game.'

'When we got to the end we used to stamp our feet and shout Bang! Bang! Bang!,' added Evi. 'If the soldier wore glasses we would change the words and call him a four eyed fool. Sometimes the soldiers would join in with us at the end and stamp their feet. They had no idea we were being rude about them. When they began to have a knowledge of Greek they used to chase us away.'

'What else did you girls get up to?'

'The soldiers were more suspicious of the boys and we used to keep watch for them. The boys would hide when they saw the soldiers coming and sneak out later. Most times the soldiers left their vehicles at the bottom of the hill and the boys would make their way down. It was quite simple for them to place a handful of earth into the petrol tank or a few small stones. If we saw the soldiers returning we would call out as loudly as possible "Kiri-kiri-coo".'

'Why did you call that out? What did it mean?'

'It's the sound the cockerel makes when it crows. The sound carries. As soon as one of us heard it she would call it and the rest of us would join in. The boys would hear and immediately go and hide. The soldiers would drive off and it was not until some time later that the vehicle would break down.'

'They did any damage they could, cutting the leather seats, breaking the door handles, loosening wheel nuts or stealing anything that had been left inside,' said Maria.

'They had another trick,' smiled Evi. 'One of the boys would have a sharp knife or screw driver and try to gouge a hole in a tyre. If they succeeded they would then push a piece of glass or sharp stone in as far as possible. They became quite proficient and knew where the weakest spots in the tyres would be. By the time the soldiers had driven back down the hill they usually had a puncture.'

'And they always used to try to make a hole in a fuel can if the vehicles were carrying one,' added Maria. 'They would use a sharp nail and bang it with a large stone until they had made a small hole and the petrol began to leak out.'

'The soldiers blew themselves up on one occasion,' Evi rocked with laughter. 'They'd patrolled the village as usual and the boys had made quite a large hole in the fuel can. The petrol began to run down the road and the boys disappeared. The soldiers returned to their jeep and lit cigarettes. Then they saw their petrol running away and bent down to investigate. One threw his cigarette down which ignited the petrol and blew the jeep up.'

'What happened? Were they hurt?'

Both the women nodded vehemently. 'They were all four badly burned and we heard later that one had died and another had lost his sight.'

'How awful,' exclaimed Elena.

'It wasn't awful at all,' declared Maria vehemently. 'We wished all four been killed. They were our enemies.'

'Did no one suspect that the boys had been the cause of the fuel leak?'

Evi shrugged. 'No one admitted to seeing them anywhere near the vehicle and their mothers insisted they had been at the house all morning helping her.'

'They were believed?'

'It couldn't be proved that anyone had damaged the fuel can. It had happened to some of the others when they were left unattended in Elounda.'

'I heard that all the vehicles that were parked in Aghios Nikolaos were found to have holes in the spare fuel cans. They must all have been faulty,' smiled Maria. 'What a waste of petrol.'

'Were they sabotaged?' asked Elena.

'I expect so, but no one was ever caught, not that I heard, anyway.'

'What would have happened to the culprits if they had been found?'

'Probably shot.'

'What!' exclaimed Elena in horror. 'Even if they were little boys?'

'Their age would have made no difference. They were committing acts of sabotage.'

'Little Christos was the only one who suffered. He was small for his age and more daring than the others. He would crawl beneath their jeeps or lorries and damage the fuel pipe to the engine. He was just about to crawl out and run away one day when a soldier came and moved the lorry. Christos was caught and severely beaten around the head to teach him a lesson. His eyes became crossed and he was unable to speak properly after that.'

'Weren't the soldiers punished for hurting him so badly?'

'No one witnessed the attack. The soldiers said he must have fallen down the hillside and hit his head on a boulder, although we all thought we knew better.'

'What happened to him?'

Maria shrugged. 'He still lives in the village. Those of us who remember his exploits consider him our local hero. People take him food and his sister looks after his cleaning and washing as best she can.'

'He's still alive? I'll have to ask my brother if he has talked to him.'

'I don't think he'd be much help. He doesn't remember what he ate yesterday so it's doubtful he'd remember what he was up to as a boy.'

'Can you remember any more about those days?'

'I remember being hungry,' said Evi. 'The soldiers made sure they were well fed and we had to make do with whatever we could find growing wild in the fields.'

'We used to collect snails and boil them up so we could remove them from their shells.'

'And you actually ate them?' asked Elena in amazement. 'The ordinary snails that lived in the fields?'

'When you are that hungry you'll eat anything,' replied Evi. 'They were a bit tough, but not unpalatable if we added a bit of garlic.'

'Why didn't you slaughter one of your sheep or goats?'

'We didn't have any. The soldiers had taken them, along with our chickens. We used to search the hedges for bird's nests and steal their eggs; we even caught birds sometimes and cooked them.'

'They were horrible,' shuddered Maria. 'Full of little bones that you had to spit out.'

'Couldn't you walk into Aghios Nikolaos and see if there was any food available there?'

'We weren't allowed to go out of our village without a pass issued by the soldiers. Sometimes a woman would risk taking the donkey trail down to Elounda and find a fisherman. She would beg him to let her have a fish, but the people there were probably as hungry as we were.'

'Didn't any of you try to reach the other villages?'

Maria shook her head. 'It was difficult. We girls didn't like being alone anywhere in case the soldiers decided to rape us. Three or four of the older girls suffered along with some of the women.'

'What happened to them? Were they pregnant?'

'They went to see Androula. She used to fiddle around inside them and give them something to drink. It seemed to work.'

'Was there no one around who could stop them?'

Evi shook her head. 'The older boys had disappeared up into the hills, some of them probably joined the resistance movement, so it was only the younger ones who were left here. There were no men around to defend us.'

'Suppose one of you was taken ill? Were you able to visit the doctor?'

'You either got better or you died,' stated Maria simply. 'You would have to get a pass from the local commanding officer and that could take days and then you had to get to Aghios. The only

143

way to do that was riding on a donkey if the owner would lend it to you. Most people just laid on their beds and waited.'

'Did many people die due to lack of medical attention?'

'People died, but it was mostly from old age or malnutrition. They just gave up on their struggle to survive.'

'That is so sad,' remarked Elena. 'What happens now if you are ill?'

'Someone will take us in their car down to Elounda to see a doctor, or into Aghios Nikolaos to the hospital. We have telephones so we can call for help.'

All the time the women had been talking Elena had been busy making notes.

'Is that the kind of information that you wanted?' asked Evi.

'Exactly. I would like you to tell me the silly rhyme again so I can write it down.'

Andreas was delighted when Elena returned and related to him the information that Evi had given her. 'You did really well getting all that information from the women at Pano,' Andreas complimented her. 'I knew about the activities of the boys, but they didn't tell me that the girls acted as look outs for them or that some of the women had been raped.'

'What about that poor man, Christos, who was injured by the soldiers?'

Andreas shook his head. 'I have to admit that I have never approached him and the men did not disclose how his injuries occurred. I thought he had been born disabled.'

'Do you want me to go up again and talk to Evi and Maria?'

'I'm sure there are more incidents they will remember now you have jogged their memories. Go up again next week. Some parts of my play need embellishing so anything else you can find out will be useful to me.'

'Have you thought about staging it here for the locals to give their opinion?'

'I'd love to, but I'm not sure if that would be possible. We can't expect the elderly people we've talked with to learn lines and act. I don't know if we'd be able to get any uniforms for the soldiers and what about the vehicles? People may have odd souvenirs stored away, but they're not likely to have an army jeep.'

John looked at the photographs he had taken of the bones that had been unearthed. They meant little to him, but he placed them in a folder and announced his intention of walking up to Plaka with Skele and showing them to Saffron.

'We'll come with you,' said Nicola. 'The children can spend some time in the playground whilst you visit Saffie. I'll ask your mother and Bryony if either of them need any books from Monika and we could call in on her at the same time. I'm sure she'll have some books suitable for the girls.'

Vasilis spent most of the morning on the telephone to the bank, explaining that he needed an extra four hundred Euros each month in cash sent to the hotel to enable Giorgos to pay Ludmila Kuzmichov the amount that had been agreed by Propenkov. He finished explaining the position to the man on the other end of the line only to be told that he would need to speak to someone in higher authority to sanction the arrangement.

Sighing in exasperation, Vasilis repeated the reason for the request only to be informed that he would need to speak to the manager and would probably have to visit the bank with Mr Propenkov to sign an authorisation. Requesting his call to be transferred to the manager he was then told that the man was out of the office until Monday. Furious at wasting so much time Vasilis 'phoned the Consulate and asked to speak to Mr Propenkov.

Mr Propenkov sounded puzzled that the bank had been so uncooperative. 'I spoke to them and they said it would be no problem. You have been appointed as the official administrator so you can withdraw whatever you consider necessary to cover the expenses. Did you explain that to the manager?'

'He's out of the office until Monday.'

'Then I suggest that you simply withdraw the extra money and list it as hotel expenses until you have made an agreement with him. It sounds as though the manager has not passed down the instruction to his staff.'

'I send through the accounts as they are submitted to me by Dimitra. How do I suddenly say that a further four hundred is needed this coming week without proof of the expenditure?'

'Mr Iliopolakis, I am not a financial adviser. I can only suggest that you visit the bank on Monday and sort out the problem.'

Cathy tried to placate her irate husband. 'I'm sure Mr Propenkov was correct when he said the instruction had not been passed through to the staff. When you 'phone on Monday and speak to the manager he'll probably apologise and the extra money will be sent through without a problem.'

'I don't want to have to go up to Heraklion again next week. I spoke to Panayiotis briefly yesterday evening and he thinks the archaeologists will be finished this weekend and I will be able to progress with the building.'

'Did you ask after Blerim's daughter?'

Vasilis looked guilty. 'I forgot.'

'Then why don't you drive down to the site and see what the position is for yourself.? You could then go into Aghios Nikolaos and visit Blerim. I'll come with you and we could sit down by the lake and watch the world go by. It will help you to unwind and relax.'

John showed Saffron the photographs he had taken and she studied them carefully.

'It's difficult to say anything definite about them. Without giving them a thorough examination I wouldn't be able to tell if there had been a disease present that caused their death.'

'What about leprosy?'

Saffron shook her head. 'The bones from the fingers and toes usually show signs of absorption which ends up with the clawing effect that you see in the living patients. None of that is evident. I can see from that photograph of the jaw that the person had an abscess. It would have been extremely painful and the poison from it could have spread throughout his body causing blood poisoning, but more than that I cannot say.'

'So they're not lepers,' said John, disappointed.

'It's possible, but I think it unlikely. There are no obvious signs on the bones that indicate the disease and those who did die from leprosy were not usually buried amongst the other villagers. There's no sign of violence that would point to them being victims of a battle and nothing apart from that abscess to indicate the possible cause of death for this man. Is there any evidence that there was a hospital in the area?'

John shook his head. 'I've looked at the old maps and there's nothing in the way of a building shown on them.'

'I'm sorry to disappoint you, John, but I think these burials are probably from the farmers and fishermen who lived in the area from a couple of hundred years ago. All I can suggest is that you wait until they have been examined by the museum staff and see what they can tell you.'

John shrugged. 'Oh well, it was a long shot on my part that you would be able to tell what they were suffering from.'

'At a rough guess I would say they probably all had ailments and infirmities that were common at the time. There could have been some kind of epidemic in the village and these were the older and less fit who succumbed. One thing I can say for certain is that they were not victims of an earthquake. The bones would show signs of fracturing or crushing if that had happened.'

Ludmila examined the map she had bought and also the bus time table. From the terminus in Heraklion she appeared to have access to most of the main towns along the coast. She decided that once she had collected her money from the hotel on Tuesday she would visit Rethymnon on the Wednesday.

The following week she would go to Hersonissos although she had no interest in visiting the town. It should be easy to find a shop there that would sell her a pay as you go mobile and the transaction would be untraceable as she would pay in cash. She had no intention of using the appliance until sufficient time had passed and she felt that it was safe to contact Ivan. Tomorrow she would walk down to the Venetian fortress and sit there for a while watching the people who milled around. Wherever she went she wanted to make certain that her movements were not being monitored and for the next few weeks she would act like a tourist visiting the area for the first time.

Vasilis drove down to his plot of land and it appeared that Panayiotis was correct in assuming that the excavation was nearing completion. Leaving Cathy sitting in the car he ducked beneath the tape that was still cordoning off the area and walked over to where Lambros was gathering up items and placing them in a carrier bag.

Lambros scowled as he approached. 'If you want to take more photographs you're wasting your time. There's nothing to see now.'

Vasilis shook his head. 'No, I was told you had finished your work and I wanted to check with you that I was able to ask my builder to return and make a start on my house.'

Lambros shook his head. 'I can't allow you to start work again yet. We need to complete some GPR on the neighbouring plot.'

'Are there burials there?'

'We won't know that until we have done the survey. It's quite likely that the graves on your land were at the end of a cemetery and there could be more on the adjacent land.'

'How does that affect me?'

'Some of them could extend a short distance onto your land. We wouldn't want them to be damaged by allowing you to continue building yet.'

'How long will that take? I need to get on with my house. I want it completed by next summer.'

'We'll work around the boundaries of your land first and if we need to excavate we'll make those graves a priority. It should take no more than another week, depending upon what we find, of course.'

'When will you start?'

'On Monday. My men deserve some time off. They've worked hard so I've sent them home early today and I'm just finishing collecting up any odd tools that have been left around.'

'Surely the men should have been responsible for the tools they were using.'

'They did a pretty good job, but it's easy to move along a bit and leave a tooth brush or spatula behind. I always like to leave a site as clear as possible so I've picked up the markers that weren't used and some lengths of bandage and string. Don't want you accusing me of leaving rubbish behind.'

'I appreciate that you have tidied up. I'll come down on Monday and see how you are progressing.' Vasilis walked back to the car, hoping that no further burials would be found that would hinder the progress of the building his house.

He smiled at Cathy. 'They have finished on my land, but want to check the boundaries to ensure no one has their head or feet buried on my plot. Lambros said they would do a GPR survey on Monday and provided they did not find anything, or should I say anyone, I can ask my builders to return.'

'Well that will give you something else to think about apart from "The Central". What shall we do first? Go into Aghios and look for Blerim or go down to the lake?'

'It would be most practical to look for Blerim. Once we've seen him the rest of the afternoon is ours. I just hope I remember where he lives.'

Vasilis took a number of wrong turns before he finally drew up outside Blerim's apartment. 'Stay here,' he said to Cathy. 'I'm sure they will invite you in, but they may not have anywhere suitable for you to sit. I'll not be long.'

Andon opened the door and looked out cautiously.

'Is your father at home?' asked Vasilis.

Andon nodded and called out in a language Vasilis did not understand.

Blerim looked weary when he came to the door. Once he saw Vasilis he smiled and opened the door wider. 'Please, come in.'

'Thank you, no. I'll not stop. We were just passing and I just wanted to ask after Lejla.'

'Slowly. She will smile sometimes now and say a few words to her mother, look at a picture book.'

'It's good to know she is making progress. Are you still working for Mr Palamakis?'

Blerim shook his head. 'Mr Palamakis say I do good work. He say council should make me refuse collector.'

'I'm pleased that you have regular work now.'

'I do not like. The men not talk to me. I like work with Mr Palamakis. All day now is dirty and smelly rubbish, but I have money each week.' Blerim shrugged. 'I not complain.'

'Is Andon doing well at school?'

'He good boy. Work hard.'

'I'm pleased to hear that. As I said, I'm not stopping, I only came to ask after Lejla's progress.'

'We grateful. Without help Lejla not get well.'

'The help will always be there until she has made a good recovery. I will call again and ask after her.' Vasilis walked back to his car. Once he was able to start work on his house he would see if it was possible to employ Blerim again, although that would mean the man had to give up his work as a refuse collector and would no longer have a reliable weekly wage.

August 2015
Week Four – Monday

Marianne could hardly contain her excitement. Elizabeth had 'phoned to say they should be arriving at Heraklion airport just after two that day and Giovanni had set off to collect them. She checked the room they had been allocated to ensure that all was in readiness and asked Bryony to help her with the cooking.

'I thought we'd have kleftiko tonight. I'll get on with preparing that, but can you make five cheesecakes for us to eat afterwards.'

'Five?'

Marianne nodded. 'You know how fond Giovanni is of your cheesecake so I thought an extra one could be useful. If it isn't eaten it can go into the freezer for a later date.'

'What topping do you want?'

'Giovanni likes a lemon and orange mixture so three of those would be ideal and two sweeter ones for you and the girls.' Marianne hoped Bryony would not notice that she was preparing extra meat and vegetables.

'If you have time afterwards could you knock up a few biscuits? Uncle Yannis and Marisa always like a biscuit in the afternoon.'

'I think we have plenty,' frowned Bryony.

'A few extra will not come amiss. Nicola often takes one for the girls.'

Bryony gave Marianne a puzzled look. 'Are we expecting visitors?'

Marianne shrugged. 'You know what it's like, people drop in at all sorts of odd times and I'd be embarrassed if I couldn't offer them a biscuit.'

Vasilis drove up to Heraklion and entered the bank, requesting to see the manager.

'He has a customer with him at present. If you would take a seat I'll let him know you are here as soon as he is free.'

Vasilis took out his mobile 'phone and called Mr Propenkov. 'I am at the bank waiting to see the manager. When I called on Friday asking for the extra money I was told I needed to come up and sign another agreement. I was under the impression that you had arranged everything.'

'I signed to authorise the further monthly payment so I imagine you need to do the same.'

'I wish you had told me that. I wasted a considerable amount of time on Friday being passed from one employee to another and finally being told that the manager was not in until Monday and I would need to see him.'

'It is only a formality. I'm sure it will take no more than a few minutes.'

'All the more annoying to have to drive all the way to Heraklion for something that should be unnecessary. If there are any more transactions in the future that need to be authorised by me I would appreciate having the full details.' Vasilis closed his mobile. He would withdraw the money in cash and take it to "The Central". It would give him the opportunity to see how the hotel was being run and also speak to Giorgos and Dimitra.

'If my wife has been released I should be also,' complained Evgeniy Kuzmichov. 'How is she going to manage on her own?'

'She has returned to the apartment and Mr Propenkov has arranged for a sum of money to be allocated to her each month. She will have sufficient to live on so you do not need to be concerned about her welfare.'

'When can I see her?'

'I'm sure that can be arranged for a few day's time. Your wife requested that she had some time to herself.'

'No doubt she'll contact her brother and ask him to arrange a flight to Russia.'

'That will not be possible. We will be able to monitor any 'phone calls that she makes and we are holding her passport. She knows that she is unable to leave Crete without it.'

Evgeniy looked at Chief Inspector Solomakis sceptically. He knew that if he were released he would contact Ivan immediately and make arrangements to leave the island even if he did not have a passport. He was sure Ludmila would find a way to escape justice and leave him to face all the criminal charges against him on his own.

Elena walked up to Pano Elounda with the intention of talking to Evi again. She hoped that now the woman had told her about various occurrences she would remember some more events that Andreas would find interesting and be able to add to his play.

'My brother was so pleased with the information that you gave me. It is certainly helping him with his writing. Do you remember any more incidents that happened whilst the Germans and Italians were here?'

Evi nodded. 'You don't ever forget the atrocities they committed. When a soldier raped Soula her daughter tried to beat him off with a broom. One of the other soldiers held her and made her watch her mother suffer; he then raped the girl although she was no more than twelve years and her mother was made to witness the act.'

'That's terrible.' Elena looked at Evi in horror. 'Quite wicked. What happened to them?'

'Soula became pregnant and when she gave birth she

153

smothered the child and made her daughter swear never to tell anyone in the village.'

'What happened when her husband returned? Did no one in the village ever tell him?'

'He didn't come back.' Evi shook her head sadly. 'Another woman who was raped hung herself in the woods as soon as she realised she was pregnant.'

'How awful.'

'It was, but compared with some areas we were fortunate. Even when some of their soldiers never returned from a patrol they did not shoot every villager as I heard later had happened in other parts of the island.'

Elena frowned. 'Why did the soldiers not return? Did they decide to defect and hide from their compatriots?'

Evi gave a throaty chuckle. 'They had been killed.'

'Killed?'

'There was a girl who lived locally. When she saw the soldiers arriving she took her father's shotgun, hid outside until they were within range and then shot them.'

'Did she kill them?'

'Of course. She was a real heroine.'

'Wasn't she punished?'

Evi shrugged and looked at the olive groves lower down the hill. 'She and her mother dug graves in the olive grove and buried them. They denied ever seeing the soldiers so how could she be punished?'

'What happened when the Germans found where they were buried?'

'They never did find out. The family kept that knowledge to themselves.'

'Have the bodies ever been recovered?'

'No, they are still there.'

'Do you know where they are?'

'Maybe. I'm not telling you and nor am I telling you the

name of the girl. Her family still live locally. They could be in trouble.'

Elena considered the information. 'Surely they could not be blamed for something that happened years ago.'

'They should have admitted to the crime and disclosed the location of the graves when the war ended. They kept quiet then and have done ever since.'

'The relatives of those soldiers would probably be grateful to know their fate.'

'Why should we do anything for them? They never did anything for us. At least it was better when the Italians came.'

'In what way?'

'They did not treat us so brutally. Many of the villagers were forced to take them in to live in their cottages. Although they all resented having them live with them it meant there was more food available as the soldiers could draw rations from the base in the town. Had they not been able to do that they would have been starving along with us. We should have left them to forage in the countryside for something edible as we had been doing. I doubt if many of them would have survived.'

'One of my relatives married an Italian soldier. She went over to Italy to live and only returned to live in Crete after he died. She was very happy with him.'

'I suppose they were not all bad,' admitted Evi grudgingly. 'When we suffered from the flu epidemic the Italian doctors treated us. Mind you, they probably brought it into the country so it was only right that they should provide us with medicine and nurse us back to health.'

Elena looked around. Down the hill she could see olive groves in all directions and wondered which one held the bodies of the three German soldiers.

Elena returned to Andreas deep in thought. She felt uncomfortable that the graves of the murdered Germans had never been discovered and their bodies given a decent burial. Andreas shrugged off her discomfort.

'There are probably a number of unknown graves across the island. Why should we be concerned about them when there are whole villages that lost their men folk? The men were often made to dig a communal grave for themselves before they were shot and their families forced to witness their execution.'

'At least they knew where they were.'

'Hardly a consolation when you have lost your husband and are struggling to feed your children and yourself, never knowing if you might be shot the next day for some reason. I'll obviously incorporate it in my play. If the villagers saw no reason to disclose the whereabouts of the graves after the war the incident is best forgotten. Who knows what trouble you could stir up otherwise?'

'I suppose you're right,' agreed Elena. 'I wouldn't want to cause a problem for Evi.'

'It could be a product of her imagination. She may well have embellished the story. Next time you go up to Pano see if you can speak to Maria and ask for her version of the event.'

Vasilis was kept waiting for half an hour before the bank manager was able to see him. 'I'm sorry, Mr Iliopolakis; there appears to have been a misunderstanding. The original agreement with you acting as the administrator for the hotel only covered the expenses incurred for the business. I am obviously happy to confirm a further agreement for you to withdraw four hundred Euros in cash each month, commencing today. Mr Propenkov visited and signed as appropriate. I thought he would have advised you of the need for a signature from yourself.'

'Unfortunately he did not. He told me all was in order. I was passed around to various employees on Friday before finally being told that you were not here again until today. I had other urgent plans for today that I had to postpone to enable me to drive up to town.'

'I can only apologise again. I will ask for the agreement to be produced from the file and in the meantime I will ask a cashier to have the money ready for you to collect.'

Slightly mollified Vasilis sat and waited until he was able to add his name below the large, flourishing signature of Mr Propenkov and the cash was handed to him.

Vasilis strode into "The Central" and immediately asked Giorgos to go into the private office with him.

'Is there a problem, Mr Iliopolakis?' asked Giorgos anxiously. 'As far as I am aware the hotel is recovering from the initial cancellations and the accounts are all in order.'

'Nothing to do with the hotel that I am aware of and I've found no fault with the accounts.' Vasilis took the packet of notes from inside his jacket. 'I have been told that Mrs Kuzmichov has been released from custody. Unfortunately she has no access to any money whilst her husband continues to be held. The Russian Consulate and myself have reached an agreement whereby she is given four hundred Euros each month to cover her immediate needs until such time as Evgeniy Kuzmichov is also released. This will be separate from the expenses for the hotel. I would like you to count the money and sign to say you have received it from me. It will be repaid when Mr Kuzmichov returns to take control of the situation.'

Giorgos nodded and counted the notes rapidly, confirming that there were four hundred Euros in total.

'Mrs Kuzmichov will come to the hotel at some time tomorrow and you will hand the money over to her. Once again a signature must be obtained. I do not want her claiming at a later date that she has not received it from you.'

Giorgos looked hurt. 'I would not dream of keeping the money for myself.'

'I know that, Giorgos. I trust you, but I do not trust Mrs Kuzmichov. She could buy herself an expensive dress or shoes and then claim that she had not received the money and request more to enable her to buy her food and any other essentials during the remainder of the month. I believe the lady has had unlimited funds at her disposal in the past.'

'I understand. I will ask for one of the other managers to be in attendance and ensure that she counts it out in our presence and signs to say she has received the full amount.'

Vasilis nodded. 'I knew I could rely on you. I will now visit Dimitra and apprise her of the situation. I do not want her to be looking for money that she thinks has gone missing. I will invite her to come for lunch with me. She is entitled to a lunch break but as her hours are being paid for by the hotel I will ensure that she is not out too long.'

Having informed Dimitra of the financial arrangement that had been made Vasilis invited her to accompany him to lunch.

Dimitra looked dubious. 'Mr Kuzmichov did not like me to go out for lunch with you.'

Vasilis raised his eyebrows. 'Mr Kuzmichov had no right to tell you who you could meet for lunch. Whilst I am in charge, however temporary that might be, if I want to invite you for lunch he is unable to object.'

'I should not be longer than an hour.'

'That is acceptable and honest of you. I need to return to Elounda when we have eaten so I am not proposing that we spend all afternoon talking whilst we have a meal. I'd just like to know how you are coping and if you think there is any problem with the running of the hotel.'

Dimitra smiled at Vasilis. 'Now you are in charge of the accounts there is no problem at all.'

Giovanni arrived early at Heraklion airport having had to take a family up in time to catch a flight to Heathrow that left at one that afternoon. He sat in the car and read his newspaper, continually looking at his watch. Finally he was able to stroll across to the

arrival gate and scanned the information board anxiously, relieved
that no delays to the flight had been announced. He had promised
Marianne he would call her the moment the plane landed.

Travellers from an earlier flight made their way through
noisily, dragging their cases or pushing overloaded trolleys with
small children often sitting on top of the luggage. Instructions
were shouted and rapturous greetings took place, often the whole
family having come to meet the arrivals.

Giovanni took out his mobile 'phone. 'Their flight has landed.
I'll call you when we reach the turn off to Elounda. Give me
about an hour.'

Marianne looked at her watch. She had plenty of time to shower
and put on a respectable pair of trousers rather than the jeans she
was wearing along with a clean T-shirt. Bryony was around should
Uncle Yannis or Marisa need anything and her mother had only
returned a short while earlier from her visit to Pano and would
probably be having a siesta. Provided Nicola did not suddenly
take it into her head to take the children out for the afternoon all
was going to plan.

As soon as Giovanni called to say he was no more than fifteen
minutes away Marianne phoned John at the shop that served the
self catering apartments.

'John, I really need you to come home now.'

'Why? What's wrong? Is it Nick or the children?'

'No they're fine, but I have a problem and I need your help.'

'Can't Dad help you?'

'He's on an airport run and I don't know where Marcus is.'

John took the money a customer was handing to him. 'I'll be
down, but I'll have to bring Skele with me. I can't leave him up
here on his own.'

'That's no problem. Just be as quick as you can.'

Marianne went in search of Nicola. 'I really need your help,
Nicola. Bring the children and come along to the kitchen.' Without
waiting for Nicola to answer her or ask why she was needed

159

Marianne returned to the patio and checked that all was ready to receive Elizabeth and Nicolas.

'What's the problem, Marianne?' asked Nicola as she arrived carrying Yiannis and the two girls following her.

'I'm not sure. I feel a bit strange. I don't know where Bryony is so I'd like you to stay with me.'

'Are you ill?' asked Nicola anxiously.

'No, it's more a fluttery feeling, like excitement.'

'Why don't you go and lie down?'

'I'm sure that isn't necessary.' Marianne looked out of the window. 'I believe Giovanni has just arrived back. I'm sure I'll be fine now.'

Nicola looked at Marianne suspiciously. 'I'll wait until Giovanni has come in. I'm sure he'll agree with me that you should go and rest for a while.'

Giovanni drew up and opened the car doors and insisted Elizabeth and Nicolas went straight round to the patio. Nicola saw her parents arrive around the corner, gave a gasp of disbelief, deposited Yiannis in Marianne's arms then ran to greet them. Marianne smiled with pleasure as Nicola clung to both of them, tears running down the faces of both Nicola and Elizabeth whilst Nicolas tried to brush his own tears away surreptitiously.

John parked his scooter and ran round to the patio, Skele at his heels.

'What's the – Elizabeth, Nicolas, when did you arrive?'

'A few minutes before you.'

'I don't believe it,' said Nicola finally. 'Why didn't you tell me you were coming?'

'We asked Marianne and Giovanni to keep it a secret so we could surprise you.'

'You're properly well again now, Dad?' asked Nicola.

'No problems at all until I get to the airport and have to admit to having a pacemaker and unable to go through the electronic screening. I have to be sensible for a while longer, no heavy lifting or undue exertion, but apart from that I feel better than I have for years.'

'Come and sit down,' Marianne encouraged them towards the table. 'Giovanni will take you up to your apartment later and drop off your luggage at the same time. It's a shame you cannot stay here with us but the house is a bit full as my mother is staying at the moment.'

'We don't mind staying in the self catering and it's only a short walk down to the house. Nicolas is supposed to walk every day, but he should avoid hills at the moment.'

Joanna and Elisabetta were looking at the new arrivals curiously. Nicola took their hands. 'This is your Grandma and Grandpa from America. They've come all the way here especially to see you. Come and say hello properly to them.'

The twin girls walked forward shyly and allowed both Elizabeth and Nicolas to place a kiss on their cheeks. Nicola took Yiannis from Marianne's arms and held him out for her parents to inspect.

'Who is he like?' asked Elizabeth.

'His father. I just hope he will be better behaved than John was when he was a little boy,' answered Marianne.

Yiannis smiled broadly and stretched out his hand towards the plate of biscuits. 'He's full of mischief, at the age of being into everything,' said Nicola as the little boy made a dive towards the plate and taking a biscuit, the sudden movement almost making Nicola drop him. 'I'll put him down. He's quite a heavy weight.'

Still clutching the biscuit Yiannis immediately made his way over to where Skele was sitting at the entrance of the patio. He sat down beside the dog, took a bite of biscuit and then gave the remainder to Skele.

'He likes to share,' remarked John. 'I'll just give Skele a bowl of water. I made him race down the road with me.' He placed the bowl of water down beside the dog 'No Yiannis,' remonstrated John as the little boy tried to pry open the dog's jaw to see where the biscuit had gone. 'You must not do that or you'll hurt Skele. You gave him the biscuit.'

Nicola called Joanna and Elisabetta over to her. 'I'd like you to go and find Aunt Bryony. Tell her Grandma needs her in the kitchen.'

'Why?' asked Joanna.

'Never mind why, just go and ask her to come along here at once.'

'And Uncle Marcus?'

'If he's there with her ask him to come as well.'

'What about Grandma Marisa?'

'She's having a rest. You can go and ask her later.'

Bryony walked out to the patio, the girls hanging on a hand each side of her. She stopped in surprise. 'Where did you two spring from? I didn't know you were coming.'

'We wanted it to be a surprise for Nicola,' answered Elizabeth.

'Now I know why Marianne was so busy cooking this morning and I was asked to make so many cheesecakes.'

'Is Marcus around? He ought to join us.'

'He should be back very soon. He's gone into Elounda to buy some light bulbs. He needed to replace one on a patio at the apartments this morning and found there were no more spares.'

Elena emerged from her room. 'I thought I heard voices that I didn't recognise.'

'I'm sorry if we disturbed you,' said Marianne immediately contrite. 'I think we all became over excited.'

'I'm not surprised. I haven't seen Elizabeth and Nicolas since my mother's hundredth birthday party. You both look very well, but where is your other daughter, Eleanor?'

'She has to attend college. It was not appropriate for her to have a holiday during term time. You're looking well also. Marianne tells me you have been staying here for some time now.'

Elena nodded. 'I'm enjoying being here. I've visited Saffie up at her shop and also met the nice girl, Monika, who has a bookshop next door. I've also been spending some time with my brother.'

'You'll have to tell Elizabeth and Nicolas what you and Uncle Andreas are up to,' smiled Giovanni.

'Later. I'm sure you all have far more important news to catch up on. Is Yiannis supposed to be drinking the dog's water?'

'Yiannis!' exclaimed Nicola in horror. 'Put that bowl down. If you want a drink I'll give you one.'

By way of an answer Yiannis tipped the contents of the bowl over his legs and onto the ground. Marianne sighed.

'He is like his father. Unless you watch him continually he always manages to do something to draw attention to himself. I'll mop this up whilst you sort out Yiannis.'

John looked at his watch. 'I ought to go back up to the shop for an hour, then I'll take Skele down to Dimitris. I'll catch up with you all later.'

'We ought to go and unpack, said Elizabeth, 'And Nicolas should have his afternoon rest or he'll fall asleep at the table this evening.'

Over their meal Elena described how Andreas was compiling the memories of the local people with the idea of producing a play.

'That sounds really interesting,' commented Nicolas. 'I'd like to go up to Pano Elounda. It's years since we have been around the area and I'm sure it has changed.'

'You can't possibly walk up that hill,' said Marianne firmly. 'I'll drive you up and leave you at the kafenion with Uncle Andreas. I'm sure the locals will enjoy hearing about your recent visit to Athens. When you are ready to come home you can call me.'

'I'd like to go over to Spinalonga again,' said Elizabeth. 'Do you still have the photograph of Anna?'

'Of course. That is something I would never part with.'

'We've found another ghost since then,' smiled John. 'Nothing to do with our family. You will have met up with Ron. She came over for great grandmother's hundredth birthday and decided to return and work here as an artist. It's quite a long story, but she inherited a house and found some old diaries there. When Nick and I translated them it turned out that her grandmother had been born on Spinalonga and her family had no idea.'

'So how is she a ghost?'

'I took Ron over there to do some painting and she became quite frightened. She insisted there was someone watching her and trying to communicate.'

'And was there?' asked Elizabeth.

'I think so. Ron finally had the courage to call out to her great grandmother who had been sent over there. She told her that her daughter, Vivi, had gone to America and had a happy life. Ron insisted that she heard someone say "thank you" and she had a quick glimpse of a woman.'

Elizabeth shivered. 'I've come up in goose bumps.'

'Do you think she imagined it?' asked Nicolas..

John shrugged. 'Who knows for sure. I know Ron was in quite a state when I reached her and insisted the event had happened. You could ask her yourself, she and Ackers have the apartment next door to you during the summer.'

'I though you said she had a house.'

'She has, but just as she had finished renovating it there was a fire. The new extension she had built on wasn't damaged and she and Ackers live there during the winter. It's too inconvenient for them to live up there during the season whilst Ron is painting and Ackers has the taverna.'

'Tell them about the bones,' giggled Nicola.

'Well,' John lowered his voice although there was no one around who could have heard him. 'The roof of the old charnel house collapsed and it was decided to remove the bones and display them in a new building. I was not prepared to have Old Uncle Yannis put on display for visitors to gawp at. I managed to persuade the work men to let me recover his bones as I knew they would be at the top. I said we wanted to bury them in the local cemetery. Saff agreed to wash them and Ron persuaded Ackers to allow her to use his kitchen. They had almost finished when a family turned up and asked for a meal. They told them the kitchen was not open, gave them a few bits and pieces and cold drinks. The boy who was with them walked into the kitchen and saw Old Uncle Yannis's skull sitting on the side. He screamed the place down and said they were murderers and cannibals.'

'What happened?' asked Elizabeth, wide eyed.

'They boxed up the bones and removed them and when the police came the next day there wasn't a sign of anything out of the ordinary. The police decided the man had been somewhat inebriated and his son had been playing a joke on him.'

'So what happened to Old Uncle Yannis?' asked Nicolas.

'He's gone home?'

'What do you mean?'

John lowered his voice even further. 'We placed him in a casket, dug a hole in the floor of the house where he had lived and reburied him.'

'On Spinalonga?' asked Nicolas.

'Of course. That was where he belonged.'

'Is he still there?'

'I hope so,' replied John vehemently. 'I go over every so often and check that he's not been disturbed.'

August 2015
Week Four – Tuesday & Wednesday

Ludmila strode imperiously into "The Central" and walked up to reception. 'I understand that the head receptionist needs to see me.'

'If you wish to settle your bill I can deal with that, Madam.'

'I have no bill owing here that needs to be paid. Please find the receptionist immediately.'

'What name shall I tell him, Madam?'

'Mrs Kuzmichov.' Ludmila glared at the man.

Aristo knocked on the door of the office and Giorgos called to him to enter. 'A Mrs Kuzmichov is here and demanding to see you, sir.'

Giorgos nodded. 'I was expecting her. Give me a couple of minutes and then show her in and stay here whilst our business is transacted.' Giorgos removed the packet of money from the safe and walked towards Ludmila with his hand extended as she entered the room.

'It is a pleasure to see you, Mrs Kuzmichov. Please take a seat.'

'I don't need to sit. I understand that you have something for me.'

Giorgos nodded and took the money from the envelope. He handed it to Aristo. 'Please count that money and tell me how much there is in total.'

Aristo looked surprised at the request and counted out the notes slowly onto the desk, making piles of twenty, ten and five Euros. 'Four hundred Euros,' he said at last.

Giorgos nodded. 'If you would now be good enough to check that, Mrs Kuzmichov. I will then ask you to sign a receipt to confirm the amount you have received.'

With a bad grace Ludmila counted out the money again and then signed the receipt that Giorgos handed her. She had planned to return later and say she had not received the full amount. With a witness checking and confirming the transaction she would not be able to claim she had been short changed. She stuffed the money into the bottom of her bag.

'Thank you. I will see you next month.'

'Certainly and if I can be of any assistance to you in the meantime please let me know.' Giorgos held out his hand, but Ludmila ignored it and swept out of the room.

Aristo looked at his immediate superior curiously and Giorgos shook his head. 'Thank you, Aristo. That lady is the wife of the Russian man who owns the hotel. Mr Iliopolakis arranged that she should call for the money.'

'I'd never seen her at the hotel and I didn't recognise her. She seemed quite put out when I asked her name.'

'Don't let it bother you. I'm sure you will remember who she is the next time she calls.'

Ludmila walked back to the apartment, removed the money from her purse and checked the amount again. She was relieved that she had no fifty Euro notes that would need to be changed for smaller denominations. She opened the safe and placed four hundred Euros inside along with the two hundred Euros of her original money. The change, along with one hundred Euros she put in her purse. That amount would have to last her the week for her food and also the bus fare for her planned visit to Rethymnon tomorrow. Provided she was frugal she would have some money left over.

'You look tired, Mamma,' observed Marianne as her mother entered the kitchen.

'I didn't sleep very well, probably too much excitement yesterday evening.'

Marianne smiled. 'It's wonderful to have Elizabeth here, and Nicolas, of course. Once she and Nicola have spent time together I hope we will be able to sit and chat the way we used to. I have no special friend over here that I can confide in and share any problems.'

'Do you have problems?'

Marianne shook her head. 'Not really. I get worried if the bookings for the apartments appear to be down, or one of the children is not well. The worst time was when John had to go to England have that operation due to that weird man who had been stalking Nicola. I had Giovanni for support, of course, but I didn't feel I could burden him with all my worries. He was as concerned as I was and we both had to help Nicola. At least everything has quietened down now and we are able to get on with our lives.'

'I'm going up to Pano again today so don't include me in any arrangements you want to make.'

'Why don't you stay here today if you're tired?'

Elena shook her head. 'I need to go up and see if Maria is around. Evi told me something and I'm not sure if she was speaking the truth.'

'I think it's quite possible that they are exaggerating events when they talk to you.'

'That's very likely, but if one confirms what the other has told me I feel inclined to believe their recollections.'

'They could be colluding and making up stories. They probably have very few visitors up there who they can talk with. Do you want me to run you up in the car?'

'I'd really appreciate that, provided it's no trouble.'

'Of course not. Be ready in about half an hour.'

Elena walked slowly up the hill. She was not sure where Maria lived and had been loath to enter the kafenion and ask the men who were already congregated in there. She decided it would be most practical to walk up further to the church and hope that she could meet the priest.

There was no one around when she reached the building and she tried the door which yielded to her touch. Inside was a woman attending to the flowers that had been placed there for the service that had been held the previous Sunday. Elena genuflected and crossed herself before approaching the woman.

'Are you able to help me, please? I'm looking for Maria and I'm not sure exactly where she lives.'

'Which Maria?'

'She is an elderly lady, a friend of Evi's.'

'Oh, that one. Do you know your way to Evi?'

Elena nodded and the woman continued. 'You need to go back down the hill until you reach the junction where you would walk up to Evi. Maria's house is two from the corner on the right hand side.'

Thanking her and placing a few coins in the box Elena lit a candle. She stood for a few moments with her head bent, saying a short prayer in memory of her late husband, Matthew.

Elena retraced her steps and could see Maria sitting outside pulping tomatoes in a jug.

'What are you doing?' she asked.

'I thought you were Greek,' answered Maria scathingly. 'You should know how to make tomato puree.'

'I do, but our tomatoes don't taste like yours. Unless you grow them yourself they are not fresh. I buy tomato puree ready made now in tins or tubes. Having just about everything you want in a large store makes you lazy.'

Maria pulled a face. 'If the youngsters were not so keen to get into the towns and work for money they would be far healthier. All this ready made rubbish isn't good for you.'

'I do agree. The problem in America is that the fruit and vegetables are often grown hundreds of miles away and have to be transported in refrigerated containers. All the flavour has gone from them. If the produce has been canned it tastes better and lasts a good deal longer.'

'We never had a problem until the war. We grew what we needed and would give the surplus to our neighbours. They would do something in return for us, chop some wood, mend a fence or replace a roof tile. It was only when all our food was taken away from us that we had to scavenge in the countryside. We soon found out that with the addition of some herbs the blandest of foods could be quite palatable.'

'Talking about the war years, I heard that a girl shot three soldiers and then she and her mother buried them in an olive grove. Is that true?'

'Who told you that? Evi, with her big mouth I expect. Why shouldn't it be true?'

Elena shrugged. 'I just find it rather difficult to comprehend. The shooting I can believe, but two women managing to dig a grave sufficiently large enough to hold three men; that would have taken a considerable amount of time. I would have expected the soldiers to have been missed and a search made for them.'

'They did come looking. No one admitted to seeing them in the area and they began to look elsewhere but eventually gave up. They were more concerned with trying to capture the andartes.'

'Were they in this area?'

'Of course. They were everywhere. They would ambush the patrols and shoot as many men as possible before disappearing into the hills.'

'Weren't they ever shot?'

'Sometimes. If they were hiding in the village whilst their wounds healed and the soldiers were seen to be coming the young women used to go out and flirt with them, trying to distract them whilst the andartes made their escape. One man carried his brother all the way to down to Plaka.'

'Was he able to hide there and recover?'

Maria nodded. 'A local woman helped him. She managed to get the doctor to come out one night and remove the bullet from his leg. As soon as he was well enough to be moved his friends came for him and took him away.'

'Oh!' Elena felt stunned by the information. 'Do you know the name of the woman who looked after him?'

'No, and she wouldn't be around now for you to question.'

'I think she could have been a relative. My mother's cousin lived on a farm in Plaka and I have heard stories that she helped the resistance movement in any way she could.'

'Then your relatives would be the ones to ask for more information about her.' Maria smiled smugly, lifted her jug and walked back inside her house.

Vasilis drove down to his land and was disconcerted when he saw Lambros and his assistants working assiduously on the neighbouring plot. The area had been cordoned off with tape and Lambros was standing next to the fence that bordered Vasilis's land and talking to one of the workmen.

'Am I able to continue with my building?' asked Vasilis.

Lambros nodded. 'You're fortunate. It appears that your land was the very end of the burial ground. We've found at least thirty more graves where we are investigating now and we haven't finished the GPR yet.'

Vasilis heaved a sigh of relief. 'When you started on my land I wished I'd bought the adjacent plot. Now I'm extremely pleased that I did not. How long do you think you'll be working there?'

'Hard to say. Provided the weather holds we should be finished by the end of the year.'

'That long!'

'Excavations cannot be hurried or we lose vital information.'

'But there's no reason why I cannot ask my man to return and continue levelling my ground and marking out the dimensions of my building?' asked Vasilis anxiously.

'Provided he doesn't interfere with our work there will be no problem.'

'And the footings can be dug to support the pillars?'

Lambros nodded. 'Of course, but if any more graves were unearthed on your land we'd have to ask you to stop.'

'Do you think that's likely?'

Lambros shrugged. 'Difficult to say, but anything is possible although we ran GPR over the whole area.'

'I'll mention that to my workmen and tell them they must consult you if they find any more bones. I hope they'll be here tomorrow. Thank you for the information. I'll let you get on with your work.'

Vasilis hurried back to his car and returned to his apartment.

'Good news,' he announced to Cathy. 'Lambros has said that I can continue building. They've found a lot more burials on the land next to mine and think that was the main cemetery.'

Cathy smiled at him. 'Well before you become totally engrossed in building again I'd like to ask Elizabeth and Nicolas to visit us.'

Vasilis nodded absently as he opened his mobile 'phone. 'I must make some calls. The sooner the work can continue the happier I will be.'

Over their evening meal Elena mentioned the information she had gleaned from Maria. 'Do you think she was talking about Aunt Anna?'

'Bound to be,' answered Uncle Yannis firmly. 'I found the man hiding up there in an outhouse and took him into Babbis's house. Mamma Anna found him and needless to say I was in trouble.'

'For taking him there?' asked Giovanni.

'No, for not telling her about him as soon as I had found him. She gave her mother a sleeping draught and told the soldiers who were billeted on us that her mother had suffered another stroke and needed the doctor. They believed her and fetched him.'

172

'Why would they be concerned about an old lady having a stroke?' asked Marianne.

'They had been told that Mamma Anna was very knowledgeable about herbs. I think they were more concerned that she would poison them if they did not do as she asked,'

'I remember that,' added Marisa. 'I was really worried about Grandma and Mamma Anna left me sitting with her whilst she took the doctor up to the wounded man.'

'But what about the soldiers who were living with you?' asked Elena.

Uncle Yannis grinned. 'I said I had seen resistance workers hiding out on the hill. They believed me and I took them well away from Babbis's house so the doctor could visit the injured man.'

'Weren't you frightened?' asked Marianne.

'I was no more than a boy at the time and I just considered it exciting.'

'What else did you do? Were you a nuisance to them like the boys in Kato and Pano?'

Uncle Yannis shook his head. 'No, I was too busy trying to help Mamma Anna to keep the farm going and I was told not to antagonise them.'

'Who told you that?'

'Michael, the English resistance worker who visited the area.'

Elena looked at her cousin. 'There is Andreas asking the men for their memories and all he really had to do was talk to you.'

Uncle Yannis shrugged. 'I did very little. I was too young to go away and join the andartes and with the soldiers living in the village if their vehicles had been damaged I would have been blamed. I had to think of Mamma Anna and Marisa.'

'Victor would have looked after me,' Marisa assured her brother.

'He may not have been able to. He had to obey orders.'

Elena looked from one to the other. 'I think I need to sit down and have a long talk with both of you. Evi told me that there was a young girl locally who shot three soldiers and she and her mother buried them in the olive grove. Was that you and Mamma Anna, Marisa?'

Marisa shook her head. 'I have never shot anyone.'

John was listening avidly to the conversation. 'What happened to the soldiers who were buried?'

'Evi told me they were never found.'

'You mean they are still there?'

'Presumably.'

'Then why don't we look for them and dig them up?'

'No, John. Evi would not tell me the name of the girl as she said her family still lived in the area. They might not even know if they have bodies on their land and if you started digging them up it could cause terrible trouble for them.'

'What a shame they were not the skeletons that were found on Vasilis's land. That would have been exciting,' smiled John.

'Poor Vasilis has had enough problems without adding buried soldiers to them. What Uncle Andreas does with this information is up to him, but I don't think we should try to find out where these soldiers are buried. If the land is developed in the future they could well be found then. Let's hear no more about that idea, John.' Giovanni spoke sternly.

Elizabeth held up her hand. 'Please tell me what you have been talking about. I've managed to pick up a word or two but you know I don't speak Greek.'

Marianne immediately felt contrite. 'I'm sorry. We are so used to speaking Greek when we are together that we tend to forget others may not understand. It's probably best if my mother explains to you. We'll try to keep quiet and not interrupt. Come and sit here, Elizabeth.'

Whilst Elena explained to Elizabeth about her brother's ideas for a play and the investigation she had been carrying out on his behalf the men continued to talk and refill their glasses.

'Will your brother really have the play published in New York?' asked Elizabeth.

'Apparently his publisher is interested. Andreas would like to stage a performance locally to gauge the reaction, but that could be difficult. There is no way army vehicles and uniforms could be hired. He's been trying to think of a way around that problem, and I have had an idea.'

'Tell me.'

Elena shook her head. 'I need to talk to Andreas about it first. He may say it isn't practical.'

Ludmila made her way to the bus station and bought a return ticket to Rethymnon. Although she had visited the town with Evgeniy she had no real recollection of the harbour area. It could be a suitable location for Ivan to come to collect her.

She walked slowly along the waterfront. It was far more attractive than the port of Heraklion where the ferries docked and disgorged their travellers from the other islands and Athens, but it was also a hive of activity. Small boats were moored in every conceivable docking space, visitors in vast numbers strolled up and down, taking photographs or looking at the menus displayed outside the tavernas that lined the area. There was no way Ivan would be able to arrive and moor without the maritime authorities being aware of his presence. Although she had been deliberately vague about the name of the boat Evgeniy may have disclosed it and that would mean that an alert had been sent out to all the ports to investigate the arrival of the craft.

It had been a wasted journey and she would console herself with a meal at one of the waterside tavernas before returning to Heraklion. Provided she had sufficient money she would visit Hersonissos next week and see if that was a more viable location.

Elena sat with her brother and asked if he knew that Yannis and Aunt Anna had been involved with the resistance. 'She said one of the andartes carried his injured brother down to Plaka. Yannis found him there and hid them in Babbis's house. He then said that Aunt Anna had managed to get the doctor from Aghios to visit.'

Andreas frowned. 'How did she manage that?'

Elena sighed. 'It would be far better if you talked to Yannis and Marisa. I'm sure they would be able to fill in the details for you and might have some other incidents that you could use.'

'I'll visit Yannis and Marisa this afternoon. I didn't think either of them could have done very much as they had Italian soldiers living at the farm.'

'You should certainly talk to them. They must know if their aunt was involved with an injured andarte. I'll tell them you'll be coming.'

Andreas shook his head. 'I'll 'phone Marianne and check that it is convenient. As she has Elizabeth and Nicolas staying she may have other plans. I wouldn't want to inconvenience her.'

'I don't think they have made any plans to go anywhere at the moment. Nicolas wants to come up to the villages and also go over to Spinalonga, but Elizabeth is insisting that he rests each day. So far all they have done is gone out for a walk along the road towards Plaka. It's flat so suitable for Nicolas to have the exercise he's been prescribed.'

'Did you manage to speak to Maria?'

Elena nodded. 'She confirmed the story Evi told me about the soldiers, but I'm not sure if you should include that. Evi said the family still lived locally.'

'That won't matter if the play is staged in New York. No one there will know.'

'I was thinking more of the performance you are keen to produce here.'

Andreas shook his head. 'I don't think that will be feasible.'

'Why not? I was talking to the family last night about the shot soldiers and I completely forgot that Elizabeth did not speak Greek. She finally asked for an explanation of our conversation and whilst I was telling her about visiting the women an idea came to me. Why don't you stage it the way they used to present plays?'

'How do you mean?'

'You have a narrator. That could be you. The men sit on chairs one side of the room and the women on the other. The soldiers don't appear at all; you just hear them tramping up and down. You say they arrive in the village and the women wail, cling together and hide their faces. The men appear to be talking together, waving their arms. One man says he's going off to join the Resistance, another says he'll join him. The women reach out imploring hands to them.'

Andreas nodded. 'Go on.'

'You will need someone who is efficient with lighting as the men need to be in darkness whilst the women do their next bit. A child says they are hungry and one of the women says something like "*We are all hungry, except for the soldiers. They have taken our food and left us to starve.*" Another woman then suggests that they collect whatever they can from the hedges and fields and they mime picking and collecting leaves and grasses. Every so often the sound of the soldiers tramping is heard again and the women cower and hide their faces.'

'And the men?'

'The light goes back onto them and each one has just a few lines saying where they went with the Resistance. Some will then claim to have been killed and slump down on the chair, or walk off; others will say they were injured. One says he doesn't want to talk about the horrors he experienced and still suffers nightmares. Their dialogue is up to you, Andreas. You're the writer.'

Andreas was already scribbling furiously on a sheet of paper. 'Give me some more ideas,' he ordered.

'The women are then lit up again and scream and plead to be left alone. One woman walks behind them and gives each of them a small glass of liquid that they drink. They shudder and then begin to clutch their stomachs. She announces that the medicine she has given them will cause them to miscarry. There could be one woman holding a doll and saying she is the most shamed woman in the village as the medicine did not work for her. We ought to have some girls singing that silly rhyme as a round and hear the soldiers stamping their feet in time with the children when the performance ends.'

'And the boys,' added Andreas. 'We need them describing how they sabotaged the army vehicles.'

'Do you think it would be viable to present it like that?'

Andreas nodded. 'I was trying to write a play drawing on the people's war time experiences and that would be fine for a professional company in a theatre. You've come up with a far more practical idea for a local presentation. When I have worked on it some more we'll go and have a word with the locals and see how they feel about performing.'

'I expect the youngsters will be keen enough, but I'm not sure about the older residents.'

Andreas shrugged. 'I'm sure we will be able to persuade them.'

Marianne answered Andreas's 'phone call and confirmed that he could visit that afternoon. 'Come about three, Uncle Yannis and Marisa will have had their afternoon rest. You're welcome to stay and eat with us and I can take you home later.'

'I can always walk back home.'

'I wouldn't hear of it. Even if you decide not to stay for a meal one of us will be available to drive you home. Nicola and the children are going up to the playground at Plaka this afternoon and I expect Elizabeth will go with them. She finds it difficult if you are all speaking Greek and doesn't like to keep asking to have the conversation explained to her. I don't know what Nicolas's father did during the war; he was in the army and stationed in Athens. Nicolas could have some interesting information for you.'

'Elena and I will have some lunch here and then have a taxi from Elounda down to you. I don't know how long I will spend talking with them but I don't want to disrupt your day.'

'You are welcome to stay as long as you want,' Marianne

assured him. 'I will assume that you are eating with us and add a few more vegetables. You won't want to think about preparing a meal for yourself when you get home.'

'That's true,' admitted Andreas. 'I will probably want to sit and write.'

'And no doubt your lunch time meal will be bread and cheese. I do hope you are looking after yourself properly.'

'I often visit my neighbours during the evening and they always offer me a meal. I take a bottle of wine with me and they seem to think that's a fair exchange.'

'You are not to bring a bottle of anything to us. You're family, remember.'

Elizabeth pushed Yiannis in his stroller up to the playground. 'We won't stay here all afternoon,' said Nicola. 'After about an hour the girls become bored and Yiannis fractious. We'll walk on into the village and you can visit Saffie if you want whilst I take the girls into Monika's shop. She'll keep them occupied whilst I walk along the waterfront and back up the main road with Yiannis and he'll probably go to sleep for a while.'

'I'm just pleased to be able to spend the afternoon with you. There's always someone around at the house and I just wanted to get away from everyone for a while. I'm not used to having people around me all the time.'

'If you want some private time make an excuse and go back to the apartments. No one will think any the worse of you. If Bryony isn't working up at Saffie's she and Marcus often spend the afternoon together in their rooms and I know that Marianne will sneak off and have a short siesta some days. Although we are all sharing the same house we have our own areas where we can be alone.'

By the time Andreas and Elena reached the house Marianne had told Yannis and Marisa that he was coming and wanted to talk to them about their war time memories.

Marisa shook her head. 'I don't think I'll be much use to him. Mamma Anna never confided in me and I just did my best to help her. Doing the washing every day for Grandma was the worst chore. I remember my hands used to be red raw from scrubbing at the sheets.'

'What about when you visited the island and watched the films with Ourania and her mother?'

'That was before the war.'

'Andreas could still be interested.'

Marisa shrugged. 'Maybe.'

Andreas sat with Yannis and Marisa, his notebook on his knee.

'So, Yannis, tell me exactly how you became involved with the andartes and the resistance. I've talked to the men locally but they've never mentioned you.'

Yannis smiled. 'Some of the boys may have boasted about their activities, but I couldn't tell Mamma Anna what I was up to. She would have forbidden me to meet Michael and become involved in any way. She was so worried that something would happen to her and then who would take care of Grandma?'

'I would have looked after her,' protested Marisa.

'You were only interested in Victor,' replied Yannis scathingly and Marisa had the grace to blush. 'Mamma Anna nearly had a fit when he asked her if he could marry you.'

'She just didn't want me to go to Italy. She was worried that if I was unhappy I would be unable to return to Crete. I was never unhappy with Victor.'

Andreas smiled. This was not the information that he wanted. 'I think your experience could be useful right at the end of the play. A "happy ever after" ending to the tragic events that had taken place over here.'

Marisa nodded happily and Andreas turned back to Yannis. 'So tell me what you got up to.'

September 2015
Week One – Tuesday, Wednesday & Thursday

On Tuesday Marianne had driven Nicolas and Elizabeth up to Mavrikiano, parking outside 'The Hope' and blocking the road to any other traffic before she went down to the official car park at the bottom off the steep hill. By the time she had climbed back up she found Nicolas and Elizabeth sitting outside on the balcony admiring the view and studying the menu.

'What do you suggest?' asked Elizabeth.

'The crab salad is magnificent; we'll need two portions as once you start eating that it's impossible to stop. Courgette balls and cheese balls are very similar so I would only order one portion of each, and the beetroot is superb. You could also have dolmades and keftedes.'

'What about taramasalata and tzatziki and should we have a salad?'

'Whatever you wish.' Marianne smiled to herself; Nicolas had certainly not lost his appetite due to his heart surgery.

They lingered over their meal until Marianne finally announced that she would pay the bill and collect the car.

'I could walk down,' offered Nicolas, but Marianne would not hear of it.

'The time is getting on and you want me to drive you through Pano Elounda and down to Kato Elounda so you can see Uncle Andreas's house. Is there anywhere else you would like to go after that?' she asked.

'I'd like to go up to Plaka again and walk around,' said Elizabeth. 'I went into Saffie's shop when I was up there with Nicola and she was just putting out some new scarves. I'd like to buy one for Eleanor.'

'We don't need to impose on Marianne to take us there,' remonstrated Nicolas. 'We can easily walk along from the apartments. We can do that tomorrow morning and then John has promised to take us over to Spinalonga on Thursday.'

'You're quite sure you don't want to go on to Plaka now?'

'No, we'll leave that for tomorrow,' said Elizabeth firmly. 'We'll walk back from your house to the apartments so that Nicolas has had his daily exercise. He can then have a rest before we walk along to you this evening.'

Elizabeth and Nicolas climbed into John's boat and he motored over to Spinalonga and moored at the old jetty, enabling them to avoid the boats that came over carrying the tourists. He led them up to the main road and back to the square where Old Uncle Yannis had lived.

'This is where we have buried his bones,' John said quietly as he indicated the corner of the room. 'We are the only people who know where he is and there is no grave marker. When I go into the church I light a candle for him and wish I could have met him. From all I have been able to find out he was much respected and it was mostly due to him that the community came together. He was not frightened to make demands on the government before or after the war.' John led the way slowly back onto the main road. 'This where the parade of shops were originally. They have made them into an information centre.'

'Oh, no,' exclaimed Elizabeth. 'That was where Marianne photographed Anna. The old shutters where Anna carved the ships have gone. Where did Ronnie think her ghost made an appearance?'

'We'll need to go back down to the main square for me to

show you where she was sitting. Do you want to walk all the way around the island or just go back down there?'

'I'd like to go to the top of the road,' said Nicolas. 'Now they've done so much work over here clearing the weeds and rubbish it's remarkable how much more you can see.'

'They've also taken down some of the houses that were dangerous. They have promised to rebuild them when all the safety work is completed,' explained John.

'I hope they will. Looking just at building foundations hardly gives you an idea of how the village looked originally.'

'There are photographs in here and also some of the artefacts that have been discovered. They have been working on the hospital and hope they will have that open to visitors at a later date. I just happen to have a key to the padlock, so if you feel able to walk up the hill I can let you in to have a look. I don't want to be accused of exhausting you both.'

Elizabeth looked at her husband anxiously. 'You're not supposed to be walking up hills yet, Nicolas.'

'I'm sure if I take it slowly I'll be perfectly alright.'

'If you decide it is too much for you we can go back down and visit another day.'

John unlocked the padlock that was fixed to the doors of the hospital. 'It may be a bit dark in here so wait until your eyes have become accustomed before you start to walk around. The last time I was here the archaeologists were excavating an area in the passage and I don't want either of you to fall down.'

'Have they found anything interesting?' asked Elizabeth.

'A considerable amount of pottery that dates back to when the Turks used the building as a hospital and a few odd coins. Where they have dug in the passage they have found a cobbled area beneath and they believe that was the original floor.' John took out his mobile 'phone and used the light as a torch. 'Watch your step here.'

Cautiously Elizabeth and Nicolas walked around the area of flooring that had been excavated to a depth of about four feet leaving a narrow walkway at the side.

'From here we go into the area where the sick people were nursed.'

'That's awful,' remarked Elizabeth. 'It's so dark and dismal.'

'The other inhabitants used to give Spiro all their oil so he could have some light up here at night. This meant they had to sit in the dark inside their houses until the electricity was finally installed. That made all the difference.'

'I still cannot imagine it being a pleasant place. Did they have beds to lie on?' asked Nicolas.

'Not at first. They had their mattresses on the floor. I understand that it was quite well organised. Soiled mattresses were changed each day and volunteers would mop them clean. During the summer months they would dry quite quickly but it was more of a problem in the winter.'

'What a horrible job.' Elizabeth shuddered.

John shrugged. 'Pretty awful, but someone had to do it. If they had been left not only would the patients have suffered but the smell would eventually have become unbearable. If we go through here this is where Doctor Stavros carried out some of the essential operations.'

Elizabeth and Nicolas looked at the stone slab that had been used as an operating table.

'On there?'

'It was practical. There was a drain underneath and it could be scrubbed clean after it had been used.'

'Did Doctor Stavros operate often?'

John shook his head. 'According to his old records that I have been able to read it was quite a rare occurrence. Most of the patients were simply bedridden and unable to help themselves due to their illness. The hospital was really more of an area where the incapable could be cared for under one roof rather than in separate houses. Sometimes a foot or hand had to be amputated if it had developed a further infection that would have been life threatening.'

'Like the girl who had her arm amputated?'

John nodded. 'Considering the conditions under which the operation was conducted it was remarkable that she survived.'

'I am amazed that anyone who lived over here survived. Having just spent some time in a modern hospital this is positively primitive. Like something from the eighteenth century.'

'It was a hundred years ago,' John reminded Nicolas, 'And the best they could do under the circumstances. I doubt that the other hospitals in Greece were very much better. I remember my great grandmother saying that she was not allowed to nurse leprosy patients. They were expected to look after each other.'

'I really do not like being in here,' said Elizabeth. 'I'm pleased you were able to show us how it was, but can we go now?'

John led the way back to the main room and back into the sunlight, replacing the padlock on the door. By the time they reached the main road Nicolas was breathing heavily and sat down on the step.

'I'm alright, just need to get my breath back. I think it was the atmosphere that took my breath away more than the climb.'

'Sit as long as you want. There's no rush.'

Elizabeth lowered herself onto the step beside her husband. 'Are you sure you're alright? We could go back now.'

Nicolas shook his head. 'I want to go down to the square and see where Ronnie thought she met her ghostly relative. We saw her yesterday and she told us the story.'

'She had encounters in various different places. Did she tell you that she thinks she has found the house where they lived? There's nothing to see up there except the foundations so I'll not drag you up the steps. If you were really keen to go there we could always come back another day.'

Nicolas nodded. He was conscious of his pace maker regulating his heart beat and realised why he had been told he should not climb hills for at least another month.

Ludmila took the bus to Hersonissos. The town was overflowing with young people. As she walked along the narrow pavements she was frequently jostled and pushed out into the road. This was busier than the centre of Heraklion. She saw a shop advertising cheap mobile 'phones and went inside. It could be sensible to purchase one here rather than in Heraklion. It was hardly likely that the assistant would remember her.

The shop keeper tried hard to sell her the latest model, but Ludmila was adamant. She only needed a cheap 'phone to use whilst she was away as she had left her usual appliance at home. Finally the shop keeper gave in and produced a cheap plastic model in lime green. Suppressing a shudder and refusing to buy a protective cover she placed it in her bag and handed over her Euros. She was convinced he had over charged her.

On leaving the shop she took a side road that led down to the waterfront hoping to avoid the worst of the congestion of tourists who milled around. Once again she was disappointed, the harbour area was full of small boats. On the beach people sun bathed beneath the umbrellas, splashed in and out of the sea, hired a paddle boat or went for a ride on the "banana", shrieking with laughter as the power boat pulling them gathered speed. It would be impossible for Ivan to bring his boat here. Unless she was able to discover a secluded cove she would have to 'phone her brother and ask his advice.

Ludmila walked to one of the cafes at the top of the beach. Originally she had intended to have lunch there, but when she saw the prices they were displaying she changed her mind. She would return to Heraklion on the next bus and visit the local supermarket before returning to the apartment and making a meal for herself.

Ludmila spread the map of Crete out before her on the table. There were villages marked down on the coast, some of them having umbrellas denoting that it was a bathing beach. There was nothing to indicate if the others were suitable for a boat to dock. She began to make a list of the ones that she thought could be feasible and then looked at her bus timetable. The only villages that appeared to have a bus service were those with the umbrellas. She was certain that the others ought to be accessible and she made a further list with the intention of asking at the bus station. She certainly did not want to have to take a taxi to any of the destinations as she was unsure how much it would cost. Having purchased the mobile 'phone she needed to be careful now with the remainder of her money.

Andreas had spent the whole of the weekend writing. Having talked to Yannis he knew it was essential that he incorporated the information he had been given into his play. Satisfied that he had done justice to both Anna's and Yannis's exploits he considered the idea that Elena had given him. It was certainly feasible.

He walked up to the kafenion and sat with the men there. They greeted him affably and asked how he was progressing with his writing.

'I've been working hard and I have had another idea. I'd like to stage a production locally.'

The men looked at him and shook their heads. 'We haven't any theatre here that would be large enough for you to have jeeps inside.'

'That would not be necessary. I would just want some of you to agree to be on the stage and say a few lines.'

'I'm not an actor,' said one. 'I used to be a fisherman.'

'You don't have to be an actor. I'd just want you to talk as you have to me. You'd relate the acts of sabotage that were carried out when you were boys.'

'And probably end up in prison.'

Andreas shook his head. 'I'm sure you wouldn't. It's too long ago for you to be accused of a crime and no one on Crete would

187

think you acted criminally. You don't have to claim that you committed any of the acts. Think of the actors you see in a film. All they do is learn the lines they are given and act as instructed. It isn't real.'

'I'll not take the chance.' Stavros ran his worry beads through his fingers. 'I ought to get back to the house. My wife will have my lunch ready.'

One by one the men declined to participate, making excuses to return to their homes until Andreas was left alone in the kafenion feeling disappointed and frustrated. He would have to call Elena and ask her to visit Pano tomorrow and see if she could persuade Evi and Maria to support him.

Elena returned from Pano Elounda feeling despondent. Neither Evi nor Maria were willing to take part in the performance.

'I'll come and watch,' said Evi. 'I'm sure my son will drive me down. I'll ask him to bring Maria at the same time.'

However hard Elena tried to persuade the two women they were adamant that they were too old to participate in such activities. Andreas was equally as disheartened when she told him. 'That's it, then. I'll just have to hope that my publisher thinks it's good enough to be put on as a play and forget the idea of doing anything locally.'

Elena walked back to Yannis's house deep in thought. How could she persuade the local people to take part?

'Why didn't you call home and ask one of us to collect you?' asked Marianne when her mother finally arrived. 'I was beginning to become quite concerned about you. Surely you haven't been up in Pano all day?'

Elena explained that she had spent most of the morning trying to talk Evi and Maria into performing and then the afternoon trying to console Andreas. 'He's so disappointed. Neither the men nor the women will agree to appear.'

'I'm sorry; he seemed so enthusiastic when he was here talking to Uncle Yannis.'

'Maybe he could write a one man show where only Yannis appeared,' suggested Elena.

'I'm not sure that would be a good idea. It would mean that Uncle Yannis had to learn a lot of lines. He's eight four, remember.'

'That's why Andreas wanted the older villagers to take part. They would only have had to say a couple of lines each and Andreas would have told the story of the men and I would tell the story of the women.'

'You would?' Marianne looked at her mother in surprise.

'I wouldn't have to learn anything as I could read it. What has everyone else been up to today?'

'Elizabeth and Nicolas visited Cathy and Vasilis. He's been told he can continue with the work for his house so he's much happier.'

'They haven't found any more bones then?'

'Not on his land, but apparently they've found a number of graves on the plot next door.'

'Good job he didn't decide to buy that then. I'm going to have a rest. If I don't appear when you're ready to serve our meal ask someone to come and fetch me.'

'Did you have some lunch with Andreas?' asked Marianne anxiously.

'Yes, but he'd forgotten to buy any fresh bread, so we just had some ham and salad.'

Marianne looked after her mother sadly as she left the kitchen. She seemed so disappointed that the performance would not be taking place.

'What's up with Grandma?' asked John. 'She hardly spoke whilst we were having our supper and afterwards she went straight back to her room. Isn't she feeling well?'

'She's just disappointed that Andreas won't be able to put on a performance of his play locally. Apparently she was going to tell the story of the women.'

'How do you mean?'

'I'm not sure. She said she wouldn't have to learn any lines, she would just read it. I didn't want to press her for details.'

'I'll see if she'll tell me.'

'Don't upset her, John,' called Marianne as her son left the room and he looked back at her reproachfully.

John tapped on his Grandmother's door. 'May I come in, Grandma?'

'Of course. I'm not going to bed yet.'

'Mum said you were rather upset that you and Uncle Andreas have been unable to persuade the villagers to take part in his play.'

'I am,' sighed Elena. 'I'm sure it will be accepted in New York, but it's the history of the local people during the war. It would mean something special to them. New Yorkers will either love it or hate it, but it won't have a personal meaning for them.'

John nodded. 'I heard Uncle Yannis telling Uncle Andreas about fooling the soldiers. Who else knows about that or many of the other things that the ordinary people did whilst Crete was occupied?'

'Only the older generation and there are not that many of them left. Once they have died their memories will be forgotten. That's why Andreas wanted to perform locally.'

'Does it have to be the elderly people who participate?'

'It's their memories.'

'Of course, but if they're not willing to share them in public why can't some of the younger generation perform on their behalf?'

'What do you mean?'

'These people are old now, but when the events took place they were young, so why shouldn't younger people take their parts?'

'I suppose that might be possible. Andreas said the men were reluctant to acknowledge whatever they had done in fear that there would be reprisals against them now.'

'That's the answer, then. Unless they want to lay claim to a particular act no one will actually know who was responsible originally. Think about it, Grandma, and talk to Uncle Andreas tomorrow and ask his opinion.'

Although she felt tired Elena could not sleep. John's suggestion seemed practical and she wished she could speak to her brother now rather than having to wait until the following day. If he agreed they would have to think who they could ask to participate and where a performance could be held.

Andreas listened to his sister when she recounted John's idea to him. 'I suppose it might be possible, but I don't know any of the younger people. They live and work down in Elounda. I only go down to do a bit of shopping occasionally.'

'You know Giovanni and Marcus and what about John's friend Dimitris? I'm sure John would know other people. He seems to know everyone. Shall I call him and ask if he can come down and talk to us?'

Andreas shrugged. 'There's nothing to be lost in talking to him.'

'I'm up at the shop at the moment,' explained John to his grandmother. 'Marcus is going to relieve me and then I have to collect some of Uncle Yannis's pots and take them into Aghios and see if I can get any of the gift shops there interested in stocking them. I can't be with you until about three. Is that too late?'

'No problem at all. Uncle Andreas wants to hear more about your idea of younger people taking part in his production.'

'You and Uncle work out exactly how and where you want to stage it and I'll see what I can do about providing him with the actors.'

Elena closed her 'phone. 'John will come up after he has been into Aghios. We need to have some ideas ready for him. He wants to know where the performance could be held.'

'It would have to be at the Municipal Centre in Elounda where they hold exhibitions and special events. Make me a coffee, Elena and I'll start to make some notes.'

By the time John arrived Andreas had pages of diagrams with scribbled comments on them. As soon as John had taken a seat at the table he immediately began explaining his ideas.

'We have the men sitting on one side and I'll be a distance behind them. I'll describe the invasion by the Germans and how they progressed down the country to join up with the Italian forces. Then I'll mention how the resistance tried to defend the villages and the formation of the andartes.'

Elena shook her head. 'I think everywhere should be in darkness to start and the women sing the silly song. When they finish that is when you have a light on you and you begin to describe the events.'

Andreas nodded and made a note. 'The light will then go onto the men. Some of them will just have a line or two saying how they participated. I'll go on to say that Spinalonga was blockaded and how the villagers were robbed of their livestock and food.'

'Can you mention Manolis? asked John. 'I could be him and say how I took supplies out to the island until I was stopped and then how I became part of the resistance movement.'

'You?'

'Yes, I want to be a part of this and I'm sure the rest of the family will be just as keen. Grandma Marisa could be Aunt Anna and Uncle Yannis could say how he helped draw the soldiers away so Aunt Anna could take the doctor up into the hills.'

Andreas nodded. 'I'll see where it fits in best. Your Grandmother is going to be behind where the women are sitting and talk about the part they played and how they suffered. We'll need someone who can work the lights so that the men are in darkness whilst the women are talking and vice versa.'

'Dimitris is your man for that. How many people do you plan to have on stage?'

'I'm not sure yet, but I think it should be an equal number of men and women.'

John began to tick them off on his fingers,' Mum and Dad, Bryony and Marcus, Grandma Marisa and Uncle Yannis, Nick and me. We need more than eight. I could ask Ackers and see if Vasi and Vasilis are willing.'

'What about Monika from the bookshop?' suggested Elena.

'That's a good idea. Saff probably knows enough Greek by now to say a line or two.'

'What about Ronnie?'

'She'd probably need a bit of coaching, but that would then make fourteen people. What's the song that you want to open with?'

Elena opened her notebook. 'I have it written down in here. The girls used to sing it as a round and the soldiers didn't realise they were being rude. At the end the girls would stamp their feet and shout "bang, bang, bang", and the soldiers often joined in, but I'm not sure what the tune was.'

John grinned. 'Give me a copy of the words and we'll see what we can come up with.'

'Evi did try to sing it to me, but her voice is very cracked and off key.'

'Can you go up again and ask her to sing it to you? I'm sure you'd get some idea however rusty her voice is now.' John looked at the words that his grandmother had passed to him. 'Oh, I like this. I wonder who made it up originally?'

'Probably better that I don't ask. Both Evi and Maria would probably claim they did. I get the impression that they are not always on the best of terms, each tries to outdo the other when telling me their memories.'

'Sounds like women,' said John with a wink. 'I'm sure you didn't have that problem with the men, Uncle. Why don't you come back with us now, Uncle Andreas? You can explain your ideas far better than I would be able to. I'll give Mum a call and say you are coming up for supper. I'm sure Uncle Yannis is waiting anxiously to know if I have taken any orders for his pots.'

'Have you?' asked Elena.

John nodded. 'Five small and two larger ones. I think it's going to be those enormous pithoi that he has a job to sell. I can only think that museums would want those. What would a private person do with them?'

Andreas explained his ideas for staging the performance to the family as they ate their evening meal. 'The older generation who have given me the information are unwilling to participate. They think they could be called to account for their actions although it was so long ago now. John has suggested that we do it ourselves. That way whoever gave me the information remains anonymous.'

'I don't mind admitting that I helped the resistance,' declared Uncle Yannis. 'I'm proud of the contribution I made.'

Andreas looked around the table. 'How do you feel?'

Giovanni nodded. 'I see no reason why we shouldn't participate, provided everyone is agreeable.'

'Have you mentioned how the Jewish population were targeted?' asked Marcus. 'If I take part I'd like to mention that, after all, I am a Jew.'

'You can certainly have that as your main part, although I'll have to do some research. Most of that atrocity took place in Heraklion and I believe that one of the ships carrying passengers was sunk.'

'Then I'm agreeable.'

'I'll write a few lines for each person and then we'll have to rehearse. We need to make sure that it is coherent and doesn't end up disjointed and muddled.'

'We can do that here,' said John enthusiastically. 'We can put the chairs in line on the patio or in the lounge. We need some extra people and I think we should ask Saff, Monika, Vasi, Vasilis and Ackers.'

'Saffie and Monika have their shops open until late. Would they be willing to come here after a day's work?' asked Bryony.

'We could ask them to close an hour early occasionally.'

'I can't see Kyriakos being willing to close his taverna half way through the evening,' remarked Giovanni.

John shrugged. 'We can but ask him.'

Marianne shook her head. 'I think they should all be asked before you make any more plans.'

'That will take ages going and explaining to everyone and asking if they will take part. Why don't we have a party before Elizabeth and Nicolas go home? I'm sure they would all come to that and Uncle Andreas can explain his idea and ask them to join us.'

Nicolas had been explaining quietly to Elizabeth the nature of the discussion that was taking place.

'It sounds really exciting. When will this happen?' asked Elizabeth.

'I don't think Uncle Andreas has decided on a date yet.'

'I wish we could be here to see it,' said Elizabeth wistfully.

'It will all be in Greek so you wouldn't understand,' Nicolas reminded her gently.

'I'm sure you could tell me what was going on.'

'If we were going to be here I'd ask to be included. We have to return home to Eleanor and cannot stay out here indefinitely. It sounds quite complicated and it could be months before Uncle Andreas feels it is polished enough to perform in public.'

September 2015
Weeks One & Two – Saturday & Monday

Marianne had 'phoned Cathy and asked her and Vasilis to come for a meal that evening and followed that with a 'phone call to Vasi.

'I know Saffie has the shop open late but if you could persuade her to close a little earlier and you both came for a farewell meal with Elizabeth and Nicolas they would really appreciate it. I've spoken to Cathy and she has accepted on behalf of her and your father. I'm going to ask Ronnie and Kyriakos, but I think it unlikely that Kyriakos will be willing to close the taverna.'

'I'm sure Saffie can close early for once. She wouldn't want to miss saying goodbye. When do they actually leave?'

'On Monday, so we thought Saturday was the best evening. If the evening goes on late they can always sleep in the following day without having to worry about getting to the airport.'

'What time would you like us to arrive and can we bring anything?'

'About eight to eight thirty would be perfect and there's certainly no need to bring anything at all.'

Giovanni tapped a teaspoon against his glass. 'Can I have your attention for a few minutes. Firstly I would like you all to ensure that your glasses are full so you can raise them and wish Elizabeth and Nicolas a safe journey home. It has been our pleasure to have them here and we hope they will be able to return again very soon.'

Nicola placed her arm around her mother. 'I'm going to miss you so much. It's been lovely to have you here.'

'I'll miss you and the children also,' said Elizabeth as she tried to hold back her tears.

'There is something else that Uncle Andreas wants to speak to all of you about,' added Giovanni as the glasses were lowered after the good wishes had been expressed. 'I'm going to ask him to explain his idea. We have found it interesting and somewhat exciting and hope you will also. He needs your support as part of the family to make his plan a success. We are relying on you. Over to you, Uncle.'

Andreas cleared his throat. 'I have already spoken with Yannis and Marisa and gained their approval so I will talk to you in English so everyone else present can understand me. As you know I am a playwright. I have been researching the activities of the ordinary people and the events that over took them when the country was invaded. Although I have written a play that I hope will eventually be successful in New York I want to put on a production over here as a way of thanking everyone who has made me so welcome in their community and also shared their memories with me. I asked the older generation to join in the project and they refused. They were concerned that any events they described would then be attributed directly to them.'

Andreas took a sip of his wine. 'John suggested that the family helped by performing. We discussed this the other evening and they have agreed, but we need more people. You, my friends, are also part of the family so now I am asking you to join us. Please, ensure that your glasses are topped up and you have a plate of food and I will tell you exactly what I am asking of you.'

As Andreas outlined his ideas for the performance he was listened to attentively but when he finished Vasilis shook his head. 'I think it is an excellent idea, but I am not an actor.'

'You do not need to act as such. Participants will only be given a line or two of dialogue and the action will be in mime. Some of that

197

will be individual, but mostly you will all do the same motions as the events described will have happened to all of you. There is a silly rhyming song that has to be learnt and sung by the ladies, but it is only a few lines.'

'I can't help,' said Ronnie. 'I can't speak Greek.'

'You don't need to be able to speak Greek; just to learn a few words. Kyriakos would help to correct your pronunciation.'

'Can I take part?' asked Cathy eagerly. 'I was very proud of my father and his work with the Resistance. If Vasilis helped me I'm sure I would be able to learn the song.'

Vasilis looked at his wife. 'If you want to participate then I will have to agree to do so also. I just hope it will not interfere with my building plans and the work I have to complete each week for "The Central".'

Andreas nodded. 'And you, Saffie and Vasi? Will you join us?'

Vasi smiled. 'I don't think we have any choice. If we refused the family would never forgive us.'

'I'll need help with the Greek,' Saffron reminded Vasi. 'I can speak enough to be understood when I go shopping, but I'm certainly not fluent.'

Andreas counted on his fingers. 'Yannis, Giovanni, Marcus, John, Vasilis and Vasi. We need more than six men. Would Kyriakos join us?'

Ronnie shook her head. 'I'll ask him, but when would you plan to rehearse? It would be difficult for him to leave the taverna in the evenings.'

'I could ask my friend Yiorgos Palamakis. I'm sure he'd be agreeable provided his wife didn't object to him being out in the evenings.'

'She could join in with us. Let me see how many women we have; Marisa, Marianne, Bryony, Nicola, Saffron and Ronnie. Six again so we really need a couple more.'

'Isn't Elena taking part?' asked Ronnie.

'Elena will be the narrator for the women so cannot take part with the rest of you.'

'What about Monika?' suggested Saffron. 'I'm sure she would be willing provided she did not have to close the shop too early.'

Andreas nodded. 'I think we need a minimum of eight women and eight men. Can you think of anyone else?'

'Dimitris?'

John shook his head. 'I know how Uncle Andreas wants to stage the production and Dimitris would be essential for arranging the lighting. What about Theo?'

'He's a possibility,' agreed Saffron. 'Monika's mother would probably be willing to join us if he was taking part as well.'

'So can I leave it up to you, Saffie, to speak to Monika and Theo?' asked Andreas. 'One of them can then ask Monika's mother. You ask Yiorgos, Vasi and then let me know if they all agree. We'll then arrange for a rehearsal and in the meantime I'll concentrate on writing the script and the miming actions that need to be learnt. Most of you will be doing exactly the same thing at the same time, so if you do forget where you are you will only have to look at your companion and copy them.'

'I have three questions, Uncle Andreas,' said Vasi. 'When and where will the performance be held and where are you proposing we will rehearse?'

'The Municipal Centre is the only suitable location. There is no fixed date at the moment, but I think it would be most practical if it took place in November. The tourists will have left by then, the tavernas and gift shops closed so the local people will be looking for something to occupy them. John suggested that we gather here to rehearse and provided that is agreeable to Uncle Yannis that seems practical.'

Giovanni quickly translated the request to use their home for rehearsals to Uncle Yannis and he nodded. 'I see no problem provided I do not have to move my pots around.'

John grinned. 'I'll take some out to the gift shops again and see if I can get some more orders. Pity we can't use them. I'm sure the soldiers would have smashed them out of spite.'

Uncle Yannis looked at John in horror. 'You cannot smash my pots. I will certainly not agree to such vandalism.'

'I'm not serious, Uncle, unless you have any that are damaged already.'

Yannis shook his head. 'I do not carry damaged stock,' he said firmly.

'John, stop being a tease,' said Marianne. 'This was supposed to be a farewell party for Elizabeth and Nicolas but it also seemed an ideal opportunity for Uncle Andreas to explain his idea and ask for your help. Now, who needs their glass refilled so we can drink to the success of Uncle Andreas's production?'

Saffron took Vasi to one side. 'I'm a bit concerned about this song that I have to learn. I haven't a great singing voice.'

'I'll see if Uncle Andreas can be a bit more explicit.'

Uncle Andreas smiled at Vasi's concern on behalf of Saffron. 'It is not difficult. Elena is going to see if she can find out the tune they used, but I hardly think that matters. It was just the village girls poking fun at the soldiers. Ask Elena, she knows the words off by heart and you'll see what I mean. I'll obviously give all the women a copy the next time we meet.'

'Do the men have to sing?' asked Vasi.

'No, they only have to learn to stamp their feet in unison.'

Vasi raised his eyebrows. 'In time with the song?'

'No, only the women are involved with the song. The men will stamp their feet to replicate the marching of the soldiers. It should be easy enough as you will be sitting down at the time.' Andreas looked down at the trainers that Vasi was wearing. 'Do you have any shoes you could wear? The villagers at that time would hardly have been wearing trainers. They'll need to have hard soles and you'll probably have to stamp quite hard so the audience can hear you.'

Vasi frowned. 'I'll see what I can do. What about our clothes?'

'You all need to be dressed alike so just black trousers and a white shirt, unless everyone happens to have a traditional Cretan costume.'

'I think that is very unlikely and I can't see a museum lending out their costume collection.'

'Shame.' Andreas shook his head. It was much simpler when a professional production was staged. A theatrical costumer was contacted, measurements of the cast given and a description of the clothes that were required was sent to the theatre for them. He walked over to where Elena was sitting.

'Well, that seems to have been successful,' he smiled. 'Can you teach Marianne, Bryony and Nicola the words to that song? I don't know how strong Marisa's voice will be, so they will need to sing loudly and that will also cover up any mistakes the English speakers make.'

'I'm sure they will all be word perfect.'

'It will be the confidence they need to perform in the Greek language. Imagine if you did not speak English and were asked to sing a song in the language. It would be very daunting.'

'You're not asking any of them to sing solo so you don't need to worry. You're such a perfectionist, Andreas.'

Having packed their belongings ready for their departure that afternoon, Elizabeth and Nicolas walked along to Yannis's house.

'I really do not want to go home,' said Elizabeth.

Nicolas squeezed her hand. 'You couldn't wait to return to the States when we lived in Athens.'

'That's true,' agreed Elizabeth, 'But you cannot compare Athens with Elounda. If we had lived here I think I would have been happier and you would not have been shot.'

'Judging by what Uncle Andreas was saying I could easily have been shot. If my father had returned to Crete I would probably have been one of the little boys sabotaging the German's equipment.'

'Don't be silly, Nicolas. You would not have been old enough.'

'My father may have married someone from the village and I could have been born earlier.'

'I'm glad you weren't.'

'What? Born earlier or shot when I was a little boy?'

'Both. When I look at Elisabetta and Joanna and hear snippets of the information that Elena has discovered I'm very grateful they are growing up now in a happy family and they are not likely to lose their father in a war or know that their mother has been molested by a soldier.'

'I agree, but many of the children suffered that fate during the war and managed to overcome the memories. Look at Marisa and Yannis. They lost both their parents, yet they grew up to be sensible, well balanced people.'

'I think their Aunt Anna has to take the credit for that.'

'I wish she was around now. She might be able to instil some sense into Eleanor. I do hope she has been going to college whilst we've been away and not caused our neighbours any problems.'

'We'll soon find out. Enjoy our last day over here with Nicola and the family.'

'Oh, I will,' Elizabeth assured him. 'I just don't want to find we return to a disaster.'

John insisted that he and Nicola accompanied Elizabeth and Nicolas to the airport. 'We want to be able to spend every last minute with you,' he said as they stood in the queue waiting for their luggage to be weighed. 'I also have something I want to tell you. I've spoken to Mum and she and Bryony are willing to look after the children so we can visit you in the New Year.'

'John!' exclaimed Nicola. 'You didn't tell me.'

'I wanted it to be a surprise. I know we'd considered it before as the girls became older, but then we had Yiannis. Could you put up with us for a week or so?' he asked Nicolas.

'It would be our pleasure. You could stay as long as you wanted.'

'I'm sure we would only be with you for a couple of weeks. It wouldn't be fair on Mum to expect her to look after the children for an unlimited amount of time.'

'You could bring the girls with you,' suggested Elizabeth.

John shook his head. 'It's a long flight and we'd have to give the girls a break in New York or Washington. We can't afford to bring them with us on this visit. We'll save up and bring all the children with us another time.'

Ludmila woke up in the early hours of the morning. Why was she looking for secluded coves where Ivan could collect her? The ideal place was the beach where she had met the refugees. She had been stupid not to think of that before. It would have saved her a trip to Rethymnon and also Hersonissos. She rose from her bed and spread out the map and studied the bus time table. It appeared that she would have to take a bus from Heraklion to Aghios Nikolaos and catch another down to Elounda. It would be quite simple then to walk across the Causeway. She would contact Ivan and tell him of her plan.

The sun was just rising and she felt too excited to return to bed. Having showered she sat and drank her coffee thoughtfully. She did not want to use the mobile she had bought whilst in the apartment as she did not feel certain that a call from that location could not be intercepted. She needed to find somewhere where her presence would not create suspicion and then make the call when she was certain she was not being watched or overheard.

The knock on the door startled her and she opened it with trepidation. Was this a call from the police to take her back to prison?

'Yes?' she said cautiously to the man who stood outside.

'I'm sorry to disturb you so early but I believe this letter is meant for you.' The man held out the envelope. 'It's probably the electricity bill and it must have been sitting in my mail box for almost a week as I've been out of town. I thought I ought to give it to you immediately.'

'Oh! Thank you.' Ludmilla closed the door and opened the

letter with trembling fingers and drew in her breath. It was the bill for her electricity, water and telephone with a demand for payment to be made within the next few days. She looked at the date; she would have to settle the outstanding amount today or the electricity would be cut off and she would be summonsed. She could not afford to fall foul of the police a second time.

Opening up the safe where she kept her surplus money she found she had just sufficient to cover the bill. She would visit "The Central" to collect her monthly allowance and ask if they would either pay the amount on her behalf or grant her some extra funds. She needed to leave Crete before any more unexpected bills arrived.

With infinite care Ludmila unpicked the hem of a pair of trousers to disclose a small length of material with numbers stitched on it. Once she had visited "The Central" she would visit Knossos and call Ivan from there on his emergency number. The site was only a short bus ride away and it was bound to be swarming with visitors and she would be able to get lost amongst them. She would find a secluded spot where she was unlikely to overheard and ask Ivan for his help.

Giorgos counted out her money and insisted that she checked and signed a receipt. He looked at her sympathetically when she asked if the hotel would be able to give her some extra funds to cover the utilities bill.

'I'm sorry. I don't have the authority to do that, Mrs Kuzmichov. I'll have to call Mr Iliopolakis and ask him if I can take it from the petty cash and he will then adjust the accounts at the end of the week. Please have a seat. Would you like some refreshment whilst you wait?'

Ludmila declined the offer of a drink. She did not want to be asked to pay for it afterwards. She sat in a corner of the lounge and watched as visitors went in and out. The hotel seemed to be functioning exactly as it had been when Evgeniy had first made the purchase. It seemed a considerable amount of time before Giorgos returned to her.

'I have spoken to Mr Iliopolakis and he has instructed that the bill should be left with me and will be settled by us.'

'I was only given the letter this morning by a neighbour and it needs to be paid today. I do not want to have my electricity or water cut off. If I pay it from the paltry sum that I am given each month I will be unable to purchase my food.'

'I had not realised that such an immediate payment was needed. I will have to speak to Mr Iliopolakis again.'

Ludmila sat there impatiently until the manager returned.

'If you care to come into the office with me I have been authorised to give you the necessary money. Once you have had the bill receipted please return it to me here.'

Giorgos counted out the Euros and insisted that Ludmila checked and signed for the amount before she left. She was feeling decidedly aggrieved. Surely she should have been allowed more money each month to cover expenses at the apartment? Having obtained directions from Giorgos she walked to the office where she had to make the payment and waited in the long queue of people. Each one seemed to have a query or was arguing about the amount they were being charged. By the time she was nearly at the front of the queue the office declared it was closing for lunch and would re-open at three.

Feeling annoyed at having wasted the day and been unable to contact her brother as she had intended she finally returned to "The Central" and handed the receipted electricity bill back to Giorgos.

'Having to spend time dealing with this really upset my plans for the day,' she complained.

Giorgos raised his eyebrows. 'I'm sorry to hear that, Madam. Did you have something else important that needed your attention?'

'I had planned to visit Knossos today.'

'Then I am pleased that your plans did not work out. The site

205

of Knossos is closed on a Monday. You would have had a wasted journey.'

John and Nicola arrived back in Elounda from the airport and Nicola went to find Marianne.

'John tells me that you and Bryony are willing to look after the children so we can go to New Orleans next year. Are you sure you'll be able to manage?'

'Provided you are willing to trust us with them I'm sure it will be no problem. We'll only have Yiannis to cope with during the mornings as the girls will be at school.'

'I'll 'phone every day,' promised Nicola. 'We can always come back if we're needed.'

'It would have to be a dire emergency for me to have to ask you to return. Don't even think about it. Where is John? Uncle Andreas called and left some papers with a request that John makes twenty copies of them. I've had a quick look and I think it's the script.'

'He's gone to collect Skele. May I see?' asked Nicola. 'Is the song there? I thought the girls might like to learn it.'

'I don't really think it's suitable for them to sing.' smiled Marianne.

Nicola scanned the words. 'I see what you mean. When John returns I'll ask him to make the copies and then I'll go up to Plaka and see if Saffie has had a chance to speak to Monika. I can take a script up with me so she can have an idea what is expected of her.'

'You'd better take some extra copies. Saffie can take one for Vasi and if Monika, her mother and Theo have agreed to take part they ought to be able to look at the script also. Tell them there will be food and drink here for them. They can't be expected to spend the evening here without having anything to eat.'

John returned and said he had spoken to Dimitris. 'His sister said he was out working so I had to track him down. I then had to explain to him exactly what was wanted and he has agreed to be in charge of the lighting. He'll come along tomorrow evening and Uncle Andreas can explain to him exactly what he wants.'

Nicola held out the sheaf of papers to him. 'Uncle Andreas brought these up to Mum with a request that you copy them ready for tomorrow. If you do that now I'll take some up to Plaka when they're ready and talk to Monika, unless Saffie has already had a chance to speak to her.'

'Have you read them?' asked John.

Nicola shook her head. 'I've had a quick look at the song. I thought I'd teach it to the girls but when I saw the words I changed my mind.'

'Good job they'll be in bed when we're rehearsing, then,' grinned John as he read the words briefly. 'Who would have thought those decorous elderly ladies would have been such naughty little girls? I wonder which one of them thought up the words?'

'Probably better not to ask. They'd either all claim to be responsible or deny knowing who composed it. Will we need anything apart from the chairs tomorrow night?'

'I don't think so. Uncle Andreas hasn't said anything about props. He only said what he wanted us all to wear for the performance.'

'He'll probably tell us what is needed tomorrow. Go and copy the scripts, John, so I can take them up to Plaka. I should be back before Yiannis needs his bath.'

Nicola waited until Saffron had finished dealing with some customers and handed her a script. 'I've only had a quick look and I admit it doesn't make a lot of sense to me. No doubt Uncle Andreas will explain tomorrow.'

'I wish it was in English,' complained Saffron. 'I can only understand a word or two.'

'I'm sure Vasi will help you. I've brought a copy for him. Have you had a chance to speak to Monika?'

'I talked to her this morning. She seemed quite overcome to be included and has promised to speak to her mother tonight. I've not seen Theo, but she may have done.'

'I'll give her a script for herself and one for her mother. If Litsa refuses to take part you can always bring it back tomorrow. I'll go over and see Theo if she hasn't had the chance and give him a script provided he's willing. John saw Dimitris when he went to collect Skele and he's coming along tomorrow to see what Uncle Andreas wants him to do.'

'Did your parents get off alright?' asked Saffron.

Nicola nodded. 'We waited until they had to go through to their boarding gate and they'll call us when they land. John had a wonderful surprise for us. He's arranged that Marianne and Bryony will look after the children so we can go to New Orleans next year.'

'How lovely That is something to really look forward to after Christmas.'

'Are you and Vasi going back to England for Christmas?'

'Yes, I know Vasi would rather spend it here with his family but he realises that I want to go back to see Marjorie. I'd like to bring her back for a week or two as the shop will be closed and I'll be able to spend time with her.'

'I'm sure she'd like to visit.'

'She enjoyed being here and going out with Ronnie's mother and great uncle. That was such a help to me. Bryony is very good about working in the shop and terribly reliable, but I feel guilty about imposing on her and guilty about being up here and not with Marjorie.'

'If only all our relatives lived over here it would make life much simpler,' sighed Nicola. 'By the way, Marianne said she'd have food and drink waiting for everyone. I must remember to tell Monika that. I hope she has seen Theo or if I have to spend a long time talking to him I'll never be back before Yiannis's bath time.'

'Can't John see to him?'

'Of course, but I like to be there as well to say goodnight to him just before he's popped into his bed. I'll see you tomorrow as early as you feel you can close the shop.'

Nicola walked next door and waved the papers at Monika. 'I'm so pleased you have agreed to take part. Have you had an opportunity to speak to Theo?'

'Yes, but I wasn't actually able to tell him very much about it.'

'Don't worry. I'll pop over to him and give him a script to read, although it doesn't make a lot of sense to me. Uncle Andreas hasn't inserted any names, just numbers. Will you ask your mother if she can join us and take part?'

'I'm sure she will if Theo is agreeable.'

Nicola raised her eyebrows.

'She often comes down and helps in the taverna after she has finished at the baker's. I think she was hoping to be down here all the time, but the girl who was supposed to be at the baker's shop turned out to be so unreliable that they asked my mother to stay on for an extra hour or two.'

'You'd think the girl would be grateful to have some work during the school holidays,' remarked Nicola.

'She only wanted the extra money to buy clothes apparently. Turns up every day in a different outfit, then needs time out to repaint her nails if one becomes chipped and has to do her hair about every hour.'

'She'd drive me crazy.'

Monika nodded. 'Mother is always pleased when Thalia calls in and says she can't come to work as she has other things she needs to do. Goodness knows what those other things are. She'll have a nasty shock one day when she marries and has children. Could you take this book back to Bryony for me? It's just been returned to the library and I know she's waiting to read it.'

'No problem. I'll see you tomorrow and hope you'll have your mother with you. I'll now go and talk to Theo.'

Nicola tucked the book beneath her arm and crossed over

209

the road. 'Just the man I want to see,' she said as she entered the taverna where Theo was wiping down the bar area. 'I understand Monika spoke to you this morning. We really are hoping you will take part.'

'I'm not sure what it's all about. Monika didn't seem to know any details.'

Nicola perched up on a bar stool and explained Uncle Andreas's idea. 'I've brought a script for you to look at and the first rehearsal is at our house tomorrow night. Please come along. If you decide that you don't want to participate after that we'll understand. Monika is going to ask her mother to join us. Marianne is providing food and drink for everyone so you really have nothing to lose.'

September 2015
Week Two – Tuesday

Ludmila had no idea what time the site of Knossos opened but according to the time table the buses went there frequently from early morning. That was probably to accommodate the workers and she decided that if she left the apartment at ten and walked to the bus station there would be sufficient time for visitors to have arrived and she would mingle with them.

Having copied down the important phone number onto a sheet of paper she placed it inside her purse. The strip of material she slipped inside her bra, fixing it securely with a safety pin. She made herself a sandwich, took a bottle of water from the fridge and placed them in her bag along with her lime green mobile.

Feeling both excited and apprehensive she purchased her ticket and joined the collection of tourists who were waiting for the bus, pushing her way inside so she was able to get a seat. The bus drove slowly through the suburbs and finally drew up outside the entrance to Knossos. To her surprise there were already six coaches parked at the side of the road and people were milling around at the entrance. She looked at them in trepidation. Would she manage to find anywhere on the site where she would be able to have a private 'phone conversation?

Having purchased her ticket, horrified that it had cost her nearly twenty Euros, she followed the crowds as they walked up to the main plaza. Groups stood around listening to a guide or posing for photographs. Trying to be inconspicuous she joined a group and was looked at suspiciously by the tourists. After a short while she turned away and wandered over to where another guide was talking, but did not stay long before walking away.

Feeling disheartened she began to wind her way through the maze of buildings, up and down steps and stairs until she reached the sign for the "Throne Room" and the "Queen's Apartments". It was impossible to see inside due to the crush of people. Lower down there was a covered area and people were only giving that a cursory glance before moving on and climbing back up to the main palace complex.

Trying to walk unhurriedly Ludmila made her way to the lower part of the site. There were far fewer people there. She walked along beside the wire perimeter fence, finally finding herself at the end of the site where there was nothing to see. She sat down on the grass and looked around. There was no one nearby.

She took her mobile from her bag and Ivan's 'phone number from her purse, pressing in the numbers carefully. To her relief he answered almost immediately.

'Ivan, it's Ludmila. I need your help. Evgeniy is still in prison. I've been released and I need to leave Crete.'

'Do you have your passport?'

'No. The police are holding it. I thought you could sail over and collect me from the beach where I met the refugees.'

'That's not a good idea. The police could be watching that area. I'll speak to Panos and call you back.'

Ludmila looked at her mobile. She hoped Ivan had a record of her number as she had not thought to write it down so she could give it to him. Feeling conspicuous sitting there Ludmila rose to her feet and walked nearer to the wire fence before sitting down again and taking out her bottle of water. She hoped that if anyone was watching her they would assume she was having a short break before continuing to investigate more of the site.

Ivan called her back before she felt the need to move on.

'Are you able to help me?' she asked.

'Don't talk. Listen. You need to follow my instructions,' he said.

'Yes,' answered Ludmila breathlessly.

'You go down to Elounda and carry on to Plaka. There you catch a boat over to Spinalonga. You will wait for me at the end of the old jetty. Take nothing with you except a shopping bag with essentials.'

'When will you come?'

'It will take me at least a week. I'll call you when I am in the bay. Go over to Spinalonga tomorrow so you know where you have to wait.'

'Suppose I am seen?'

'Hundreds of tourists go over every day. No one will notice you.'

Ivan closed the call and Ludmila continued to sit on the grass. She had hoped to be able to talk to her brother and describe her own detention by the police and receive his sympathy. Their conversation had been so brief that she could have called him from anywhere and not wasted her money by visiting Knossos. If it was going to take Ivan a week to sail over from wherever he was at present she did not need to go to Spinalonga the following day. She would have to count her money and ensure that she had sufficient to last her until the following month if Ivan was delayed for any reason. She would be unable to go to "The Central" and make a request for more money.

Andreas arrived early at Yannis's house. 'I thought I ought to get the chairs organised so we don't waste any time this evening. Have you looked at the script and have any of you learnt the song?' he asked Marianne.

'No one expects you to move chairs around. John and Marcus will do that. Do you want to be out on the patio or down in the lounge?'

'It should be warm enough outside.'

'Then sit down and relax over a glass of wine. We've all looked at the script, but we don't really understand it.'

'I'll explain when everyone is here. Have the other people you asked agreed to join us?'

'I think so, at least they are coming this evening. They may change their minds when you tell them what is expected of them.'

'It isn't difficult,' said Andreas firmly. 'I'm sure they are all quite capable of following my instructions.'

'We are none of us professional actors,' Marianne reminded him gently. 'John has spoken to Dimitris and he is willing to talk to you about the lighting arrangements.'

'He will have to understand that the timing is crucial.'

Marianne placed a glass of wine and a bowl of olives in front of her uncle. 'Relax. You'll have to make allowances for all of us tonight.'

Andreas shuffled his papers and looked at his watch. 'Was everyone told what time they had to be here?' he asked.

'Saffie and Monika have to close their shops before they can leave Plaka. John and Nicola have to put the children to bed, but I expect everyone else will be arriving shortly.'

'Then we need to get the chairs arranged.'

'Sit down, Uncle. Here's Marcus and he can make a start until John arrives.'

'I want one each side at the back and then the others can be in a line in front with a gap between each eight.'

'This isn't very practical; they'll take up too much space,' commented Marcus as he moved the chairs around.

'Then they can go into a semi circle, but everyone must be seen by the audience who will be sitting at the front.'

'What kind of chairs are you planning to use, Uncle?' asked Marianne.

'Just the plastic ones they have in the Centre.'

'They will take up less space than our chairs. Why don't you put them like this?' Marianne moved the chairs so a V shape was formed.

Andreas nodded. 'That might work.' He looked at his watch again. 'I wish everyone would hurry up. I want to talk to them all at the same time.'

'I'm here,' announced Marisa from the doorway.

'You're not a problem. You sit there and just go along with whatever the other women do in the way of actions. I'll tell you when I want you to speak.'

'What am I supposed to say? John gave me a script and I saw my name but nothing afterwards.'

'I want you to pretend to be Aunt Anna and describe going up to tend to the injured andartes.'

'Just like that?'

Andreas nodded. 'You and Yannis will talk as you did to me. I can make you some notes so you can think about what you need to say but I'm not writing a script for you.'

Marisa sniffed. 'It's alright for Yannis. He knows what he did. Mamma Anna never confided in me.'

'Then make it up as you go along,' replied Andreas irritably. 'Pretend you're Anna and have to think how to fool the soldiers and bring the doctor from Aghios.'

'Are we late?' asked John.

'Only for helping to put out the chairs,' replied Marcus. 'Bryony is in the kitchen with Marianne, but Elena and Uncle Yannis haven't appeared yet.'

'I'll go and chivvy them along,' said Nicola. 'I'm sure everyone else will be here very soon.'

'There's Dimitris,' John beckoned to the young man to come onto the patio. 'Now you can talk to him about the lighting effects.'

'I'm an electrician, not a lighting specialist,' protested Dimitris.

'You only have to follow instructions. Can you put a side table over there for Elena and another one for me with a table lamp on each one?'

John raised his eyebrows and looked at Dimitris who shrugged.

'Elena,' said Andreas, turning towards her as she walked out from the kitchen. 'Do you know the tune to that song?'

Elena shook her head. 'Not really. Evi and Maria had such old voices it was hard to make out any tune at all so I've made up a very simple one myself.'

'Let me hear it.'

'You want me to sing it?'

'Yes, you'll start it with Marisa singing after you and then I'll decide on the order for the others to join in.'

Blushing with embarrassment Elena sang the first two lines. *'He's a fat faced fool, smells like a mule; Cut out his liver and drown him in the river.'* She stopped. 'That is the tune. It's just repeated.'

Andreas nodded. 'That's suitable. It was the children who sang it, not opera stars. Can you teach the tune to the others during the week so that everyone knows it in time for the next rehearsal?'

'I'll do my best

Andreas frowned and was about to make a cutting remark when Vasilis and Cathy arrived followed by Ronnie.

'I hope we're not the last,' apologised Cathy. 'Vasilis saw Panayiotis just as we were leaving and wanted a quick word with him.'

'You're not last,' Saffron assured her as she and Vasi arrived, followed by Monika, Litsa and Theo.

'Take a seat,' ordered Andreas. 'Men on the right hand side and women on the left. I'll sort you out as I want you after I've talked to you. Elena, you sit at the back on a level with me.'

'At least let them have a glass of wine and plate of food before you start to talk. Sit down everyone and we'll bring some supplies over to you.'

'You can't have that table,' said Andreas as Nicola was about to move it next to Cathy. 'I need that where it is.'

'I feel like birds in a row or ten green bottles,' giggled Nicola as she finally took a seat next to Monika after handing around the food with Bryony and Marianne. Marcus had poured glasses of wine for everyone except himself and Bryony, with the offer of a soft drink if they preferred.

'Everybody settled?' asked Andreas and was answered by nods. 'I know most of you have been told my idea, but I will repeat it briefly for the new comers. If any of you are not happy please feel free to leave and we will have to find someone else to take your place.'

He gave a brief outline of his talks with the village men and then how Elena had spoken to the women. 'I understand you all have a script and it probably makes little sense to any of you. There are no names, just numbers and I'll give each of you a red pen so you can underline when you need to say a line or two. You'll need to know the line or action that comes before your part. Elena has suggested that we start and finish with the song. You all have the words and Elena will give you the tune. Ready, Elena?'

Elena stood and cleared her throat.

> *'He's a fat faced fool, smells like a mule;*
> *Cut out his liver and drown him in the river.*
> *His feet smell of meat, left out to rot;*
> *Rancid and sweet, he ought to be shot.'*

Andreas waited until the smiles and titters had subsided. 'The children used to sing it as a round and that is what I want you ladies to do. At the end you stamp your feet and so do the men. Once the song is finished I will read out information about the invasion and how the Germans and Italians spread across the country terrorising the inhabitants.' Andreas placed his papers on the table next to him and moved in front of the chairs.

'This is when you start to mime. The men will stamp their feet in unison as if they are soldiers marching. You ladies will cower together, clutch each other, wail. Imagine you are petrified at the thought of rough soldiers being amongst you. Let me see you do it.'

He watched them critically. 'Put some *feeling* into it. You're all like stone statues. You're frightened. How do you usually react when you're frightened? Think of something that terrifies you, a spider, a mouse, a snake and react as you would to suddenly seeing one in your house. Now, let's try it again. Men, stamp your feet and ladies show some fear.'

Andreas made them go through the scene three more times before he sighed. 'We'll move on. I continue to read; the soldiers begin to go up to the villages, stealing the food and livestock. Number One, Nicola you be Number One and read that line. Marianne you are Number Two so you answer her.'

'Mamma, I'm hungry. May I have a rusk?'

'We are all hungry. The soldiers have taken our food.'

'All together now,' called Andreas. *'What are we going to do?'* Bryony, you be Number Four. Change seats with Saffron and remember your number. Saffron say the line for Number Three.'

Taken off guard Saffron stammered her way through the line. *'I caught a bird and my mother cooked it.'*

'Vasi, please help Saffron when you are at home. Bryony – your lines.'

'I hated it when Mamma cooked a wild bird. They were so small and full of little bones that I had to spit out. I thought I would swallow one and choke.'

'Monika, Number Five.'

Hastily Monika drew a five and underlined the words. *'Mamma took me up to the fields and we collected the weeds that grew there. I also carried a bucket and any snails that I found I put in there and took them back home. One day I found a hedgehog and Mamma cooked it.'*

'Litsa, be Number Six.'

'I had to sort the weeds out carefully. Some of them could be poisonous. I wish I could have given those to the soldiers.'

'Ronnie, Number Seven.'

'*I had to take the snails from their shells after Mamma boiled them.*' Ronnie shuddered. Kyriakos would have to help her. Surely she had not understood the context of the line?

'Right, we'll go through that once more and then I'll begin to go through the parts the men have.'

Cathy looked confused and a little hurt. 'I haven't been asked to say anything,' she said.

'Your turn will come,' Andreas assured her. 'Now, men, I will continue to read and then you will describe your activities.' Andreas looked around. 'We're one man short.'

'Yiorgos is willing to take part but he couldn't come tonight. He'd promised to take Barbara to the cinema.'

Andreas nodded. 'Right. You men know that the Germans have invaded. Start with you, Giovanni. '

'*I went into the hills and joined the andartes.*'

'Vasilis.'

'*I joined up with the allied forces and became part of the resistance movement.*'

'Vasi.'

Vasi shook his head. 'I think that next line should be said by Yiorgos. He has Manolis's boat '

'What's that to do with it?' frowned Andreas.

'Manolis took an English Resistance worker around the coast to deliver a radio and ended up at Preveli.'

Andreas shrugged. 'I don't mind who says which line. Just remember which number you are and make sure you sit in that order again at the next rehearsal.' Andreas scribbled quickly on his copy of the script. 'Yiorgos can be Number Three. Move down so his chair is vacant. This makes you Number Four, Vasi and when he has said his line it is your turn Cathy.'

Cathy heard her name but had no idea what was being asked of her. 'Please, tell me in English.'

Andreas repeated his instructions and indicated the words to her. 'You say "I was very proud of my father." when Vasi has said his line. I will point to you today, but I will expect you to remember when you have to speak in future. Vasilis will be able to you help you.'

Andreas turned and pointed to Vasi. 'You have a new line. Write it down, please. *I sailed with the boatman to deliver a wireless to the Resistance.'*

Vasi read out his new line and Andreas pointed to Cathy. 'Now you.'

Cathy nodded and made a reasonable attempt at the words.

'Theo, be Number Five.'

'When the Germans came to my village I was arrested along with the other men and taken to work at the salt pans.'

'John, you are Number Six.'

'My father was shot when he tried to defend my mother from the soldiers.'

'Marcus, Number Seven.'

'I was not in Heraklion when the soldiers rounded up the Jewish people and transported them to mainland Greece. We only found out their fate when the war ended.'

Andreas smiled. 'Not bad for a first attempt. We'll move on to the next scene. The men stamp their feet again as if they are soldiers marching. When I hold up my hand you stop and Elena reads some more. She will describe how the women would warn the village that the soldiers were approaching and giving any andartes who were hiding there time to escape. When she has read that Marisa will call out the words "Kiri-kiri-coo" and one by one the women will join in until you are all calling out the signal. Understand?'

'What is 'kiri-kiri-coo'?' asked Saffron of Marianne.

'The sound a cockerel makes.'

'Oh, of course.' Saffron blushed at not recognising the call. She heard it regularly in the mornings where the man down the road from them kept chickens.

'Elena will then read a little more before Yannis describes how he became involved with an injured andarte. I just want you to describe the events as you told them to me the other day. Marisa will talk after you and pretend she is Aunt Anna. After that we will return to the men who will boast of their sabotage attempts when they were boys.'

Marianne looked at her watch surreptitiously. 'Uncle Andreas, I know this is very important to you, but I think we should stop now. Everyone is tired.'

Andreas frowned. 'We ought to have a complete run through.'

'Not tonight,' said Marianne firmly. 'Now we know how you want us to perform the next rehearsal will proceed more quickly. Give us a chance to learn the words of the song and our lines.'

Marisa yawned. 'It is definitely past my bed time.'

With a deep sigh Andreas agreed to call a halt. 'I would like to mention a few more things to all of you. The men must wear hard soled shoes so the noise of the marching can be heard. I don't expect any of you to have authentic clothes, so just a black skirt for the ladies with white blouses, black trousers for the men with white shirts.'

'If we had a cummerbund we could stick a gun or knife in it,' suggested John. 'They sell the knives with a ram's horn handle at the souvenir shops for the tourists.'

'We'll go into more detail about accessories later. Are you in a hurry to leave, Dimitris, or can I talk to you about the lighting that is needed?'

Dimitris gave a pleased smile. He had felt totally excluded from the proceedings.

'Does that mean the rest of us are dismissed?' asked Theo. 'When you have decided on the date for the next rehearsal I will take Monika and Litsa home.'

'They could come with us,' offered Vasilis. 'We are going back to Elounda.'

'Can everyone come on Thursday?' asked Andreas anxiously.

"If any of you have knowledge of any other events that I should include please let me know. At this stage I can add or change anything. I'm planning to add more words to the script for the men and women to say. We'll need a number of rehearsals so that the production is slick.'

'What have we let ourselves in for,' groaned John.

'It was your idea,' Nicola reminded him. 'Too late to back out now.'

Marcus and Giovanni began to move the chairs back into position on the patio as Andreas explained to Dimitris how he and Elena should be highlighted when they were talking and then the lights must be on either the women or the men when they acted their parts.

'I'll need to make some notes and also see what facilities are available at the Municipal Centre. Ideally we need spot lights and a control panel and I doubt if they will have either. The Centre is usually used for exhibitions.'

'Why are we numbered and not named?' asked Vasilis.

'You are not representing individuals; just relating the experiences of the people generally. Only Yannis and Marisa will be speaking personally,' explained Andreas.

'Maybe Yiorgos could relate some of the experiences Manolis had when he and my father were travelling to Preveli,' suggested Cathy to Vasilis.

'That's a good idea. Tell me some more tomorrow and I'll make some notes to give to Uncle Andreas.'

'Manolis told Yiorgos and I some of the adventures they had. I'm sure Yiorgos won't mind talking to an audience. He usually gives his passengers information about Manolis taking supplies over to Spinalonga before they were blockaded. That event should be mentioned as well,' added Vasi.

'I think we need to be a bit careful. If the performance goes on too long the audience will become bored,' said Saffron. 'Are you ready to leave now, Vasi? I really am tired and we ought to offer to take Uncle Andreas home.'

Marisa and Yannis retired to their rooms and Marianne and Giovanni waved everyone goodnight as they left. Giovanni poured a glass of wine for himself and offered one to Marianne who shook her head.

'I was so busy handing around the food that I didn't really have very much to eat so wine now would not be a good idea.'

'Go and get some; there's plenty left. I could do with a bit more. Once Uncle Andreas started I didn't like to be eating in case I was suddenly called upon to say something.'

Bryony rose. 'Let's all have something. It was quite an exhausting evening.'

'Bring a plate for me,' said Elena as she joined them.

'Aren't you tired, Mamma?'

'I don't feel tired. I want to know what you think about Andreas's script.'

'Well,' answered Bryony cautiously, 'So far the parts we have to play are not taxing. There's only the song and a few simple lines to learn. Will it become more difficult later?'

Elena shook her head. 'I don't think so. You just have to remember when you need to say your part so you need to know the lines above yours.'

'Uncle Yannis and Grandma Marisa have the most to learn.'

'They don't have to learn lines, remember. They can just talk.'

'I hope they won't get confused and start to tell events in the wrong order,' said Marianne as she dipped some bread into a dish of taramasalata.

'I might suggest to Andreas that he rehearses them separately. He can then see if there is a problem,' added Elena as she helped herself to a small cheese pie. 'I prefer these when they are warm.'

'Do you think everyone will have learnt the song by Thursday?' asked Bryony.

'Learning it should be simple but I think Ronnie and Saffie may have some difficulty when it comes to singing it.'

'I'm sure Vasi and Kyriakos will help them.' Bryony yawned. 'I'm more tired than I realised. I'm off to bed.'

September 2015
Week Two – Thursday

Ludmila had spent the previous day sorting out her belongings. Although Ivan had said she could take nothing but a bag with her she wanted to ensure she had some clean underwear, spare socks and a jumper as she knew it could often be cold out at sea. She also needed a washing kit, hair brush and comb.

Carefully she packed the large cloth bag she planned to carry with her. There was sufficient space for more items so she added an old T-shirt to sleep in, another jumper and a pair of trousers. She debated whether to remove the second jumper and replace it with a pair of shoes. She tested the weight of the bag and decided that a pair of shoes would make it too heavy and unwieldy. Once they reached a port well away from Crete she could borrow some money from Ivan and buy whatever else she might need.

It was annoying to have to leave before she could go to "The Central" and request her next month's allowance. She hoped Ivan would be able to provide her with a passport so she could travel back to Moscow and have access to her account there. She sighed. She knew Ivan would do his best to help her, but that it would also come at a price.

Picking up the shopping bag and her handbag Ludmila walked to the bus station and waited for the bus to take her down to Aghios Nikolaos. When she had driven down the journey to Elounda had taken no longer than an hour. She felt anxious each time the bus stopped and picked up more passengers. They all seemed to be visitors intent on going down to the town and spending the day there. She reasoned with herself that it would be foolish to get off at Malia or Hersonissos and wait for the next bus. That one was likely to be full of tourists also and no one seemed to be taking any notice of her.

Reaching the bus station in Aghios Nikolaos she alighted and looked around. Where was she supposed to catch the bus to Plaka? She walked into the ticket office and took her place in the queue, again most of the people appeared to be tourists.

'Where do I catch the bus to Plaka?' she asked when she finally reached the counter.

'Ticket.'

'Yes, I will buy a ticket, but I need to know which bus I have to catch.'

'Elounda bus.'

'I want to go to Plaka.'

The ticket clerk sighed. 'The bus goes to Elounda and then on to Plaka. You want a return?'

'Yes, I think so.'

'Cheaper to have a return.'

Ludmila handed over a five Euro note and waited for the ticket and the change.

'No change. Return ticket five Euros.'

'What time is the next bus?'

The clerk looked at the clock on the opposite wall. 'Thirteen hours.'

'Isn't there one before then?'

He shook his head. 'Eleven, then thirteen.'

'What time does the bus return?'

'Seventeen fifteen. Last bus.'

Ludmila was being pushed by the people behind her who wanted to purchase their bus tickets and she moved to one side. She had over an hour to wait. When she came down to meet

Ivan she must catch an earlier bus from Heraklion. She was not used to having to calculate bus times into her journey. For years she had had a car at her disposal to make whatever journeys she wished. Placing the ticket safely in her purse she walked outside and looked for a seat in the shade. So far her journey had cost her over twenty Euros and she still had the boat fare to pay.

The time dragged and the sun moved round in the sky leaving her in the full glare of the rays. There were no free seats in the shaded area and she did not want to stand for another half an hour. She waved her hand in front of her face hoping to move a little air towards herself. She must look for a hat when she returned home. Finally she could bear the burning sensation on her skin no longer and walked back inside the ticket office, appreciating the cold air that was being blown around. She would watch the clock and when there were only ten more minutes before the bus departed she would return outside and hope to be first in the queue of passengers.

The journey to Plaka took longer than she had anticipated and she was worried that she would have missed the boat going to Spinalonga or might be unable to return in time to catch the bus back to Aghios Nikolaos. She certainly did not want to make the journey again tomorrow and she could not afford to stay in the town over night unless she slept on the beach.

'Plaka, Spinalonga,' called the driver and Ludmila scrambled to her feet and pushed her way off the bus with the other passengers. Following the sign for Spinalonga boats she hurried down the hill.

'Eight Euros.'

Horrified Ludmila produced another note from her purse. 'Can I come back on that ticket?' she asked.

'Last boat eighteen hours.'

'I want to come back before then. I have to catch the bus to Aghios.'

'Boats every half hour. Hurry, loading now.'

Treading carefully, Ludmila hurried down the uneven stone

steps to where a man was helping passengers aboard a small fishing boat. She held out her ticket and he nodded, took her bag from her and placed it on the deck before taking her elbow and helping her jump aboard.

As the motor propelled the boat across the water Ludmila looked at the island anxiously. How long would it take her to find the old jetty? It could be on the opposite side of the island and take her an hour or more to walk there. It was imperative that she returned in time to catch the last bus back to Aghios Nikolaos. How she wished Ivan had agreed to collect her from the beach across from the Causeway.

The boat swung around the island and tied up at a beach where there were other boats of all sizes moored. Someone was using a loud hailer, calling passengers back to the largest of the boats before it left to return to Aghios Nikolaos. Ludmila cursed herself for not enquiring about the cost of the trip. It would have saved her the bus and boat fare and ensured that she arrived back in time for a bus to Heraklion.

She looked around; Ivan was obviously not expecting to meet her down on the open beach area where so many tourists were gathered. She walked up the ramp and was about to enter a tunnel when she was asked for her ticket. Ludmila held out her boat ticket and the woman shook her head.

'Ticket from kiosk.' She pointed to a small wooden building where people were queuing.

Ludmila tried to walk through again, but the woman effectively barred her way with her arm. 'No ticket, no entry.'

Frustrated and furious Ludmila had no choice but return and wait until she had purchased a ticket costing her a further four Euros before she could proceed through the tunnel.

'Old jetty?' she asked, taking a chance that others would have asked the woman for directions and her request would not appear strange.

'Through tunnel, up path.'

Ludmila was not sure if she was being directed to the jetty or just onto the island generally. She hurried through the dark entrance and emerged into a small square. The path continued and she walked up, taking little notice of the buildings on either side. Finally she could see the sea from the top of a flight of steps and assumed they must lead down to a beach.

The steps were uneven and she made her way down carefully with one hand on the wall. Her bag, although not unduly heavy, was certainly putting her off balance. At the bottom of the steps she stood to one side and looked around. Plaka was almost directly opposite and she could see Elounda further around the bay. This must be where Ivan planned to meet her.

She was conscious of the sun again and took another drink from her water bottle. There was little left and she hoped she would be able to purchase another before she had to make her bus journeys. Retracing her steps she saw that the path continued onwards. She would need to continue also to ensure that there was not another jetty on the far side of the island.

The buildings came to an end and she saw that the path led on around to the side of the island that was totally exposed to the open sea. The path was narrow with a steep hillside rising on one side and a steep drop down to some wicked looking rocks below. In places there was a wooden fence and this finally gave way to a stone wall, gradually curving inwards and downwards until the beach where she had landed came into view.

Ludmila sighed with relief. She now knew where Ivan expected her to be waiting for him.

Back on the beach she tried to find some shade beneath one of the trees that grew there. A man moved slightly to one side.

'Hot, isn't it?'

Ludmila nodded and drank the remaining amount of water she had with her and threw the empty bottle into the bin. She did not want to get into conversation with anyone. A boat arrived and more tourists came ashore and the man called out 'Plaka, boat to Plaka.' Almost at a run Ludmila joined the people who were being helped aboard.

'You weren't there long,' he remarked.

'I have a bus to catch. I will come again when I have more time.'

He was not really interested how long his passengers spent on the island.

Back at Plaka Ludmila looked at her watch. She had missed the bus that left at three and would have to wait until five for the last one back to Aghios Nikolaos. She would wander around the shops to help to pass the time.

She walked slowly up the steep hill crossing from side to side looking in the shops. She lingered longest in the shop that was selling a selection of blue and green items, admiring the dress that was on display in the window. At one time she would not have thought twice about going in, trying it on and purchasing the item whatever the cost. Sighing with regret and frustration she continued up the hill; all the other shops seemed to cater for the tourists who wanted souvenirs to take home.

Ludmila entered each shop and browsed to pass the time. She reached the top of the hill and walked into the gift shop there. Saffron looked up and Ludmila backed out of the doorway hurriedly. She did not want to be recognised.

Saffron frowned, she was sure she knew the woman but could not put a name to her or recollect where she had seen her before. Ludmila walked up to the taverna on the main road and walked along the small parade of shops, spending some time looking into the jeweller's window. The taverna was busy serving food and drinks to every table. She could not afford to eat there and it did not look like a place where she could buy a bottle of water.

She retraced her steps to the top of the hill where "The Pines" was situated. It appeared to be serving drinks rather than food. She slipped into a vacant chair and waited.

'What can I get for you?'

'I really only want a glass of water.'

The waiter frowned. 'I can bring you a bottle. We do not serve water separately in glasses.'

'That's fine. Whatever I do not drink I can take away with me.'

Saffron looked out of her door. She remembered now; the woman was Ludmila Kuzmichov. She had no wish to make her acquaintance a second time and returned inside the shop, wondering what had brought the woman to Plaka.

Ludmila poured some of the water into the glass the waiter had brought and looked at the bill he had left in the glass. She should have found a supermarket; a bottle of water would have been cheaper purchased from there. She was concerned about the amount of money she had spent that day. The same amount would be needed the following week to enable her to meet Ivan. If he did not arrive she would have very little money to live on in the following weeks.

Andreas accepted the ride he was offered by Vasilis to Yannis's house and was waiting down by the church when Vasilis arrived.

'I'm hoping we can really make progress this evening. Have you learnt the words to the song, Cathy?'

'Vasilis has helped me with the line I have to say and I think I have that right now' answered Cathy avoiding answering Andreas's question.

'Vasi has talked to Yiorgos about the part you want him to play and he'll be coming along this evening,' said Vasilis, knowing that Cathy had only learnt the first two lines of the song.

'Good, good. Provided everyone turns up on time all should go smoothly.'

Vasilis certainly hoped Andreas would be satisfied and would not ask for another rehearsal that week. Now he had been able to resume work on his building he wanted to be able to devote all his spare time to the project.

John and Marcus had the chairs arranged by the time they

arrived and Marianne was putting the finishing touches to the food. 'I'm afraid Giovanni is going to be a little late. He's had to do an airport run.'

'How late?' frowned Andreas.

Marianne shook her head. 'I can't say for certain. Provided the flight lands on time he should be here within the hour.'

'Has anyone said they are unable to come?' asked Andreas.

'No one has called to say they won't be here. Uncle Yannis has been wandering around muttering to himself all day and when I asked him what was wrong he told me he was trying to remember everything he wanted to say. Marisa is in a panic and Uncle Yannis has promised to tell her all he can remember about Aunt Anna.'

'If she really is unable to relate the events coherently I may have to ask you to take her place, Marianne.'

Marianne shook her head. 'I wouldn't want to do that. She would be so hurt if she thought you considered her useless.'

Andreas shrugged. 'It would be for the good of the production, not personal.'

'I'm sure she will be fine. Try not to fluster her.'

'I particularly want her and Yannis. They are the only older people who have agreed to take part and they will truly be relating their memories. Vasilis tells me that Vasi has spoken to Yiorgos. When they arrive I'll talk to him and tell him what is required.'

'Uncle Andreas, please remember that none of us are professional actors and we'll do our best. You will have to make allowances for our short comings.'

Finally everyone was assembled except for Giovanni and Andreas stood in front of them. 'I'm not going to read all my part this evening and Elena will not read all of hers. I'll just read the last couple of lines and go straight into the men stamping and continue from there. I hope you all remember your parts. We'll start with the song and try it later as a round.'

After two renditions of the song Andreas declared himself reasonably satisfied, although he knew neither Cathy nor Ronnie were singing. 'Now I will read and we will proceed from there. If Giovanni does not arrive in time I will say his words.'

The women performed their parts and Andreas read on to where the men appeared. After Vasilis had said his words Andreas pointed to Yiorgos.

'Now you, Yiorgos.'

'I was a boatman taking supplies to Spinalonga until it was blockaded by the Germans. I was asked to collect a package from Mohos but when I arrived it had been moved elsewhere. I continued to ....'

'Stop,' called Andreas. 'That is sufficient for now. You can say more later on. The other men continue and you will say your line later on, Cathy. Monika, you will no longer say you caught a hedgehog. Cathy will say that line and change seats with you. Make the alterations on your script, please so that you remember.'

Vasilis smiled and shook his head. Cathy was going to have trouble saying hedgehog in Greek.

Andreas held up his hand when the men had finished saying their lines. 'I need more feeling from all of you. When you say you joined the andartes or resistance sit up straight, point to yourself and say the words proudly. Those of you who witnessed the bad events shake your heads and let your shoulders slump. You have to portray sadness. We'll go through those lines again and then move on.'

Giovanni arrived, apologised for being late, collected some food and a glass of wine and took his seat.

'You're just in time,' remarked Andreas. 'We've been through the first thing the men say and I want to move on to your next appearances. I hope you've all looked at the script where you relate the sabotage activities you got up to as boys. We'll start with you, Giovanni, and follow on in the same order as previously.'

Giovanni swallowed his mouthful of food rapidly. *'I had a catapult and I would hide until the soldiers had left their vehicles. I was an accurate shot and used to aim at the windows. I rarely missed breaking them.'*

'Have you got a catapult?' asked Andreas and Giovanni shook his head.

'I can make one,' offered John. 'They're not difficult.'

'I'll add that to the list of props. Giovanni can hold it up when he says his lines.'

Vasilis followed with his line. *'I would remove the cap from the petrol tank and place a handful of earth and stones inside.'*

'If they had left the windows down so they could not be broken I would reach in and cut their seats with a knife.' Yiorgos was longing to talk more about the exploits of Manolis than the one liners that appeared to be his part at present.

'I would break their wing mirrors and door handles.' added Vasi.

Theo smiled. *'I would search for snakes and if I found one I would place it beneath the seat inside the cab. I would have liked to see the soldiers reaction when they found it.'*

Giovanni stood up. 'I'm not prepared to sit in the same room as a snake.'

'It would only be a grass snake, Dad. You know how good Skele is at finding them.' John grinned wickedly at his father.

'I mean it,' said Giovanni firmly. 'I'm not taking part in this at all if there's going to be a snake around.'

'I'm sure we can find a plastic one in a toy shop. You don't need to worry about that at the moment. Let's just get on. John, your line,' Andreas said irritably.

'I would push a stick into the radiator grill so the engine would over heat.'

Marcus was ready with his line. *'I used to carry a pocket full of stones and push them into the exhaust pipes.'*

Andreas nodded. 'Remember you have to say the lines as boastful little boys who thought it exciting to make a nuisance of themselves. Elena will now read the next section. When she says that you used to warn the boys by calling 'Kiri-kiri-coo' she will repeat that, then Marisa will join in along with the rest of you in turn so that eventually you are all calling out the word. The men will duck their heads down and pretend to be hiding. Understand?'

Andreas appeared satisfied with their first attempt, simply saying that they must make the call louder. 'You are warning the boys who are way down the hillside. They need to be able to hear you and run away to hide. Elena will now read some more and I will indicate when you have to sing the song, ladies. Marisa will start it. As she reaches the end of the first line you will start the first line again, Nicola, and so it will go on for all of you. I will point to each of you when you should start to sing the first line whilst the others continue with the next lines. When it has been sung through twice you will shout "Bang! Bang!" and stamp your feet. The men will also stamp their feet as the soldiers used to do and that will add to the sound.

Cathy, Saffron and Ronnie were not at all sure what they were supposed to be doing and none of them were prepared to ask Andreas for further explanations.

As Elena finished reading Andreas pointed to Marisa. Her voice was off-key and trembly, but Nicola sang the words strongly. Saffron coped with the first two lines and then lapsed into silence whilst Ronnie and Cathy shook their heads when Andreas pointed to them.

'It isn't difficult,' he remonstrated. 'Just a few lines. If you haven't memorised them yet read them but you have to join in or the continuity is lost. Now, we'll do it again.'

Feeling like disobedient school girls they tried to sing the words that were on the script.

'If it really is too difficult for them they could always mouth the words and the round could continue on without them,' suggested Elena.

'Once they have learnt the words they'll have no trouble,' announced Andreas confidently. 'We'll try it again now they know how it is to be done.'

Ronnie rolled her eyes. She understood how Andreas wanted

it sung, but she was not sure if she would be able to join in at the right moment. When he pointed to her she placed her hands over her ears and stared fixedly at the words, managing to virtually block out the words the others were singing, but when Cathy tried to pick up her line she only managed the first few words.

'We'll concentrate on that next time,' said Andreas with a sigh. 'You read on, Elena, and then the women will say their next lines.'

They all turned the pages of their script and Marisa turned two pages and stared at it in puzzlement. Nicola realised her dilemma, took the pages from her, turned the page back and pointed to the line.

'That's where you start when Elena has finished the line above.'

'The soldiers knew there were no men folk to defend us and frequently came up to the village to molest us.'

Nicola added her lines. *'I tried to beat a soldier off my mother when he attacked her. I was not successful. His companions held me and made me watch her humiliation. Then they turned their attention to me.'*

Marianne followed on. *'Many of the women were raped. They would visit the local medicine woman who would give them a remedy to drink.'*

'All of you, bend over, rub your stomachs as if in pain,' Andreas directed.

'If that did not work she would move a crochet hook around inside them.' Saffron shuddered at the thought.

'I was unlucky. Neither remedy worked for me and I gave birth to a healthy child. I smothered him before he had time to draw more than two breaths.' Bryony felt her eyes fill with tears. She had always wanted a child so much that she did not think she could have disposed of a newborn infant so callously.

Monika closed her eyes and cringed as she remembered the brutal way Manu had treated her to make her pregnant. Litsa squeezed her daughter's hand and Monika sat up straight and pointed to herself.

'I had heard of the atrocities the soldiers carried out. I saw three of coming up the hill and took my father's old gun. When the bullets hit them they dropped to the ground as inert as the rabbits that I shot.'

Litsa gave a surreptitious look at Theo when Monika mentioned shooting rabbits, nearly forgetting that she had to speak next.

'I helped my daughter to dig a hole in the ground amongst the olive trees and we pushed the dead soldiers in there and covered them up.'

'They could not expect any mercy from us as they had shown us none.' Ronnie spoke her lines haltingly.

'Ask Kyriakos to help you, Ronnie. Vasi, help Saffie with the words, but keep in the shudder. That was a good reaction. I'll read the next bit and then it will be your turn, Yiorgos.'

'I tried to take supplies to Spinalonga and the Germans shot at me so I turned back. The priest in Aghios Nikolaos asked me to take a message to Pahia Amnos and when I reached there I was sent on to Mohlos and then told to go further down the coast. Finally I met up with an English man who was working for the Resistance. He was taking a wireless to his compatriots even further down the coast. Once the wireless was delivered we were asked to take some allied troops down to Preveli where they hoped to get a ship to Egypt. We stayed down at Preveli and I ferried supplies up to the local villages. The Germans arrived and we took sanctuary in a church where the priest hid us under the paving slabs in the aisle. The Germans had found my boat and it was riddled with bullet holes. My companion, the English man, wanted to return to his village to visit his wife and child. We had no choice but to walk across the whole of Crete, avoiding soldiers on the way.'

Yiorgos took a breath and looked at Andreas who nodded at him to continue.

'We were unable to walk down the coast road to Aghios Nikolaos so we commenced to walk back over the hills, using the

donkey trails and goat paths. On our way we met up with andartes and joined them. I took part in the fighting, and narrowly escaped with my life. Once we heard that the Germans had surrendered and were leaving Crete we began to make our way back to the coast. I was able to sail across to Spinalonga and was horrified at the situation I found there.'

Andreas held up his hand. 'Stop after saying that you made your way back to the coast. Elena will read some more and when she says 'Kiri-kiri-coo' all the women will join in again as before. Then Yannis will speak.'

'We'll have to stop after Elena has said her Kiri-kiri-coo'. Giovanni had noticed that Marisa's eyes were closing. 'We'll make a date for the next rehearsal and carry on from there then.'

Andreas shrugged. He would happily have continued however late it became. 'Before we finish I'll speak quickly about the props the men will have. We need the toy snake and the knives as John suggested. They must have sheaths, we don't want any accidents. All of you must have a stone in your pocket that you can bang against the chair frames when you are talking about the damage you did to the vehicles. Bring those things with you next time and we'll go through that part again.'

'Should we bring Manolis's hat with the bullet holes?' asked Yiorgos.

'Do you have it?'

Yiorgos nodded. 'He gave it to Vasi and myself after Flora's funeral. It's very precious to us and Vasi keeps it safe.'

'That would be ideal. When you mention narrowly losing your life you could hold it up and show the holes.'

'Can I stand up when I talk?' asked Yiorgos. 'I think it would give more emphasis to my words.'

Andreas considered Yiorgos's suggestion. 'I see no reason why not. It would break up the monotony of having everyone sitting. How about you, Marisa and Yannis? Would you be willing to stand?'

'I'd need to have my stick to lean on,' said Yannis.

'That's no problem. Both you and Marisa can have a stick for support if that helps.'

Ronnie walked over to Andreas. 'Are you sure you want me to take part? Wouldn't someone with a better knowledge of Greek be more suitable?'

'It's too late now to start changing people around.' frowned Andreas.

'I thought I could be more useful if I designed some posters and the programmes.'

'I'd be grateful if you could manage that also. Once I have seen them and agreed on the design and wording I'm sure John would be able to run them off for us. I suggest we meet again on Monday and could you all try to learn your lines by then and be more confident with the song.'

Cathy wished she had had the courage to ask Andreas to find someone to take her place. She had no idea how she would pronounce the word hedgehog, but she did want to be able to give credit to her father and say how proud she was of him.

September 2015
Week Three – Monday & Tuesday

Vasilis had arranged for Vroukinas to resume work on his land and had telephoned Mr Sfyrakos to tell him that the building was now able to proceed. He drove down to the building plot and was pleased to see that the ground was now completely level and all the rubbish had been removed. He would call Mr Sfyrakos again and ask if he could visit him the following day and discuss how the building could proceed.

Cathy had spent the morning trying to pronounce the Greek word for hedgehog and finally gave up. She would have to ask Vasilis when he returned home. She would also have to ask him for further help with the words she was expected to say and also the song. She had learnt the words as they were written down, but was sure her pronunciation was incorrect. If she was going to take part she needed the audience to understand her and not titter at silly mistakes. It was a drama, not a comedy.

'Do you want to come to Heraklion with me tomorrow?' Vasilis asked Cathy.

'Not really,' said Cathy. 'I have nothing to do in Heraklion and you'll probably be hours talking to your architect. I'd rather stay here and try to learn the lines of that song. It would be much easier if we didn't have to sing it as a round. I'm never sure when Marianne has finished her line.'

'Ask her to give you a nudge when you are supposed to join in. You could probably help Saffie by doing the same.'

'I'm going to try to count off the lines on my fingers because I'll be expected to sing a different line the next time around.'

'Why don't you ask Marianne to cover for you and you just open and shut your mouth? The audience will be sufficiently far away not to notice.'

'They may not, but Uncle Andreas will,' replied Cathy morosely.

'I'm going to suggest to him that he only has the natural Greek speakers singing it. That way there will be no pressure on you, Saffie or Ronnie.'

'Now that is a really good idea,' Cathy smiled at him. 'I know we are all worried that we will make a mess of it and we none of us want to let Uncle Andreas down.'

'Leave it with me. I'll speak to him on Thursday.'

'I'd better learn the lines anyway. He might insist that I sing.'

Ronnie had also spent time with Kyriakos as he corrected her pronunciation.

'Greek is simple to say,' he said airily. 'You just split the syllables up.'

'Show me,' demanded Ronnie and looked as he wrote down the words. 'If I say it like that it will sound stilted.'

Kyriakos had smiled at her. 'This is to show you where you put the emphasis on a letter. The word is said as one, not split up into two or three. Listen to me when I read the words individually.'

Patiently he explained to her and finally Ronnie smiled. 'I think I understand now. I'm not very conversant with the Greek alphabet so I'm going to write out the words using the English spelling and underline where the emphasis should be on each one. I'll ask you to listen to me later and correct me. I did suggest to Uncle Andreas that he found someone else to take my part and I offered to do the posters and programmes. He said it was too late for me to leave now, but he took me up on my other offer.'

'Do you know what he wants?'

Ronnie shook her head. 'Not yet and I hope it won't be too complicated.'

'Why don't you sketch out a few ideas to show him? You don't want to wait until the last minute so you have to do a rush job.'

'I think I ought to learn my lines properly first. He's expecting all of us to know them when we go along this evening.'

Andreas was pleased to see that everyone had turned up; after Ronnie suggesting that she should be replaced he had been concerned that she would force his hand by not being there or maybe influence Saffron to withdraw.

'We'll run through the song first as a round then move to where I talk after Yiorgos. Elena will talk after me and then Yannis will describe how he found the injured andarte. When he finishes it will be you, Marisa, pretending to be your Aunt Anna and saying how you brought the doctor to the wounded man. Everyone understand? If so we'll make a start.'

Yannis spoke confidently, describing finding the andartes hiding in a shed on his father's derelict farm. *'I stole some food from the house and took it up to them, then I moved them into my father's house where I thought they would be safer. I asked Mamma Anna about the herbs that could be used to help to heal a wound, saying one of the sheep had cut her leg. Mamma Anna was suspicious. Later that day she went up to my father's farm. When she opened the door she could smell smoke and went to investigate. As she entered the room a man pointed his gun at her. Mamma Anna stood her ground and asked what they were doing in her brother in law's house. The man disclosed that I had taken then there and had also been taking food up to them. She was very cross with me for not telling her sooner and also for putting our lives in danger. She forbade me to go up to visit them again. She realised that the injured man needed a doctor to remove the bullet that was in his leg and gradually poisoning him. That was when she formed a plan.'*

'Stop,' called Andreas. 'That's fine, but now I want Marisa to explain what happened next.'

Marisa frowned. 'I'd rather tell it as I remember it than pretend to be Mamma Anna.'

'Go on, then.'

'One morning Grandma did not wake up and I thought she was dead. Mamma Anna assured me she was breathing, but had probably had another stroke and the doctor needed to visit her. I offered to ask Victor to go to Aghios for the doctor but Mamma Anna said I was to wait until later. She sat beside her mother all morning and in the afternoon she asked for Victor or Mario to go and ask the doctor to come out urgently. Mamma Anna took Yannis to one side and talked to him quietly. He seemed excited and not concerned about his grandmother. As the doctor arrived he rushed in and declared he had seen andartes up in the hills when he had been searching for a lost sheep. Victor and Mario asked him to lead them up there. As soon as they left Mamma Anna told me to sit with Grandma and she took the doctor up to my father's house. They were gone a long time. When they returned their shoes had mud on them that they cleaned off before the soldiers came back. The doctor said that Grandma would probably be better by the morning and asked one of the soldiers to drive him back to Aghios Nikolaos.'

'Yannis, now you again.'

'I led the soldiers up the hill in the opposite direction of my father's house. I hoped we did not find an andarte hiding up there or I would have felt very guilty about betraying him. I took a steep route and walked slowly, wanting to keep the soldiers up there as long as possible as I had no idea how long the doctor would be operating. Of course there was no one to be found and eventually I had to lead the soldiers back. I was very relieved when I found the doctor was there and waiting to be taken back to Aghios Nikolaos.'

'Marisa.'

Marisa looked up surprised. She thought she had said all that was required of her.

'What happened next?' Andreas prompted her.

'I had been sent off to bed and in the morning Mamma Anna told me I must not mention the visit from the doctor to anyone. Grandma appeared to have recovered, but she was still rather sleepy. Mamma Anna often walked up to the hills leaving me looking after Grandma. She said she was looking for herbs, but after the war was over she admitted she had been visiting injured andartes who were hiding in some caves up there.'

'That's good,' Andreas nodded, 'Say it like that on the night. You and Yannis can practice that together. Now, back to the ladies. I'll make it a little easier for some of you now. Marianne you begin and are followed by Bryony, then Monika and finally Marisa. Mark your scripts accordingly.'

Cathy, Saffron and Ronnie gave a collective sigh of relief.

Marianne looked at the words. *'It was easier when the Italians were with us. They were not as brutal as the Germans.'*

'Not all of them were bad. They often helped us with repairs to our houses,' said Bryony.

Monika had her finger on the line she was to say. *'When we had a bad flu epidemic in the area their doctors treated us. Without their help many would not have recovered.'*

Marisa looked up from her script with a broad smile on her face. *'I married one of the Italian soldiers who had lived with us. He was a good, kind, man and we were very happy together.'*

Giovanni gave a little cough to hide the emotion he felt at his mother's words. His father had been good and kind and he wished he was still with them to enjoy his grandchildren.

'Yiorgos, tell us what happened when you finally returned to Aghios Nikolaos,' continued Andreas.

Yiorgos wrinkled his brow. *'I sailed over to Spinalonga. I had been warned that many people had died from starvation. I had fallen in love with a girl who lived over there and I was petrified that she would be one of the casualties and I would never see her again. I could not believe it when I saw she was still alive. The English Resistance worker who had shared so many experiences with me also returned to his home. He found his wife and child had been massacred along with the other villagers. The Germans had taken out their revenge for their defeat out on the villagers as they retreated.'*

Cathy felt a lump come into her throat. 'Can I add something, please.'

Andreas nodded. 'Tell me in English and I will translate it for you.'

'My father was broken hearted at the death of his family. He commissioned Manolis to erect a large memorial in memory of the villagers. Later he met my mother, but Katerina was always close to his heart.' Cathy's voice broke and tears began to run down her face.

Andreas shook his head and spoke gently 'Cathy, that is too emotional for you to be able to say and there are some difficult words there for you to learn. Let me think about it and maybe Litsa can say a part of it.'

Cathy nodded and Bryony handed her a tissue to wipe her eyes.

'Has anyone else anything they would like to add? Think about it and let me know at the next rehearsal. You've most of you done well to learn the words you will say. Next time we will try it without you looking at your scripts and we still have to work on the song. I think a slightly earlier break is called for tonight. Are you willing to put up with us all again on Thursday, Marianne?'

'It's no trouble at all. It's far easier for John and Nicola to be here because of the children.'

Ronnie walked over to Andreas. 'Have you any ideas for the posters?'

'No date for the performance has been decided upon yet.'

'That can be inserted later. Kyriakos suggested I made some sketches and showed them to you. You can then say if you think my ideas are suitable and let me know the size. I'll use A4 paper, but I can scale it up.'

'I also need to think about the programme,' frowned Andreas. 'I'm not used to having to worry about publicity.'

'That should be quite easy as no one is a named character. It can be an A4 fold which is relatively cheap to produce so you wouldn't have to ask more than fifty cents for a copy.'

Andreas shook his head. 'I wasn't planning to ask for any money. This is a performance to commemorate how the local people suffered during the occupation, not a money making project. I plan to ask the audience for a donation when they leave that can be given to the hospital in Aghios Nikolaos.'

Dawoud sat with his companions in the hostel. 'I've been considering our options and I'd like to know your opinions. I think it very unlikely that we will be allowed to travel on to England and I certainly do not want to be sent back to Syria. I'd like to apply for asylum here in Greece.'

'Why would they grant us asylum here when we entered the country illegally?' asked Chadhi.

'We are professional people who could be useful to them.'

'But we don't speak the language,' remonstrated Hazim.

'We've been given books so we have had the opportunity to learn,' replied Dawoud.

'I can't understand it. If the letters were spelt the same way as the English it would make more sense. If we want to stay here we'll have to learn the language. It will take years before we can speak it properly and until we have done that we won't be able to get any work. What will we live on?' Chadhi shook his head. 'I'd rather go to England.'

'We brought money with us and we ask to have that returned. It is legally ours,' argued Dawoud.

'I expect someone has hidden that away somewhere safe,' remarked Nazim.

'We were told it was in the bank.'

'Yes, whose account?' replied Nazim sceptically.

Dawoud sighed. 'I think we should speak to that policeman again.'

'What good would that do?' asked Chadhi.

'We could ask him if we can have our money back. The weather will get colder in a month or so. I'm already wearing my jacket in the evenings. I'd like to be able to buy a warm jumper to put on.'

'I think that's reasonable,' Nazim nodded, 'But I'm not sure about asking for asylum here. How long would our money last?'

'We should be able to find temporary jobs, casual work.'

'Like what?'

Dawoud shrugged. 'I don't know, waiting at tables, kitchen work, cleaning. Things like that. Think about it and let me know.'

'We ought to ask for our money to be returned. That I do agree with. I'm not sure about asking for asylum, though.' Farsal spoke for the first time.

'Well, that's a start,' agreed Dawoud. 'We can't just sit here and do nothing or they'll probably forget about us.'

Vasilis sat in Mr Sfyrakos's office with the plans for his building spread out before them.

'Your side and back wall will need to be approximately twelve feet high. It would be most practical to build them up to six feet, lay the concrete base and then increase their height by another six feet rather than try to build that high in the first place. You won't need footings as the concrete will keep them stable.'

'What about the back wall? That will have to be higher as it will be the rear of the house where the kitchen is planned.'

'The same arrangement. Build the wall to the same height as the others. The walls will be extended at the side of the building and a wall built up at the front to enable you to have a concrete base laid as a level area for you to build on.'

Vasilis frowned. 'If there is a high wall at the front how will the workmen have access to the rear?'

Mr Sfyrakos took a sheet of paper. 'Here is the area of your land.' He drew a dotted line. 'These are the walls at the back and the side walls extend down to the pavement. There will be a further wall at the front with another at the side, leaving access to the rear. This is the area that will be filled with concrete.' Mr Sfyrakos cross hatched the area.

'When you have the front wall built and the rear wall raised you will need scaffolding. In both cases you will have a double row of bricks and they will be tied in for additional stability.'

'I want to have the front terraced,' frowned Vasilis.

'That will be dealt with later. If you are in agreement I will contact a structural engineer and ask him to pass the plans. He will probably want to visit the site to assess the feasibility. Assuming there is no problem he will give you permission to commence the work and will arrange to make regular visits to check that the safety procedures are being carried out.'

'How long will this take?'

'If I speak to him now he should be able to give you an answer within the week.'

'I'm hoping to have the building completed by June.'

'Then I suggest you contact a reputable building firm and explain to them what is required,' smiled Mr Sfyrakos. 'If they are willing to do the work it can commence as soon as the structural engineer gives his permission. Whether the building will be completed by June is another matter. That will depend not only on the number of men you have working, but also the weather over the winter.'

'May I take this diagram with me?'

'I'll make you a temporary copy and then draw up one with accurate measurements for the engineer. I will send you a copy of that when I have completed it.'

Vasilis took the sketch Mr Sfyrakos had produced. At least it would give the builders some idea of his requirements and he hoped he would be able to explain it to them. He would consult

Mr Palamakis, although he thought it unlikely he would be able to undertake such extensive work, he might be able to recommend a reliable building firm.

From Heraklion Vasilis drove to Aghios Nikolaos and drew up outside Christos Palamakis's house.

'You can't leave your car there,' announced Palamakis when he saw where Vasilis was parked.

Vasilis nodded. 'I know. I'll move it up to the car park. I wanted to make sure you were at home first. Give me ten minutes and I'll be back.'

By the time Vasilis returned Palamakis had put on a clean shirt and trousers.

'Are your men available for some work?' asked Vasilis immediately.

'Not at the moment. They all have work. What did you want?'

Vasilis spread the sketch out on the table. 'I've just left my architect. I need these walls built around my land so that cement bases can be poured.' Vasilis traced them with his finger.

'That's a considerable amount of wall that needs to be constructed. How quickly do you need the work completed? My boys are busy at the moment up at Miss Ronnie's. She asked us to make a start on repairing some of the interior of the big house during the summer whilst she wasn't living up there. It will take a long time before it is restored to the way it was before the fire.'

Vasilis looked disappointed. 'Mr Sfyrakos said he would speak with a structural engineer today and provided the man was happy he would pass the plans and work could start immediately afterwards.'

'Have you accurate measurements for the height and length of the walls?'

'I think so.'

Mr Palamakis raised his eyebrows. 'They need to be exact or you'll end up with some walls higher than the others. What did your architect suggest?'

'He said it would be most practical to build the walls six feet high initially. When the concrete was laid they could then be built higher, except for the wall that forms the back of the house and the one at the front. Those walls will need to be considerably higher and will need scaffolding.'

'How high is higher?'

'They'll need to be about twenty feet, maybe a little more.'

Mr Palamakis shook his head. 'Well, Yiannis is a good brick layer but we couldn't cope with that amount of work. You need a team of men; four brick layers at least and someone keeping the cement mixer working along with a general handy man to fetch and carry for them. Even so I reckon it will take two to three weeks before the area is ready to have the cement poured and once it's cured you want to have the walls built higher. I wish I could help, but it just isn't possible. If you want us to do some of the other work later on I'll be delighted, but the work you are describing at the moment is beyond us,'

'Can you recommend a reliable building firm?'

'I can, but I don't know how busy they are.'

'I'll ask them; and if they can't do the job then I'll have to go to someone else that they recommend.'

'Calculate the number of bricks you will need to complete the low back walls. You don't want to have to pay for extra.'

'Any that are over can be used later,' said Vasilis complacently.

'True, but if you have no idea how many are being used initially how do you know if you have sufficient or need more? One unscrupulous character could take twenty bricks home in his car each night and then you'd be asked to buy more. I'm not saying the firm I will recommend isn't trustworthy but I'm not acquainted with their workmen. You'll need to make unannounced visits to the site to keep an eye on what is going on until you have confidence in them.'

Vasilis nodded. 'I'll take your advice. How do I work out how many bricks will be needed?'

Palamakis smiled. 'Total up the length of the walls and divide that by the long side of the bricks. You need to know the depth of each brick and then you can multiply that measurement with the height. That should give you an approximation of the number required. You could use breeze blocks for the perimeter walls. They are larger, lighter to deal with and cheaper than bricks.'

Vasilis looked at him, thoroughly puzzled. 'How do I find out the dimensions of brick and breeze blocks?'

'The easiest way is to go to the builders' merchants with a rule.'

'Would you be willing to come with me? You know what you're talking about.'

'I can. When do you want to go?'

'Would this afternoon be convenient?'

Palamakis nodded. 'I'll need a while to work out the dimensions of the perimeter walls and you can decide which materials you want to use. We can find out the cost of the bricks and the number needed for the other walls can be calculated later.'

'Couldn't I have breeze blocks for all the walls?'

'Not those you plan to have as supporting walls. The structural engineer would not agree. You could use them internally to divide up the rooms as you're only building one floor.'

Vasilis frowned. 'Could I retain you as my site manager? I need someone I can trust to ensure the structure is built to my specifications and is safe. No short cuts that can be covered up.'

Palamakis looked embarrassed. 'I appreciate that you trust me. I'll accept your offer.'

Marianne answered her mobile 'phone with a sinking heart as she saw it was her sister Helena calling.

'We're in London, Marianne. It seemed foolish to waste our time in Washington. We can stay there longer when we return and take mother with us. I'm sure she would appreciate a change of scenery and being in a city again after spending so long with you in the middle of nowhere. I've enjoyed visiting Harrods and

Selfridges and we leave London this afternoon for Paris. We'll probably spend about five days there as I want to go to Galleries Lafayette. Then we are going to fit in a quick visit to Rome and then a further five days in Athens. This means we will be arriving in Crete in October, probably the fifth, but I will let you know that date is definite when we are in Athens.'

Marianne scribbled a quick note of the date on the pad next to her.

'I am relying on you to arrange for Vasi to have a room ready for us,' continued Helena. 'Greg is going to hire a car and we will drive down. That will also mean we can do as we please whilst we are there.'

'That's fine with me, Helena and we'll look forward to seeing you. I'll speak to Vasi and I'm sure he will be able to arrange your room.'

'I want it on the first floor at the front. I'm not prepared to have to keep waiting for the lift to take us up to a higher floor. It's always busy and so slow. We must have a decent balcony so we can sit out there and look at the view whilst we decide what to do each day.'

'I can't make any promises on Vasi's behalf, but I'm sure he will do his best to accommodate your requests.'

'We're giving him plenty of notice so there should be no problem.'

Marianne sighed. At least Helena had given her a definite date for their arrival and not expected Vasi to have hotel accommodation available at the last minute. She hoped Vasi would have a free room that would suit Helena's demands.

'Tell mother that we'll make arrangements to take her back with us the following week.'

'That's not possible, Helena.'

'Why not? Is she ill?'

'Not at all, but she is involved with a production that Uncle Yannis is putting on.'

'I'm sure that isn't vital.'

'On the contrary, she is absolutely essential to the production. You'll have to discuss a return date with her, but I know she will not be willing to leave here until at least mid November.'

'That is ridiculous and alters all our plans. Part of the reason we are making this visit is so we can take her back to New Orleans.'

'If you wish to cancel coming here that is no problem. You could spend more time in Italy, maybe visit Venice,' suggested Marianne.

'Not at all. I'm sure mother will change her mind once we have arrived. Must go. The taxi to take us to the airport will be here within the hour.'

Marianne shook her head. She would have to tell her mother of Helena's plans and she did not think Elena would agree to return to New Orleans before the performance had taken place.

'Certainly not,' said Elena adamantly. 'Helena has no right to try to organise my life and I have no intention of returning to New Orleans with them. If we stopped off in Washington it would only be for Helena to visit the hairdresser or go shopping. If you want to get rid of me I'll go and stay elsewhere, but I'll not let Andreas down.'

'Mamma, you know you are welcome to stay with us as long as you want. You're no trouble at all and Andreas is relying on you. I'll talk to Helena when they arrive and make her understand that there is no way you are going back with them.'

Elena gave a relieved smile. 'I do find it difficult to stand up to her. She just ignores whatever I say.'

'Well she won't ignore me,' declared Marianne. 'I just feel sorry for Greg. I'm sure he would have liked to visit more interesting places than shops and Helena has probably spent far too much money on unnecessary items that took her fancy at the time.'

September 2015
Week Three – Thursday

Chief Inspector Solomakis sent for Orestes. 'I've received a message from the hostel. The men would like to speak to someone. They say it's important.'

'Do you think they are going to request asylum or to return to Syria?'

Solomakis shrugged. 'How would I know? You go along and find out what their problem is. They are probably going to complain about the length of time they have been held. If that's the case ask the Immigration Authorities to pay them a visit. It's nothing to do with us how long they spend at the hostel.'

'When do you want me to go?'

'May as well go today. There's nothing urgent here.'

Again Dawoud acted as spokesman for the group when Orestes arrived.

'We appreciate that you have responded to our request so quickly. There are two important matters that we wish to discuss. The first is that we have decided to request asylum in Crete.'

'That is not a police matter. You will need to speak to the Immigration Authorities.'

Dawoud smiled. 'I expected you to say that and I hope you will be able to arrange for us to have a meeting with them. The second thing is regarding our money. We handed over our money

254

to the woman who met us in good faith, expecting it to be used to cover our expenses in Crete and flight to England. This money has not been used and we were told it was being kept safely at the bank until our futures had been decided. We would like to have it returned to us now.'

Orestes raised his eyebrows. 'With what object in mind?'

'We need some warmer clothes for the winter. We only have the few items we brought with us. We do not expect you to purchase them for us, so we need some of our money to allow us to shop for them. We have all attempted to learn Greek from the books that were sent in to us, but it is very difficult without help. If we can read the words we are unable to pronounce them. If we had our money we would be able to pay to have private lessons in the language. That would indicate to the Immigration Authorities that we are prepared to be useful members of the community and hopefully they would look on this favourably when considering our asylum application.'

Orestes shook his head. 'I am unable to authorise the return of your money. I was only asked to come and speak to you. I will have to advise Chief Inspector Solomakis of your request. It is not unreasonable for you to want to buy yourselves some winter clothes and he may be able to release a small sum to each of you. To pay for private language lessons could be a waste of your money if asylum is not granted and you return to Syria. You would need your money once you were back there.'

Dawoud nodded. 'We did not expect to have an immediate decision from you, but please ask for our requests to be considered. We are already feeling cold during the evenings and spend our time wrapped in a blanket.'

'There is heating in the hostel.'

'I know, but I do not know when it will be turned on and how warm that will be for us. We are used to cold nights, but we always had plenty of additional clothing to wear.'

Orestes felt sympathetic towards the refugees. 'I'll certainly ask for you to have some money returned to each of you for winter clothes, but I can do no more than that.'

'And the Immigration Authorities?'

'I can advise them of your decision and ask that they arrange to visit you.'

Orestes returned to the police station to report to Chief Inspector Solomakis.

'The men have decided they want to apply for asylum here.'

Solomakis nodded. 'Contact Immigration and they can sort that problem out.'

'They also want to have their money returned to them. They say they need warm winter clothes and would like to pay for private Greek lessons.'

The Chief Inspector shook his head. 'I can arrange for a small sum to be made available to each of them and a variety of clothing taken to the hostel for them to purchase. We can't have them wandering around the town on their own.'

'What about the Greek tuition? The schools are still on holiday at the moment so one of the teachers should be available and pleased to earn a bit of extra money. They could go to the hostel.'

'If the men are prepared to pay for their lessons and you can find someone willing to visit them that could be arranged. Provided they realise that a knowledge of the language will not guarantee them the right to stay in Crete.'

'I think they hope it will be in their favour. It will show that they have made an effort to become conversant with our language.'

'Let me know if you are able to arrange anything.' Solomakis turned back to his paper work. He had more important things to deal with than Greek lessons for illegal immigrants.

Ludmila opened her lime green mobile, her heart beating with excitement. Only Ivan knew that 'phone number and she hoped he would be arranging to collect her.

He began to speak without preamble. 'Go down to Plaka and over to Spinalonga today. Sit on the edge of the jetty and remove your shoes. Panos will collect you.'

'What time should I be there?' asked Ludmila, but the line was dead. She looked at her watch. However much she hurried she was unlikely to be in Aghios Nikolaos in time to catch the eleven o'clock bus and would have to wait until one o'clock.

She was about to pick up her bag and leave the house when she thought about her shoes. She was wearing strappy sandals with a low heel. They were hardly suitable for wearing on a boat deck. She rummaged in her wardrobe and drew out the pair of canvas deck shoes that she had worn when she drove down to meet the immigrants. If she was going to wear those she would need to change her skirt for a pair of trousers. Feeling rushed and frantic she pulled out the first pair of trousers that came to hand and dragged them on before slipping her feet into the deck shoes.

Although she was resigned to missing the eleven o'clock bus from Aghios Nikolaos to Plaka she was desperate to leave the apartment and be on her way. If the police should come looking for her for any reason she did not want to be there and delayed by them. Checking her purse to ensure she had her money and her door key she picked up her bag and hurried down the road.

Ludmila bought her ticket to Aghios Nikolaos and sat in the shade waiting for the bus driver to appear. She looked at her watch constantly. Provided there were no delays on the road the journey should take no more than an hour and it was only ten thirty now; giving her ample time to arrive and catch the one o'clock bus to Plaka. Her stomach rumbled, reminding her that she had not stopped to eat any breakfast. She should have thought and made herself a sandwich. It was too late now to return to the apartment; she would have to rely on purchasing a snack in Aghios Nikolaos when she arrived.

When the driver finally appeared and called out that the bus was destined for Aghios Nikolaos she hurried forward and produced her ticket. He punched a hole in it and she mounted the bus steps and made her way to the back, sinking into the seat with a sigh of relief.

The bus crawled through the outskirts of Heraklion, collecting passengers on its way. Tourists chattered excitedly together and pointed out various landmarks to their companions through the windows. Ludmila sat immersed in her thoughts. She felt a certain amount of guilt in placing all the blame for the venture on Evgeniy, but had she not implicated him fully she would still be in a holding cell and awaiting a criminal trial. She felt convinced that Evgeniy would be able to extricate himself; he knew influential people.

As the bus drew into Aghios Nikolaos the passengers disembarked eagerly, some making their way towards the town and others checking the time of the next bus to Plaka. Having purchased her ticket she looked around for a snack bar, disappointed that she was unable to see one in the vicinity. She really was feeling hungry now and dared not walk away from the bus station as she did not know her way around the town, despite having visited with Evgeniy and buying suitcases. She sat miserably on the hard wooden seat willing the time to pass, with only mouthfuls of water to assuage her hunger.

As the bus travelled down the road to Elounda the view drew "Oohs" and "Aahs" from the passengers and many of them alighted at Elounda whilst more passengers climbed on to make the short journey down to Plaka.

As they arrived, to her annoyance, Ludmila saw a boat pulling away from the jetty.

'What time is the next boat to Spinalonga?' she asked of the man behind the bar at "The Pines".

'Every half hour,' he answered without looking up.

'Am I able to get anything to eat here?'

'What do you want? We only do snacks.'

'Anything; a beefburger or bag of chips. Something I can take away with me, and a bottle of water.'

'Have a seat.'

'I don't have long. I have to be on the next boat.'

'You'll not get on it any quicker by standing up. Sit outside and I'll bring you a beef burger and chips to take away.'

Clenching her fists in irritation Ludmila watched the boat's ponderous journey across the sea and it seemed no time at all before a boat left the island and made its way towards the shore. Her beefburger and chips were placed on the table in front of her contained in a small cardboard box, along with a bottle of water. She counted out the Euros for the bill and placed them inside the small glass before pushing the box on to the top of her bag and walking hurriedly down the hill to purchase her ticket for the boat ride. Waiting for the boat to finally dock she ate some of her chips, but did not want to take out the beefburger in case she had to move swiftly.

Once down at the small harbour Ludmila looked out across the bay. There was a boat moored, but the prow was towards the island and the stern towards the land so she was unable to read the name. She hoped it was Ivan, but there was no sign of anyone on board. Had she misunderstood? Was she supposed to be waiting on a jetty at Plaka for him? Her stomach lurched. What would she do if he was not there?

Ludmila tried to curb her impatience as she queued for her ticket and then followed the visitors up to the entrance tunnel. They seemed to move so slowly, looking at everything and blocking the path so she could not get through. Once they reached the square the way became clearer and she was able to walk around people and continue on her way to where the entrance to the old jetty was situated. She walked down to the edge, trying to appear nonchalant, then sat on the edge and removed her shoes.

There was no space for them in her bag with the cardboard box containing the beefburger. She ate that whilst looking out for Ivan to arrive. When finished she scrunched the cardboard box up as small as possible although there were still some uneaten chips inside. To put it in the rubbish bin would mean replacing her shoes and walking to the top of the jetty. Instead she tried to drop it inconspicuously into the sea and then watched it bob around embarrassingly, hoping no one would know she was the culprit.

Whilst eating Ludmila kept her eyes on the boat that was moored between the island and the mainland. The only other boats in the vicinity were those who took the visitors across to Spinalonga. It had to be Ivan. She had an overwhelming desire to stand up, wave her arms and shout "I'm here."

The tourists who walked down through the archway and onto the jetty hardly gave her a second glance. As the afternoon drew on the number of visitors thinned and Ludmila felt panic setting in. What would she do if Ivan did not arrive? Should she stay on the island over night or catch the last boat back to the mainland? If she hid on the island would she be found and forced to leave? The stone of the jetty was becoming painful and she moved her bag so she was able to sit on it.

She had been waiting there over two hours before she saw a dinghy leaving the boat and approaching the jetty. As it came closer she could see that Panos was rowing and she drew a deep breath of relief. He stopped at the end of the jetty, steadying the small craft with his hand on the rough wall.

'Throw in your bag and get in,' he ordered and Ludmila hurried to comply.

As her bare feet hit the damp rubber base of the dinghy they slid from beneath her and she ended up in an ungainly heap.

'Stay lying there, you're safe enough and if you start to move around you'll draw attention to us.'

Despite the discomfort she was suffering Ludmila obeyed him and he rowed away strongly. As they reached the boat Panos attached the dinghy to a line that was hanging over board next to a rope ladder and spoke to her again.

'Put on your shoes and climb up the ladder. I'll bring your bag.'

Tentatively she took a grip on the ladder and began to haul

herself up slowly. The rough rope cut into her hands and her feet slipped continually on the rope rungs. She did not feel at all safe and was pleased to know that Panos was behind her, hoping he would be able to save her should she fall. Ivan pulled her unceremoniously aboard.

'Go below. Say nothing.'

To Ludmila's surprise when she opened the cabin door eight men looked up at her expectantly. She stood there uncertainly, wondering what was expected of her. She could hear movement up on the deck and the boat rocked as Panos and Ivan pulled the dinghy back on board. She leaned against the wall of the cabin to steady herself and one man indicated that she could sit on the bunk bed between him and his two companions. She shook her head. If they had any intention of molesting her she would rather be standing close to the door in the hope that she could make a desperate dash for the stairway that led to the deck.

She heard the engine start and felt the movement of the boat as it travelled through the sea. One of the men spoke to her in Arabic and although she understood his words she remembered Ivan's instructions to say nothing and simply smiled at him.

As they moved from the shelter of the bay Ivan raised the sails allowing the freshening wind to fill them and increase their speed. Once satisfied that he was well away from the coast he went below deck and opened the cabin door.

'Come with me,' he said to his sister in Russian.

Dutifully Ludmila followed him up onto the deck. The brisk wind made her shiver and he passed her bag to her. 'I hope you thought to pack a jumper.'

She delved inside and pulled the jumper over her head, grateful for the extra warmth.

'Did you speak to the men in the cabin?' asked Ivan.

'One of them spoke to me and asked if I was also a refugee. I just smiled and pretended not to understand. Where are you taking them?'

261

'Turkey. They should be able to travel on from there.'

'Do they speak Turkish?'

'I've no idea. They just want to get to Europe. I took a chance coming to Crete to collect you, rather than sailing direct.'

'I'm very grateful,' answered Ludmila humbly.

'The port authorities may have been told to keep a look out for my boat. I'm going to have to risk making a stop at Naxos and again at Lesbos to refuel. When we reach Turkish waters I'll refuel again at Gokceada and take the men up to Enez. Once I have disposed of them we will sail through to the Sea of Marmara and dock at Istanbul. How did you and Evgeniy get picked up?'

'I think the police were informed and were keeping watch on the canal and the beach. When they questioned me they said that some immigrants in England had asked for asylum and described their journey. I was extremely careful when I collected them but someone must have said they'd seen me. I had no idea there was anything amiss until the police came to the apartment.'

Ivan nodded. 'I guessed something had happened to disrupt our plans when Evgeniy did not call me and say they had arrived. I waited twenty four hours and then sailed to a different port and decided I could no longer use any Greek island as a safe destination for travellers.'

'I understand they tried to close the hotel down. Evgeniy came to an arrangement through the Russian Consulate that it could remain open. It has been put into administration with the previous owner being responsible for the finance. When they allowed me to leave the prison I told them I had no access to any money and they arranged for me to collect four hundred Euros each month to cover my living expenses.'

'What about the money that the men took with them?' asked Ivan.

'I put that in the safe as usual. The police removed it. They asked me where it had come from and I said I had followed Evgeniy's instructions and placed it in the safe when I arrived home. I expect they questioned the men and they would have said that it was to cover their onward journey.'

'I wonder what else they told them?'

Ludmila shook her head. 'I don't know. I said Evgeniy had been responsible for arranging their escape from Syria and he had blackmailed you into using your boat to transport them. He's still being held in prison. I was not going to involve you as you were my one hope to leave the country. They obviously believed that I was only acting under Evgeniy's instructions as they released me.'

'Did they return your passport?'

'No.'

Ivan frowned. 'That could cause a problem.'

'I have my passport in my maiden name at the apartment in Moscow.'

'You'll not be allowed ashore anywhere without a passport.'

'So what am I going to do?'

'There's only one thing we can do. When we reach Istanbul I'll have to contact someone and ask them to produce another one for you.'

'Would you be able to get two for me; one in my maiden name so I am able to access my bank account in Moscow?'

'At a price.'

'Until I am able to go to the bank there I have no money. Can you pay and I'll repay you later?'

'I suppose I have no choice. Once I have disposed of the men I'll make some 'phone calls. Remember whenever we are within sight of land you must stay below with the men. I don't want to be asked why I am carrying passengers who have no passports.'

Ludmila nodded. 'How long will it take us to sail to Turkey?'

Ivan shrugged. 'I'm getting low on fuel having had to collect you from Crete. I don't want to run the motor unless it's necessary. It's too expensive. We should reach Naxos tomorrow and I can refuel there, then another day to arrive at Lesbos for another fuelling stop. Provided the wind does not become too strong we can use the sails. To ensure I have enough fuel, whatever the circumstances, I'll make a stop at Gokceada. Once I've dropped off the men we can sail into the Bay of Marmara. The lighter the boat the less fuel is used. We can take some more on at one of the ports along the coast if necessary. It will probably take us a week to reach Istanbul.'

Ludmila shuddered. It was not a pleasant thought to have to stay cooped up below in the company of the men for four or five days and nights.

'Cathy, I have written some words that I hope you will find acceptable. You will say "My father was broken hearted at the death of his family." Bryony can follow you by saying "He commissioned a large memorial to be erected in memory of his wife and child and the other villagers who were massacred." Cathy nodded approval. 'Then Yiorgos can say "Later he met an English lady whom he married and they had a daughter who helped to heal his mental wounds." You then say again "I was very proud of my father." We'll change the earlier wording to say "He was a very brave man" How does that sound?'

'Thank you, Andreas. I do want a fitting tribute paid to him, but I know I'm not capable of saying it in Greek.'

''Right, now let's get on with rehearsing.'

'I have a suggestion to make,' said Vasilis. 'Cathy is really struggling with the song when it is sung as a round. Saffie and Ronnie are also having a problem. Could the singers be readjusted so that only the ladies who speak Greek fluently take part?'

Andreas frowned. He had been frustrated at the hesitancy and errors that had been evident since the first rehearsal. 'I suppose that could solve a problem. Let's try it through that way. Marisa, you start, then Marianne, followed by Bryony, Monika and Litsa. If I'm satisfied then you can alter your scripts accordingly.'

'There are only four lines,' said Marisa. 'Why don't you just have four people singing them as a round?'

Marianne nodded. 'That makes sense, Uncle Andreas. We're less likely to get confused about which line we're supposed to sing.'

Andreas sighed. 'You'll have to sing loudly if there are only four of you.'

'I'm sure we can manage that. Shall we try it?'

'I suppose so. I really want to get on with rehearsing the lines and your actions tonight. Have you managed to find a toy snake, John?'

'I have it in my pocket.' John pulled out the plastic imitation and his father shuddered at the sight as John wriggled it around.

'Are you sure that isn't real?' asked Giovanni.

'Quite sure, Pappa. Do you want to look at it?'

'No, don't bring it anywhere near me even if it is a toy.'

'I've also made a catapult.' John held it up for inspection, 'And bought some knives.'

'You four ladies sing the song and then we'll be able to move on,' said Andreas irritably.

Marianne, Bryony, Monika and Litsa sang lustily and it was certainly far simpler for all of them to render their line at the appropriate moment.

'Right, you sing it through twice and when you should start for a third time is when each one of you stamps your feet in turn and shouts "Bang! Bang!". The second time you shout and stamp everyone, including the men join in. Understand?'

After three attempts Andreas declared he was satisfied that they understood. 'You'll have to sing louder than that on the night or you'll not be heard by the audience at the back. The same applies to all of you when you say your lines; you have to be able to project your voice. I'm hoping that when I've discussed the lighting arrangements with Dimitris we will be able to have some time in the hall to rehearse. I'll be able to stand at the back and wave at you if I can't hear.'

'That could be a problem,' frowned Nicola. 'I can't leave the children here alone and I don't know who I can ask to baby sit.'

'I'm sure you'll find someone,' answered Andreas airily.

Nicola looked at John dubiously. Their children had only ever been left with a member of the family to look after them, not a stranger.

'Maybe your sister would be willing to look after them when she's here?' suggested Giovanni to Marianne.

'Don't be silly. She would consider it demeaning to have to look after small children for a few hours, even if they were in bed and asleep. She'll probably complain that we have to spend some evenings rehearsing whilst they are here rather than spending every evening with them.'

'They can always go out on their own for a meal. They probably think they are being kind in inviting us to go with them.'

'I'm sure Helena only does it so she can wear a different expensive dress every evening.'

Giovanni felt guilty. Marianne never asked him for expensive clothes. 'Would you like to go into Aghios Nikolaos and buy something special?'

Marianne shook her head. 'I've three dresses and two tops that I can dress up a bit. I don't need anything new just to try to impress my sister. Helena really is a nuisance deciding to come and visit us now.'

Giovanni did not reply. He felt that his sister in law was always a nuisance whenever she decided to pay them a visit.

Evgeniy sat in his prison cell. He could not complain about the treatment he received; he was allowed to shower each day, have two hour's exercise in the grounds along with the other men and given three meals regularly. Having been informed that Ludmila had been released he had expected her to visit him but she had not put in an appearance. Finally he requested to see Chief Inspector Solomakis.

'How much longer am I going to be held here?'

Solomakis shrugged. 'I have no idea. The Greek justice system moves slowly.'

'Why has my wife not been allowed to visit me since her release?'

'She has not applied for a visitor's permit,' answered Solomakis.

'Did you tell her that she was able to visit me? I'd like her to bring me some clothes from the apartment. Contact her with my request, issue her with a permit and tell her to bring them when she visits me.' Evgeniy spoke imperiously.

'I am not an errand boy,' replied Solomakis. 'I will ask one of my men to call on her when they have time and give her your message.'

September 2015
Week Three – Friday & Saturday

Ludmila hated being confined to the cabin with the men. She was reluctant to use the shower and contented herself with a quick wash. When Ivan drew into the harbour on Naxos he had told them they were not to speak until after he had refuelled and they were back out at sea. The smell of the diesel permeated the cabin making Ludmila feel sick. She sat with a T-shirt held across her mouth and nose trying to breathe in as little of the fumes as possible.

Once back out in the open sea Ivan went below and opened the porthole to allow some fresh air to enter.

'You may talk quietly again and prepare yourselves some food.'

'How much longer are we going to be on board?' asked one.

'We will have to stop for fuel twice more and then we will be able to leave you at a safe haven in Turkey.' Ivan spread a map on the floor and the men craned forward to look.

'There is a suitable landing area here,' he placed his finger on the coast line. 'You will be taken ashore in the dinghy; four of you in each trip. Once on the beach you will stay there until daylight and then it is only a few kilometres to the nearest town. From there you will be able to get transport in a truck to take you across the country.'

'Will we have our possessions and mobile 'phones returned to us?'

'Of course,' Ivan assured him, not mentioning the fact that he had removed the chip from each phone and rendered them useless. 'I will also return your money once I have deducted your expenses.'

'Will we be able to use our money in Turkey?'

'You will need to go to a money exchange bureau to have it converted into Turkish Lira, but that should be no problem. Do not go to a bank or you will be asked for your passports as identification and questions could be asked. I will give you a 'phone number to call so your onward journey can be arranged.'

Ludmila looked at her brother dubiously. He made it sound so simple.

Dawoud and his companions appreciated being able to rummage through an assortment of jumpers and trousers that had been brought into the hostel and after completing their purchases they had a little money left over from the amount they had been allowed.

'Do you think we could ask them for some socks and underwear?' asked Faisal.

'I think that's a reasonable request,' agreed Dawoud. 'We should have thought about that when we asked for jumpers. We should have sufficient to pay for them.'

Dawoud spoke to the guard on the entrance desk of the hostel and asked for a further visit from Orestes. He was pleased to be able to make the request in halting Greek although he was unable to understand the reply.

Achilles called at Ludmila's apartment on his way to the police station and was surprised to find that she was not at home early in the morning. He rang the bell a second time and then banged on the door. If she was still asleep that should have woken her.

'What's the problem?'

The man from the apartment above opened his window.

'I'm trying to contact the lady who lives here. I have a message for her.'

'I don't think she's there. I called yesterday to give her another letter that had arrived for her and there was no answer.'

'Did she tell you she was going away?'

'I only see her occasionally. We're not friends so she'd be unlikely to tell me her plans.' The man closed his window leaving Achilles standing there wondering what to do for the best.

Achilles rang the bell and knocked on the door again. There was no movement or sound from inside. An awful thought struck him. Had the woman taken an overdose of sleeping tablets, or even worse, cut her wrists?

He took out his mobile 'phone and called Chief Inspector Solomakis relating his fears to him and requesting that a female officer be sent to the address. 'I'll keep trying to get an answer until she arrives and then I'd like permission to break down the door. Ask her to bring a crowbar with her.'

With a deep sigh Solomakis agreed. It sounded ominous and he would not relish the task of breaking the news to Evgeniy Kuzmichov that his wife had committed suicide if that was the case.

Agate arrived and Achilles smiled at her. 'Sorry to have to call you out. I'll go in first and have a look around. If resuscitation is needed I'll ask you to start whilst I 'phone an ambulance.'

Achilles took the crowbar and inserted it against the hinges of the door and applied all his strength. There was a loud crack as the wood splintered and Achilles attacked the area around the lock until it fell away. He placed the crowbar beside the door and walked inside calling loudly as he entered. Agate followed him and waited whilst he opened each door and looked inside.

'There's definitely no one here,' he announced. 'I'll let Solomakis know and then we'll have to arrange for the door to be blocked up securely. Whilst I do that you have a look around and see if you think anything is missing.'

Agate opened the wardrobe and drawers. She had no idea if any clothing was missing. In the bathroom she noted that tooth paste and a tooth brush was not in evidence and nor was there a brush and comb in the bedroom.

'I think she has gone away for a few days. She's obviously not moved out permanently as most of her clothes appear to be here.'

Achilles nodded. He was cross with himself for jumping to conclusions.

Chief Inspector Solomakis received Achilles's report with both relief and annoyance. Where would the woman have gone? She could not travel far without her passport so must be somewhere on the island.

'Call Mr Propenkov,' he ordered Achilles. 'He may know where she is.'

Propenkov assured Achilles that he had no idea where Ludmila Kuzmichov would be if she was not at her apartment. 'I have not seen her since she was released. I can contact "The Central" and Mr Iliopolakis to see if they have any information.'

Giorgos was puzzled when he received the telephone call from Achilles. 'I've not seen the lady since she brought her electricity bill in and asked if we could pay it on her behalf. I received permission from Mr Iliopolakis and she had to bring the receipted bill back to me. I can look up the date for you if necessary. I remember it was a Monday she was not best pleased. She said she had been planning to visit Knossos that day and I told her the site was closed on a Monday.'

Vasilis was in the lounge of Vasi's hotel with Mr Palamakis when Achilles contacted him and confirmed he had no knowledge of Ludmila's whereabouts. Vasi frowned and held up his hand.

'Saffie told me she had seen her briefly in Plaka. She obviously recognised Saffie as she walked in and out of her shop without stopping to look around. Saffie couldn't place her face at first, but then she saw her over at "The Pines" and realised who she was.'

Vasilis relayed the information to Achilles who thanked him. The police man thought it most likely that the woman had been on her way to visit Spinalonga if she had also visited Knossos. She was probably taking advantage of sight seeing whilst she had time on her hands. That could mean that she had travelled up to Chania and was staying up there or even in Aghios Nikolaos with the intention of visiting the sites in that area.

Vasilis continued his conversation with Mr Palamakis. He was not interested in Ludmila Kuzmichov, but he did wonder where she had suddenly found the money to visit Spinalonga. Even travelling down to Plaka by bus and over to the island would have cost her almost fifty Euros. With an allowance of only four hundred Euros each month to enable her to buy her food that was a considerable amount to spend in one day. He would speak to Cathy when he returned home and ask her how much she would expect to spend if she was living alone on a limited income.

Cathy was intrigued by Vasilis's enquiry. 'Why? Am I spending too much?' she asked.

'Not at all. I had a call from the police when I was down with Vasi. Ludmila has disappeared apparently. Vasi said Saffie had seen her at Plaka. Why would she spend the money to go down there if she only had a hundred Euros each week to live on?'

'Maybe she is being very frugal and wanted to visit the area in day light.'

Vasilis shook his head. 'She collected the men from the beach on the other side of the Causeway so why would she travel on to Plaka?'

'She might have made a mistake with the bus stop or decided to visit Spinalonga.'

'That would have cost her almost fifty Euros in total. That's a good deal to spend on a visit. There's something niggling at me.'

'Shall I 'phone Saffie and see if she can tell us anything more?' suggested Cathy.

Saffron was surprised to get the call from Cathy. 'She literally walked into the shop, looked at me and walked out again. I saw her again a short while later sitting over at "The Pines". Do you want me to ask Theo if she said anything to him about going to Spinalonga?'

'Might as well, but I doubt if he'll remember her.'

To Cathy's surprise Saffron 'phoned her back within the hour. 'Theo does remember her. He said she only wanted some water the first time, but he remembers her clearly when she returned yesterday. She seemed in quite a panic and wanted to know how often the boats went across to Spinalonga. She also wanted something to eat and he gave her a beefburger and chips to take away.'

'What did she do then?'

'Once she had her food she hurried off to get a boat ticket so she must have gone over to Spinalonga. He didn't see her when she came back.'

Cathy repeated to Vasilis the information that Saffron had supplied. 'I'm going to see if Panayiotis is at home and ask him for his opinion. Something doesn't feel right to me.'

Panayiotis listened carefully to Vasilis. 'There's really very little to go on. The woman is not under house arrest so can go where she pleases. I agree she doesn't appear to have much money at her disposal, but it is hers to spend as she wishes. I'm not sure if I can do anything to help.'

'Would you be able to speak to the boatmen? They might remember her and she may have said where she planned to go next, asked for directions or the time of a bus; something like that.'

Panayiotis shrugged. 'I can, but with the number of visitors they have each day to the island they are hardly likely to remember one woman. I can go down tomorrow morning before I have to go on duty, but don't expect me to have any information for you.'

Nicola spoke to John regarding arranging a baby sitter for their children. 'I should have thought of that before,' she said miserably. 'I'm not prepared to leave them with a stranger. I think I should tell Uncle Andreas that I will have to drop out.'

John looked his wife in consternation. 'I admit it hadn't really occurred to me that we would be spending time in the Municipal Hall to rehearse. I only expected to be there for the one evening and we could have taken the children with us. The girls would probably be interested in watching and we could have taken them some colouring books to keep them occupied if they did become bored. Yiannis would probably be asleep and he could be settled down beside them.'

'I don't think it is a suitable production for the girls. They're not old enough to understand. I'd like to know that someone responsible was looking after them at home.'

'I'm sure we will be able to find a baby sitter.'

'They need to know them. If they woke up and found a total stranger here they'd be frightened.'

'Ask my Mum. She might know of someone who would be suitable.'

Although John appreciated that Nicola's fears and objections were reasonable he felt confident that someone known to them could be found.

Andreas called on Dimitris and asked if he had been able to gain access to the Municipal Hall.

'I have, but I need to know your exact requirements. There are electrical sockets around, but they only use them if additional lighting is required to illuminate a display. If the dancing is being held there they just leave all the lights on.'

'Ideally we need spotlights for when the men and women are talking. Elena and I will be at the back and we'll need lights to be able to read our scripts. I can't expect Elena to learn hers by heart and I doubt if I could. I'd probably realise that I'd left out something important and it could be too late to add it in at a later date.'

'Would it help if I came to your next rehearsal?' offered Dimitris. 'I could mark on the script when lights were needed.'

'That would be a help, but what about the spotlights?'

'A number of small theatrical productions are put on in Aghios Nikolaos. There could be a firm there who hires out stage lighting. How long would you want them for?'

Andreas considered. 'We ought to have at least three rehearsals there with the lights and then we'll need them on the night. Find out where you are able to hire them from and see how much they charge on a daily basis.'

Dimitris considered the request. 'I'll make enquiries. It would probably be cheaper to hire spotlights for a week rather than for odd days.'

Andreas frowned. 'If we did that we would need three rehearsals in one week. I don't know if everyone would be able to manage that.'

'Do you have a date in mind for the production?'

'I think Thursday fifth November would be suitable. The tourists will have left by then and most places closed down. That will give us another month in which to rehearse and time for Nicola to find a baby sitter. She says she'll withdraw rather than leave the children at home on their own.'

'That's understandable. My sister wouldn't leave her child alone in the house.'

'Then ask her if she'd look after the children that week.'

'There's no spare room at her house for them.'

Andreas sighed. 'Ask your sister and if she is willing you can ask Nicola if she can go and stay at their house for the week.'

'She doesn't know the children very well.'

'Then tell her to get to know them,' answered Andreas impatiently.

Vasilis had to wait until Panayiotis arrived home the following day before he could ask him about his visit to Plaka.

'Well, it was interesting. I spoke to Theo at "The Pines" and he confirmed that the lady seemed very concerned about catching the next boat and wanted some food to take with her. He didn't see her again after she left and went down to the ticket kiosk. One of the boatmen remembered taking her over the previous week and bringing her back. He remarked that she hadn't stayed very long and she said she planned to return another time. He happened to take her over again on Thursday. He said he definitely remembered her as he had seen her on his return trip sitting on the end of the jetty and she threw her take away carton into the sea. He was surprised to see her still sitting there two hours later. On his final trip that day he saw a dinghy very close to the jetty and there was no sign of her after that, although she was not on the beach waiting to go back to the mainland.'

Vasilis frowned. 'She could have caught the boat back to Elounda.'

Panayiotis shook his head. 'Her ticket only allowed her to return to Plaka. According to the boat man there had been a rather nice sailing boat moored between the island and the shore and the dinghy appeared to be returning to it. Are you thinking the same as I am?'

Vasilis nodded. 'That was her brother picking her up! It's too much of a coincidence that a dinghy should be close to the jetty and she then disappears into thin air. Did the boatman spot the name of the boat?'

'He did. It was rather worn around the area as though it had been removed and then painted back on. He said it was either "Sea Spirit" or "Sea Sprite". He couldn't be certain.'

'Would you be willing to call Chief Inspector Solomakis and tell him all you have just told me?' asked Vasilis.

'I don't see why not. He may not act on the information, of course'

Chief Inspector Solomakis listened to Panayiotis. 'It's very circumstantial. The best I can do is put out a call to all the maritime police to look out for the boat in their waters and a request to apprehend it. Even if the lady is found on board provided she is within Greek waters she has not broken the law, but if she is with her brother we'd definitely like to interview him.'

The coastguard at Naxos called Solomakis back with the news that the boat had refuelled at the port the previous day and a short while later a message from Lesbos was received confirming that a boat of that name and description had stopped there for fuel about five hours earlier.

'How long does it take to refuel?' asked Chief Inspector Solomakis.

'Depends upon the size of the boat. A tanker would take two, maybe three days, but we couldn't cope with anything that size.'

'So how long was this boat there with you?'

'No more than three hours.'

'Get after her and stop her before she reaches Turkish waters. Arrest whoever is on board and bring them back to Lesbos.'

'I'll do my best, but I suggest you contact the coastguard at Limnos. They will be able to reach her more quickly than us. Do you know if they are armed?'

The thought had not occurred to Solomakis. 'I don't think so, but it would be as well to be prepared.'

Andreas accompanied Dimitris to the Municipal Hall and Dimitris showed him where the electrical sockets were situated.

'You'll have to use that end of the hall for your performance otherwise the audience will be walking on and past the staging area. There are the same number of sockets on each wall.'

Andreas examined the area. 'I'll want a small table and chair on each side at the back. Next to each one I will need a light that can be adjusted to the correct height and the beam directed where it is required. I will be using one and Elena the other. We will need to be able to switch them on and off as necessary. When our lights are off you will be directing the spotlights on either the men or the women, depending who is speaking.'

Dimitris nodded. He wished they would be able to have more rehearsals in the hall with the lights. Depending where Andreas wanted the spotlights positioned he might have to use an extension lead, tape it to the floor and cover it with a piece of carpet for safety.

'I'll go into Aghios on Monday and see what's available. I'll come to the rehearsal on Monday and then let you know. I ought to sit through it a few times so I know exactly what you expect of me.'

'Have you spoken to your sister about looking after the children?'

'She says she's willing and is going to speak to Nicola.'

Having refuelled at Lesbos Ivan continued along the route under sail. The wind had strengthened and at times the boat rolled and pitched alarming Ludmila.

'Is it safe to continue. Ivan?'

'Of course. I know what I'm doing. If you're worried put a life jacket on or go below.'

'Couldn't we put in somewhere until the sea is less rough?'

'The nearest coast is Turkey and there are few safe harbours along this stretch of coast. The wind is not helping our progress. I'll furl the sails and use the motor to ride this out.'

Feeling frightened Ludmila donned a life jacket, but decided she would prefer to stay on deck. If by any chance the small craft did capsize she would be unlikely to escape from the cabin. She sat and shivered, as much from the cold wind as from fear.

Ivan started the engine and Panos began to haul down the sails. Without the contrary wind Ivan was able to steer his boat into the waves rather than them meeting him at the side. He frequently cut the engine to allow them to ride over the waves and the violent rolling movement lessened much to Ludmila's relief.

She negotiated the stairs down to the cabin gingerly with the intent of bringing up a blanket to wrap around herself. As she opened the cabin door she reeled back. The men were in various stages of sea sickness and few of them had made it to the bathroom. There was no way she was prepared to enter the cabin.

Feeling thoroughly miserable Ludmila sat on the deck with her legs pulled up and her head bowed to gain as much shelter as possible. She heard Panos shout to Ivan and Ludmila looked up in alarm. There was a much larger vessel approaching their stern.

'Who is it?' asked Ludmila.

'A coast guard cutter.'

'Are they going to help us?' asked Ludmila.

Ivan did not answer her. The sound of the engine changed as he increased the power.

'Hold on,' he called. 'I'm going to try to out run them and get into Turkish waters.'

As Ivan attempted to turn towards the coast a second cutter appeared and cut across their bows, effectively blocking his route to the Turkish waters.

'Cut your engines. Drop your anchor. We are preparing to board you.' The words came over a loud hailer and were distinguishable despite the wind and a mounted gun was pointing in their direction.

Ivan gritted his teeth. With a gun pointing at them he had no choice but to obey. 'I'll do as they say and try to stall them.'

Riding at anchor without the aid of the motor the boat began to roll again alarmingly. The cutter arrived alongside and threw a rope to Panos who caught it deftly. Ludmila gave a sigh of relief. At least if they did sink help was at hand.

'What do you want?' Ivan called back.

He received no answer and as the two boats closed together a coast guard jumped onto the deck.

'I'd like to see your maritime papers and passport.'

'They're below deck. I'll have to get them.'

'I'll come with you. It will be easier to talk out of this wind.'

'There's no need. My papers are all in order. Once you've seen them we can be on our way.'

The man took no notice and followed Ivan down to the cabin, his hand resting on his revolver. As Ivan opened the door eight frightened men looked up at him and the smell was unbearable. The coast guard stopped.

'I don't think I need to inspect your papers at this moment. You're under arrest. We'll tow you to Limnos and you can produce your papers and the passports of your passengers there.'

Back on deck the coast guard took out his radio and spoke to his ship. 'Prepare to receive passengers. We'll have to winch them across. Some are in a bad way.'

More hands appeared on the deck of the coastguard cutter and a life belt attached to the winch was sent over to Ivan's boat. Ludmila was helped into the life belt and safely secured before being swung off her feet and over to the deck of the coastguard cutter. Once she was aboard the life belt was sent back and the men from the cabin were ordered up on deck to repeat her journey.

Tow lines were attached to Ivan's boat and the journey to Limnos began. The coastguard cutter powered her way through the sea easily whilst Ivan's boat bobbed around like a cork, the waves washing over her deck regularly.

Having ascertained that none of the passengers were actually injured, but only suffering from sea sickness, they were given blankets to wrap around themselves and bowls placed beside them. Once they were back on dry land they would soon recover.

The coast guard radioed to Limnos that he was returning and would need to be met by the police as he had eleven people to be taken into custody and questioned.

'Let that police Inspector on Crete who gave us the tip off know that we have picked them up along with some other passengers.

We'll make arrangements to send them all on to him as soon as possible.' If, as the coast guard suspected, the eight men were refugees they were not wanted on Limnos to swell the numbers who had already arrived there.

October 2015
Week Two – Monday & Tuesday

Chief Inspector Solomakis received the news of the arrest of Ivan Kolmogorov and Ludmila Kuzmichov along with a deck hand with pleasure and complimented the coast guards from Limnos for their prompt and efficient action. He was not so pleased when he heard that they wanted to send the eight refugees on to Crete.

'I'm not prepared to accept them. They are able to claim refuge in the first safe country they reach so they will have to stay on Limnos. I'm sorry to add to your problems but we have a complicated case here regarding the Kuzmichovs and the six men who were brought into this country in August. I really do not want additional refugees arriving. Now we have all the traffickers in gaol I am going to ask the Court to fast track their trial. Once that has been settled we can agree between us how to proceed. In the meantime I have to ask you to look after the additional men. We will probably be calling on them for evidence at a second trial involving the boat owner and his deck hand.'

Mr Propenkov was not amused when Chief Inspector Solomakis telephoned him and gave him the news of the arrest of Ivor Kolmogorov and his sister, Ludmila.

'You may wish to visit them as I am planning to fast track a trial for all of them as people traffickers.'

'Naturally they will appeal.'

'I think they will be wasting their time. We have irrefutable proof. Not only do we have the men we arrested at the hotel, eight more refugees were found hiding on Kolmogorov's boat. He tried to out run the Greek coast guard and reach the safety of Turkish waters. Not exactly the action of an innocent man carrying legal passengers. The boat was searched at Limnos and Syrian passports were found along with a large quantity of American dollars.'

'There could be an innocent explanation,' protested Mr Propenkov.

'Then I would be interested to hear it. I think your countrymen could be looking at rather a long gaol sentence.'

'Should the charges be upheld against any one of them they might request that they serve a sentence in Russia.'

'I'd be quite happy for Russia to be responsible for them provided it was guaranteed that they would serve their time and not be released as soon as they arrived in the country.'

'That decision would have to be made by the Russian judiciary. I'll meet with Mrs Kuzmichov and her brother tomorrow and hear their version of events.'

'Fine, but I really cannot think what sort of defence they will be able to offer.'

Panayiotis was surprised when he received a call from Chief Inspector Solomakis thanking him for his assistance in the arrest of those aboard Kolmogorov's boat.

'I'm very pleased to hear that the operation was successful. May I relay the information to Mr Iliopolakis?'

'You may and I suggest you compile a written report of the information you passed to me. You could be called upon to give evidence.'

Dimitris's sister Antonia, arranged to meet Nicola when she collected the twin girls from nursery school and accompanied them up to the playground at Plaka.

'We have at least a month in which you can get to know them properly. If you can come and meet them with me every day we can then go back to the house and you can play with them for an hour or so and then one of us will drive you home. By the end of that time they should be quite happy to be left alone with you.'

'I'm not sure I could come every day. I have to think of Despina.'

'You can always bring her with you. The girls are just beginning to enjoy a simple board game and she could always join in or read a book. I can get a selection suitable for her age group from Monika.'

'I think I'll ask the mother of one of her friends if she can look after her for my first few visits.'

'You can both spend the night at the house when we go to the rehearsals and the performance,' Nicola assured her.

'Her father will be at home then, so I wouldn't need to bring her with me, but I would appreciate being able to stay when you are going to be late. You'll all be tired and I can't afford to have a taxi home.'

'You'll have to let me know how much you charge for baby sitting. After you have paid your bus fare into Elounda and then spent time with us I shall owe you for two hours for each daytime visit.'

Antonia looked at Nicola in surprise. She had not expected to be paid to visit and play with the children.

'How do I tell them apart?' she asked, looking from one to the other of the twin girls.

'It can be difficult,' agreed Nicola. 'They are supposed to wear name tags when they are at nursery, but they often swap them over. I'll embroider their initial on their pyjama tops, but I can't guarantee that they won't change with each other. By the time you arrive to look after them they should be asleep and then they are no problem at all. Even if they did wake up you can explain to them that we are out and will soon be back. They are sensible.'

'What about Yiannis?'

'He usually sleeps all night but if you really did have a

problem you could call me on my mobile and I would come home immediately. Uncle Andreas would just have to do without me, even if it was in the middle of the performance.'

Ronnie showed the A3 programme she had designed to Kyriakos.
'Do you think Uncle Andreas will approve?'
Kyriakos scrutinized it carefully. On the inside fold Ronnie had listed "girls/ladies" with their names beneath and below that Elena's name as the narrator. On the opposite page she had done the same entitling it "boys/men" and listing the participants' names with Andreas's name beneath.
'It looks perfect to me, but I think you ought to add Dimitris's name and give him credit for the lighting effects and also thanks to the Municipal Centre for allowing you to use their premises.'
'Now I am going to ask you for your help to write that information out in Greek for me.'
'What about the front cover?'
'I have no idea,' admitted Ronnie. 'I'll have to ask Uncle Andreas if he has a name for the performance. Provided he has decided on a title I can design a poster and the front cover of the programme could be the same.'
'And the back?'
'I thought I could leave that blank.'
Kyriakos nodded. 'You could always add small photographs of the participants with their names underneath.'
Ronnie shook her head. 'I don't think that's practical. There are thirteen people taking part, fifteen if you add in Elena and Uncle Andreas. The photos would have to be very small and it would look cramped. Elena and Uncle Andreas could have their photos and names on the back. I'll see what Uncle Andreas says.'

Panayiotis called on Vasilis as soon as he returned to Elounda when his duty at the police station ended. 'I thought you'd like to know that the information you gave me about Mrs Kuzmichov being in Plaka resulted in the coastguard detaining the boat and the occupants arrested.'

Vasilis smiled in delight. 'I'm pleased to know you were successful.'

'It was also due to an observant boatman. He saw the name on Kolmogorov's boat and also noticed that Mrs Kuzmichov had been sitting on the end of the old jetty for some considerable time. When a dinghy passed close by she had suddenly disappeared.'

'I wonder why her brother decided to pick her up from such a public place rather than the beach where he dropped off the refugees?'

'He probably thought we would be watching that area and with so many people visiting Spinalonga that she would not be noticed. He did not give credit to the Cretan people for their excellent memories for faces.'

'May I tell Saffie and Theo? I'll be seeing them this evening when we rehearse.'

'Rehearse?'

Vasilis nodded. 'We are arranging to give a performance next month at the Municipal Hall. It is to commemorate the bravery of the local people during the occupation.'

'Let me know the date and I'll arrange to have that evening off so I can attend. I'll spread the word to the other officers. I'm sure they will be interested. Many of them lost their grandparents during that terrible time. You only have to look at the names on the war memorials to see how many people from one family died.'

Andreas declared himself happy with the programme Ronnie had designed when she showed it to him.

'Kyriakos translated it into Greek for me. I couldn't possibly attempt that.'

Andreas smiled. He had spotted two spelling errors. 'There needs to be one addition at the bottom. It needs to say that people will be asked for a donation at the end of the performance and the money collected will be given to the hospital in Aghios Nikolaos.'

'I could put that on the back,' suggested Ronnie and Andreas shook his head.

'No, it has to be inside. Many people will not see it if you put it on the back. They won't turn the page over to look.'

'Have you decided on a title?' asked Ronnie.

Andreas nodded. 'I thought it could quite simply be called "Memories" and the dates that Crete was under occupation printed below. It would then indicate to the audience that it was going to contain memories from that era.'

Ronnie nodded agreement. 'That's a good idea. Do you want some illustrations on the front cover? I could add the Greek flag, soldiers, guns, things like that.'

'No, put the Greek flag on the back cover. Take up the whole area. Give me some ideas of small illustrations to go on the front and I'll decide which are the most appropriate.'

Andreas was pleased with the way the rehearsals were progressing. Marisa had become far more confident with her description of Aunt Anna's involvement and everyone had learnt their single lines and was saying them on cue.

'Let's concentrate a little more on the acting this evening when you say your lines. You're all sitting there like dummies at the moment. There needs to be feeling expressed and transmitted to the audience. Ladies, you are frightened, look around as if to see if anyone is coming near when you say your line and think about the content of it. Saffron shuddered the other day; it was involuntary at the time but that's the kind of reaction that needs to be kept in.'

Andreas consulted his notes.

'Another thing, ladies, when you are little girls singing the rhyme, clap your hands together without making a noise and giggle. You are children having fun, remember. Men, when you say you joined the resistance sit up straight and puff out your chests; you are proud of the part that you played. When you mention the sabotage you carried out remember you are little boys, pretend to whisper together and hold up the implement you used or bang the metal legs of the chairs with the stones as the line is finished. When you hear the ladies call "Kiri-kiri-coo" you duck down in your seats and hide your head.'

All but Marcus marked their script accordingly. 'I cannot be proud or boastful when I deliver my line. The ethnic cleansing that took place was one of the worst atrocities of the war.'

Andreas considered. 'Having said your line I suggest you place your head in your hands as though you are shedding tears. Does that sound reasonable?'

Marcus nodded. 'I could have a handkerchief with me and mop my eyes.'

'Yes, if you are comfortable with that add it in. Now, can we get on? Elena and I are only going to read the lines that give you cues so you'll need to concentrate.'

'Are we going to start with the song?' asked Marianne.

'No, I've changed my mind. I'll commence with my narration and then continue with the soldiers marching and the song can come in later. At the finale you can sing it again, but not as a round. That way all you ladies can sing and even some of the audience who remember it might join in.'

'We could ask them to do so.'

'Yes!' Ronnie exclaimed excitedly. 'The words can go on the back of the programme with the Greek flag underneath. What about that, Uncle Andreas?'

Andreas nodded. 'That's an excellent idea, but remove the flag and put a small version on the front cover above the title. I also think after two renditions of the children's song I ought to call a halt and speak to the audience, thanking them for attending. We should then sing the Greek National Anthem. We are proud to call ourselves Greek and that we resisted the occupying forces.'

'I'll see if I can fit the words of the song inside and put the Anthem on the back, although I'm sure most people know the words.'

Andreas smiled at her enthusiasm. 'Do you know there are one hundred and fifty eight stanzas? It is the longest hymn in the world. We'll have to content ourselves with just the first and second verse.'

Ronnie looked at him in amazement. 'I had no idea it was as long as that. First and second verses it will be and I'll have to ask Kyriakos to help me. I would hate to spell any words incorrectly; it would be insulting.'

'Show it to me when you have it typed out and I'll check it out for you. Now, everyone in place, please and we'll get on with the rehearsal.'

Mr Propenkov was shown into the interview room and Ludmila was escorted there to speak to him. She had been devastated when she had been imprisoned in the holding cell that she had occupied previously. In retrospect she should have been grateful to have been given bail and content to await the outcome of her husband's trial. Once she had been completely exonerated she would have had her passport returned and could have left Crete legally.

He looked at her coldly. 'So, Mrs Kuzmichov, I understand you were trying to leave Crete although you had no valid passport.'

'Certainly not,' replied Ludmila with as much indignation as she could muster. 'I was simply accompanying my brother on a sailing trip. If you check the facts you will see that we were apprehended in Greek waters. I have not violated any law.'

'Maybe not, but I would like you to explain why it was necessary for your brother to collect you from Spinalonga. If you just going sailing with him why didn't he put into the harbour and allow you to go aboard in the conventional manner?'

'He did not want to have to waste the time with the port authorities. It seemed quite simple for him to collect me from the island and continue with his journey.'

'Quite, but if he was in such a hurry to proceed why did he spend most of the day anchored off the coast at Plaka?'

Ludmila shrugged. 'I don't know. Maybe it depended upon the currents. You would have to ask him that question.'

'I intend to do so,' Mr Propenkov confirmed. 'When did you arrange to go on a sailing trip?'

'I'm not sure exactly. After I was released. Ivan thought a change of scenery and a chance to relax would be beneficial for me.'

'Very considerate of him. How did he make this arrangement with you? I understand you have not made any calls on your mobile and whenever the police have tried to contact Mr Kolmogorov they have been told the number is not in use.'

'I bought a cheap mobile and used a number he had given me years ago. He had said I should only use that if it was an emergency.'

'And you felt that arranging to leave Crete was an emergency?'

'Not at all.' Ludmila smiled and tried to appear at ease. 'I wanted to let him know the fate of my husband.'

'According to the Chief Inspector you made no arrangement to visit your husband once you had been released. I find that difficult to understand. I would have thought if you were sufficiently concerned about his welfare to contact your brother you would have wanted to ensure that your husband was in good health and being looked after in a fitting manner.'

'I had no reason to suspect otherwise. I could not complain about the treatment I received whilst in detention.'

'I hope you will find it as amenable on this occasion. I understand that you are going to be detained until such a time as the case against all three of you goes to Court. I am unable to ask for your release a second time due to lack of evidence against you.'

'But I am innocent,' declared Ludmila. 'You have to believe me. The reason I did not visit my husband was because I knew he would expect me to implicate my brother and Ivan was only acting under duress.'

'Really.' Mr Propenkov raised his eyebrows. 'I will be

interviewing Mr Kolmogorov tomorrow and I am sure it will be interesting to hear his version of events.'

Mr Propenkov read over the notes he had made. He did not believe any one of the trio was innocent of the charges that were probably going to be brought against them, but as they were Russian citizens he had to do his best for them. It could be to their advantage to serve time in a Greek gaol as he knew if they were released Russia would like to have them extradited. Kuzmichov's business activities were being thoroughly investigated and it appeared that all three were involved to a certain extent.

It would be interesting to find out where the eight Syrians had expected to be taken and he requested permission from Chief Inspector Solomakis to visit them now they had arrived from Limnos.

'I'll have to ask Orestes to go with you. I expect they will all speak English and he will be able to translate their statements into Greek for you.' Solomakis sighed. 'If we are going to have more Syrian refugees arriving here I'll need some more officers who are proficient in English.'

'I'm hoping that once this affair has been brought to a conclusion you'll not be troubled with more arriving. There are other islands closer to Syria than Crete, or even a short boat trip from Greece into Turkey would be more practical.'

The men, having recovered from their sea sickness and fear were willing to talk. They felt resentful that their lives had been put at risk.

'We were assured that the journey was perfectly safe at this time of year.'

'I don't think your lives were in actual danger at any time, although I do agree that sea sickness is most unpleasant. The owner of the boat is a proficient sailor and knew the procedure for riding out a storm. On another occasion the passengers might not be so fortunate.'

'We were all most relieved when he was stopped and we were

taken aboard the other boat. At least we were treated humanely there. He had left us down in the cabin to wallow in our own vomit.'

'Where exactly was he planning to take you?'

'We were bound for a place called Enez on the coast of Turkey. He said that there was a town close by and we would be able to find transport to take us over land to the border. From there it would be a simple matter of bribing a lorry driver to take us across Europe to France or Spain.'

'And you believed him?'

'When you are desperate to arrive in a safe country you believe all you are told. We had money with us and our mobile 'phones. He said he would return our belongings when we reached Enez.'

'Unfortunately your 'phones would have been very little use to you as he had removed the chip. How much money he planned to return to you I do not know, but it is unlikely that it would have been sufficient for you to bribe any driver to take you very far. Even had you managed to reach one of the neighbouring countries you would have been detained as you need a valid passport to pass through.'

'What is going to happen to us?' asked the Syrian apprehensively.

'You will be kept here in custody and may well be called upon to give evidence when the owner of the boat comes to trial. It is an offence to smuggle people out of their own country and into any other. The best advice I can give you is for you to contact any of your friends who are contemplating making the same journey and telling them that it would be most unwise for them to attempt such an undertaking. You can relate your own distressing experience to them.'

'How can we do that when you say our mobiles do not work?'

'I am sure a small amount of the money that was found on the boat could be used to purchase either a new chip or cheap mobile for you. You should ask anyone that you are able to contact to pass the message on to their friends and acquaintances.'

Mr Propenkov telephoned Chief Inspector Solomakis. 'We have finished talking to the refugees and Orestes was most helpful. He will now return to your office and type up their statements. With your permission I would like to interview the deck hand this afternoon. His name is Panos Colonakis, I believe. Do you wish to be present?'

Solomakis sighed. 'The interview should be recorded so I'll need to be there.'

Mr Propenkov ate a leisurely lunch before returning to the police station and waited in the interview room for Panos to be brought to him and the recording system set up.

Panos denied all knowledge of the smuggling operation. 'I was employed as a deck hand. I was not privy to any other business with Mr Kolmogorov.'

Propenkov raised his eyebrows. 'You must have been aware that there were passengers aboard?'

'Of course, but I was given to understand that their presence was nothing to do with me. I was just to obey Mr Kolmogorov's instructions.'

'And what exactly were those instructions?'

'I was told to take the men ashore when we reached their destination.'

'We know that you took men through the canal at Elounda and landed them on a small beach on no less than thirteen occasions. You must have been aware that you were acting illegally.'

Panos shrugged. 'I had no choice. I considered staying with the men and not returning to the boat, but that was not practical.'

'Why was that?'

'Mr Kolmogorov had possession of my passport.'

Chief Inspector Solomakis shook his head. 'I do not believe you, Mr Colonakis. When you were taken on board the coastguard cutter you produced your passport. It was not locked away in the safe with the passports belonging to the refugees. I believe you were as much a part of this people smuggling operation as the

Kuzmichovs and Mr Kolmogorov. How much were you paid for your assistance? You might as well tell us, Mr Colonakis, as I am sure Mr Kolmogorov will implicate you as he tries to extricate himself.'

'One thousand dollars,' muttered Panos.

'Was that for each trip or for each man?'

'For each man.'

'Quite a considerable sum for a journey that took no more than ten days. That amount must have made you quite a rich man. If my calculations are correct you have accumulated seventy eight thousand dollars.'

With the various other supplies of drugs and small arms that he had helped Ivan to deliver he had considerably more than that amount hidden away and he hoped their other journeys would not be investigated. He was already looking at a lengthy prison sentence for helping to transport the refugees; he did not want his other activities scrutinized and the extent of his involvement with Ivan Kolmogorov brought to their attention.

'How long have you been in Mr Kolmogorov's employ?' asked Chief Inspector Solomakis.

Panos shrugged. 'I don't remember.'

Solomakis looked at him sceptically. 'Maybe if you thought about it for a while you would be able to recall the amount of time. You are going to be kept under arrest and charged with aiding and abetting the arrival of illegal refugees. I am planning to fast track a Court hearing and you will be called upon to give evidence against your employer. We have recorded this interview so I suggest that you do not try to deviate from the details you have given us.'

October 2015
Week Two – Wednesday & Thursday

Ivan Kolmogorov sat uncomfortably in the interview room with Chief Superintendent Solomakis and Mr Propenkov. The Russian Consulate representative had given permission for the interview to be recorded and the Inspector went through the formalities.

Solomakis asked first about the removal of Ludmila Kuzmichov from Spinalonga. 'Why did you sail to the island and collect your sister in such a fashion? Were you abducting her?'

'Certainly not. She had asked me to rescue her from an impossible situation. Although she had been allowed to return to live at her apartment the allowance she had been given barely covered her food. Evgeniy had always controlled their finances and she had no money of her own. He paid for everything and without him to control her every move she felt very alone and insecure.'

'So where were you planning to take the lady?'

Ivan shrugged. 'I thought she would be happier living on board my boat and sailing around. I could look after her financially.'

'Yet you sailed into the teeth of a storm after refuelling at Lesbos.'

'That arrived more quickly than I had been led to believe by the forecast. Had I realised the severity I would have stayed in the port until it had blown through.'

'How would you have explained away the presence of your passengers to the port authorities?'

Ivan spread his hands. 'I had shown my maritime papers to the port commander and paid for my fuel. He had no reason to come aboard and ask to see the identity of anyone else. It would have been different if they had wanted to go ashore.'

'So you travelled from Lesbos to Limnos – where were you planning to go after that?'

'A refuelling stop at Alexandroupolis and then return via Limnos, Lesbos and Khios before going over to the Cyclades. I would then return my sister to Crete.'

'Quite an extensive trip. The men who were with you, were they also going to accompany you on the return voyage?'

'Of course. They would then disembark when we reached Syria.'

'Mr Kolmogorov I do not believe you. When your boat was searched a large quantity of American dollars were found in the safe, along with mobile 'phones and Syrian passports.'

'Of course.' answered Ivan easily. 'The men had asked me to place their possessions there for safe keeping.'

'They claim that over half their money was to be paid to you to cover the cost of their trip. You were planning to take them to Turkey where they would be able to continue on over land. It was noted by the port authorities that the mobile 'phones had had their chips removed. Once these men had been placed ashore they would have had no way to contact anyone for help.'

Ivan sat there mutinously. He should have realised that the men would have been interrogated and told the police of the arrangements that had been agreed. No doubt Panos had also implicated him in the operation. Had he not agreed to collect Ludmila from Spinalonga the coast guard would not be trying to apprehend them. Her movements must have been under surveillance.

Helena and Greg arrived in Crete the early afternoon and Helena called her sister.

'Hello, Marianne. We have just arrived and Greg is collecting the car we have hired. We'll stop off for something to eat and should be in Elounda by about four. Obviously we'll go to Vasi's hotel and drop off our luggage and then come along to visit you.'

Marianne sighed, anticipating a difficult few days. 'We'll look forward to seeing you and you'll join us for a meal this evening, of course. We'd like to hear all about your travels.'

'That will give us time to unpack and freshen up. I expect we'll be with you by about seven.'

Marianne wondered just how much luggage Helena and Greg had with them if it was going to take them that amount of time to unpack and shower. She pressed in the numbers for Vasi's mobile. He needed to be aware that they planned to arrive that afternoon and ensure that the room they had requested was prepared immaculately for them. She was immensely relieved that her sister and husband were not going to be staying with them.

Vasi called the housemaid to him who was responsible for the first floor rooms. 'I know your work is always excellent, but I have a very difficult lady coming to stay. Please ensure that there is not a speck of dust anywhere, don't forget to check beneath the bed and in the wardrobes. I would also like you to sweep the balcony and make sure the tables and chairs out there are clean. The shower must also be spotless and well stocked with toiletries.'

The maid nodded. She was scrupulous when she cleaned those particular rooms as they were always let out to the most important guests who usually returned each year and Mr Vasi would not be pleased if he ever received a complaint.

Marianne called Giovanni and informed him that they would have Helena and Greg coming for a meal that evening.

'Am I expected to fetch them?' he asked.

'Helena said Greg was collecting a hire car and they were driving down so there is no reason for you to have to act as their chauffeur.'

'Will I be expected to dress up?'

297

Marianne laughed. 'There's no reason to be formal. I expect Greg will just be in slacks and a shirt, although Helena will probably arrive wearing an evening dress. I'll let everyone else know they are coming so they can be on their best behaviour.'

Elena heard Marianne's news with trepidation. 'You won't let Helena take me back to New Orleans when they leave, will you?'

'Certainly not,' Marianne assured her mother. 'You have a commitment here with Uncle Andreas and cannot let him down. I suppose I should call him and invite him to come this evening. If they are interested he can tell them about the proposed performance.'

Andreas refused Marianne's invitation. 'I have arranged to meet Dimitris at the Municipal Hall this evening. I need to discuss with him exactly how the lighting will be arranged. He's been to Aghios and hired some spotlights ready for the week. We need to decide on their positioning so we do not waste time dealing with that when we go there to rehearse. I'll see you tomorrow evening and I may be able to meet Helena and Greg another day.'

Marianne had forgotten that they were due to rehearse the following evening and she must remember to tell her sister that they were not available to join them for a meal should they be invited.

Helena swept into Vasi's hotel leaving Greg to unload their luggage from the car and take it into reception. She put her finger on the call button for the lift and when it arrived she held it open until her husband had placed all the cases inside.

'You'll have to go up and take them out. Send the lift back down for me.'

'Have you registered and been given the key?'

'I always leave you to do that.'

'Then I'd better get that over and done with before I take the luggage up. I ought to take it out of the lift. Someone else may need to use it.'

'Rubbish,' stated Helena imperiously. 'They'll have to wait their turn. I'll hold it here until you return.'

Greg waited until the receptionist finished her call with a customer and asked to be booked in.

'I have to ask you to complete this form with your passport details, please.'

Greg returned to where his wife was waiting. 'Can you give me our passports, please. I need to fill in their details on a registration form.'

'How ridiculous. We should be known here.' Helena took her finger off the call button and delved into her handbag. The lift door promptly closed and the lift began its slow ascent. 'Now look what's happened!' exclaimed Helena.

Greg returned to the reception desk, feeling guilty that he had not emptied the lift of their belongings. No one would be able to use it until he had unloaded them.

Helena continued to press the call button impatiently and finally the lift returned to the ground floor with a man and woman inside, one with crutches and the other using a stick.

'Where is our luggage?' asked Helena.

'Oh, does that all belong to you? We asked the maid to remove it into the hallway as we needed to use the lift. My husband cannot manage the stairs with his crutches.'

'Which floor are you on?' asked Greg.

'The second. We were told that our usual room on the first floor was unavailable for our visit this time.'

Helen held the lift door a second time. 'Go up there and retrieve it before it is stolen,' she ordered her husband. 'Send the lift back down for me when you have taken it to our room.' She gave the couple a venomous look. 'Some people are so inconsiderate.'

The woman retorted immediately. 'Not as inconsiderate as people who hold the lift so others who need it are kept waiting.'

'I am sorry,' apologised Greg. 'It took us longer to register than I had anticipated. Why don't we both go up to our room,

Helena? I can then go up to the next floor and collect our cases.'
He almost pushed his wife into the lift.

Helena looked around the lounge critically. She wished theirs was as large. If she had a house the size of Yannis's her acquaintances would consider her very rich and in her eyes appearance was everything. She greeted her mother with a show of affection and said how much she had missed her.

'Really?' said Elena. 'I was under the impression that I was rather a nuisance to you.'

'Certainly not. You are never a nuisance, you just give me cause for concern insisting that you live alone in that big house.'

'I'm quite capable of looking after myself. I know I can call on you if I have a problem.'

Marianne rescued her mother by going over and placing her arm around Helena's shoulders. 'It's so good to see you. I thought we'd have some drinks out on the patio and eat in here later.'

'Greg must not have too much. He's driving.'

'Of course, and I expect both of you are tired after all your travelling so we won't expect you to stay late.'

Giovanni had to turn away to stifle his laughter. Marianne had very adeptly told her sister and brother in law that they were not welcome to stay until the early hours of the morning.

Nicola and John had settled Yiannis down for the night but allowed the girls to stay up a little later to greet their American visitors.

'Aunt Helena is Grandma's sister so she is your great aunt.' he informed them. 'She has come a long way to see you, so I am relying on you both for best behaviour.'

Both girls nodded solemnly and accompanied their parents out to the patio.

'Ready for bed, I see,' observed Helena. 'Very sensible. Children are really not welcome at an adult's gathering.'

'Come and say hello to me properly,' said Greg and held out his arms.

The girls approached him shyly and he looked them up and down before shaking his head. 'You'll have to tell me which one of you is which. You are so alike.'

'I'm Jo. She's Lisa.'

'Well, I'm very pleased to meet both of you. You were babies the last time I saw you.'

'Yiannis is the baby now. He's in bed.'

'I hope I can meet him another time.'

'We go to school now,' Joanna advised him.

'Really? Then that must mean you are both very grown up. Go and say hello to Aunty Helena. She's been waiting to meet you all day.'

Helena ignored them and continued to talk to Bryony until Joanna touched her dress.

'Please do not put your sticky fingers on me,' she said swiftly and moved away. 'This dress was very expensive.'

Joanna looked at her hands. 'They're not sticky,' she replied indignantly. 'I've had a bath.'

'Uncle Greg said we were to come and say hello to you.'

Helena looked at them with a ghost of a smile on her lips. 'You can say hello without touching me. I see you are wearing your pyjamas. Are you off to bed soon?'

Jo put her head on one side. 'Pappa says you are our great aunt. That must mean that you are old like Uncle Yannis. You don't look as old as him.'

'I should hope not,' answered Helena. 'I am no older than your grandmother.'

Both girls turned and looked at Marianne.

'You look older than Grandma,' observed Lisa. 'Is that because of the stuff you have on your face?'

Helena stiffened visibly. She had spent over an hour applying her make-up and was sure Marianne would not have bothered to apply as much as lipstick. 'I think it is time your mother took you both off to bed and left the grown ups to talk sensibly together. Nicola, it must be their bed time.'

Nicola suppressed a smile. 'Of course.' Nicola looked at her watch. 'Goodness, girls, do you see what the time is?' She knew that neither girl could tell the time. 'It's very late and you have to be up in time for school tomorrow. I'll say goodnight to everybody for you.'

Obediently the girls took Nicola's hands as she led them from the room, but Lisa could be heard singing *"He's a fat faced fool"* and then Joanne interrupted loudly, 'No, <u>she</u> is, and she smells.'

Marianne looked at John and they both began to laugh.

'What's the joke?' asked Giovanni and Marianne whispered in his ear. A broad smile spread across his face. 'A very perceptive little girl. Maybe we should ask Andreas to include them in the performance.'

Marianne shook her head. 'It isn't really a suitable song for children. I hope Helena did not hear.'

'Actually.' added John, 'I hope she did.'

Helena helped herself sparingly to the food that Marianne and Bryony had prepared. 'I have to be conscious off my figure. I don't want to end up with middle age spread.'

Marianne shrugged. 'There's no point in worrying about it. Provided you eat sensibly and keep active you're unlikely to put the weight on.'

Helena looked pointedly at Bryony who could no longer be described as plump. However hard she had tried over the years she always seemed to increase her weight, but that could have been due to her liking for baklava.

'I really needed to speak to mother,' said Helena. 'We need to decide on a return date for her.'

Marianne shook her head. 'I've told you, Mamma is not returning to New Orleans with you.'

'I'll come up tomorrow when there are fewer people around and talk to her then. I'm sure she will change her mind once I have spent some time with her.'

'You're welcome to come during the morning and have coffee.'

'The afternoon will be preferable. I have made an appointment for a massage during the morning.'

Marianne shook her head. 'I'm sorry, that's not convenient. We'll have to make it Friday morning.' She was not prepared to have her mother stressed just before a rehearsal.

Andreas felt satisfied after he had visited the Municipal Hall with Dimitris. He had discussed the seating arrangements with the manager and it had been agreed that the two spotlights that Dimitris would hire would be placed at the back of the hall. Their electrical leads would need to be taped down safely onto the floor and the audience would be warned to step over them when they arrived.

Dimitris arranged and rearranged the chairs under Andreas's direction until Andreas was satisfied that those taking part would be seen by the audience wherever they were seated. On each side behind the chairs there was to be a table with a standard lamp that he and Elena could switch on to illuminate their script when the spotlights were not being used.

'The sooner we can come here to rehearse the better. Elena will have to remember her cue to switch on her light and the others will have to get used to having a spotlight on them.'

'I've been thinking about that,' said Dimitris. 'It could be difficult for you both fumbling for the switch in the dark. Would it not be more practical if you each had a torch? It could be left on permanently and when not in use stood on the table so that the beam is not visible. When it is needed you would only have to pick it up.'

Andreas considered Dimitris's suggestion. 'That could be a very sensible solution.'

'Why don't you try rehearsing in darkness a few times? I could stand by a light switch and put lights on when you want. You and Mrs Pirenzi could have a torch and become used to picking it up when you have to read.'

303

Andreas nodded. 'I'll speak to Giovanni and see how we get on with that arrangement tomorrow. Can you buy two torches? I expect there are some at the house but we don't want to have to waste time searching for them and then find they need new batteries.'

Vasilis was pleased at the way his building was progressing. He had visited the builders' merchants with Christos Palamakis and under his guidance had ordered the quantity of bricks and breeze blocks that were going to be needed for the walls. Now they had been delivered to the site they looked a vast number and he hoped he had not inadvertently doubled up on the number required.

'The cement mixer is due to arrive tomorrow morning and then the men will be able to commence work properly,' Mr Palamakis assured him.

'What about the visit from the structural engineer?'

'Let me worry about that. I'll know when he needs to check the construction for safety. It won't be until after the enclosing walls are completed to the height where they will receive the concrete base. The back wall of the house will have had the strengthening rods inserted by then and he will be more interested in checking those than garden walls at that time.'

'What happens if he is dissatisfied and says the walls are not safe?'

'In that unlikely event he has to give us a written reason for his objection and how he wants the work remedied to meet with his safety requirements. Don't worry, Mr Iliopolakis. Provided the weather holds you'll have the skeleton of a building by the end of November.'

'Talking of skeletons, what happens should some more bones be unearthed when the men are digging footings?'

Mr Palamakis looked across at the neighbouring land where the archaeologists were hard at work exposing the graves and carefully lifting the bones.

'I'm sure that any bone that should be found will belong to an animal and there will be no need to report it. I'll have a word with the brickies and tell them to ignore anything further that comes to light.'

'Is that legal?'

Palamakis shrugged and indicated the workers on the spare plot with his thumb. 'They have more than enough to do currently. If you start saying that more bones have been found on your land you're likely to have to wait until they have finished next door before they return to you. That would mean your building had to come to a halt for a considerable amount of time. Better to keep quiet about it.'

'Suppose they were found at a later date?'

'Once your footings are complete and the concrete laid the only way anything beneath would be found would be if it was dismantled. You say the archaeologists went all over your land with their GPR so I don't think you have anything at all to worry about. How are your rehearsals going?' asked Palamakis to move the discussion away from how any skeletons would be dealt with should they be found. 'According to Barbara Yiorgos never stops talking about it.'

'I hope you'll all come to see it in November.'

'We'll definitely be there. Do we have to buy tickets?'

'No, Uncle Andreas is going to ask for donations at the end and the money will be given to the hospital. It might be a good idea if you let me know how many of you will be attending and I can ask for seats to be reserved for you.'

Andreas arrived early for the rehearsal and Marianne looked at her watch. 'Is it that late?'

Andreas shook his head. 'No, I want to speak to Giovanni about the lighting this evening. Dimitris is coming up and we are going to try to run through in darkness and put the lights on when appropriate.'

'You and Mamma won't be able to read your words.'

'Dimitris is bringing two torches with him and we are going to see how successful that is for Elena and myself. How are Helena and Greg?'

'They both appeared well. Helena wanted to come up this afternoon to try to talk Mamma into going back to New Orleans with them when they leave, but I told her she would have to come tomorrow.' Marianne placed a glass of wine at his elbow.

Andreas looked at Marianne in alarm. 'She isn't planning to go before we have had the performance?'

Marianne shook her head. 'Mamma won't hear of going back with them. She is as enthusiastic about the production as you are. I didn't want arguments and Helena upsetting Mamma just before a rehearsal.'

Andreas gave a sigh of relief. 'It would ruin everything at this late stage if she was not able to be the narrator for the women. When I've spoken to Giovanni I'm going to call Ronnie and ask if she has a draft programme ready to bring with her. Kyriakos has helped her, but his spelling is not perfect.'

'I doubt if anyone in the audience will notice a spelling mistake. The Greeks seem to spell words as they fancy. You only have to look at some of the shop signs and names of the towns. It isn't important to them.'

'I also want her to make some additions. I think Marisa should be credited for being Aunt Anna, along with Yiorgos as being Manolis. Yannis can be named as himself. I'm hoping there will also be space for the song so that the Hymn to Liberty can be on the back with another picture of the Greek flag.' Andreas frowned. 'I'll have to speak to John and ask if he can print the Greek flag in colour.'

'Decide on the final layout of the programme and then ask him to run off a copy. If you're satisfied you'll have to tell him how many you want.'

'Dimitris and I calculated the chairs for the audience when we were at the hall. There's sufficient space for at least two hundred. We thought we'd arrange a hundred. More chairs can be added if necessary at the last minute, but it's better to have them all filled and not a lot of empty spaces.'

'I'm sure once word gets round you'll find you have a full house.'

'When the posters have been printed I'll take some up to Kato and Pano and show them to the people. I thought Elena could come with me and talk to the women. I know she'd like Evi and Maria to come.'

'I'm sure she'll be willing. You ought to ask Litsa if she can ask the baker to display one in his window.'

'I thought we'd stick them up on the outside of the windows or doors of the shops that will have closed down by then. They'll be no inconvenience to anyone and people will stop to read them.'

Giovanni had no objection to a rehearsal being held with Dimitris in charge of the main lighting. Ronnie produced the programme she had worked on and hoped Andreas would approve.

'I want some additions,' he declared and Ronnie's face fell. She hoped she was not going to be asked to design something new.

'Beneath the names of the women and girls I want you to add "Marisa Pirenzi speaking for Anna Christoforakis. Beneath the men and boys I want "Yannis Christoforakis relating his own experiences" and then "Yiorgos Palamakis acting as Manolis the boatman".'

'That should be no problem,' agreed Ronnie.

'I also want the words of the song on the centre fold. Two verses on each side. That will leave the whole of the back cover with sufficient space for the first two verses of the Liberty Hymn with the Greek flag above.'

'I have to fit in Dimitris as being in charge of the lighting and also thanks to the council for allowing the use of the Municipal Hall in that centre fold.'

'I'm sure you'll manage it. Just adjust the spacing a little if necessary. I've checked the spelling that I asked you to correct and I'll check the words to our anthem before I finally agree to the printing. How is the poster coming on?'

Ronnie unrolled the A4 sheet and showed it to Andreas.

'I think it needs to be larger. People will hardly see this'

The title with the years beneath was in bold type. Above it Ronnie had drawn in the Greek flag and coloured it. Down the side of the page were illustrations of a cockerel, jeep, motor cycle, guns, soldiers and civilian men and women.

'We also need the date of the performance and the location. At the bottom it needs to say that entrance is free and donations are going to the hospital.'

'That's no problem. I just need to know the date you have finally arranged. I'll do some re-jigging of the programme and buy a piece of poster size paper. I can then scale everything up and add the date. Beneath the venue I'll say that entrance is free. I should be able to complete it over the weekend and bring it with me on Monday.'

October 2015
Weeks Two & Three – Friday & Monday

Helena arrived at Marianne's in a thoroughly bad humour. 'There is a most objectionable woman at the hotel. Whenever she sees us she makes a derogatory remark about us that we can hear and I'm sure she hit my leg deliberately with her stick this morning.'

'I'm sure she didn't mean to hit you. She probably didn't realise that she had done so,' said Marianne placatingly.

'I'm going to get Greg to speak to Vasi this afternoon and ask if they can be made to leave.'

'That is a bit extreme. They haven't actually committed any crime so he has no reason to ask them to go elsewhere.'

'I am not prepared to have rude remarks made about me. Who does she think she is?'

'Whatever she said may not have been directed at you.'

'Oh, it was. They had to wait for the lift on Wednesday whilst we took our luggage up. This morning she said, very loudly, "I do hope those people do not hold the lift for their convenience again. They have no consideration for others who need to use it." She looked directly at me as she said it. Well, they won't be able to use it for a while this morning. I've made sure of that.'

'What have you done?' asked Marianne fearfully.

'I've pushed cotton wool all around the buttons and then painted them all over with nail varnish, except for the first floor.'

'I hope you haven't actually damaged the mechanism.'

'It's only nail varnish and cotton wool. Unfortunately I didn't have any super glue.'

Marianne turned away and poured their coffee. She would have to call Vasi and make him aware that there could be a problem with the lift. She sighed, Helena could be so vindictive on occasions. He would be within his rights to ask her and Greg to leave his hotel.

'Add to that the fact that there is building work going on virtually next door means there is continual noise. There is a cement mixer working from early in the morning. It should not be allowed.'

Marianne thought it more tactful not to mention that it was Vasilis's land where the work was taking place.

'The building workers always start early before it becomes too hot. I don't think there is anything you can do to prevent them from working.'

Bryony walked out onto the patio singing quietly to herself and Marianne smiled. 'You sound word perfect.'

'I hope I am. I've had Marcus sing it with me so that I know when to join in. It's more difficult than I realised. I don't know how the girls managed it.'

'They probably made all sorts of mistakes and don't remember now.'

'I'll ask your mother if she can ask them when she visits them next.'

'Talking of our mother,' interrupted Helena, 'She is the reason I have come along this morning. Where is she? I had to change my hair appointment to this afternoon as you said it was not convenient for me to come along yesterday.'

Marianne looked at her sister's immaculate hair and wondered why she needed to go to a hairdresser. She pushed a stray strand of her own that had come loose from the band that held hers back in a pony tail.

'She could be in her room or with Uncle Yannis or Grandma Marisa. I'll find her and tell her you're here.' As Marianne left the kitchen she began to sing the song starting at the beginning as Bryony finished and she heard Bryony giggling.

'I can't come at the moment,' said Elena when Marianne found her mother sitting with Marisa. 'Marisa is going through her speech as Mamma Anna and has asked me to listen and tell her if she misses anything out.'

Marianne nodded. 'Come along when you're finished. I'll explain to Helena.'

'What do you mean, she's rehearsing with Marisa? Rehearsing what?'

'Uncle Andreas and mother have planned to put on a production commemorating the events during the occupation. Grandma Marisa is going to talk as if she was Aunt Anna and tell of her exploits with the Resistance. Uncle Andreas has planned it out really well. He is going to be the main narrator starting with the invasion and describing how the troops went into the villages and terrorised the inhabitants. The men will then say how they tried to sabotage the soldiers' army vehicles by puncturing their petrol tanks or the tyres and the women will describe some of the events that were suffered by the female villagers. Mother is going to be the narrator for the women's stories.'

'You sound quite enthusiastic.'

'I am. We're all taking part. Marcus is going to mention the persecution of the Jewish community.'

Helena raised her eyebrows. 'So if you are all in it what are Uncle Yannis and Giovanni doing?'

'Uncle Yannis is going to relate how he took a group of German soldiers up into the mountains giving some Resistance workers time to escape from Plaka. Giovanni is just going to be one of the boys and men. He was asked to play the part of Manolis and describe how the boatman took Resistance workers to different locations and ended up fighting with them, but Giovanni said it was more fitting if Yiorgos Palamakis took that part as he has Manolis's boat.'

'I'm surprised anyone remembers those days now.'

'On the contrary, Oxi Day is very important to all of us. This year the girls will be taking part in the parade for a short while as they are at nursery school. Cathy is very proud of the part that her father played in the Resistance.'

'Really?'

Marianne nodded. 'Vasilis is also very proud of his father in law. If you and Greg are planning to leave next week I suggest you come along to one of the rehearsals.'

'Maybe.'

Marianne smiled. She doubted very much that her sister would attend a rehearsal. 'What do you and Greg have planned for tomorrow?'

'Not much. There isn't very much to do here. There aren't any decent shops so we'll probably go to Aghios Nikolaos.'

'The shops here are mainly for the tourists. Of course, if you and Greg took off in the car and travelled the side roads you'd end up in some very old villages that have an interesting history. You'd be given a warm welcome at the local taverna and traditional Cretan food.'

'I'll see what Greg says.'

Marianne knew very well that Greg would do whatever his wife wanted and that would probably mean driving down to the coast road and stopping for a drink before driving on to Aghios Nikolaos for lunch and Helena would then spend the remainder of the afternoon wandering around the shops.

Elena appeared and sat down wearily in a chair. 'Good morning, Helena.'

'Coffee, Mamma?' asked Marianne.

'Yes please. I've heard Marisa go through her lines three times and I'm exhausted. You have to listen so carefully to make sure she isn't repeating herself and is relating events in the correct order.'

'Forget that, Mamma said Helena irritably. 'It isn't important. I've come over specially this morning to collect your passport and arrange for you to travel back to New Orleans with us next week.'

'Then you've had a wasted journey. I have no intention of returning with you.'

'Don't be silly. Just give me your passport and you'll have nothing to worry about.'

'You are not having my passport and I am not returning to New Orleans until it suits me to do so.'

'You have to think of us, Mamma. We have put ourselves out to come over here to collect you.'

'No one asked you to come. I am not a child or an imbecile to have to be "collected" like a parcel. I am involved with Andreas in this production and if his publishers accept it as a play I may well go to New York with him and become involved in the production there.'

Marianne hid a smile. She had never heard her mother speaking so forcefully.

Helena stood up. 'There's obviously no way I can talk sense into you so there's little point in me staying. Where's Greg? Can you find him, Marianne, and say I'm ready to go home.'

'I believe he's in the office with Dad,' said John who had been standing quietly on the edge of the patio listening to the exchange between his aunt and grandmother. 'I'll get him.'

Helena bade her mother a frosty goodbye and did not look back as Greg drove away.

Marianne hugged her mother. 'Well done. I'm really proud of the way you stood up to Helena.'

'If the Cretan people stood up to the Germans and Italians I should be able to stand up for myself against Helena,' said Elena with a satisfied smile.

'I'm really proud of you too, Grandma,' smiled John. 'You have the Cretan spirit.'

'I have to thank Andreas. Going up to the villages and hearing from the women all they endured made me realise what a coward I was to allow Helena to dictate to me.'

'Do you really plan to go to New York with Uncle Andreas?' asked John.

Elena smiled. 'I doubt very much that he'll need me around. The idea just came to me on the spur of the moment as an additional excuse to give to Helena.'

Greg telephoned Marianne whilst Helena was at the hairdressers.

'I'm not sure what your mother said to Helena, but she was furious when I took her back to the hotel. It took me well over an hour to calm her down.'

'I'm sorry you ended up with a problem. Helena wanted to take our mother back to New Orleans with you next week and mother refused to contemplate the idea. She's so involved with Andreas and the performance and really enjoying herself.'

'Giovanni was telling me about that. I wish we were going to be here to watch.'

'I invited Helena to come to a rehearsal. There are still some wrinkles to be ironed out, but Mamma and Uncle Andreas are working on it constantly and I'm sure that it will be perfect eventually. Maybe you could persuade her to come on Monday evening and that way you'd be able to see it for yourself.'

'If she is in a better temper when she returns from the hairdresser I'll see what I can do. I don't want to go back to New Orleans without some sort of reconciliation between Helena and her mother.'

Vasilis sat and examined the accounts that Dimitra had sent through to him and then telephoned the bank and authorised their payment.

'There is a problem, Mr Iliopolakis,' said the bank manager. 'The compensation money to the travel companies for the cancellation of bookings in August is still outstanding. I have received two letters threatening legal action unless the money owed is paid to them within the next thirty days. I cannot take the sum from Mr Kuzmichov's account as that is frozen.'

Vasilis frowned. 'It cannot come from the hotel accounts. I

am only authorised to pay the bills for the hotel. I'll have to try to speak to the man from the Russian Consulate and see if he can help. Can you e-mail the letters from the companies over to me? If he agrees to approach Evgeniy Kuzmichov to authorise the payment from his account he'll need proof and the amount that is necessary.'

'Certainly,' the manager sounded relieved. 'I will leave it in your hands, Mr Iliopolakis.'

Vasilis read the letters the bank manager had sent to him and frowned. He was certain that the travel companies were demanding far more money than they were entitled to, but he was not prepared to become involved in a legal argument. He would accept the amount at its face value and hope that it would be paid from the Russian's bank account without question.

Vasilis telephoned the Russian Consulate and waited impatiently to be put through to Mr Propenkov.

'This is Mr Iliopolakis speaking. I am the administrator for the "Central Hotel" accounts.'

'Yes, is there a problem?'

'I have had a conversation with the hotel manager and he has e-mailed me the letters he has received from the travel companies that are requesting compensation for lost bookings. They are demanding payment within thirty days. I am not prepared to sanction this withdrawal from the hotel accounts. I think it should come from Mr Kuzmichov's own bank account. It was due to his actions that the situation arose.'

'Yes, I understand, Mr Iliopolakis, but it may be necessary to get a Court action to allow access to Mr Kuzmichov's account.'

'Surely it can be done as an agreement by him the way it was arranged for me to be the administrator?'

'There needs to be a third party involved who will take responsibility for the payment.'

Vasilis sighed. 'So what can be done?'

'The easiest solution would be for you to have the money

transferred through to yourself, with Mr Kuzmichov's agreement, of course.'

'Me? I don't want his money transferred through to my account. The transaction could be open to question and my accountant would certainly not be happy.'

'I'm sure you would be able to explain to your accountant.'

'I'm not prepared to do so. I have some extremely large bills coming in at the moment where I am in the midst of constructing a new apartment. It could be thought that I was using the money from Kuzmichov for myself.'

'I'm sure no one would doubt your word, Mr Iliopolakis. Why don't you speak with your bank manager and open a separate account? The money could be transferred there and the outstanding amounts paid. Once the debts are cleared you could close the account.'

'That will mean I have to visit Heraklion and to open a new account in my name will take at least a week.'

'I'm sorry, Mr Iliopolakis. That is the best I can do for you. I'll apprise Mr Kuzmichov of the situation and ask him to agree to the transfer once the new account has been opened. Let me know when it will be operational.'

Vasilis ended the conversation feeling dissatisfied. He would now have to explain to his bank manager why he needed to open a separate account. He must also contact Giorgos and find out if money was owed to any other travel companies and if so ask them to produce their claims immediately. Provided the bank manager was agreeable to the arrangement he would then have to compose letters assuring the travel companies that the money would be paid to them within the thirty day limit to prevent them from taking Court action.

Cathy found him sitting at his desk with his head in his hands. 'What's wrong? They haven't found any more bodies on your land, have they?'

'That really would be all I needed to make my day complete!

Giorgos has sent me through threatening letters from two travel companies.'

'But that isn't your problem. It was agreed that they would be paid by Kuzmichov.'

'His account is frozen so the bank cannot touch it. I've spoken to Mr Propenkov and he has suggested that I open a second account and have the money transferred there so I can pay them. This depends upon Kuzmichov agreeing.'

'And if he refuses?'

Vasilis shrugged. 'I'd have to pay it myself and hope to reclaim the money later.'

Cathy shook her head. 'There is no way you should do that. Kuzmichov is a crook and he would never repay you.'

'I'll have to 'phone the bank again and hope the manager hasn't left for the day. It means I'll have to go up to Heraklion on Monday.'

Vasilis called the bank as soon as it was open on the Monday morning and agreed to go to Heraklion that afternoon.

'I'll need to speak to the man at the Russian Consulate,' he advised the manager. 'If Kuzmichov has refused to co-operate I'll call you back and cancel my appointment.'

Vasilis telephoned the Russian Consulate and asked to speak to Mr Propenkov only to be told that he was out of the office at present and requested to call back later. Feeling helpless Vasilis called again half an hour later only to be given the same message and this was repeated when he 'phoned next.

'I don't know what to do,' he confessed to Cathy. 'I don't want to drive up to Heraklion only to find that I have had a wasted journey as Kuzmichov has not agreed, but nor do I want to miss my appointment with the bank manager.'

'You ought to keep the appointment at the bank. If you open an account and it isn't needed you can always close it again. You could try to contact Mr Propenkov again whilst you're there. It's possible that he's with Kuzmichov at this time making the arrangement.'

'I suppose that makes sense,' agreed Vasilis. 'I'll have some lunch and go up afterwards. Do you want to come?'

Cathy shook her head. 'I'd far rather stay here. I have a good book so I'll sit and read.'

'Vasi told me that Marianne's sister has been rather a nuisance at the hotel. She has upset some of his regular guests and actually damaged the lift.'

'What?'

'She told Marianne about the lift and Marianne called Vasi as soon as Helena had left them. He had found the damage, luckily it was only cotton wool and nail varnish placed over the lift buttons so it would not travel up to the higher floors. A wipe over with acetone removed it, but he's going to have to ask a mechanic to come and have a look as the buttons are sticking where is must have seeped behind them. Whenever someone wants to use it they have to be escorted by a member of staff just in case it gets jammed between floors.'

'How stupid of Helena and embarrassing for Marianne.'

'Vasi says that if they ask to come and stay again he's going to refuse them. He's managed to placate the guests that Helena upset but is not prepared to have other guests upset in the future.'

'I don't blame him. I know Giovanni won't have them to stay in his house or at the self catering apartments. I like Greg, but I cannot bear Marianne's sister.'

'Unfortunately most people feel the same. I'll be off in a few minutes. Is there anything you want me to bring you back?'

Cathy shook her head. 'I can't think of anything. Drive carefully, and don't forget we have a rehearsal tonight.'

'I've arranged the dates with the Municipal Hall,' announced Andreas. 'The performance will be on the fifth of November. That gives everyone time to close down and have a few days relaxation, but they won't have made any arrangements for travelling to visit relatives for Christmas at that time. I've booked for us to be at the Hall to rehearse on the Monday, Tuesday and Wednesday so please make sure you all keep those evenings free from any other engagements.'

'Good!' exclaimed Ronnie. 'I've brought the poster with me to show you and you can tell me exactly where you want the date inserted.'

'Where's Vasilis?' asked Andreas.

'He had to go to Heraklion this afternoon and he called me about an hour ago and said he was stuck in a traffic jam. Apparently there has been an accident. Nothing serious, but the vehicles are blocking the road.'

'Oh, no. I hope John isn't involved.' Nicola began to press in the numbers of her husband's mobile 'phone. 'He was delivering some pots for Uncle Yannis and I had expected him back much earlier.'

'I'm absolutely fine,' John assured Nicola. 'It's a bit of a long story and I had to return to Heraklion to make a statement to the police. I wasn't allowed to make any 'phone calls until I had done that. I kept telling them that you would be worried but they took no notice of me.'

Nicola drew a breath of relief. 'You're not injured?'

'No, and tell Dad that he only needs a new bumper.'

'Where are you now?'

'Just getting into the car. They insisted that it was checked over before I was allowed to drive it home, so there's nothing to worry about.'

Andreas frowned. 'I'm relieved to know that John is safe, but until Vasilis arrives that means we are two people short for rehearsing. We'll look at the poster that Ronnie has designed whilst we wait. If any of you see anything that you think should be changed speak up.'

Ronnie also produced the programme with the alterations that Andreas had requested and after scrutinizing it carefully he declared himself satisfied. 'I'll ask John if he can run off two hundred and fifty copies. That should be more than sufficient, but I'd rather have some left over than find we are a lot short. Now until Vasilis and John arrive we ought to get on. Marcus, you be John and Theo you can read Vasilis's part.'

They had only just taken their places when Marianne heard footsteps coming around to the patio and looked up in surprise as Helena and Greg arrived.

'Excuse me a minute,' she said and walked over to them. 'I'm pleased to see you both, but is there a problem?'

Greg shook his head. 'I persuaded Helena that we should really come and watch a rehearsal. That could help her to understand her mother's refusal to return to New Orleans. She thinks her mother only has a few words that could be spoken by anyone.'

'That is not so. She is an integral part of the performance. Help yourselves to some food and drink and have a seat over there. It's a shame you don't speak Greek. We're two men short at the moment as Vasilis and John have been held up. You could have played their parts tonight.'

Greg grinned sheepishly. 'Giovanni explained the general idea to me, but I'd love an English translation at a later date.'

'I'm sure we can manage that. We're going to start and the others will take their parts until they arrive.'

Vasilis arrived half an hour later, apologising for not being there earlier, and slipped into his vacant seat. Giovanni indicated to him where they were up to in the script and Vasilis nodded. He had only missed saying his lines as a little boy.

Helena sat with a bored look on her face, whilst Greg was evidently fascinated, despite not being able to understand the dialogue.

The rehearsal was nearly finished by the time John arrived. He stood outside of the patio until he heard them begin to sing the song. He waited until they had finished it and then walked inside.

'I am very sorry, Uncle Andreas.'

'Good job it wasn't the night of the performance. What happened, John?'

'Tourists, of course. They took the corner far too fast and ended up on the wrong side of the road. It was lucky I was three cars behind the one they hit head on. That one is a write off.'

'What about the passengers?'

'They're injured, but nothing life threatening, thank goodness. The car behind the one they hit has had the engine stove in and the rear isn't much better as the one in front of me couldn't stop before hitting it. I managed to stop but the car behind me ran into my bumper and we were locked together. That left me stranded with the rest of them.'

'Why didn't you call me immediately?' asked Nicola.

'I was expecting to be allowed to continue to drive home once the cars had been untangled. There were more important things to be dealt with at that particular moment. One man and woman were checking on the injured and those of us who were not hurt jumped out and did a bit of traffic control until the police and ambulance arrived.'

'So why were you kept waiting so long in Heraklion?'

'They interviewed the owners of the more badly damaged cars first so I was last on the list. I tried to tell them that I needed to call my wife and assure her I was alright but I wasn't allowed to make a call from inside the police station and I was not allowed to go outside. Even once I had given my statement I had to wait there until I was told my car was safe to drive. Bureaucracy gone mad. I could easily have gone outside and made a 'phone call. There were plenty of police around who could have acted as an escort to me. Never mind that, how did the rehearsal go? Was I missed?'

'Not a bit,' answered Giovanni. 'Marcus read your lines.'

John sighed. 'And there was me thinking I was the star of the show. I'll just grab a bite to eat and then you can tell me if there's anything I need to know ready for the next rehearsal.'

'I hope my pots weren't damaged,' remarked Yannis.

'I had already delivered them. Luckily it was on my journey home that the incident occurred.'

'What did you think, Greg?' asked Marianne, deliberately ignoring her sister.

'I couldn't understand the words, of course, but I was able to follow the actions and know what was being portrayed.'

'Really? Uncle Andreas will be delighted to know that.'

'I don't see why mother had to have such a large part. She could just have been one of the women,' remarked Helena.

'Mamma had written a good deal of her script as the narrator through spending time with the women up in the villages. She wasn't just reading it, she was *feeling* the emotions and suffering they went through. No one else could have done that so effectively.'

October 2015
Week Three – Tuesday & Wednesday

Brian Cavanagh turned his television on each morning. It had become a habit to listen to the local Greek news whilst he shaved. It always seemed to contain political wrangling that did not affect him, but it was useful to keep abreast of affairs. This morning the headlines were about a group of people who had been been arrested the previous week for taking refugees into Crete illegally and he stopped shaving and walked back into his lounge to listen more attentively.

There was a photograph of a boat, although the name was not visible, that was stated to have been used and the newsreader declared that the men had fled from Syria paying an extortionate amount to the owner of the craft. There were no names mentioned as the investigation was continuing.

The information that followed was about a car crash that had occurred on the main road from Heraklion and caused long delays to travellers. Brian returned to his bathroom and finished his toilet. He would have to make some enquiries and find out if the people who had been arrested were those who had sent the refugees on to England. If that could be proved it would add weight to the case for the prosecution.

Mr Propenkov was not amused to see the report on the news and 'phoned Chief Inspector Solomakis angrily.

'Who gave permission for that news release?'

'I did,' replied Solomakis smugly. 'The Cretan people have a right to know that we take people smuggling seriously.'

'You realise that Mr Kolmogorov could sue you for showing a photograph of his boat without his consent?'

'As far as I am aware there is no proof that it was his boat that was shown. It could belong to anyone. I also think that Mr Kolmogorov could have far more serious problems to deal with than a photograph of his boat, assuming it is his, of course. I am presenting papers to the Court today asking for a date to be set for a hearing.'

'Have you seen the news?' asked Giovanni of his wife. 'It sounds as though that could involve the Russian who bought Vasilis's hotel.'

'What will happen to the hotel if the man is convicted and sent to prison?' asked Marianne.

'No idea. Although he might own it I can't see him being given permission to continue to run it. It may have to be closed.'

'Poor Vasilis. He blames himself for having sold to him in the first place.'

'Maybe he'll buy it back. If the Russian is sent to gaol it will probably go at a knock down price.'

Marianne shook her head. 'I don't think he would do that. He and Cathy are happy living down here and it would mean they had to return to Heraklion. I'm going to 'phone Helena in a while and ask if she and Greg would like to come over for a meal this evening.'

'They were here last night,' protested Giovanni.

'Yes, but we were all busy with the rehearsal. Greg insisted they came yesterday evening in the hope of a reconciliation. They leave tomorrow so we ought to have some family time with them and give Helena the opportunity to say goodbye to Mamma properly.'

Giovanni shrugged. 'She's your sister. I can tolerate her for one more evening for the sake of your mother. I'm going to call Vasilis and ask what he thinks of the news.'

Vasilis was composing letters to the travel companies, hoping that Propenkov would be able to negotiate a release of funds from the man's bank account. He would ask Marianne to look at them before they were finally sent to ensure that he had not written anything that could be misconstrued.

'Did you see the news?' asked Giovanni.

'Yes, but I don't know how it will affect the situation at "The Central".' He ran his hand over his thinning hair. 'The sooner the whole affair is settled the better.'

'Marianne thought the hotel might have to be sold and you might want to buy it back.'

'No way. I made my decision to retire and I certainly do not want to go back into business again. Giorgos is making a good job of managing everything.'

Mr Propenkov sat with Evgeniy Kuzmichov and explained that the travel companies were claiming compensation for the bookings they had needed to cancel.

'That is nothing to do with me.' Kuzmichov shook his head. 'That is the hotel and I suggest you speak to Mr Iliopolakis regarding settlement.'

'I have already done so. Mr Iliopolakis is the administrator for the hotel at present. He has pointed out, quite correctly, that you were responsible for the problem, not the hotel and therefore it is your responsibility to make a settlement.'

'And if I refuse?'

'You will be sued by the companies involved and they are very likely to have their claim upheld. That would mean you also had to pay their legal expenses.'

'They cannot sue me. I'm in gaol,' replied Kuzmichov smugly.

'Being in custody will not stop them from bringing a law suit against you. It will just add weight to their claim. A judgement against you would probably be made without you having the opportunity to put up a defence.'

'I don't see why the money should have to come from my personal account,' argued Kuzmichov. 'I understand that my safe at the apartment was raided and the money in there seized by the police. Where is that?'

'Chief Inspector Solomakis arranged for that to be held by the bank until further notice.'

'Then use that to pay these companies.'

Mr Propenkov shook his head. 'That money cannot be touched. It was paid to you by the refugees that you and your brother in law brought into the country illegally. It is quite likely that it will eventually be repaid to them.'

'It was to cover their expenses.'

'A proportion of it maybe, but they paid both you and Ivan Kolmogorov an exorbitant sum. I know some was used to procure their false passports but you did not pay Maziar the amount that you charged them. You also used their money to book their flights to England and gave them a small amount in sterling to take with them. Even taking those events into account and paying you a reasonable amount for their stay at your hotel each man should have at least six thousand dollars returned to them. The men who were arrested at the same time as yourself should have the full amount reimbursed as they did not stay at your hotel.'

'This is preposterous!'

'No, Mr Kuzmichov, the only way to settle your debts to the companies is to sign an agreement that the money can be transferred from your personal account to a separate one that Mr Iliopolakis has agreed to open. Once the money has been paid over to the travel companies that account will be closed and your personal account will remain frozen for the foreseeable future.' Mr Propenkov produced the document from his briefcase.

'I would like you to read that and sign it now. Negotiations can then begin with the bank. This is a one off transaction until you have to pay my expenses and those of a defence lawyer at your trial. A separate agreement will have to be put into place for those payments which will be nothing to do with Mr Iliopolakis.'

'I was not expecting a bill from the Consulate!' exclaimed Evgeniy.

'My first visit to you was free, but my subsequent visits to you, your wife and the refugees, along with liaison with the police have to be paid for. Whilst I am visiting you I am not completing my other work.'

'I thought you were going to represent me?'

Mr Propenkov smiled. 'I am an ambassador. Although I am fully conversant with the legal system I am not qualified to act as a defence lawyer. I can ask the Consulate to send you a list of men capable of handling your case. When you have decided who you would like to represent you I will ensure that they have all the facts. I do have to advise you that you need to consider this very carefully. If you plead not guilty the trial is likely to be prolonged for months whilst lawyers argue and you are kept in custody. I do have to warn you that a prolonged trial is very expensive. You may find that it becomes necessary to sell your hotel to cover the costs. It could be in your best interests to plead guilty.'

'If I plead guilty will I need a lawyer?'

Mr Propenkov shook his head. 'The facts of the case will be presented by a lawyer chosen by Chief Inspector Solomakis. If you decide to plead guilty there will be no necessity to call witnesses so a decision will be made immediately. If you want to appeal against whatever the Court decides you will certainly need a lawyer. Now, could we deal with the matter in hand. I will ask one of the officers to come and act as a witness to your signature on the agreement. There will be four copies; one for the bank, another for Mr Iliopolakis, I will keep one in my records and you are obviously entitled to a copy.'

Evgeniy thought about the conversation after Mr Propenkov

left. He had not been expecting a bill from the Consulate and had assumed Propenkov would conduct his defence and he would not have to pay for that either. He wished he knew how Ludmila would plead. She had plenty of money in her account in Moscow and could well afford to pay a lawyer to defend the charges against her.

Mr Propenkov telephoned Vasilis and also sent him an e-mail copy of the agreement that Evgeniy Kuzmichov had finally been persuaded to sign.

'I can take the agreement to the bank and it will be up to you to speak to the manager there. I don't know how long they will take to act upon Kuzmichov's instructions.'

Vasilis gave a sigh of relief. He had thought he might have to drive to Heraklion again with the agreement. 'I really appreciate your help, Mr Propenkov. As soon as the funds are cleared I'll instruct the bank to pay the companies. I have letters prepared for them and I can now confirm that a settlement for the full amount they are claiming is being negotiated.'

Brian Cavanagh called Stuart at Immigration on his own mobile 'phone during his morning break. He never made a private call on his office 'phone, although he only intended to repeat to Stuart the information he had heard on the news.

Stuart was pleased to know that at least some people were in custody. 'Are they the ones who arranged for the refugees we have here to be brought over?'

'I can't say as no names were mentioned. As soon as I know anything more I'll let you know.'

'Can I tell Barry and pass the information on to Peter? His wife certainly deserves some credit for bringing the situation to our attention.'

'You can certainly tell them the same as I have told you. It was on the local news this morning so it isn't confidential. What is going to happen to the men who have requested asylum in England?'

'No decision has been made yet, but I think it is likely they'll be allowed to stay. They all speak good English and have professions that would be an advantage to our country.'

'At least that will be some compensation for them having spent so much money to get there.'

'I heard some interesting news today,' said Peter to Lucy when he arrived home. 'Barry called and said he had heard from Stuart that some people involved in the trafficking of the refugees on Crete have been arrested. He said to compliment you on spotting them in the first place.'

'I'm pleased to hear it. I just hope others won't take their place. Did he say what was going to happen to those who have requested asylum here?'

'The decision hasn't been made yet, but he thinks they'll probably be allowed to stay.'

'Will they get some of their money back?'

'I've no idea. It could be argued that the money was used to cover their costs.'

Lucy snorted in derision. 'It doesn't cost a quarter as much as they claim to have paid to get to England. They should certainly have at least half of it returned to them.'

'That will be nothing to do with Stuart. He'll have to abide by whatever decision the Greek courts make.'

Helena and Greg arrived to spend the evening at Yannis's house. Helena had a fixed smile on her face when she entered.

'We can't stay late. There's all the packing to be done before we leave tomorrow.'

'I'm just pleased you were able to spare the time to come. Please do not spoil the evening by asking Mamma to return with you. She is determined to stay here and becomes upset when there are arguments.'

'I also become upset when she behaves like a foolish old woman,' replied Helena acidly. 'Where has Greg disappeared to?'

'Probably gone to find Giovanni. Let me give you a drink, Helena, and then I'll go and tell Mamma that you're here.'

As Marianne left the patio she began to sing to herself quietly. Bryony appeared almost immediately with a loaded tray, also singing to herself.

'Hello, Helena,' she said brightly. 'Did you enjoy watching the rehearsal last night?'

'It made a change from listening to the inane conversation of the people around me at the hotel.'

'Well I doubt if our conversation is any more interesting. We rarely go anywhere or do anything exciting.'

'Why don't you visit the States? There's always plenty going on over there.'

Bryony shook her head. 'I never want to go back there again. It would bring back too many memories of Hurricane Katrina.'

Greg walked out onto the patio humming to himself.

'Not you as well!' Helena rounded on her husband angrily. 'I'm sick of hearing that silly tune.'

Greg grinned. 'I know, but once it gets into your head it won't go away.'

'What is that irritating little song?' asked Helena. 'You were all singing it last night and I've heard you and Bryony singing it every time I've visited. The words don't make sense.'

Elena heard the comment with amusement. 'That's because to you it's out of context.'

Marianne smiled. 'It's a silly rhyme the children of the village made up and used to sing at the soldiers. The soldiers didn't realise the children were being rude as they did not understand Greek. At the end everyone stamps their feet and shouts bang.'

'Can you tell me the words in English?' asked Greg and Marianne complied.

Greg laughed, but Helena sniffed derisively. 'Sounds very childish to me.'

'It's meant to be. There was so much tragedy at the time that inserting a little bit of humorous nonsense will help to lift the atmosphere. Now, do come and help yourselves from the table. John and Nicola will be along in a moment and you know how John can clear a table.'

Vasilis 'phoned whilst they were eating and asked Marianne if she would be willing to look over the letters he had composed. 'I can e-mail them over to you.'

'Is there any urgency? We have Helena and Greg here at the moment as it's their last evening.'

'No, Mr Propenkov has spoken to Kuzmichov and he's given permission for the amount to be moved from his account. Now I know that has been agreed I can send these letters, but they can easily wait until tomorrow. I'd just like reassurance from you that I haven't left them any negotiating options and have made it clear that they are being repaid the full amount they are claiming.'

'Have you been able to check that the amount is correct? They could have doubled it.'

'I asked Giorgos to send me a comprehensive list of the cancellations when he e-mailed me the letters. They have all added on an amount for administration expenses and added VAT, of course. I'd rather get the matter settled than have to enter into arguments with them.'

'I'll look at them first thing tomorrow,' promised Marianne, 'and get back to you. It was good news about the arrests, wasn't it?'

Greg looked at her questioningly. 'What arrests were those? I didn't think you had very much crime in this area.'

'You tell them, Giovanni. It's quite an involved story starting from when Vasilis sold his hotel in Heraklion.'

Greg listened avidly as Giovanni related how Vasilis had been out fishing with his neighbour when there was the first sighting of the men being landed near the Causeway, followed by the arrest of Kuzmichov at the hotel and detention of the immigrants.

'It's Vasilis I feel sorry for,' ended Giovanni. 'He sold the hotel and his apartment in Heraklion in good faith looking forward to a quiet retirement down here. He bought a ground floor apartment in Elounda and then also bought some land along on the seafront. He had just started the clearance work when some skeletons were found. At the same time he was asked to take over the financial administration of "The Central" and goodness knows how much longer he will be expected to deal with that.'

'Do you mean that land by the hotel where the building work is taking place belongs to Vasilis?' asked Helena sharply.

Giovanni nodded. 'Now they've finished excavating the graves he's been given permission to continue whilst they work on the land next door.'

'Had I known that land was his I would have insisted that Greg 'phoned him and told him to stop work. There is a cement mixer working there from early morning and I find it most annoying.'

Greg spread his hands and shrugged an apology. He was very relieved that Helena had only just discovered the owner of the land.

Giovanni shook his head. 'I don't think he would have agreed. He's desperate to get a certain amount of work completed before the weather breaks.'

'They only seem to be constructing the garden walls,' complained Helena. 'Surely there is no urgency about completing those.'

'Vasilis is planning to have the building elevated. Once those walls have been completed a concrete base is going to be laid and then the walls will be made higher.'

'He should still not have been allowed to work there when the hotel had guests.'

'I've not heard of any complaints from anyone else. Most people are up early and then off out for the day or up by the swimming pool. I'm sure Vasi would have spoken to him if there had been any problems.'

'Some people just do not have the courage to complain,' remarked Helena darkly.

'Hey, Dad, I've had an idea.' John entered the room whilst Nicola followed shaking her head. 'Why don't we get someone to let off some fire crackers when the soldiers are supposed to be marching? It would add authenticity.'

Elena frowned at her grandson. 'That is not a good idea, John. It would be dangerous to let them off inside and many people would be disturbed by the noise. They will have heard more than enough in the way of gun shots when they were young.'

'No one stops them from letting them off on Oxi Day,' argued John.

'That's because they're celebrating. This is not a celebration, this is a commemoration,' Elena said firmly.

'Oh, well, I thought it was a good idea. I'll see what Uncle Andreas thinks.'

'You are not to mention it to him,' said Marianne sternly. 'Your grandmother is right, the audience don't want to be frightened thinking someone is shooting a gun.'

John grinned and whispered in Nicola's ear. 'I should have bought some and I could have let them off as Aunt Helena was leaving.'

Nicola suppressed a giggle. 'You do have the most wicked ideas.'

Helena had bade her mother goodbye at the end of the evening, but could not resist adding that it was not too late for Elena to change her mind and return with them. 'We could always change the date of our flights to give you a couple of days to pack your belongings.'

Elena shook her head. 'You already know my answer, Helena. We have had a very pleasant evening, please do not spoil it now by starting an argument with me. I'll let you know when I decide to leave Elounda.'

'But what about your house?'

'It can remain closed up. I would appreciate you visiting and checking that all is well occasionally. If there is anything that needs the attention of a builder please deal with it and pay the bill. You can then e-mail the invoice to me and I will transfer the money to your account.'

'Your post could have something urgent in it that needs your attention,' persisted Helena.

'Most unlikely. Utility bills are paid monthly from my account and I do not owe anyone else any money. Just place anything that comes for me on the table in the lounge, but I expect it will be circulars that can go straight in the bin.'

To Vasilis's relief the bank manager confirmed he had received the agreement signed by Kuzmichov.

'The transfer can be effected immediately, Mr Iliopolakis.'

Vasilis shook his head. 'No, I'd like it held for a week. That will give me the opportunity to send e-mail letters to the companies and add a date when they can expect payment to reach their account. I don't want to appear too eager to settle as if we have been intimidated by their threat of court action. They have given us thirty days. I am sending you copies of their invoices and I am relying upon you not to transfer anything more than the total involved.'

Mr Propenkov thought it only courteous to inform Chief Inspector Solomakis that he was not going to represent Kuzmichov in court.

'I will send him a list of competent lawyers and it is up to him if he wishes to use one. If he has any sense he'll plead guilty and save himself the expense.'

'You consider him guilty, then?'

Mr Propenkov spread his hands and shrugged. 'It is not up to me to judge him, but from all he has told me and the fact that he was arrested along with six illegal immigrants the evidence against him appears overwhelming. I am so pleased that I am not entitled to represent him and present a case for his defence. It would go against my conscience.'

'What about his wife?' asked Solomakis.

'I don't know if she gained financially but she is obviously guilty of taking part in the operation. I will have to visit her and give her the same advice as I have given to her husband. She would most likely be given a more lenient sentence if she pleads guilty to acting under duress.'

'Personally I think she was a willing participant. Why else would she ask her brother to collect her from Crete?'

'If Kolmogorov is to be believed he was only taking her on a sailing trip and would then return her to Crete.'

'A pack of lies in my opinion. I think he planned to head for Turkey, dropping off the refugees on the way. Once he was in the Sea of Marmara they would both be well away from Greek jurisdiction and an extradition order would be needed to bring them back. Dealing with Turkey is never easy and by the time that was granted they would both have disappeared, along with the boatman who was accompanying them.'

'I wanted to ask you about the money that was taken from Mr Kuzmichov's safe.'

'It was all accounted for, both by my men and the bank. I insisted that photographs were taken every step of the way. I didn't want my men or myself to be accused of pilfering.'

Mr Propenkov shook his head. 'I am sure you were scrupulous, but I wanted to ask if any agreement has been reached whereby the money is returned to the refugees? When I told Mr Kuzmichov he would be liable for his lawyer's expenses along with mine he seemed to think they could be paid from that money. I told him that was out of the question.'

'I'll have to contact the British Embassy in Athens. I agree that the men should be repaid but it could be wise to wait until an asylum decision has been made. If they are allowed to stay in England that money could give them a useful start.'

'Provided Kuzmichov is unable to claim it for himself it makes no difference to me if the men wait a month or a year for it. He did try to tell me it was to cover their expenses, their false passport, flight and his hotel expenses.'

Chief Inspector Solomakis shook his head. 'He had taken the money from them to pay for the passports and also their flights. He cannot claim that as owing to him. I'll ask Mr Iliopolakis how much visitors pay to stay in "The Central". That could be a legitimate claim, but it would then be repaid to the hotel accounts.'

'That sounds very satisfactory to me. I'll hand all my interview notes over to whoever Kuzmichov selects to represent him and wait to hear the date the Court set for his trial.'

Mr Propenkov shook hands with the Chief Inspector. He hoped now that his involvement with Evgeniy and Ludmila Kuzmichov was at an end. Neither Ivan Kolmogorov nor Panos Colonakis were entitled to his services as neither of them held a valid Russian passport.

November 2015

Elena had visited Evi and Maria and given them a programme. She was unsure if either of them were able to read and she pointed out the time and place to them.

'Will your son be able to take you both down to Elounda in his car?' asked Elena. 'I'll make sure that seats are reserved in the front row for all three of you.'

'I'll have to ask him when he takes me to church on Sunday.'

'You won't forget?' asked Elena anxiously. 'If he says it's not possible then I'll arrange for someone to come with a car and collect you.'

'Will they bring us back?' asked Maria.

'Of course. I'm not sure what time the performance will end, but I will be around and look after both of you. I wouldn't dream of leaving you stranded. I'll come up on Monday and check arrangements with you. You'll need to be in your seats by eight so make sure you are ready to leave here by seven thirty. Do you want me to write that down on the programme?'

Evi nodded. 'Might as well. I'll pin the programme to my calendar to remind me.'

'I'll not forget,' remarked Maria. 'I have a good memory.'

'So have I,' rejoined Evi immediately, 'But it can be useful to have a reminder sometimes.'

'You forgot to ask your son to buy you some soap last week.'

'I hadn't written it on my shopping list for him.'

'You forgot,' said Maria triumphantly.

Elena could tell there was about to be a full scale argument between the two old ladies and rose to go. 'I know neither of you will forget. You can keep reminding each other. I'll see you both on Monday.'

Ronnie and John had taken the posters around Elounda, asking the shops that were still open to display them and taping them to the doors or windows of the establishments that had already closed down for the winter.

'I'm going to ask Pappas Matthias if I can put one on the church notice board. Everyone always looks at the board when they pass the church.'

'Do you think he would mention it after church on Sunday?' asked Ronnie.

'I can ask him. I'll give him a programme so he knows exactly what is going to happen and offer him a seat in the front row.'

'Should we take some posters into Aghios? Yiorgos lives there and could put some up, also Dimitris.'

'No harm in asking. I can always run off another twenty if they're needed.'

Andreas was suffering from worse nerves than when he had attended the opening night of one of his plays in New York. If anything went wrong there was no one to blame except himself. He was the writer, producer and stage manager.

'Nothing will go wrong,' Elena assured him. 'We all know our lines and our cues. I've shown Marisa and Uncle Yannis how to use the microphones and they know when they need to switch them on.'

During a rehearsal at the Municipal Hall Andreas had decided that the voices of Marisa, Elena and Uncle Yannis were not strong enough for their words to carry to the audience in the back seats.

He had also decided that he needed one or by the end of the performance he might no longer be able to speak loudly enough.

'I'm worried that Marisa will suddenly dry up.'

'I'm sure she won't. I've spent time with her going over her part as Aunt Anna. If she is thrown by the occasion I can always say "What happened next, Aunt Anna?" or ask "What did you do after that happened?" I think you may have more of a problem getting Yannis and Yiorgos to finish their speeches. Besides, you have to realise that we are not professionals and I'm sure the audience will excuse any slight hitches.'

'Remind the men to bring some stones If anyone forgets a stone there need to be a few around that they can have. Check that they'll have their black trousers and white shirts and will be wearing proper shoes with hard soles. The same with the ladies. Black skirts and white blouses and hard soled shoes.'

'I'm sure we're all organised in that respect. Ronnie has borrowed a black skirt from Saffie as she only had a pencil skirt. She saw the look you gave her at the dress rehearsal.'

Andreas smiled. 'What could I say? It was a black skirt. I had a quick word with Bryony and she said she'd willingly lend Ronnie a skirt, but that it would be far too large for her. The problem has obviously been sorted out with Saffron's help.'

'Will the men be expected to wear ties?' asked Elena.

Andreas shook his head. 'Open neck shirts. They are country folk, not city dwellers going off to work in an office. I will wear a tie, of course, as I am the narrator.'

'I'm sure Giovanni and John will be relieved to know that. I think they only possess the black ties they wear to church.'

'Don't forget your torch.'

'I won't,' Elena assured him. 'I've also practised using the hand held microphones along with Marisa and Yannis. They are definitely happier not having to try to shout their words.'

'I should have thought of it before. I don't think Yiorgos will have a problem, but if he does then Yannis will have to hand his

microphone along to him. Before we start I'll ask the audience
to raise their hands if they are unable to hear us. I hope those
who need them will have remembered their hearing aids. I'm
adding more chairs as John has told me he has run off a further
fifty programmes. Just about everyone who has heard about the
performance wants to attend.'

As the performance ended Dimitris closed all the lights. The
audience sat in silence and when the lights were turned back on the
men and women were standing in front of their seats with Andreas
and Elena between them. They held out their hands towards the
performers at each side of them who then smiled and bowed.

The audience broke into applause and Marianne felt tears
coming into her eyes.

Andreas stepped forwards. 'This is a tribute to the brave people
who suffered so atrociously under the occupying forces and
fought against them so courageously; not just here, but throughout
Crete. I am indebted to those of you who were willing to share
your memories with us. I would like to thank you all for coming
and express my appreciation to everyone who gave so willingly
of their time to take part. I particularly have to thank my sister,
Elena. Without her valuable assistance this would not have been
possible. The presentation was entirely her idea.'

Marianne's tears were now running down her face.

'What's wrong?' asked Giovanni.

Marianne shook her head. 'Nothing, I just found it so
emotional. I think many of the audience found that also.'

It was true, the women were dabbing openly at their eyes and
many of the men were rubbing their sleeves across their face or
wiping their eyes.

Elena looked at Andreas and smiled. 'Congratulations on your
success. That was magnificent and the audience were spellbound.'

'We will finish by singing our National Anthem, our Hymn to
Liberty. I'm sure you all know it but the words are on the back

page,' announced Andreas. He turned to the performers on the stage and nodded for them to commence.

The audience stood and joined in lustily, hardly any of them needing to look at the printed words. As the last word of the Anthem was sung there was a moment's silence and then the audience broke into a further round of applause, with the actors on stage joining in.

'I must go and have a quick word with Evi and Maria before Evi's son takes them back to Pano Elounda.'

'We should sing the song again as the audience leave,' announced Andreas. 'Straight through, not as a round. Start it, Marianne.'

The ladies on the stage began to sing, taking their cue from Marianne. Before Elena could reach the elderly ladies she could hear they were singing the rhyme. With a delighted smile on her face Elena joined in and indicated that the other women in the audience should sing also. The volume rose and the women stood together, their arms on each other's shoulders.

Father Matthias approached Andreas with a beaming smile, although his eyes were moist. 'You have done something remarkable for the community. It is the first time the women have had their sacrifice acknowledged publicly. It has always been the men who have been honoured in the past.'

'I feel quite exhausted,' confessed Elena as the hall finally emptied. 'I was so worried that the audience would not like it and Andreas would be upset.'

'I should not have expected so much of you,' answered Andreas, immediately contrite. 'You were magnificent, as was everyone else. I could not have asked for more from a professional company.'

'Now, how is everyone getting home?' asked Marcus. 'I understand that Mr Palamakis is waiting for Yiorgos, but I'll be happy to take Dimitris and Uncle Andreas.'

'Kyriakos is meeting me,' said Ronnie. 'It would probably be easier if we took Uncle Andreas. We'll be driving past Kato.'

'I'll be responsible for Monika and Litsa,' confirmed Theo.

'We'll take our mothers and Uncle Yannis. There's enough space in the mini bus for all of us, including Nicola and John,' said Marianne. 'Vasilis, you and Vasi both brought your cars didn't you?'

Both men nodded affirmation.

'In that case we just need to clear up. I'll collect any discarded programmes whilst Vasi and John stack the chairs,' said Nicola. 'Dimitris ought to take those hand microphones home with him. He can then return them to the hire shop tomorrow and arrange for the collection of the lights.'

Marianne stood and looked around at the deserted hall. 'I think we ought to have a celebration tomorrow evening. Everyone is invited to us. Yiorgos, ask Barbara and your father to come and Ronnie don't forget to bring Kyriakos with you. You'll bring Monika and Litsa, won't you, Theo?'

'I'd be only too delighted.'

'We can collect Uncle Andreas,' offered Vasilis. 'Is there anyone we've forgotten?'

'Only Evi and Maria,' said Elena, 'but I'm sure they wouldn't come. It was quite an adventure for both of them to come here this evening. They'll probably talk about it for months.'

John raised his eyebrows and Nicola nodded. She knew what her husband was suggesting.

Once satisfied that the hall was cleared of any of their possessions they walked out silently feeling sad. It had been an exhilarating evening and now there would be no rehearsals to look forward to or a final performance.

Ronnie led Uncle Andreas over to where Kyriakos was waiting beside his car.

'I hope you won't mind sitting in the back, Uncle Andreas. My mother is in the front.'

Ronnie was completely taken aback to see Kyriakos's mother sitting there. 'Good evening, Mrs Mandakis,' she managed to stutter in Greek.

'Good evening, Miss Vandersham,' replied Mrs Mandakis stiffly.

Much as Ronnie was longing to ask Kyriakos what he had thought of the performance she did not feel she could speak to him with his mother sitting there. She was most relieved when he stopped before his mother's house and helped her out of the car.

'Good night, Mrs Mandakis.'

Kyriakos's mother turned and gave a curt nod in Ronnie's direction.

Kyriakos returned to his car and sat in the driving seat and turning to face his passengers in the back. 'I would like to tell you how much my mother enjoyed this evening.'

'Really?' Ronnie was delighted. 'How did you manage to persuade her to come?'

'I did not give her a programme until we were in our seats and it was too late for her to leave. She didn't know you were taking part.'

'Good job you didn't tell her beforehand.' Ronnie turned to Uncle Andreas. 'Kyriakos's mother does not approve of me. I am American, my grandmother was born on Spinalonga and I am an artist.'

Andreas chuckled. 'Silly lady. She should be pleased that her son has found such an intelligent and attractive partner.'

'I think it is being American that she disapproves of most. If I was a local Greek girl my other sins might be forgiven.'

'She did say that your Greek had improved,' smiled Kyriakos.

'That was due to all the work you put in to correct me. I may be able to say "I had to take the snails from their shells after Mamma boiled them" perfectly, but that is about all I can say apart from very basic sentences.'

'I wish I could have taken part,' said Kyriakos enviously.

'Being a taverna owner means you have to be open in the evenings. I could not afford to close two evenings each week to attend rehearsals.'

Nicola sat at the breakfast table with Antonia and described the performance to her. 'It was amazing the reception it received from the audience. Many of them were in tears at the end.'

'Will you be putting it on again during the day so I could come to watch?'

'I don't know if Uncle Andreas has any plans to do that. I can suggest it to him. Now, John will take the girls to nursery school, drop you home and collect Skele at the same time.'

Antonia felt quite sad that she would no longer be spending time at Uncle Yannis's spacious villa. The house she shared with her husband, daughter and brother was cramped and small and Despina had to play outside in the street rather than on a patio that overlooked the bay.

Bryony entered the kitchen singing the rhyme that had been used in the performance. 'I don't think that silly little song will ever leave my head. Is Marianne around yet? I want to know what food she is planning for this evening and then I can go shopping for anything we need. We'll need to eat inside as it will be too cold now to use the patio.'

'I'll go shopping. Let me know what you want and when John returns I can take Yiannis with me in the car. We ought to move. The girls should not be late for school.'

Nicola was pleased to have the excuse to leave the villa for an indeterminate amount of time. It would enable her to visit Evi and Maria and invite them to come to the house that evening.

Having purchased the items Marianne had given her on the shopping list Nicola parked and placed Yiannis in his stroller. She was not prepared to carry him up the steep hill to Pano Elounda and it would be asking too much of him to expect him to walk.

When she arrived Evi was sitting outside her house in the morning sunshine with Maria beside her. They looked at her curiously.

'Remember me?' asked Nicola. 'I was in the performance last night.'

Evi nodded. 'I'm pleased my son agreed to take us to watch.'

'Did you enjoy it?'

'It made a change' said Maria.

'I've come to give you another invitation. We are holding a party this evening at Yannis Andronicatis's house. We would like you to come.'

'We won't know anyone,' demurred Evi.

'Yes, you will,' Nicola assured her. 'You know my grandmother, Elena. She will be there. I'll be there as well as the other members of the family and those that took part. We really would like you to come.'

'My son can't be expected to drive us backwards and forwards again tonight.'

'He won't have to. My husband will collect you at seven and bring you back when you wish to leave.'

'I've not got any party clothes,' said Maria and shook her head.

'You don't need to dress up specially. Whatever you wore last night will be fine. We won't be dressing up, it will be very informal. It will just be a way of thanking Uncle Andreas for his hard work and both of you for contributing. Please come.'

Evi and Maria looked at each other. 'Well, if we're going to be taken up and down by car I suppose we could come,' agreed Evi finally.

Marianne and Bryony spent the afternoon preparing meze food for the evening so everyone could help themselves whilst Nicola took her children up to the playground.

'I think there will be about twenty five people coming if you include us. Do you think we have enough?' asked Bryony anxiously. 'Maybe we should have asked Nicola to buy some more bread.'

'I have plenty of rolls in the freezer that were brought back from the taverna. I'll get some of those out in case we need them. We'll probably have too much, but we don't have to put out everything at the same time. If we hold some items back we can top up plates when they begin to be emptied. If there's anything left over we can always eat it ourselves tomorrow.'

Elena sat and watched them. 'I feel terribly lazy just sitting here, but I really am tired. I couldn't get to sleep last night. The performance kept going round and round in my head.'

'You're not being lazy,' Marianne assured her mother. 'You worked far harder than us. I expect Uncle Andreas is feeling the effects today. I know Marisa and Uncle Yannis are drained. They've already retired to their rooms for the afternoon. You all put so much emotion into your parts.'

'I'm not sure it was a good idea for you to arrange a party for this evening. We'll all be too tired to enjoy ourselves.'

'Not at all. If we had left it until next week the moment would have passed. Bryony and I are organised and the men will arrange the lounge and dining area so there really is nothing we expect you to do. Why don't you go and have a long rest? As we're at home you can go to bed whenever it suits you this evening. You won't be expected to stay up until the last guests leave.'

Elena hesitated. 'Well, I might go and read for a while, but I doubt if I'll sleep.'

As their guests arrived Marcus offered them a choice of wine or a fruit juice and Marianne instructed the to help themselves from the table that was overflowing with food.

'Where's John?' asked Marianne. 'Everyone is here except him.'

'He won't be long. He's taking Skele back to Dimitris's I think.'

'I thought he did that earlier.'

Nicola shrugged. 'I'm not exactly sure where he is. I'll call him and find out.'

'I was a little delayed, nothing to worry about. All is going to plan and I should be with you within the next ten minutes. When I open the door make sure you start to sing that silly rhyme and get Mum and Bryony to join in.'

Nicola walked over to where Monika and Litsa were talking to Ronnie. 'Can you come over by the door with me? We have a surprise arranged for Elena and we'll need to sing our rhyme. I'm going to ask Mum and Bryony to join us.'

The women clustered together, expecting a presentation of some sort to be made to Elena. John opened the door and ushered in Evi and Maria.

'Now,' said Nicola and began to sing with the others joining in.

Evi and Maria stood inside the doorway uncertainly. Andreas saw them first and called to his sister.

'Elena, you have some special visitors.'

Elena rose from her chair, a look of disbelief on her face.

John placed his hand beneath the elbow of each woman and propelled them forward. 'Come over and sit by Elena and I'll get you both a drink. We all want to talk to you. Mum will bring you over some food and you can help yourself to anything more that you want. It seems to be disappearing rapidly so don't be shy.'

December 2015

Once again Vasilis sat with his head in his hands. The bank manager had called him to say that Evgeniy Kuzmichov had decided to sell the hotel and suggested that Vasilis might like to re-purchase the property.

'It will obviously be at a reduced price under the circumstances. If you refuse there is no guarantee that anyone else will come forward and the premises will eventually have to be closed down.'

'How long do I have before I make a decision?'

'The sooner the better, but I can give you a couple of weeks.'

'What should I do, Cathy? I don't want to buy the hotel back and have the responsibility that entails. I also don't want to know that the hotel is going to be closed down and all the staff will lose their jobs.'

'I don't know, Vasilis. It isn't fair that you should be put in this position. Why should the hotel have to be closed? You say it is running at a profit.'

'It's a question of ownership. The bank cannot accept money in and paying bills indefinitely when there is no owner who is overall responsible. If the compensation money to the travel companies had been paid from the hotel accounts rather than from Evgeniy's personal account there would not have been sufficient funds available.'

'Why don't you ask Marianne's advice? She suggested that Evgeniy should be responsible for the debt.'

Evgeniy Kuzmichov sat in his prison cell, both furious and unhappy. He had been sentenced to ten years for smuggling refugees into Crete. The money from his safe that had been held at the bank had been transferred to a bank in England. This would be divided equally between the asylum seekers after a deduction of two hundred pounds for each man had been made and repaid into the hotel accounts to cover the cost of their stay.

Although he had pleaded guilty and saved the expense of a defence lawyer the bill presented to him by Mr Propenkov for both himself and Ludmila had drained him of money. He had protested at having to pay Ludmila's fees, but Mr Propenkov had pointed out that she had no resources of her own and as her husband he was responsible for her debts.

Added to his fury was the fact that Ludmila had not received a gaol sentence. She had insisted that she had acted under duress and had not been reimbursed in any way for driving the refugees from Elounda to Heraklion. She had visited him, a smug smile on her face, and told him that having had her passport returned she would be travelling back to Moscow at the earliest opportunity.

'You'll not get away with this, Ludmila.'

'I already have.'

'You have been a traitor to me. You were never under any pressure from me to help with the scheme and you always received your fair share from any activity you participated in. You must have a very healthy bank balance,' Evgeniy ended bitterly.

Ludmila shrugged. 'Prove it. You taught me how to be devious and sparing with the truth. I'll see you in about ten years.'

Evgeniy watched her be escorted from the room. The one consolation to him was that Ivan and Panos were still in custody and awaiting trial.

Marianne sat and listened to Vasilis carefully. 'Have you been happy to work as an administrator for the accounts at "The Central"?'

'Dimitra is scrupulous with the accounts now. She checks and double checks before sending them on to me for payment.'

'And you say the hotel is making a profit?'

'Exactly. It would be wrong to close it down if a buyer cannot be found.'

'And you won't contemplate buying it back?'

Vasilis shook his head. 'I'm nearly seventy four. I want to devote my remaining years to Cathy, not to a hotel.'

'Would Vasi be interested?'

Again Vasilis shook his head. 'It wouldn't be practical. He'd either have to move back to Heraklion or spend part of each day driving up and down.'

'So what about the senior managers at the hotel?'

'They'll lose their jobs along with everyone else,' replied Vasilis gloomily.

Marianne shook her head. 'That is not what I meant. If they were willing to make a financial investment they could form a consortium. That would mean that they all had ownership. It would have to be agreed that they would receive a percentage of the overall profit made by the hotel over the course of the year. It would also mean that if there was a shortfall they could be asked to invest more money to keep the business afloat. Provided you were willing you could continue to act as the administrator and everything would continue to run as it is at present. It's similar to having stocks and shares. You put money in for the firm to use and receive a dividend payment each year.'

'Suppose it was agreed and then one of them wanted their money back?'

'The way to safeguard against a large amount being withdrawn at any one time would be to put a limit on the amount any one person could invest and a clause to say that it could not be withdrawn until after a certain date. Alternatively you could offer everyone working there at the moment the opportunity to become a share holder and it could become a co-operative.'

'You mean the chamber maids and cleaners would be able to invest as well?'

Marianne nodded. 'They might only be able to put in five Euros at present so it would be too little for them to receive an annual dividend, but they could have the option of adding to it each month. Find out exactly what the asking price is going to be, then make a list of the staff. Those who have been there longest have the most to lose and also probably have some savings. Work out exactly how much you would have to ask them to contribute and then meet with them and gauge their reaction. You have nothing to lose, Vasilis.'

'If this idea of yours works and I agree to continue to act as administrator am I also able to invest a sum?'

'There's no reason why you shouldn't, but be careful. Don't invest too heavily or you could end up as the owner again. If the staff are agreeable you'll need to have legal papers drawn up for everyone who is investing, including yourself. You will need to account for that in your calculations.'

'Suppose I died within the next few years, how would that affect Cathy and Vasi?'

'You would have to discuss that with your lawyer, along with the option of the staff making investments. Provided he agrees there should be no reason why Cathy cannot inherit your share and you can nominate Vasi as administrator in your place.'

Feeling happier, Vasilis drove away from Marianne and along the seafront road to check how his building work was progressing. The concrete had been laid and the men were building the perimeter walls higher. He sat and looked across the bay. He had been foolish not to sell "The Central" years ago and then this current situation would not have occurred. The hotel would not have been bought by a Russian and there would not be a refugee crisis with unfortunate victims desperate to escape to Europe.

'Mamma and Uncle Andreas are going to remain in Elounda for Christmas,' Marianne announced to Giovanni. 'Mamma says she would far rather be here than have a miserable Christmas like last year when she had to go to Helena's.'

'Anything would be better than having to go to Helena's,' remarked Giovanni. 'If it wouldn't cause a volcanic eruption I'd invite Greg to come over, on his own, of course.'

'I was wondering about Evi and Maria. I expect Evi will be invited to her son, but I don't think Maria has any family. She seems to get on particularly well with Marisa and Elena likes her. We could take her to the midnight service and she could come back here and stay the night.'

'Actually I hope she refuses,' replied Giovanni. 'I have nothing against her coming to stay but it could cause trouble between her and Evi. If Evi wanted to come as well that could cause a rift between her and her son.'

'I wouldn't want to be the cause of that. I'll pay them a visit and see if I can find out their arrangements.'

'You can always take them some Christmas gifts; gloves, blanket, a food parcel, something like that,' suggested Giovanni.

'That could be a more practical idea. It might be better if I say nothing about a visit.'

Giovanni nodded. The house would be overflowing with guests, but the addition of an elderly lady whom nobody knew well could be a strain on the festivities.

'What is happening with your mother this Christmas?' Ronnie asked Kyriakos.

'I will take you both to the midnight service. You do not have to sit together. I will then visit her the next day after I have taken you along to Yannis's house and join you there as soon as possible.'

'I don't want to be the cause of trouble between you.'

Kyriakos looked at Ronnie steadily, remembering how she

had given him an ultimatum and told him he must choose between his mother or her.

'My mother has to realise that she is only penalising herself by not accepting you. One day she will see reason.'

'We've been invited to go to Yannis's house on Christmas Day, Mamma. Shall I accept on your behalf?' asked Monika.

'And Theo?'

Monika smiled in amusement. Her mother and Theo appeared to be inseparable these days. 'Of course.'

'In that case I'll accept the invitation on behalf of both of us.'

Saffron telephoned from England where she and Vasi had gone to visit Marjorie. 'Would it cause you any inconvenience if we invited ourselves for Christmas Day?' she asked Marianne. 'Mr Goldsmith has been admitted to a Care Home and although Marjorie has visited him regularly he no longer knows her. We were planning to bring her over for a visit in the New Year, but I'd like to return earlier. It will be rather miserable over here, just the three of us.'

'Of course,' answered Marianne immediately. 'We'd be delighted to have you all join us.'

Vasilis looked at his building plot. The perimeter walls were complete and the back and front walls in the process of being heightened. He had spoken to Palamakis and been told that once the Christmas break was over the scaffolding would be erected and all the house walls could be raised to the required height. Once that had been done the roof could be completed and a start made on the inside area.

He had consulted his lawyer about the feasibility of approaching the employees about forming a consortium and the idea had been agreed in principal. He then spoke to the bank manager and asked him not to consider selling the property until he had met with the senior employees at the hotel and agreed to give the manager a firm decision in January.

Earlier in the week he had spoken to Panayiotis and asked after Blerim and his family. Panayiotis had assured him that they were well and Lejla had definitely shown an improvement due to the therapy she was receiving. Vasilis had given his neighbour some money and asked him to buy appropriate gifts for all of them. Panayiotis had agreed to take them up on Christmas morning before he commenced his duty.

'I always volunteer to do a double shift on Christmas Day. That means the men who have families can spend the day with them.'

Vasilis drove along to Yannis's house feeling cheerful, determined to put all his problems behind him for the day and enjoy himself with the extended family.

Marianne, Bryony and Nicola had roasted a chicken, turkey and leg of lamb, along with sausages and making moussaka. Salad was piled high in large bowls and bread, dips and olives were strategically placed on the table so everyone would be able to reach and help themselves. The girls and Yiannis had been allowed to join the adults and given a glass of mango juice and told they were not to drink it until after Uncle Yannis had spoken. Marcus was busy ensuring everyone had a full glass ready for a toast.

Yannis stood up and looked around at the faces before him. 'I am pleased to welcome all of you into my home on this special day. It has been an eventful year for all of us, particularly Andreas, Elena and Vasilis. I hope we will all be blessed with good health throughout the coming year as I look forward to inviting all of you again next Christmas.' Yannis raised his glass. 'Let us drink a toast to the ladies who have produced this marvellous spread.'

As the glasses were replaced on the table John winked at Nicola. 'I've had another idea for Uncle Andreas Why doesn't he write a play about Old Uncle Yannis's life on Spinalonga? What do you think, Uncle Andreas? Shall we drink to that?'

To My Loyal Readers

This seems like an ideal place to take a temporary break from the Cretan 'family'.

I do have ideas for two more books, but I need some respite to complete outstanding commitments. It is also possible that I will need to have my cataracts removed during the coming year.

Please keep reading and, I hope, enjoying my books and recommending them to your friends and relations. I desperately need the storage space in my home to accommodate further publications.

I have another book planned for publication in December 2020.

Do continue to contact me as I always appreciate hearing from you along with any comments or criticisms you wish to make on my books.